Sprite
Peter Meredith

ISBN 13-978-0988898042

Fictional works by Peter Meredith:

A Perfect America
The Sacrificial Daughter
The Horror of the Shade Trilogy of the Void 1
An Illusion of Hell Trilogy of the Void 2
Hell Blade Trilogy of the Void 3
The Punished
Sprite
The Feylands: A Hidden Lands Novel
The Sun King: A Hidden Lands Novel
The Sun Queen: A Hidden Lands Novel
The Apocalypse: The Undead World Novel 1
The Apocalypse Survivors: The Undead World Novel 2
The Apocalypse Outcasts: The Undead World Novel 3
The Apocalypse Fugitives: The Undead World Novel 4
Pen(Novella)
A Sliver of Perfection (Novella)
The Haunting At Red Feathers(Short Story)
The Haunting On Colonel's Row(Short Story)
The Drawer(Short Story)
The Eyes in the Storm(Short Story)

Chapter 1

"Don't screw this up for us, Odd," her mother warned. "Get up here and smile as pretty as you can." Taking small steps Audrey Wyatt climbed onto the rickety little porch and reached up to push her glasses firmer onto her little bump of a nose.

Thinking that Odd was about to take them off, her mother smacked her hand away. "Keep those on, damn it! You don't want to freak them out do you? Jeez! If my brother turns us away..."

Odd knew. It meant going back to the shelter. Odd hated the shelter. She hated the people there, most of whom were runny-eyed bums. She hated the day-old food, and the filth, but most of all she hated the smell. It always stank of stale urine and fresh vomit. Being there for any length of time gave her a headache.

Her mom stank as well. She reeked of cigarettes and had since Odd could remember. This gave Odd a headache, too.

"Here we go," Karen Wyatt said. In the fading December afternoon, the woman took a deep breath and knocked. At the age of thirty-three, Karen seemed to be fading faster than the light. Odd thought she looked closer to forty-five. Her hair, once a tawny gold, was now a dirty blonde with more dirt than blonde. A million cigarettes had discolored her teeth, and an uncountable number of vodka tonics had given her a worn-out look that no amount of make-up could cover. Somewhere over the last few years wrinkles had set in around her eyes and lips. There would only be more coming.

They waited on the porch, both smiling with insincere happiness. From inside a TV went low and they heard footsteps approaching.

"Who is it?" a muffled voice asked.

"Hey Mattie. It's Karen Wyatt" Odd hadn't expected her mom to mention that she was there too. As always, she was only an afterthought.

"Yeah?" The single word held deep suspicion.

The faux-happy look didn't last as Karen's lips pursed. "Well...I want to say hello. Is my brother home?"

Before the door opened they could hear the chain being slid into place. If ever there was an ill omen that sound was it.

"You want to see your brother?" Matilda Wyatt asked in a high voice. She was a small woman with dark hair and dark flashing eyes. She seemed strangely outraged in Odd's opinion. "You are simply amazing, Karen," Odd's aunt seethed.

Before the door had opened Karen had re-applied her fake smile and now it struggled to stay in place. "I know it's been a few years," she replied. "But we can let bygones be bygones. If you just let me talk to my brother, he would..."

Mattie interrupted, shaking her head in astonishment. "Your brother's been dead for two years. So if you want to see him, you'll have to go out to the cemetery on Third Avenue."

Odd could only remember having met her uncle once; even so the news of his death impacted her more than it did her mother. Karen had been far more upset the day before when she had thrown herself down on the couch and had accidentally squashed a pack of cigarettes.

"Dead? Two years...hmmm," Karen said, clearly thinking how this was going to affect her. Behind the chain Mattie rolled her eyes and Odd went a shade pink at her mom's calculating tone.

As well as feeling embarrassment, the little girl also felt decidedly queer. Even though she was only twelve she had seen her share of death. It was the consequence of living as one of the dregs of society. Death was a part of life in the back alley slums and the seven dollar a night motel rooms in which the little girl had been raised.

Yet this one death out of all the others was different. It twirled a strange sensation through her guts. John Wyatt had been family. As far as Odd knew, her only family—other than her mother.

"Did he happen to mention me?" Karen asked, almost coming across in an offhand way.

Mattie's eyebrows locked together. "Mention you? He was shot in the head... a burglar killed him. He died instantly."

"No, I meant in the will. You know, in that way."

At this Mattie looked up at her ceiling and began laughing tiredly. Ashamed, Odd glanced away and saw a face looking at her from behind a set of blue curtains at the large front window. The face was bone white and not human. Where the eyes should've been were two deep holes, hollow and black; the thing's nose was long, pointing down over a pit of a mouth that was rimmed with huge triangular-shaped teeth. There were more of these teeth, running in rings down the creature's throat. Though its skin was the color of alabaster, it ran with golden cracks like the seams of a strange puzzle

Odd screamed at the vision and stumbled back, falling down the steps of the porch. The fall jarred her spine and her hands hurt from where she had put them out to catch herself. When she looked back up to the window the dreadful face was gone and another was in its place, that of an aging cocker spaniel. The dog stared out at Odd with huge round eyes.

Irritated, Karen stared down at her daughter. "What the hell's wrong with you?" The question had barely passed her lips when her eyes came open in alarm. She hurried down the stairs and knelt down next to Odd. She wasn't overly concerned if Odd had been hurt or not, she was only concerned that Odd's sunglasses had fallen off. "Get these back on," she whispered handing over the glasses.

Straightening, Karen turned back to her sister-in-law. "I think she might have tripped on your stairs, and I'm pretty sure she sprained an ankle. Can we come in?"

Mattie turned to the dog in the window and commanded, "Dayton, get down!" It disappeared with a rustle of blue curtain.

When it did, Odd blinked, clearing the horrific image from her mind. After her initial fright she had calmed in a second. This wasn't the first time her mind had distorted the confused images her eyes sent it. This sort of thing was prone to happening if she turned her head too quickly. Doors would appear to bend, sidewalks would curl like a strand of DNA, and faces would contort as though they were looking out of funhouse mirrors at her. This one image just happened to be a little worse than usual.

"I'm ok," she said to her mother. Karen turned her head and glared in response—shaking her head in tiny back and forth movements that Mattie wasn't supposed to see. It took a second for Odd to catch on and then she said, "Except my...my ankle. I think, maybe I twisted it?"

Karen gave her a little nod and then went back up to the porch. "Yeah, I think she might have turned it. Can we come in and get some ice for it and maybe..."

"No, you may not," Mattie said, cutting across her. "Take your scams somewhere else."

"Look, Mattie, I'm not trying to scam you or anything," Karen said in a pleading tone. "We're just really hurting—financially. You think we could maybe stay for the night?"

"No."

"Oh, ok." Karen dropped her head in a display of despair. From her vantage on the ground, Odd could see her mom's eyes going back and forth, a clear sign of her scheming. "I guess we have to go...wait, you never answered me about John? Did he leave anything? For me? In the will? Any insurance money?"

Mattie's face twisted into a sneer. "You're such a ghoul! You're nothing but a grave robber. Whatever John left, he left for me. He hated you. Don't you remember that? I bet he's rolling over in his grave at the thought of you back in town begging at his door. Now get off my porch!" Mattie slammed the door in Karen's face.

Karen clenched her fists and Odd thought that she was about to explode, but then she leaned up against the door, looking weary, but not yet defeated. "What about for Audrey? She's never hurt you. Can't you help her out? She hasn't had a decent meal in days."

This was true. Her mother's drinking took precedence over everything including food. Odd's malnourishment was one of the reasons she could pass as a second grader.

Mattie seemed unmoved by the statement and no sound came in response. After a long minute of standing there, Karen let her shoulders droop. She came off the porch to stand with Odd, who was freezing where she stood. Karen had a nasty look for her daughter.

"This is all your fault," she hissed. "All you had to do was stand there and try not to be a freak. You couldn't even do that. Come on." Karen grabber her daughter by the arm, but just then, Mattie's door opened a smidge and a small rain of green was thrown out.

"That's all I have and that's all I'm going to give," Mattie said. "I don't want to see either one of you ever again." The door shut a second time with a bang and the lock sliding into place was clear in the last of the afternoon light.

"Eighty-four dollars," Karen said, thumbing through the bills a minute later. "What a bitch. But at least this keeps us out of the shelter for a while. Come on, let's go back to that bar, the one with the pretzels. You're going to get us some drinks and this time, no pouting. You ruin everything when you start in."

The drinks would be all for Karen. Only rarely did Odd ever get a Coke out of the deal. The little girl hung her head, letting her blonde hair fall across her glasses. "I don't like it when you make me look like a freak just to get free drinks. It's not fair."

"There you go pouting already!" Karen huffed. "You want to go back to the shelter then? Is that it? We can do that if you want. We can go and sit among all those stinky people and get preached to...or we can go find someone who'll take care of us. We're not going to find a man at the shelter, believe me."

Odd let out a long breath. "I don't want to go to a bar or the shelter. The people at the bar aren't much better than them over at the shelter. They're all so...so skanky. We don't belong there."

Her mother started walking, her thumb jutting out before she hit the street. "Come on," she said in anger. "We're going to the bar. When we get there you had better take a good look at all them people you think are no good. Take a hard look and then you look in the mirror...*without* your glasses and then you tell me who doesn't belong."

Chapter 2

Five days later, Odd sat on the stained cover of a motel bed with a fear squirreling around in her belly as she squinted at a note her mother had left. Unfortunately the note was written in cursive. Her eyes weren't good for cursive—really they weren't good for any sort of reading, but cursive was the worst. The letters slithered atop each other like snakes.

Odd didn't need to read the note to know she was in trouble, because sitting next to it were nine dollars bills and fourteen pennies. The only other time Karen Wyatt had ever left money lying around there had been a note as well.

It was the year before when they had stopped for a while in Toledo. Karen had hooked up with some salesman who took her on a week long tour of the mid-west. He sold his wares and she...she did that thing she does to get men to pay for their meals. That time Odd had been left twenty-four dollars. It had been the most miserable lonely week of her life.

Odd took the note to the window and held it at an angle. It didn't help. Pocketing the cash, she went to look for someone to read the note for her—someone trustworthy. This ruled out everyone at the motel and most of the people on the streets. But she knew where to go. She went to a nearby park where old men sat on benches and played chess or checkers.

She had done this every day since the two of them had been abandoned in the city a couple of weeks before by one of her mother's boyfriends. He had pulled over to get gas and when the two of them had gone to the lady's-room he had simply driven away with all their meager belongings. Karen blamed Odd, as did Odd. No one could stand being around her very long—once they knew her secret.

"Hey, it's Stevie Wonder!" One of the old men called out as she came and sat at her usual bench. This was greeted with laughter, but it wasn't cruel or mocking so she smiled in response.

"Mr. McCew, what's that mean?" Odd asked the man she always sat nearest to. They were all old black men on the benches and she had chosen Mr. McCew because he had the warmest smile, the loudest laugh, and talked the most. "Who's Stevie Wonder?" she asked him.

"Who's Stevie Wonder?" he asked right back, causing everyone to laugh again. "He's a Ray Charles wannabe." This brought out even more laughter, but only confused Odd all the more. Mr. McCew saw this and smiled broad. "He's a blind singer. Jonny B over there just called you that cuz you wearing them glasses all the time."

"Oh...I just think they're cool looking." Odd never mentioned her eye problem to anyone unless she had to.

"Ole Jonny B didn't mean nothing by it," Mr. McCew said with a last smile before returning his gaze to the checkerboard. Odd liked it better when he played chess. Compared to checkers, chess progressed at a glacial pace, making it easier for her to follow.

Because of her eyes she couldn't watch TV or read. Sitting in the park, watching the old men play was her favorite form of entertainment. She was learning chess quickly—Mr. McCew would talk out every move he'd make before making it.

Checkers was a different story.

"You see that, Odd?" Mr. McCew asked pointing at the board. For a second, the straight grid of the board twisted and she thought the pieces would all slide off. Before she could blink away the illusion, what looked like a half-dozen hands jumped around snatching the little round discs. "He's just giving me the game," Mr McCew added with a laugh.

Odd smiled her encouragement, not knowing what was going on. The action was just too quick for eyes to catch up with. Her old black friend must have been right, as the game ended soon after.

"No good, bad luck cracker," Mr. McCew's opponent snarled getting up from his side of the bench and storming away.

"Don't be like that, Earl," Mr. McCew hollered after him, patting Odd's leg. "She's a good luck cracker! You're just jealous cuz she's *my* good luck cracker." He turned his muddy brown eyes to her. "Don't fret none about the 'cracker' talk. No one means nothing about it."

"Ok," Odd said. She would fret anyway. When Mr. McCew said it, she knew it was just in joking, but the way the other man had said it struck a warning note within her. She would have to steer clear of him from then on.

"Who's up next?" her friend said, rubbing his hands against the cold.

He played another game and then another. Odd bundled her heavy coat tighter around her and watched and waited. She was patient for a twelve-year-old.

Eventually, the cold caught up to the men and they began drifting away.

As was usual, Mr. McCew wouldn't let the elements get in the way of his competitive spirit and with trembling hands he finished off his last opponent. When he got up to leave Odd brought out the note.

"Excuse me, Mr. McCew can I ask a little favor?"

His reaction wasn't what Odd had expected. He drew back with narrowed eyes. "Depends, don't it? What sort of favor?"

"I can't read this note my mom wrote me. I have dyslexia." Odd didn't have dyslexia, but people knew that word—most people that is. Odd for one didn't know it, not really. It was just what her mother told her to say when she was forced to explain why she couldn't read.

Mr. McCew looked down his nose at the girl in the sunglasses. "Dyslexia? That's meaning you can't read?" She nodded which made him scowl. "Then why the hell did your mom write you a note? That doesn't make any sense."

"She knew I'd find someone to read the note for me," Odd answered in a little voice. She hadn't expected this reaction at all.

The old man's brown eyes smoldered into hers for a moment before he reached out and took the note. He read in a slow, deep voice:

Odd,

A really good chance has come up for the both of us. Last night I met this guy, Jared. He really likes me and has a good job. He's a trucker who does runs out to California and back. He says he's not into kids, but I think that by the time we get back, I'll have changed his mind. I've paid for the room till Sunday. Don't spend all the money right away, make it last or you'll be hungry.

Mom

Once Mr. McCew finished reading out loud, his eyes went back to the page a second time, while his lips formed nearly silent words. He shook his head as he reread the note.

"Your mom left you to drive around the country with some guy she met last night?" he asked in an outrage. What could Odd say? She only shrugged in response. The old man reached out and grabbed her hand. "Come with me. We'll call my daughter-in-law. She's a social worker. You'll love her. She can cook like nobody's business."

Odd snatched her hand away and backed up quick. "No thank you, Mr. McCew. I don't need a social worker. I'll be ok. You read the note. I have a place to stay and...and some money."

'Some money' was a stretch. The nine dollars felt like nine pennies just then.

The old man made a face, pursing his lips. "Look at you, all skin and bones. You're practically starving already." He stepped toward her and Odd skipped back further. Mr. McCew stamped his foot like a toddler not getting his way. "You know this ain't right. You don't need to protect your mom!"

"I'm not protecting my mom," Odd answered truthfully. She was protecting herself. A social worker meant only one thing: foster-care. She'd been in foster-care before. It had been a disaster. Three different homes in five weeks. In all of them the other kids had mercilessly picked on her and the parents had trouble looking her in the face. She'd been passed on like a hot potato and everyday had been a torture.

"I'll be ok, Mr. McCew. Don't worry about me." She started to walk away and then remembered she'd had one other question. "Just one other thing. What day is this?"

"You don't even know what day it is and you expect me to believe that you'll be alright?" he asked. She shrugged, still backing away. "It's Tuesday," he yelled.

Odd's mind did a quick spin over the number of days till Sunday—six and the amount of money she had—nine dollars. It meant she would have a dollar and fifty-two cents a day to spend on food. The amount seemed so small that she ran them again in her mind.

"Oh boy," she said, a knot forming in her chest. Waving a last good-bye to Mr. McCew she headed off to the nearest supermarket, fearing that her money wasn't going to last and fearing what would happen to her when she ran out.

Chapter 3

It was indeed a hungry week for Audrey Wyatt.

After an hour of going up and down the aisles, staring at the prices until the numbers stopped jumping over each other, Odd discovered that her money would stretch, but only just barely. A loaf of bread, a jar of peanut butter, a jar of jelly, and two cans of peaches ate up her entire budget.

She had enough bread for one-and-a-half sandwiches a day. The peaches were supposed to last the week, but even though she tried to hold back, they were gone by Friday. It made for a long week. Every day she went about feeling jittery from the lack of calories. Sunday was the worst. She ate her last sandwich in the morning, hoping her mom would come back early.

That didn't happen. By nightfall Odd felt light-headed and her hands shook as she scraped out the remains of the peanut butter and jelly, licking the plastic knife almost like a dog. Fighting sleep, she waited up for as long as she could, but her mom never showed.

Monday morning dawned bright and cold. Odd was in a panic. She had no food and her rent had run out the day before. When a ten o'clock knock came, Odd almost ran to the bathroom to hide. She felt small and vulnerable. She *was* small and vulnerable.

"Who...who is it?" Her voice quivered.

"It's Phil from the front desk. I need the rent."

She had seen Phil and didn't like the look of him. He seemed constantly hung-over and surly was his only disposition.

Odd's hands began to twist around themselves. "My mom had to leave town...my uncle died. Can she pay you when she gets back tomorrow?"

Through the door the tired sigh came clearly to her ears. She thought that it was a good sign, but before she knew it the lock began turning. Odd squeaked and ran to the other side of the bed, not knowing what to do. Phil stepped in wearing a sour look on his unshaven face and a mustard stain on his shirt. He looked all around the room; checking the bathroom and even under the bed. While he did this Odd plastered herself to the wall.

"No luggage, no extra clothes, no nothing." He shook his head, looking crankier than ever. "Just one little girl. Is your mom really coming back?"

"Yes. I know she is," Odd said emphatically, clutching her hands to her skinny chest. "Maybe even today...soon." Her feeling of vulnerability grew, making it difficult for her to breathe. Phil was a large man with a near-to-bursting beer gut. He loomed over her, blocking the sunlight streaming in through the window.

Phil didn't care about how nervous he made her. He cared about his money. "Tomorrow. Have the rent tomorrow or you're out. And don't try to give me some bull sob story. It ain't gonna work." He didn't hang around for Odd to thank him.

One more day. She went back to waiting, but she did so holding her mid-section. There was a growing pain in her stomach that was part fear, part hunger. It gnawed at her relentlessly.

What if her mom didn't make it back on time...or wasn't coming back at all? This thought ran through her mind in a torturous repetition. Over and over. No answer came to her...that is no answer that didn't entail freezing to death or starving to death.

Finally, just after one in the afternoon, Odd couldn't take the waiting any longer; she had to do something. She cinched up her old, green cast-off coat and went out in search of her mom. There was a chance that she had come into town the night before and was either shacked up in another motel or drinking in a bar somewhere.

She could be anywhere but, if Odd had to guess, Karen Wyatt would be somewhere along the Broadway strip. Without a car, her mom didn't like to venture too far from an area she knew.

With this in mind, Odd started walking; stopping into every motel and bar she came across on the west side of the road. She walked south until the neighborhood started looking nicer. That was her cue to turn around. Karen didn't like people with too much money and they didn't seem to like her right back.

The little girl crossed the street and did the same thing, checking in at bars and motels heading north four miles before turning back. This time from exhaustion.

Five hours after leaving her room, freezing, exhausted, and walking on aching feet, Odd could see her motel again. There were only two more bars to go before she reached it. She wanted to skip them both and go straight on, but her feet were killing her in the shoes that she had outgrown the month before. She had to sit down, at least for a little while.

Easing into the first bar, a dark fetid hole-in-the-wall, she saw it was the "one with the pretzels". Suddenly she didn't care about her mom. It had been almost two days since her last meal and just then all she cared about was getting some food in her belly—even if it was just pretzels. Keeping her head down Odd climbed up onto the nearest bar stool and reached for the basket.

"What can I get for ya?" the bartender asked before she could get a handful. Odd remembered his name was Gary. Perhaps because her eyesight was so poor, her memory was better than average.

"Hi Gary...I'm actually looking for my mom. Have you seen her?"

The bartender peered at her with a little curl to his lip. "I don't know you. How am I supposed to know your mom?"

"It's me, Odd." To help jar his memory she dropped her sunglasses. His eyes came open wide.

He stared until she pushed the glasses back up onto her snub nose. Only then did he give a shaky laugh and said, "Oh right, the girl with the red eyes. Sorry, I haven't seen your mom in like a week."

"Me neither," Odd grumbled. Right after this her stomach grumbled as well. "Do you have any work I can do around here? I can clean stuff...toilets even, or floors."

Before answering, Gary first looked around his bar at the scattered patrons and then at her. "How old are you...really?"

His gaze was so intense that she didn't think about lying. "Twelve."

He shook his head, sadly. "Naw, sorry. I can't give you any work. I'd get in all sorts of trouble if anyone saw you." He gave her a commiserating look.

"Yeah, well thanks anyways." She sagged on her stool. On their own, her eyes slid to the small, brown bowl of pretzels. The truth was that she wasn't much for pretzels, but then again she wasn't much for starving either. "Can I sit here for a little bit and warm up?"

"You can stay for a bit, but not at the bar," Gary said and then pointed at booth near the door. "Take that one back there."

It had a full basket of pretzels sitting dead center on the table. Her empty stomach rumbled louder in excitement. "Thanks," Odd said and then limped over to it.

For the next ten minutes she slipped pretzels into her mouth whenever Gary wasn't looking. Unfortunately he seemed to be looking far too often and she barely was able to sneak a thing. Finally, he went into the kitchen and she stuffed a huge handful into her mouth and stuck another handful into the pocket of her coat. Just then Gary came back out and it looked to her as though he was going move her along. She considered grabbing another handful and running, but thought it would be too rude after he'd been nice enough to let her sit for a while. Instead she swallowed as fast as she could.

"Hungry were you?" he asked.

"Yeah...I...only had just a few," Odd said, still trying to choke down the last of them.

"Here, eat this." Gary slid a cheeseburger in front of her. Next to it on the plate sat a mound of fries the size of her head. Odd stared open-mouthed for a moment, taking it all in. Then her eyes dropped.

"I can't. I don't have any money," she confessed, with her chin lowered to her chest.

This struck Gary as funny and he laughed loud enough for the other customers to turn and look. "No duh, you don't have any money," he said. "Anyone can see that. The burger's on the house." He leaned and spoke low, "Now, this is a onetime deal. I don't let beggars in here, ever. So don't come back without money." He then held up a brown bag. "And don't try to eat all of it at once. Take the rest home with you."

The sudden bonanza had Odd on the verge of tears. "Th-thank you," she stammered. He smiled and left to go pour drinks.

The burger was delicious. The fries heaven. She could feel her stomach like a swollen bag by the time she had eaten half of what was on the plate. The rest went into the sack as Gary had suggested.

He came back when she was nearly done, plunking a coke in front of her. She had it sucked gone before he could sit. This brought another smile to his lips, however it faded in seconds.

"So where's your mom?" he asked. Again his gaze was of such intensity that she didn't bother to lie. It would've been silly to even try. A bartender on this side of town had probably heard every kind of lie ever told. Besides she wasn't much of a liar.

Odd examined the ice cubes that were forming strange and interesting shapes in her glass. "She took off with some guy," she said at last, without looking up.

"She coming back?"

"I don't know," Odd replied. "She said she'd be back yesterday, but..." She left off with a shrug.

Gary reached out and patted her hand. "She'll be

back, but that isn't necessarily a good thing. Your mom's trouble. I shoulda kicked the two of you out of here the other day...I mean the way she was treating you wasn't right. You're not a circus freak to be shown off like that."

Odd continued to stare at the glass; she didn't like to be reminded of how bad she had it. She let half a minute of silence pass before she asked, "So why didn't you kick us out if it was so bad?"

A grunt escaped the man and he rubbed his face with his hands. "Because we had a full bar for the first time in a long time. Because the place was really hopping...you don't know what it's like to see your bar go downhill the way..." He stopped in mid-sentence and sat shaking his head in disgust.

Odd thought that he was mad at her and she shrunk lower down into the booth.

But he wasn't mad at her. "The real reason? Because I was stupid. The whole time I'm thinking that your mom is this big bitch...I mean, sorry...that she isn't a nice person to do that to you. And now I realize that I'm just as much to blame by letting it happen. I'm sorry about that."

Odd didn't know what to say. No one ever apologized to her. "It's ok, I'm not mad or nothing," she said. "It's just how we get money and drinks and stuff. And, besides, I am a freak...or a demon-child."

"You aren't!" Gary said, pounding the table with his fist. "You're just a girl, that's all. Not a freak."

Odd slid out of the booth. "Thanks for the burger, Gary."

"Wait," he called after her. "Please, don't think of yourself that way."

"I don't think it matters what I think," Odd replied before heading out into the early night.

She paused just outside the door, zipping up her coat and trying to rid her mind of the conversation. This sort of thing happened to her every once in a while. Someone would take a moment out of their busy lives to feel bad for her. Then the moment was gone. She'd move on, or they'd move on and what did it change things? It never did change anything. She was still a freak. They felt bad and so did she. So what?

Once on the street she slipped off her sunglasses and gazed around.

She had her eye out for trouble. Freak or not, a skinny, little girl like her could be a magnet for it, especially now that she was all alone...without a mother. Traffic still moved on Broadway, meaning she would be relatively safe as long as she didn't stray too deep into the shadows dousing the alleys.

In the slummy part of town, shadows held all sorts of dangers. Awful sorts of people lingered in them: half-crazed winos, gang-bangers looking to sow chaos, pimps eyeing new flesh to hawk. Her mother had warned her and Odd had taken the warning to heart. She hurried toward the neon lights of her motel, wincing from the pain in her feet as she went.

The last bar she decided to skip. Men loitered around the entrance smoking. They eyed her as she walked by and she could feel their gaze follow her up the street. To consider what was going through their minds gave her the shivers. She knew what men did. It frightened her—just like everything else in life.

Her motel room sat empty and cold. Quiet as well. All week Odd had the TV on during the day. She couldn't watch it—the fast moving images bothered her eyes too much—but she could listen. The sound of people talking was her only company and was, in a way, comforting. At night, however, she turned it off, not wanting to draw attention to her room. This night was no different. In the dark she sat and waited.

Chapter 4

The cold of winter had a steel grip on that Tuesday morning. Looking out the motel window at the wind whipping by sent Odd's stomach into a spin. If her mom didn't show up soon, she'd have to go out into it. And then what? She had no idea. She couldn't go back to the shelter even if she wanted to. They would never take her without her mom. All they'd do is call Social Services on her, and that meant foster-care.

Odd began to pace, glancing at the digital clock every so often. The red numbers would blur if she tried to read them as she walked, so she'd pause and stare until the minutes came into focus. The time zipped by. She expected Phil at ten, but he didn't show. By eleven, a giddy hope that he had forgotten all about her began to build within her chest.

By noon she stood shivering on the sidewalk—Phil had not forgotten. Her sole possession, a half-eaten hamburger, sat in the front pocket of her old coat. Odd started walking with no idea where to go. It didn't take long for her feet, in their sprung Converse sneakers to go numb and her teeth to start chattering. Still, she walked until the pain became too great.

Ahead she saw a Goodwill and ducked into it, hoping for a moment of warmth.

She got more than a moment. Odd went up and down the aisles, pretending to shop. She filled a cart with clothes, then emptied it again and in the process killed an hour this way, regaining feeling in her toes. As she meandered through the store she had to fight the temptation to leave and go back to the motel to ask Phil if her mom had shown up yet.

It was too early. She'd go back later that afternoon if she hadn't frozen to death first.

"Can I help you with something?" A not-so pleasant voice asked her from behind. She'd been daydreaming and when the person spoke, Odd turned too quickly. The clerk's head squeezed in at the eyes and they disappeared. His nose became a dot, while his mouth ballooned large, his white teeth becoming monstrous.

"Oh!" Odd flung a hand to her face and turned away. When she looked back, this time slow and deliberately, the clerk was normal looking. Unfortunately he was also rather pissy looking.

"Are you going to make a purchase today?" he asked with eyebrows raised. Obviously he wasn't expecting her to.

"Do you have anything...that's free?" Odd asked in a little voice. She desperately needed new shoes. Hers were splitting at the seams and they were no protection against the cold whatsoever. The clerk rolled his eyes as an answer. This befuddled the girl. "But...but you get all this stuff for free," Odd said. "It's supposed to be for the poor and I'm really poor."

"What's a white-girl like you know about being poor?" the clerk, who was black, asked her. "Why don't you go back to suburbia and cry poor-mouth out there."

"But I am poor...and I don't know where suburbia is," Odd said, not really comprehending the word suburbia. She thought it was another city.

"Just head south till everything gets pasty

white," he replied, taking her by the elbow and leading her to the door. "Have a nice day." With a gentle shove he pushed her out the door.

The wind struck her immediately sending ice fingers down the neck of her open coat. Forgetting the rude clerk, Odd quickly cinched her coat up as tight as she could against the cold. It was easy to forget the man. Rude was all she got half the time; it was the pleasant people that she remembered.

Going south to Suburbia wasn't an option. The wind blew directly north up Broadway and it hurt Odd's face to look into it. Instead she went where the wind blew her. For an hour she walked north through the cold until she realized that to get back to the hotel would mean heading back into the wind. This thought made her not want to bother. In her heart she knew her mom wouldn't be there.

But without any other option she went anyway, yet not directly down Broadway. She zigzagged through the neighborhood just to the west. It made for a longer journey, but those times where the wind wasn't on her were almost heaven. Heaven or not, the cold seeped into her bones and she was forced back to Broadway to slip into coffee shops and auto dealerships to catch a minute or two of warmth.

Unfortunately, these breaks were short lived and she was always moved on before she could make any headway against her shivering. Time and again a stern voice or sour face would force back out onto the streets and, eventually the wind pushed her back off the main thoroughfare. With chattering teeth, she wandered again along the roads west until she decided that she couldn't go any further. She was done with the cold.

Odd decided that the next place she went into would have to call the police to get her out. The next place she came to was a church. Even with the numbness becoming a searing pain in her hands and feet she hesitated to go into the church.

Her life had been seedy motels, dive bars, and scrounging for food wherever she could get it. Her one role model was virulently anti-religious. Her world held much more hate than love. Yet all this did nothing to stop her from entering the building. However, the remembered words of too many children did.

"Don't ever go into a church, Odd. You'll catch fire and burn up!"

"Yeah, God hates demons like you."

"Odd is the devil; run or she'll get you!"

She paused, with her hand an inch from the door, afraid that what everyone said about her was true. It wasn't just children who referred to her as a demon-child; adults had as well...including her own mother.

What would happen if a demon-child really did touch a church? Would she burn up? "I'd be warm at least," Odd whispered, making up her mind. With a final breath she grabbed the handle.

It did indeed burn her hand...yet it burned with the intensity of frozen metal. She pulled open the door and slipped in. Blessed heat rushed over her as she stood staring about. She was in a foyer and beyond that was the inside of a church. It was pretty much as pictured in books: lots of wooden pews and a big white altar.

She barely gave it so much as a glance. Her whole attention focused on a huge bowl sitting on a marble pedestal in front of her. Though it was brass, it was so highly polished that she mistook it for gold and thought that a fortune sat right there practically free for the taking.

Odd touched its smooth surface, marveling. Inside it, filling it about halfway, water shimmered. Holy water? Would it hurt? Again with hesitation she reached out to touch the water. It was wet. She gave it a sniff and then a taste...nothing. It was only water.

Movement in the chapel caught her attention and quick as a wink she ducked down behind the pedestal. Peeking out she saw a man in black walking through the pews. He stopped every once in a while to stoop over or to fiddle with books that Odd could barely see.

Other than the pedestal there wasn't much in the way of cover in the foyer and Odd sat with her back against it, hoping not to be seen. With the heat, she soon found herself drowsing and twice she flopped over onto the floor before waking up. She was there for a long time, but eventually a door could be heard closing somewhere in the chapel as the man in black left.

Her curiosity over the church had her up in a flash. What was this all about, she wondered as she entered the main room. She understood, in a vague childlike way, about God. He was a super-powered being who had created the world. She understood praying. You asked God for stuff and, if you were good, he gave it to you. Kind of like an adult's version of Santa Claus.

It was all the rest that was beyond her. The goofy outfits, the singing, the million of rules, all the candles, and weird colored windows. But more than any of that, what confused her the most hung suspended from the ceiling. It was a slightly larger than life sized sculpture of Jesus—crucified.

Odd stared and stared. She could see the blood running from his hands and feet. She could see the thorns stabbing into his forehead. She could see the misery on his face.

Why? Why on earth would anyone worship that?

"These people are sick," she whispered, still with her head craned way back.

"Unfortunately, it's the world that's sick and it's our job to help to heal it." The man in black had come back into the main room and had snuck up on Odd. In an instant panic, she spun too quickly and the chapel appeared to fold in half. Pews were now over her head and she put an arm up to ward them off. She must have looked crazy because the man put a hand out to steady her.

"Are you alright?"

Odd shrugged off his hand, blinking away the wrong images. "I'm ok...just don't touch me."

All priests are nothing but a bunch of child molesters, her mom had said on more than one occasion. Did they molest twelve-year-old girls? Odd wasn't going to take any chances. She backed up away from the man.

He put his hands out to show he was harmless. "Hey it's ok. I won't hurt you."

She was sure all child molesters said something very similar. "I wish I could trust you, but..." She bit back what her mom had said about priests.

"You don't trust me, yet you walk into my church?" the priest asked with a smile. "Shouldn't I be the one not trusting you?"

There was logic to that. "I guess you're right," Odd admitted. "But my mom said...I was told..."

"What? That you can't trust a priest?" He knotted his brows at this. "That's silly. I've always..." He paused and understanding filled his eyes. "Oh, you're talking about what happened before...the molestations. Yes, that was a very sad time."

"You mean it doesn't happen anymore?" Odd asked, skeptically.

The priest shrugged and then went to sit in the front row pew. "I'm sure it does. There are always bad apples in any group. But, sad to say, you are in a hundred times more danger of being molested at home or at school than in a church. Especially now. The Vatican has finally started cracking down."

Odd didn't know what a Vatican was. "Oh, good," she said as way of a reply.

He smiled at this tepid answer and asked," So, what brings you to church today?"

To get warm was the truth. However, Odd also had a thousand questions about God. Whenever she considered them they filled her head and buzzed around, but of all of them, one stood out. It was a stupid question, but a burning one nonetheless. "What do you know about demons?"

Chapter 5

"A little I suppose," the priest answered. "I'm not a demonologist, but I know some stuff. It comes with the territory I guess you could say."

"Does God hate demons?" Odd asked. Even with her dark sunglasses on her pert little nose she couldn't look the priest in the face when she asked this. Instead she stared at the red carpeting.

The man looked up at the figure of Jesus dying on the cross before answering, "The short answer is yes. I think he does. Normally I'd tell you that God doesn't hate the sinner, he hates the sin. However a demon may be made of only sin....so, yes I think I can safely say that God hates demons."

"And demon children?" Odd's voice was barely a whisper. "What does he think about them?"

The priest's lips pursed and he nodded gently in understanding. "You're not a demon-child. Whoever might have told you that is wrong."

In Odd's world, that meant either *everyone* was wrong or this one man who didn't know her was wrong. She dropped her head and asked, "But what if?"

"What if you were? Then God would judge you by your actions, not by who your parents are." The man slid a little nearer to her. "If you are a good person then you have nothing to worry about."

Odd didn't like the idea of the priest getting any closer and she put the length of the pew between them. "I don't know if I'm a good person or not," she said truthfully. People were either nice or mean and she didn't know if that equated to good or evil. "I think I am. I try to be nice and all, but I'm not sure."

"Well, do you sin a lot?" he asked. She shrugged at his question, so he tried to explain, "Do you lie or cheat or steal? These are some sins."

Odd wasn't much for cheating, but she had lied and stolen. She had lied to Phil about when her mother would be back in town and she had stolen pretzels from Gary.

"Yes," she said in a little voice.

"Are you sorry that you did these things?" the priest asked in a gentle tone.

Am I sorry? She asked herself.

Not really. She hadn't hurt anyone by lying to Phil; she'd only been trying to protect herself just in case he tried anything. And she wasn't exactly sorry about stealing the pretzels either. They were meant to be eaten by the people at the bar...and she was a person after all. Kind of.

"I don't think I'm sorry," Odd answered. "What does that mean? Am I going to hell?" She had a sinking feeling in her guts that he would say yes.

The priest sat back and flung an arm over the pew. "As a little girl? Oh, I really doubt it. But..." he held up a finger at her, "...if you continue sinning, and you can't see that there's something wrong in it, there is a chance that you will. I don't want to scare you, but facts are facts."

Whether he meant to or not, he had scared her. Her mind conjured up visions of a fiery torment—of demons with bright red eyes just like hers, and of whips and screams and blood.

"I have t-to go," she stammered. "My mom's waiting for me."

You just lied again! A voice in her mind screamed. Odd started backing down the aisle. "I mean, I have to find my mom."

The priest stood slowly, again with his hands out. "You don't have to leave. We can call your mom and have her pick you up here."

"She doesn't have a phone...or a car. And she'll be mad if I'm not...home when she gets there." Odd wasn't lying about this. If Karen Wyatt got back from her trip and Odd wasn't at the hotel waiting, there'd be trouble. It didn't matter that her mom was already two days late.

The priest nodded at this. "You're welcome back anytime, if you need to talk." She nodded back to him and then waved goodbye. The man waved as well and then noticed her small fingers were bare. "Where are your gloves?" he called out. Odd gave him a half-shrug. "You don't have gloves? In this cold? Wait here. You can borrow mine."

For a full minute she waited. Then she pictured the priest not searching for a pair of gloves, but calling Social Services instead. Odd zipped up tight and headed out into the cold hurrying to put distance between her and the church.

The wind had gotten worse. So biting had it become that it drove out any chance for her to think on the priest's words. She pushed through the freezing air, bent over as if walking up hill and gradually she worked her way back to the motel. The gloves would have been nice, but her hands, shoved deep into her pockets, weren't her problem.

By the time she got into the motel lobby her feet were like hunks of wood and her cheeks stung and felt raw. It hurt even to smile, but she did regardless.

"H-hi Phil," she said with a toothy grin.

Phil sat with his feet up on the counter watching TV. "Yeah?" He had barely looked at Odd.

"I w-w-was w-wondering if my m-mom had shown up yet?" In her heart, Odd knew her mom hadn't. She had gone to California where it was warm and beautiful; where everyone was blonde and pretty. Why would she want to come back here? The only thing she had to come back for was her demon-child.

"Nope," Phil said.

Odd stood there quaking not knowing what to do. Her eyes began to blur with tears. "Do...do you have a room I can stay in? I won't make a mess, I promise. And...and I can clean for you. Toilets, beds, everything."

"Nope," Phil said again. "That's what I got the Mexicans for. I don't need two sets of free-loaders."

"I don't know what to do." Odd's eyes overflowed and she put her hands up under her glasses and pressed them there.

"I know what you can do," Phil drawled. "You can shut-up so I can watch my show."

This struck Odd like a kick in the stomach. She felt suddenly too weak to care about anything. Turning she went to the door and stared out at the fading afternoon light. It would be dark soon and the cold would only grow worse.

Chapter 6

Odd left the office in a daze. Her feet, as if programmed by the last two weeks, turned to the left and made their way up the stairs. It was only when she saw the door to what used to be her room that she reacted at all. Her reaction was to hurry forward and test the knob on the off chance that Phil or one of the Mexicans had left it unlocked...or somehow her mom had come back.

It was cold and stiff in her hand. Despite that she gave it a desperate yank.

"Hey, whatcha doing?"

Two doors down a boy stood leaning against the railing overlooking the parking lot, smoking a cigarette. Odd had seen him before. Always smoking. The boy had long legs and he always wore a blue work shirt, though Odd had never seen him going to or from a job. He seemed only to smoke.

"Just waiting for my mom," Odd said to him.

"Where is she?"

Odd shrugged, but the movement got lost in her over-sized coat. "California, I think."

"She gonna be back soon?" Mitch moved closer to her. On the shirt the word "Mitch" had been stitched in large enough lettering for her to be able to read it. Odd began to get nervous about Mitch.

"In an hour or so," she lied. The lie was so small that it hardly counted, yet after her talk with the priest it echoed in her mind. She warped the lie into a form of the truth by adding, "Maybe." Karen *could* come back any minute after all.

"Do you want to wait in here where it's warm?" Mitch asked, putting his hand out to the orange glow of his room. She wanted to say no, but he added, "A pretty little thing like you shouldn't be wandering around by herself. It's dangerous out there."

Pretty? Did he just call her pretty? This had never happened to her before. Not once, not even close. Odd snugged her dark glasses higher up on her nose and said, "Ok...thanks." He was right after all; it was dangerous on the streets.

Mitch's room was a mirror image of her old one; same ugly stained bedspread, same dinky TV. Even the one piece of art on the wall was the same. Odd went to the heater and leaned up against it, while Mitch lounged back on the bed.

"So, California..." he said this with a raised eyebrow. "Your mom must think you're pretty mature to be here all by yourself. Are you? Mature?"

Odd didn't think so. Everything in life frightened her. Even buying her nine dollars worth of groceries had been an ordeal. She sort of tilted her head in answer.

"Well I think you're mature. How old are you? Fifteen? Sixteen?"

She had to laugh at that, though the sound was more of a giggle. "Twelve," she said around her hand.

"Twelve?" He sounded surprised but his eyes didn't match the tone. "I guess it must be the glasses. They make you look older. They're pretty cool. Can I see 'em?"

He thought she looked cool...and older...and

pretty? The thoughts were staggering, but not so much that she'd hand over her glasses and ruin the moment. "Sorry...I don't want to lose my coolness."

He liked that. Mitch tucked an arm under his head and smiled. "You're only twelve...weird. I'm only seventeen. I just turned it not too long ago." This surprised Odd who thought that he had to be at least twenty. She believed him, however. Who, other than someone really old, would lie their age downwards?

"So what are you doing on your own?" she asked. "Where are your parents?"

"My parents? I left them ages ago. They were so useless." He then made a face and said in a high voice, "Go to school, clean your room, take out the trash...for what? You should be happy your mom's gone. Speaking of which, is your name really, Odd? Like in odd-ball? I heard your mom calling you that."

Odd fought the urge to drop her chin to her chest. "My names Audrey, only everyone calls me Odd," she said. "And I'm not like you I guess. I...I miss my mom."

"You only miss her cuz your scared of being alone. Come here." Mitch beckoned to the bed. Odd didn't budge, instead she thought about how the door seemed suddenly so far away. He laughed at her. "I'm not going to hurt you. You're just stealing all the heat."

Odd smiled in embarrassment and came and sat her skinny butt on the bed. She was being silly of course, he couldn't want her in that way...the way men wanted her mother. She was too much of a stick, too underdeveloped. When she looked at herself she still saw a kid.

"You know what your problem is? You're too

uptight." He fished about in a dresser that sat next to his bed and took out a little box. From it, he pulled out a joint and stuck it between his lips. "For medicinal purposes," he said with a grin.

Odd got back up and went to stand next to the heater.

Mitch lit the joint, taking a heavy drag as he did. After a long second he blew out grey smoke. "Don't be like that. Pot's good for you. The government even made it into a medicine. You wouldn't act like this if you had a headache and I was giving you aspirin. It's the same thing."

"What's it do?" she asked. Odd wasn't tempted in the least. She had seen too many crack-whores, meth addicts, and heroine junkies ever to start down that road. But she was curious.

"You mean other than get you high?" he asked smirking so much that his eyes practically disappeared. "Oh, it just relaxes you...gets you in the mood." He took another pull at the joint.

"In what sort of mood?" Odd was honestly confused. She knew that alcohol put some people in a happy mood and others into a tearful mood, while still others seemed to want to fight.

"For dancing," Mitch answered with a smile. He jumped up. It wasn't an aggressive move, but it was so quick that Odd's eyes couldn't adjust. By the time she blinked things into focus, he was right on top of her. He took one of her small hands in his large one and then tucked his arm around her waist. In a second she was dancing with the tall boy. He smelled of old sweat and cigarettes.

She was nervous as she could get. A thrumming

began in her chest that ran down into her hands—hands that shook as Mitch squeezed them right to the point of pain.

"Relax," he said, giving her a playful little shake. "We're just dancing. See? Back and forth...back and forth."

"Ok...but sh-shouldn't we have some music?" She tried to do her best to smile up at him, but her lips kept quivering down at the corners. He didn't seem to notice.

"Music would be good. You're right." Mitch turned to switch on the little clock radio and when he did, Odd dashed for the door. She had felt what sort of mood he was in and it had felt fearfully big and hard. As they had danced he had pressed it up against her. The idea of that inside her, scared her beyond the ability to think past the moment.

She raced for the door which, because of her eyesight went from something shaped like a standing rectangle to a weird, squat trapezoid. Her hand had to scramble around it to find the doorknob and by the time she did, Mitch had her by the shoulder and swung her around.

"Hey Baby, whatcha doin?"

"M-M-Mitch....I-I don't wanna dance. Ok? I don't want to dance." Her voice shook with her fear. He was so big and she was so tiny.

"I don't want to dance either." As he said this, his hands ran up and down her scrawny body. He pressed himself against her and she backed to the wall.

"Don't. Please. I'll...I'll scream."

"If you do, I'll shove my sock down your throat," he said. His hands now squeezed her arms painfully tight. She could feel his nails biting into her flesh and she grimaced. "Do you want to taste my socks? Or do you want to be a good girl?"

She didn't want either. Her head went in three directions at once, saying yes, no, and maybe all at once. He took it that she wanted to be a good girl. With strength that amazed her, he picked her up and dropped her on the bed. Before she could scramble away, he was on top of her and with one hand he ripped down her loose fitting jeans. Odd could hear one of her buttons bounce off the nightstand.

She was so afraid she could barely breathe. "No, please, please," she whispered, clamping her legs together with all her might. All her might was nowhere near enough, he pried them apart easily.

Tears came now. Sobbing tears that made him shake his head in disgust. "Do you want the sock?" he asked. She shook her head, afraid of the idea of choking to death on an old sock. As she did her glasses slipped.

"What the hell?" Mitch asked, squinting into her face. To Odd, there was one thing worse than being raped and that was for someone to see her eyes. She pulled a hand free and shoved her glasses back into place.

Mitch ripped them away and stared. He saw her eyes as they were never meant to be seen. In the harsh light of the room her irises blazed a bright crimson, while her pupils were perfectly formed wheels of hot red, and the whites, what little she had, formed only a slim border, accenting the demon-look to its fullest.

Mitch stared with a slack jaw, leaning in to get a better look. The sudden movement, ripping her glasses away, had Odd's vision turning Mitch into a funhouse monster. Except this time it worked to Odd's advantage. Mitch's eyes were perfect baby blues. The one on the left had shrunk to a pinpoint, while the one on the right was huge. A huge target. Acting on instinct and fueled by terror, Odd drove her claws at him— her left thumbnail went square into the Mitch's gaping eye.

Odd hadn't meant to scratch him, or even to hurt. She meant to blind him.

Mitch screeched like a girl and threw himself off of her, desperate to get away from the sharp object piercing his eye. When he did, Odd was off the bed in a flash, yanking her pants up and stumbling for the door, frantic to get away. She didn't trust her eyes; she knew they would betray her. Instead she closed them and put her trust in her memory.

Her left hand found the door and her searching right found the knob a second later. With a blast of sharp air she was out into the freezing night, running. She didn't scream for help. It wouldn't do anything but invite spectators. No doors would open to her pleas. It would only cause a hundred faces to peek out through a hundred curtains to watch another human's misery.

The stairs were under her feet before her eyes could adjust and it was only by a miracle that her hand found the railing and kept her from pitching down headfirst. The stairs spun and spun in her vision, forming an endless kaleidoscope. She shut her eyes hard and went down them, forcing her feet to go despite feeling the world spin around her.

At the bottom Odd felt like she was going to be sick, but angry shouts from behind had her running again. She had no idea where she was running to. She just ran.

Chapter 7

Odd ran blindly. In more ways than one. The sun had set and the headlights of the rush hour traffic were like lasers in her eyes. They had her mind reeling with distorted images. To get away from them she ducked down the first alley she came to and staggered on with her hand to the brick to keep her upright.

"You ok, Sugar?"

She jumped and blinked at the words. Three black men were leaning against the walls of the alley, smoking. The men were very dark skinned and after the lights of Broadway she hadn't even seen them. She practically ran into the closest.

Odd shied away, one hand holding up her pants, the other clutching her coat at her chest. Her mental state was well beyond fragile.

"Don't hurt me...please," Odd begged, backing away.

The men looked at each in annoyance. "Who said we was gonna hurt you?" the nearest man asked. His lip curled with the words. "I just wanted to know if you was ok."

Another scoffed, "Stupid cracker whore. You see a black man and you immediately think he's gonna hurt you?"

Odd didn't know what to think about anything. She felt like a fawn in a world of wolves. No one and nowhere felt safe. With a cry she turned and fled. The men sneered and mocked her; one flicked the remains of his cigarette at her. It struck the wall in a shower of sparks near her head. The sudden light dazzled her eyes, making the world seem to turn upside down. Odd's body shifted in response and she crashed to the frozen pavement a second later.

In tears, not knowing right from wrong, or even up from down, she scrambled out of the alley. Knowing she had to get off the main avenue, she reeled like a little drunk to the next street and headed west. She moved away from the bright lights and the immediate danger.

With nowhere to go Odd wandered in the twenty-degree night, feeling numb. The feeling went from her mind to her toes. After her near-rape, she couldn't think straight. Nothing made sense. What kind of person would want a skinny little girl like her? A psycho? A child molester? And if one wanted her that way, that had to mean that more did. How many others were out there like Mitch?

The thought kept her away from people. Any house with lights and laughter coming from it had her crossing the street. When she spied a couple walking their dog, Odd turned and ran.

For how long she walked Odd didn't know, but eventually the elements caught up with her. The cold made each step a frozen nightmare and she began limping with her toes curled in. Her face burned from the exposure and she took to grimacing. If anyone saw, they didn't care.

Odd was done caring as well. The cold went so far as to push Mitch out of her mind and she stumbled along in agony not knowing what to do.

Her salvation came, oddly enough, in the form

of a church. It was the same church that she had been in earlier in the day. This time she didn't hesitate to enter and it was a good thing too. As soon as she walked in, lights began to go down in the main chapel. In a few seconds half the church sat in near complete darkness.

In the semi-dark, Odd could see the priest moving across the front pews. He was a second from turning down the main aisle and when he did, she'd be quite visible to him. But, out of the blue, he stopped at the altar and went down on one knee. Odd dropped to her knees as well...and began crawling.

Making less noise than a whisper, she crept between a row of pews. There she laid down hoping that the priest wouldn't look in her direction as he passed toward the foyer. He didn't and soon he was gone, locking the girl in.

Only then did she relax...mentally that is. Physically, she shivered, huddled in a ball for over an hour trying to get warm. When she had thawed enough to get up, Odd went about exploring the church. There wasn't much to it. Other than the pews and the altar, the only thing of note in the main room were a series of doors along one wall.

Each opened onto its own separate and very tiny room. These were no bigger than closets and could fit little besides the chair which sat in each. The purpose of the rooms was beyond Odd's ability to fathom.

"Is this some sort of punishment?" she asked aloud, sitting in one of the chairs. It didn't seem to be. The chair was wide and comfortable. It had a soft velvety cushion to it that Odd took to stroking. If anything the chair made the hard, wooden pews look like punishment.

Shrugging the rooms off as a mystery without answers, she then went to a door at the back of the church. It opened onto a short hallway and the first thing she saw was a sign for the restrooms. Feeling a sense of urgency that she had been long repressing she hurried to the ladies room wondering how long it had been.

Next she explored the remaining rooms. Two offices, a changing room—hung with a multitude of robes in all sorts of colors, and last, and definitely best, a small kitchen. Right away she went to the refrigerator and looked in. Her last meal had been the day before at the bar with the pretzels.

She still had the half-eaten hamburger in her pocket and had planned on eating it all day; she just hadn't had the chance. But if there was something better in the fridge...

It was then that Odd remembered the talk she'd had with the priest about stealing. She stared at the white door of the refrigerator for a moment without opening it. Instead she pulled out the grease stained, brown bag. The burger inside had been frozen and thawed at least three times that day. Was it still good?

"I'll find out, won't I?" she murmured.

It wasn't bad. Not after microwaving it hot and loading plenty of salt onto it. Still it didn't come close to filling her, but she didn't go back to the fridge. The thought of stealing in a church—especially in a church where they nailed people up on a cross—made her a little nervous.

With that on her mind, Odd went back into the main room and sat on a wooden pew staring up at the figure of Jesus. "I just don't get it," she said for the second time that day. She wondered why this church didn't have the Santa Claus God. The one that was supposed to bring you stuff if you were good.

"I'm pretty good," Odd said, looking up at the ceiling. "I didn't sin today and I'll be good tomorrow. I promise. Now...can I have my mother back, please?"

She waited, not really expecting her mom to appear before her, but all the same not knowing what to expect. When nothing happened she wondered if she was in the wrong sort of church. Maybe it was one of those churches where they sacrificed goats and chickens. Her mom had told her about those. And with the man hanging limply from the cross, she guessed that it was.

Next to her on a pew, sat a book.

"Holy Bible," she read this easily. The lettering was large and distinct from the background. The words inside were a different story. The letters were tiny. To her, they looked like a billion ants crawling all over the pages. She flipped through the book, hoping for some pictures that would make sense of it all.

There were none. Odd tossed the book back onto the pew. She then got up to inspect the altar. To her it was just a big fancy table and nothing special. However, sitting on it was something that caught her eye. It was another bible, but this one was huge. It's cover had actual gold on the spine and edges. In her mind it had to be worth a fortune, yet despite that there was no temptation within her to take it.

The only form of stealing that Odd ever engaged in was the taking of food. Even that was petty in the extreme, such as how she snatched pretzels from Gary's basket. Had her eyesight been better, who knows what she would've been like, but as it was she always felt that normal people could see her smallest actions. She attributed to them, not only the eyesight of an eagle but hyperawareness of her as well.

Odd wasn't too far off about the hyperawareness. Even with her sunglasses on she attracted attention. She never really fit in with her surroundings. Little girls weren't supposed to be walking the streets alone, or hanging around the park with a bunch of old timers. Nor should they be sleeping in shady bars at midnight while their mothers were out in the parking lot working for their next meal.

Odd flipped open the book, again hoping for pictures, and again was disappointed. Yet the lettering was different from the other book. The letters were large. She found that she could read this book.

"In the beginning God created the heavens and the earth," she read aloud, pausing to blink largely every few seconds. "Um... And God said, 'Let there be light,' and there was light...Um...God saw that the light was good, and he separated the light from the darkness. God called the light 'day,' and the darkness he called 'night.' And there was evening, and there was morning—the first day."

After reading further on, Odd leaned back and made a little, "humph," noise. This version of how the world was made was certainly different from how her mom described it. Karen had said the world was just one big accident...she also said the same thing about Odd. Except, that is, when she had too much to drink. Then Odd would go from being an accident to a mistake and then a drink or two later she'd refer to Odd as a curse.

Odd almost closed the big book, thinking it silly. Judging by how her life had gone so far, she had to agree with her mom; the world was just a big accident and she was the biggest accident in it.

She didn't close the book, however. For one, there wasn't anything else for her to do but read.

Chapter 8

At ten pm the furnace shut off and the chapel began to cool. Odd's eyes were wearying her anyway, so she shut the book, but not after marking her place with one of her long, blonde hairs. She then went to the changing room she'd seen earlier, pulled down some of the robes and took them back to the first of the little closet-like rooms.

Here she built herself a snug nest and was soon fast asleep.

She didn't mean to sleep as long as she did. The sound of a vacuum woke her. Odd sat up, blinking slowly, her lids flapping up and down like a bat's wing. Where was she? It took her a moment to recognize the tiny, cell-like room. When she did, she scrambled out of the snow-white robes that had been her bed and went to the door.

Cracking it slowly, she peeked out into the church. A crew of Mexicans were cleaning the church; vacuuming, polishing the wood pews, and dusting everything in sight. Now, they might not have been Mexicans, but Odd, who had a very limited knowledge of geography, relied upon the mis-teachings of her mom.

Karen Wyatt, if she had been in that little, wood paneled room, would've called them a bunch of 'Dirty Mexicans'. Odd didn't quite understand this sort of talk, since for such supposedly dirty people they sure spent a lot of time cleaning.

But Karen Wyatt wasn't in the little room. Only Odd was in the room, feeling smaller than ever. What would the Mexicans do if they caught her there? Gently, she shut the door and began picking up the robes as fast as she could. Putting them back on their hangers, she neatly laid them across the chair.

"That's better," she whispered, glancing her red eyes toward the sound of the vacuum.

She then waited, standing up against the far wall, keeping the chair between herself and the door. The Mexicans cleaned for a long time, though for exactly how long Odd didn't know. She wore no watch, nor even a speck of jewelry. Once she had owned a silver necklace that she had found in a gutter, but that had been stolen from her years before.

She was always being stolen from. If ever she acquired anything of value it never remained in her possession for very long. Even her mother was guilty of stealing from her. On those rare occasions when someone would pity Odd and give her cash to buy a decent meal, Karen was quick snatch the money away. Then off to the bar she'd go.

So it was that Odd didn't fear that the Mexicans would take anything from her, she feared they'd call the police on her. The police would then call Social Services and Social-Services would call...foster-care.

Odd waited but, just as she heard the cleaning crew leaving, a new sound came to her ears—music. It was the sound of an organ. This perplexed her greatly since she hadn't seen an organ in the church. Slowly, Odd peeked out again. The church was filling with old people. They were milling around the entrance.

Was this Sunday? Isn't that when they did

church? Odd tried to count the days. She was supposed to have been kicked out on Monday, but Phil gave her an extra day, so that meant the day before was Tuesday and this was Wednesday. Church on Wednesday? That didn't make any sense.

Singing now accompanied the music. Odd again cracked the door. Forty or so people, mostly old and mostly white stood amongst the pews. They didn't see her; their faces were turned downwards toward their hymnals. Walking up the main aisle was the priest she'd met the day before. He took slow, solemn steps; measured against the invisible organ.

Odd had never seen a Mass before and her curiosity over whether there would be a sacrifice kept her rooted in place. Her reading from the night before had only cemented in her the idea of animal sacrifice. It was mentioned more than once as a way of pleasing God.

But there was no sacrifice. There was a lot of talk by the priest, a lot of singing by the people, accompanied by a lot of sit, stand, kneel. Odd tried to follow along, however the priest seemed in a hurry, buzzing through his prayers and the people weren't exactly articulate when they responded, either.

Visually, at least, it was a treat for her. The slow pace allowed her to watch without the confusion that her eyes could generate. The priest in his floor length green robe stood in contrast to the pure whiteness of the altar. Atop the table was the bible she had read from the night before, two chalices and a plate of shining gold. Again she marveled that no had taken them.

"Maybe they put them in a safe?" Odd mused to herself. She began imagining a hidden vault beneath the altar. In her mind it was filled with not only golden plates but jewels and coins as well.

With her daydreaming, the Mass seemed to be over before she knew it. The old people began lining up to greet the priest, or so she thought.

"The body of Christ," the priest said to the first person.

"Amen," the man replied.

Body of Christ? What did that mean? The priest then gave the man something small to eat. Odd's stomach immediately grumbled at the sight. She was suddenly starving.

The priest then picked up one of the chalices and held it up; it was filled with a red liquid. "The blood of Christ," he said with great solemnity.

Odd's stomach did a flip-flop. Blood of Christ! They were drinking a man's blood! With her heart suddenly thumping in her thin chest, Odd shut the door and gripped the knob with both hands. There had been a sacrifice after all. Her mind reeled with the knowledge. How could this be legal? And what would they do with her if they caught her? The knob became slippery with her sweat.

The procession of people waiting to get their taste of blood seemed to go on forever but, eventually, the singing began again. All during that time she held fast to the knob, not daring to let go. Soon a murmuring commenced that suggested the congregation was making its way to the door. Odd began to relax. Her plan was to wait until the room had quieted completely and then she'd make a break for the exit. After that she'd call the police and leave an anonymous tip.

Her plan went awry when, after only a minute or

so of silence, footsteps could be heard coming right to her hiding spot. Odd gripped the doorknob with all her strength, but it was to the room next door that the person went.

There was one strange feature to the room that Odd hadn't been able to fathom. It was a sliding window that opened onto the little room next to hers. A screen between the two rooms made it difficult to see into the next room.

The person who had just entered gave a little knock on the screen and announced: "I'm ready."

Ready for what? Odd's red eyes were huge. She didn't know whether to run or not. If he knew she had been hiding there it likely meant the door in the foyer was either locked or guarded. She was trapped.

He knocked again.

With one hand on the doorknob, Odd reached over and slid the window partially back. "Yes?" she said in a small voice.

"Hi...this is Father Marino. You may begin anytime."

It was the priest. He seemed very calm for having just served blood at a church. "I don't know what to say." Odd was altogether clueless as to what he wanted.

"That's ok," the priest replied, still relaxed. "Has it been a long time since you've been to confession?"

So that was it. He wanted her to confess what she had done. What would he do to her when he found out she'd spent the night? The thought gave her a shiver; he could do anything to her.

"You have to believe me," she said in a teary rush. "I didn't mean to see anything. I had no choice but to come here. I—I would've frozen to death. And...and the robes, I...I only borrowed them. I wasn't going to steal them. I promise." Her voice was embarrassingly whiny, but she didn't care.

"Robes?" he asked, perplexed. "Could you start at the beginning?"

Odd wiped her eyes and took a deep breath. "My mom hasn't got back yet. She went to California. I know I told you that I had to find my mom, but that wasn't true." Though her mouth was as dry as dirt, she paused to swallow. When she did the priest spoke up.

"Wait. Is this the little girl from yesterday? The one who thought she was a demon-child?"

"Yes...and like I said, I didn't mean it." Odd's tears kept coming and she began to sniffle loudly.

"Hey relax," the priest said through the screen. "It's going to be ok. Tell me what's going on. Just start at the beginning."

Father Marino had a soothing voice that comforted her. It sounded the way a dad's should—protective and concerned. Because of this, Odd broke down and told him almost everything that had happened in the last couple of weeks. It was 'almost everything', because she didn't mention Mitch and what he had nearly done to her. That was still too painful to even think about. When it did break the surface of her thoughts, she wanted to crawl into a hole and hide there forever.

"You've been on your own for a week?" he asked.

"Yeah." Strangely, after telling her tale and confessing her minor sins, she felt hollow, but in a good way.

"Have you eaten?"

Was he offering her something to eat? The idea got her heart thumping again. "Some stuff. But...but, I don't want blood."

"Blood?"

"Yeah, like what you gave to all them people just now."

His loud jovial laughter made her quickly realize that she had made some sort of mistake. When he could speak he said, "I was thinking of eggs and toast. I make a mean omelet, or I can do scrambled, or sunny-side up?"

All of this sounded wonderful to Odd. She only had one problem. "Can I eat in here?"

"We have a kitchen with a table and everything. Why would you want to eat in a confessional? Do you have some more sins that you want to confess?"

If she did, she couldn't remember them. "No. I...I just lost my glasses is all. I don't want anyone to see me. My eyes...my eyes..." Odd started to choke up again. "My eyes aren't normal."

"They won't bother me," the priest replied in the soothing way of his. "Now come out. We'll get this eye business out of the way and then we'll go eat."

Chapter 9

"Did God really make the whole world in a week?" Odd asked around a mouthful of scrambled eggs.

The priest smiled at this, her hundredth question. She had asked about everything, from the drinking of blood—it turned out to be only wine—to the golden cups—they weren't gold, but a brass/aluminum alloy—to the fancy robes—they were indeed fancy.

"Yes. Every part of the bible is true." The way he said this Odd knew that a *but* was coming. "But it's our perceptions that may be false. How long is a week to God? A billion, trillion years? Or seven seconds? Remember, everything is possible with God."

"Even finding my mother?"

His grim smile said that yes it was possible, but perhaps not desirable. "Your mom should be finding you."

"I know." Odd began pushing her eggs around on her plate. "She's not the best mom, or even a good mom, but she's my mom. Without her I don't have anything but these clothes...speaking of which, do you have any string?" She was beyond humiliated to have to hold her pants up with one hand when she walked. Of course without her glasses who would even notice if her pants fell down to her ankles.

A half-hour earlier, when she exited the confessional, Father Marino hadn't been able to hide his shock upon seeing her eyes. He had stared for a bit and then nodded sagely and pointed to the kitchen.

"Let's go eat," he had said with a genuine smile. The subject of her eyes hadn't been brought up again, but she knew it would. It was one of the reasons for all her questions. She wanted to put it off for as long as possible—maybe even forever.

"I'm sure we have some string around here somewhere." He pointed at her plate. "A third helping?"

Odd's belly was nearing capacity, yet, with the likelihood that food would continue to be scarce until her mom returned, she nodded to the plate. The priest went back to the stove and dropped two more eggs into the skillet. A silence came between them. Odd tried to think of something to say to forestall the coming question. Nothing came to mind quick enough.

"Are you ready to talk about your eyes?" he asked.

"I guess." Odd wasn't and never would be.

The priest glanced back at her. "You're not a demon-child, ok? There has to be a scientific explanation for your eyes to be that way."

Still looking at her plate, she shook her head. In her mind, science could explain away anything, even demons. They'd use super-long words but it would amount to the same thing.

"There is an explanation," Odd said, picturing how her mom had looked when the doctor had explained it to her. Karen had been lost in the details after two seconds. "They say I have ocular albinism, nystagmus, and a congenital defect of the retina where the first two layers are fused into one."

At first the priest frowned in concentration, then

he smiled and gave a little laugh. "I don't know what any of that means. Do you?"

Again she shook her head. "No. I heard the words and memorized them, but what they mean..." she ended with a shrug. Walking out of the doctor's office, her mother had an explanation for Odd—*That's all fancy doctor talk meaning you're a demon-child.* Karen had fortified herself with gin before Odd's examination, afraid of the outcome. When Karen was angry or drunk, the word demon slipped out of her mouth frequently.

"Is there any treatment or cure?" the priest asked.

"No...except for this part." She opened her eyes wide and pointed at them. "See how they twitch back and forth. That used to be a whole lot worse. I have an eye exercise I do every day that keeps it from getting too bad."

Anyone seeing her eyes jittering in their sockets became instantly unsettled. Father Marino swallowed loudly. "Oh, good."

There wasn't much more to say. Another silence came upon them and for some reason Odd felt sorry for the priest. He had been trying to help and now it was awkward between the two of them.

"My doctor tried to make it sound cool when he told us what the problem was," Odd said with as much cheer as she could manage. "He said I was the rarest person on the planet. That nobody had eyes like mine."

The priest responded to her lighter mood. "He was definitely right about that. You are a special girl, Audrey." Father Marino straight out refused to call her Odd. "I don't know any twelve-year-olds who could last a week without their parents, especially with..." He waved a hand toward her face.

She nodded in understanding. "It certainly wasn't easy. I used to like peanut butter and jelly sandwiches, but now I'll probably barf if I so much as see one. My mom used to... never mind."

Her mom used to make her peanut butter and jelly sandwiches. That had been long ago, however. Odd had been making her own sandwiches since before the first grade. Suddenly back to being depressed Odd asked the one real question that had been on her mind.

"Father, if I'm not a demon-child, why is God punishing me like one?"

He sat down and looked into her blazing red eyes and said, "First, you're not a demon-child and second, God isn't punishing you. If anyone is, it's your fellow man and they will have to answer to God for every mean thing they've ever done to you."

"You're the only one who says I'm not a demon-child. How do you know?" Odd asked, feeling suddenly listless with her bulging belly. "What would one look like, if she didn't look like me?"

"They'd be ugly, I'm sure. Which is something you are definitely not. And they'd have horns and a red tail. Do you have horns?" He rubbed her head, smiling as he did.

She smiled back, but it was a lie. It was clear the priest was throwing out anything to try to make her feel good. "What will hell be like?" she asked.

His smile dropped off his face. "You're not going to hell. Not if I have anything to say about it. Please remember that God loves you—even if you think that no one else does or nobody can—he does."

"Then why does he send people to hell if he

loves them? That doesn't make any sense." There was a lot about religion that didn't make sense to Odd.

The man sat back in his chair. "How do I put this...Just because you love someone doesn't mean they love you back. God loves you, but if you run from God, if you deny him, then there is no place for you to go but hell. People say hell is the absence of God. So the easiest way to keep from going to hell is to open your heart to God."

"Ok, I guess." It made sense to Odd and under other circumstances she might have been cheered by this, however the words: *Just because you love someone doesn't mean they love you back*, rang in her soul. Was this why her mom was still in California? Did her mother not love her?

A lump like charcoal sat in her throat. Could there be any other reason she hadn't come back for Odd?

Yes.

She could be in jail. She could've been ditched by the trucker. She could be dead. Odd swallowed the lump in her throat and shook the last thought out of her head. That was no way to think; it would just bring her down. The point was, there were other reasons her mom wasn't back yet. Odd just had to be patient and give her mom a few more days. Then she'd be back.

Father Marino had his eyes hard on hers, watching her think his words over. "Do you understand now?"

"Yeah, I think so," she said feeling a little bit better. "But what about Jesus? Why do you pray to a dead guy? And what about Noah? How did he get every animal on board his boat? Wouldn't they have all gone crazy. It would've been like a cage match. And why..."

"Stop. Stop. Hold on," he said, putting out a hand to her. "I'll answer each one of your ten-thousand questions, but first I have to make a call," he said this while looking her square in the face.

Odd's eyes went wide. "No! You can't. Please don't call them. I have to be here for when my mom gets back."

"That could be days or weeks, or..." His lips turned down—or never, his face implied.

"Father, please. They'll send me to foster-care...I don't belong there." Odd began to blink. Panic started forming in her chest. "Why can't I stay here with you? I'm not at all messy and I can sleep in that little room and I'll clean whatever you want me to clean. Please."

The tears came. They magnified the crimson in her eyes. The priest stared for a moment, then looked away.

"I would if I could, Audrey. It's not you...it's the law. I can't legally harbor a minor under these conditions. But, look, there are good foster-homes out there. I've seen them."

He was right. Of the three foster-homes that Odd had been in, two were wonderful and she would've been quite happy in them—if she had been normal. She saw how the other kids fit in, how there was a sense of belonging. However, Odd didn't belong. The parents couldn't stop staring. The kids couldn't stop teasing. They'd pretend that they couldn't eat with her around. They'd gag and retch. They'd call her names, and when she couldn't take it anymore, Odd had run away.

It wouldn't be any different this time. Odd, again, had the desire to crawl into a hole. Listlessly, she said, "Make your call." Then she walked from the room and went back to the confessional and buried herself once more in the white robes.

Chapter 10

Two hours later someone stepped into the other little room that adjoined Odd's.

"Audrey Wyatt?" a woman asked from behind the screen.

"My name is Odd," Odd replied coldly from beneath the robes.

"You know, Audrey sounds much nicer. It's a pretty name."

"Well, I'm not pretty. I'm Odd."

The lady sighed. "I'm sorry but I'm going to have to call you Audrey. If my boss heard me calling you Odd, I'd get in trouble. You wouldn't want me to get in trouble would you?"

"I don't care what happens to you," Odd said, truthfully. "No one cares about me. Why should I care about anyone else?"

"That's not true. Father Marino cares about you. He's afraid that you'll starve to death, or freeze to death, or that something bad will happen to you. That's why he called me. If he didn't care, he would've just kicked you out on the street. Right?"

The robes bounced once in response to her shrug. "I guess."

"My name is Jenny," the woman said. "You know, I've never been in one of these..."

"It's a confessional," Odd filled in the blank. "You tell your sins to the priest and God forgives you." Father Marino had explained to her the purpose to the room.

"Right...it's so weird telling a stranger all your secrets. Don't you think?"

Odd pulled her head out of the robes. It was getting stuffy under them. "They made me go to a therapist last time I was in foster care. It was kinda the same thing."

Jenny laughed. "I guess you're right. It's probably cheaper too. Do you want to hear one of my sins?"

The question made Odd blink. "I—I don't know. Maybe, I guess."

Jenny took a deep breath. "Now, this is true so don't laugh or make fun, ok?"

"Sure." Odd never laughed at or made fun of anyone.

"When I was your age, I had this friend—my best friend—her name was Sam. And I don't know why I did it, but I stole money from her. She had these rolls of quarters. Whole stacks of them and...and one day I took one. It was stupid. I don't know if she ever even knew the money was missing, but I knew. I knew that I screwed up and from then on I couldn't really look at her. We just stopped being friends after that."

"Oh," Odd said. "And are you sorry?"

Jenny laughed bitterly. "Yeah. It was so stupid. I'd take it back if I could."

"Then go and sin no more," Odd said, seriously. During breakfast she and Father Marino had talked of sin and confessions. These were the words that he said Jesus had used.

Now Jenny's laughter was loud and genuine. "Father!" she called. Audrey has the makings of a priest."

Father Marino was closer than either of them realized. "I heard," he said jovially from just outside the door. "Only if she had been a priest, she would've made you say a half-dozen Hail Marys and another half-dozen Our Fathers."

"Did I say it wrong?" Odd asked, not knowing what a Hail Mary or an Our Father was.

"No, you did it the way Jesus taught," the priest answered. "So good for you."

Jenny pressed her face to the screen. Her smile was distorted once by the screen and a second time by Odd's eyes. The little girl looked away from the fearsome sight. The face was more demonic even that her own. "Thanks, but I wasn't looking for forgiveness," the social worker said.

This didn't make sense. She was in a confessional, confessing her sins...Why wouldn't she want forgiveness? "Then why did you tell me this?" Odd asked.

"So you'd be my secret keeper. You know something about me that no one else knows. I want you to keep my secrets and I want you to know that I will keep yours. Do you trust that I will?"

Odd didn't know. It had taken guts to confess to stealing like that. "Should I trust her, Father?"

"Yes. I think so," he replied. "What Miss Voorhees did just now was not easy. I should know. The reason why Catholics confess their sins out loud is *because* it's so difficult. She's putting a lot of faith in you."

"Ok, I guess," Odd said.

"Will you come out now?" Jenny asked.

She'd have to eventually. "Let me clean up first," she said with a little edge of worry to her voice. The little girl rushed to hang up the robes, ashamed at having made a mess of them a second time. When she was done she brought them out and held them up for Father Marino to take. He did so with a warm twinkle in his eyes.

Jenny Voorhees was a middling tall, young woman with shoulder length blonde hair. Odd thought she would've been pretty if she had put on some make-up. As it was she looked sort of like a man.

Jenny stared at Odd until the little girl dropped her chin in embarrassment. The social worker then lifted her face back up with both her hands. "Don't turn away and don't be ashamed. This isn't your fault. I bet it's been tough to live with, but..."

Odd broke in rudely. A rare thing for her. "Tough? It's been more than tough! You don't know."

The woman nodded at this. "You're right. I don't...but maybe you don't know either. There are kids born without arms and legs. They'd kill to have your eyes if it meant they could walk. I'm not saying this to piss you off; I just want to keep you from wallowing in misery. There are people out there way worse off than you and they're living happy, healthy lives. That can be you."

That didn't seem possible. Those other people probably had family or friends who loved them...what's more, they probably weren't demons. Odd pulled back and cast her face down. "What are you going to do with me?"

"Hopefully I'm going to show you that there are people out there who would love for you to be a part of their family."

"Until my mom comes back, right?" Odd asked.

Jenny flicked her grey eyes at the priest before answering, "It's going to be a little longer than that. What your mom did, abandoning a minor, is a criminal act. She may be looking at jail time before you two can be together again."

Jail time! How many years would that be? Odd grew desperate. "But I won't press charges. It was really nothing. She left me with money and a place to stay."

Jenny's eyes were hard. She clearly didn't believe Odd. "How much money?"

Odd looked at her converse and saw two toes peeking from the right one.

Father Marino answered for her. "She told me that she was given nine dollars and rent for a week over at the *Lucky U*. But that ran out on Sunday."

The social worker nodded, while blowing slowly out through her nostrils. "That's abandonment. It's criminal, but who knows what a judge will do. I have seen cases way worse than this get thrown out entirely. For all I know you could be with your mom in a couple of days. But she has to come back first. The longer she's gone the harder it'll be."

Jenny turned away to run her hand on the smooth finish of a pew. "Sometimes I just don't get the world. If you were my daughter I would move heaven and earth to get to you. Do you know what I'm saying?"

"Yes. You're saying that my mom doesn't love me." This was a reality that was repeatedly smacking Odd in the face. She gritted her teeth against it.

"No. I'm saying her priorities aren't right," Jenny replied. "She probably does love you quite a bit, however she's letting things get between you and her. Does she do drugs?"

"No. Not anymore. She can't afford it."

"She drink?" It took a keen eye to see Odd's head moving up and down. Jenny saw it. "What about your dad? Do you know where he is?"

"I don't even know *who* he is." All she knew was that he was the demon. Her mother had cursed him with that title many times in fits of drunken rage. For some reason Odd never knew, her mother hated her father.

"Yeah...yeah that happens a lot these days," Jenny said. "What about other relatives?" Odd thought about her aunt for a second. The woman had said she never wanted to see her again. Odd believed her. Another sigh escapes the social worker before she looked to the priest. "Thanks, Father for everything. Ok, Audrey. It's time to go."

The priest stuck out his hand. Odd looked at it. She ignored it and walked up and put her face in the black of his shirt.

"Please let me stay here," she whispered.

"I wish you could."

Chapter 11

Jenny made one stop on the way to the Social Services building. She dashed into a convenience store and came out with two Cokes, a pack of cherry Lifesavers, and a cheap pair of knock-off aviator sunglasses, which were way too big for Odd's face. She shoved them on, grateful to be able to hide behind them.

"Thank you," she said, very relieved.

"Father Marino mentioned that you lost yours," Jenny replied. "He says it happened about the same time you got that scratch on your cheek. You want to tell me what happened?"

Mitch above her. Leaning his weight against her open thighs. His penis eager and hard. Then the pause. He saw something. Odd, straining with all her might, pulls an arm free. She pushes her glasses back in place. He slaps them away. Her demon-eyes flare wide. His mouth comes open. His right eye is huge. Seemingly on its own her thumb drives into the soft orb...

"I-I just lost them is all," Odd stammered. Her eyes had saved her. It was the first that her deformity had come in handy.

Jenny shared the candy between them. It didn't take much for Odd to like a person. Yet when she did, she was always disappointed. It meant they'd be gone from her life quick. Jenny was sweet and caring and understanding. And she was the intake counselor, which meant that after two hours of questions and paperwork, Jenny Voorhees assigned Odd to a caseworker and left her, going on to the next troubled child.

It didn't take much for Odd to dislike a person either.

"Alright let's see those peepers," Beth Chan demanded almost as soon as they were alone. "I gotta see what I'm working with here."

Odd wanted to argue, but most adults scared her and Beth's flat face, which seemed exceptionally devoid of emotion, was unreadable. Odd lowered her glasses.

At the sight, Beth sighed, either in frustration or anger. "Well, I don't know what to say. Jenny told me you were sweet but shy. I need you to work on being more sweet than shy...and keep the glasses on as much as possible."

"Ok." Odd hadn't planned on taking them off. She'd sleep with them on if she could. "But why do I need to be more sweeter?"

"It's like this," Beth said, pulling Odd to the window. "See those kids over there?" A bunch of older teens were playing basketball in the cold. They were kids Odd would have detoured wide around had she been on the streets. Even the girls were a very unpleasant looking lot.

"Those kids live in the B wing." Beth explained. "The B Wing is for kids that we can't place in foster-care. Either they're too violent, or they steal, or whatever. What it comes down to is that no one wants them. For the next three days you'll be in the A wing. You'll have your own room, your own bathroom, but," Beth paused a long time—a significant time. "But, if in those three days we can't find a placement for you, the regulations say that I have to move you over to the B wing until we find you a home."

Odd looked back to the kids on the court. They were tattooed and pierced in many places. Their faces seemed perpetually twisted into sneers of hatred for everyone around them. She didn't want to go to the B wing. She was too small, too weak, too shy, but most of all she was too much of a freak. Turning back to Beth, she unfurled a smile in her direction.

The caseworker was unmoved. "You'll have to do better than that."

Odd did her best. It wasn't good enough. In the first two days she met with five families. In each case she was as outgoing as she could possibly be, and everything would seem to be going fine, yet always there came the question of her eyes. And when she would remove her glasses the excuses would start to flow. She was suddenly too old or too young—or too something.

The third morning had Odd moving slowly. She felt like a condemned prisoner waiting for the gallows, but then Beth bustled in. "Let's get moving. You may have caught a break."

"My mom came back?"

The caseworker waved away that possibility with a flick of her wrist. "Hardly. A placement has opened up in a foster-home. Get your stuff. We'll move you in today."

"This *is* my stuff," Odd said, touching her ratty coat. It was now clean at least. "The pajamas are borrowed."

"Well good, the packing's done then. Let's go."

Dragging her along by the wrist, Beth pulled

Odd to the front office where her paperwork waited. After a few signatures, she was out in the cold air of the city once again.

"How do you know they'll take me?" Odd asked. Her stomach was in knots over the idea that they wouldn't.

Beth walked them to an aging blue truck. It looked diseased. Rust, creeping up from underneath, had begun ravaging the side panels. Odd pictured her foot going through the floorboards so she climbed in as delicately as possible.

"They'll take you. They take anyone." Did that mean they were nice people—generous people? The way Beth kept from looking at her had Odd thinking that wasn't the case. Beth drove for a while and then sighed one of her agitated sighs. "Look, because of your disability, we're not going to able to place you with your typical white-bread family."

"I don't care if they're white," Odd said, looking out the window. Just then she wished that she had allowed Mr. McCew to call his daughter-in-law the social worker. Maybe Odd could have stayed with her.

"Don't ask me why, but the state does." Beth took a turn and added in a huff, "They want you kids placed—bam-bam-bam—as fast as possible, but then they say, 'Oh she can't go there and he can't go here'. It's stupid. Either way, you'll be staying with the Fedorovs. Vadim and Lena. They're from Russia...and they're a little rough around the edges."

Maps and globes, with their tiny words and thousands of undulating lines, were unreadable to Odd. She'd had heard of Russia, but had no idea how near or far it was. Nor did she know what Russian people were like. However, she knew what 'rough around the edges' meant—it meant mean.

Her heartbeat began to pick up in pace. Why had her mom left her? This was all her fault. Foolishly, Odd looked out of the truck's window, hoping to see the motel they'd been staying at, but instead, images of the world sped by—broken and twisted—assaulting her eyes. In seconds she looked down at her knees, straining to keep her breakfast inside her.

She was still a shade of green when Beth pulled up in front of a ramshackle ranch house. With the car stationary, Odd chanced a look out. Now she could feel the beat of her heart in her hands. Two large dogs stood growling behind a six-foot high, chain link fence. Generally she liked dogs, just not those with so many teeth.

"They won't bite," Beth said. Nevertheless, the caseworker's eyes kept close tabs on the dogs and she put her large purse between them and her. Odd didn't have a purse. She had to content herself by snugging her hands up the sleeves of her jacket and keeping as close to Beth as she could.

The dogs followed them up the cracked cement walk, and so nervous was Odd that she stumbled into Beth at the front door. The girl had walked with her head cranked around, fearing to take her eyes off the beasts.

"Bet! So glad you come."

The front door opened, sending out a harsh aroma of cigarettes and unwashed dog. A very large woman filled the doorway. She had uniformly grey hair, except for the hairs on her upper lip and chin. These straggles were black. Despite her pleasant greeting, Lena Fedorov's eyes were hard and appraising.

"Come." The woman waved them in.

The house was small and dark. A man, large, round and greasy, sat on a couch. Between his lips a lit cigarette dangled. Odd thought her eyes were playing tricks on her again. The man sat square in the middle of the couch and it seemed to be lifting up at either end, as if he was bending it with his bulk. She blinked but the image remained.

He turned a very red face to the three women. "What is this? I want boy, not this." He waved his hand at Odd. "She too skinny. Who gonna run lawnmower? Not me."

Lena barked at him in Russian, to which he simply made a face and threw his hand up before turning back to the television.

"Don't worry about him. He likes you—he just funny," Lena explained. "Come. We sit in dining room."

The house resembled an indoor junkyard. There were piles of everything imaginable stacked here, there, and everywhere. Odd got dizzy trying to see it all; magazines, clothes, dishes, cardboard boxes, teacups, car parts.

"Come sit," Lena said; still with the fake smile and still with her hard eyes on Odd. The dining room lay between the living room and the kitchen. It too had piles of this and that all about it, but the table itself was clear. Odd's chair was stiff and heavy; she had trouble moving it, especially with the collection of hubcaps that stood between it and the wall.

Beth sat and, though her face still hadn't

registered obvious emotion, she kept her hands to her chest as if she was afraid to touch anything.

Lena sat and as she did both she and the chair groaned. "So, what's wrong wit girl?"

"There's nothing wrong with her," Beth said. "Our placement facility..."

With a snort, Lena interrupted. "This me, Bet. She is level two. That means something wrong wit her. Does she steal?" Lena didn't wait for an answer from the caseworker. She turned to Odd and glared. "Do you steal? You don't steal from me! This you don't do."

Odd shriveled under the gaze of the woman. Beth spoke up for her, "She doesn't steal. She has an eye problem, but it won't affect the placement at all."

Lena leaned back. "Eye problem? That's it? Can she see? Can you see?" Odd nodded her head. "Can you talk?" the big woman added.

"Yes," Odd said in a whisper.

"Take off your glasses, Audrey," Beth commanded.

Slowly Odd removed them. Immediately Lena cried, "What is this?" Repulsed, the woman turned her head and held up a large flat hand towards Odd. "Bet! Why you do this to me? This isn't right."

"Stop it Lena," Beth ordered. "There is nothing wrong with her. She'll keep the glasses on. Right, Odd?"

Odd nodded and slipped the over-large sunglasses back onto her small face as quickly as she could. She didn't know what to think. No adult had ever reacted to the sight of her eyes with such revulsion. Mostly they'd stare, or make a comment, but this...this was extremely hurtful. Odd felt her face go hot red and her eyes started to fill with tears.

"Nothing wrong?" Lena said in shock. "I have children here to worry about. Think of the nightmares. I don't know..." she left off, shaking her head. Beth didn't reply to this. She only sat there, waiting. Finally, after the silence had carried on for half a minute or so, Lena added, "Maybe if she was a three, I could do this."

Beth sighed. It was a combination of weariness and disgust that she breathed out. "She's a two. I already tried to get her bumped up. It's not happening."

Now it was Lena's turn to sigh, as if she couldn't believe she was contemplating taking Odd on. "What about clothing allowance? She can't go around like that."

"You'll get the full allowance."

"And her mom?"

Beth opened the folder that she had brought in with her. "Criminal abandonment. She's been gone for at least two weeks already."

"Oh good," Lena said. She turned to Odd and smiled. "Your mom, very bad. You stay wit Lena." She then patted the girl on the arm, suddenly cheerful.

The abrupt change in Lena had Odd's mouth hanging open. What was going on?

Chapter 12

It took a half-hour for Beth and Lena to fill out the paperwork. Odd just sat there becoming gloomier with each passing minute. The Fedorovs did not seem like pleasant people. The house stunk heavily of grease. The dogs scared her. And it didn't seem to matter to anyone that Odd was miserable.

Beth didn't help. She began to leave as soon as the last paper was signed. "Excuse me, Beth? Can we talk?" Odd asked, feeling desperate. Once again she felt like a hot potato—first her mom, then Father Marino, then Jenny, and now Beth was passing her along.

Lena had a sour look on her face over the idea of a private conversation; Beth didn't care, "Sure, let's go to my truck."

The truck had gone cold in the short time they had been in the house. The cold immediately seeped through Odd's ratty jeans and she began to shiver—although it might not have been just from the cold. She had a sinking feeling that the Fedorovs weren't good people. Especially Vadim. He had mumbled under his breath in Russian a good deal and each time he did Lena had pursed her lips and looked uncomfortable.

"I don't get it," Odd said, once Beth climbed in. "Lena didn't want me and now she does?"

Beth stared at the steering wheel as she answered, "She always wanted you. She was just trying to get more money for you."

More money? Was she being sold? Odd couldn't

make sense of this. "What do you mean more money? How can she do that?"

"Foster parents get a monthly stipend to help cover the cost of raising you," Beth explained. Odd could see her jaw working as she spoke. The muscle sat as a knot under Beth's skin.

"Was she haggling over me?" Odd asked. Beth set that hard jaw and shrugged to answer: yes. Was this really happening to her? Odd wondered. She had become a piece of fish to be quibbled over. But there was something worse nagging at Odd. "And why did Lena seem so happy that my mom could be in trouble with the police?"

"She wasn't trying to be mean," Beth said. "The Fedorovs try only to get long-term or permanent placements. Which is understandable, if you ask me. They don't like change. New kids coming in every other day can be disruptive to a home."

Home? Odd looked back at the little ranch house. The dogs. The fence. The closed-in feel. The hard, uncaring eyes of Lena. The vile, bitter, hung-over feel emanating from Vadim. This wasn't a home, it was a prison. "This can't be permanent. You should tell them that. My mom will be back soon. I have to be with her."

Beth smiled in her unamused way. "Audrey, I've been doing this for too long and so I'm not going try to blow rainbows up your butt. It doesn't do anyone any good to live in a fantasy world. This is going to be your home...like it or not. The Fedorovs are not easy people, but they won't hurt you. You'll be clothed and fed and kept warm...but they won't love you. Sadly, they do the minimum that the state demands and nothing more."

"But my mom..."

Beth grew cross. "You're not listening. *If* your mom comes back, she's looking at jail time. Up to five years. Do you think she'll come back for you at the end of that?" Beth's little black eyes turned away from Odd. "Remember what I said about you not being a priority to your mom? Well, it's time for you to shift your priorities, too. You need to give up the dream. She's not coming back...they never do. This is your home now. I suggest you make the best of it." As if to underline the finality of her statement, Beth put the key in the ignition and started the car.

Odd felt a yearning to cling to Beth and beg her to find another home. She resisted, knowing that it would be a waste of time. Beth wasn't the only one who had been around the block, and the Fedorovs weren't the only ones doing the minimum the state required. Beth's job was to find a home for Odd. She'd done that and she wasn't going to do anything more. The thought was like a cold, dead stone in her heart.

What could Odd do? Not knowing where she was, or really where she'd been, made running away seem impossible. And if she did run, where would she go? California? Was that ten miles away or ten-thousand? And what direction was it? And if she ever made it there, how would she find her mom; one woman out of millions of people?

Odd had to face facts: she was trapped here. She had no past to go back to, and no future to look forward to. The little girl let out her own long sigh. "Bye," Odd said, opening the truck's door.

"Hey, I'll be back in one week to see how you're doing, ok?" Beth said. "And then monthly visits after that. You'll be fine."

"Sure," Odd replied, not caring. In a week Odd would be the same: alone. And the same would be true in a month. Whatever people said about her mother, she had at least stuck with Odd...until now. And who knew? Karen Wyatt could be struggling to get back to her right at that that very moment.

With a final squeal of rusting metal, Odd slammed the door shut. Behind her Beth looked at her through the glass. In front of her Lena stared from the other side of her own glass. In a way they seemed as trapped as she was.

Chapter 13

"You have good talk, I hope?" Lena asked. Odd nodded. "Your name Odd-ree?"

"Just call me, Odd."

Lena smiled, a mouth smile only. It never touched her eyes. "Odd. Good. Come. I show you house. This is living room. Don't bother Vadim. He likes his shows. Don't bother him or he get mad."

The woman then pointed to two doors. "That. My room. Don't go in there. That. My other room. Don't go in there. Go in there and you in troubles. You understand?"

Odd nodded. She knew what troubles were: being hit, being screamed at, having her hair pulled out in clumps. Odd knew all about this; she'd had her share.

"Now. This kitchen," Lena said, taking a grip of Odd's shoulder. "Stay out of this room unless I say. Get Vadim beer if he ask. If no...don't come in here. I feed you good. I make you fat. Don't steal food. Understand?"

Water bugs had scurried under dishes the second they'd walked in. Odd got the shivers at the sight, while the smell of old cabbage turned her stomach in a slow roll. She wasn't going to steal food. She was worried about eating anything at all in that house. It was the bugs mostly; they grossed her out to no end.

"Mell-ney!" Lena yelled. The power of her voice shook the plates. "Come do your chore! She lazy.

You no lazy, right?" Odd nodded, but didn't know if that answered the question properly. However she was feeling far too overwhelmed at her new 'home' and her new 'family' to say much of anything. A second later, a doughy looking girl with drab, brown hair came into the kitchen from a set of back stairs.

"Sorry, Mrs. Fedororv," she said. Except for a flick her eyes at Odd, she watched the Russian closely. Odd saw how the girl kept her hands up close to her chest. "You said you wanted us to make sure our rooms were clean and I...ow!"

Lena had reached out one of her large hands and given the girl a sharp pinch on the neck. "You can't do two things? You are teen. You can do this if you no so lazy."

"Sorry, Mrs. Fedororv," the girl repeated, red-faced. "I'll do it right now."

"Yes, you will," Lena said. "But first. This new girl. Odd. This Mell-ney." The two girls glanced once at each other and then both quickly looked back at Lena. Odd was afraid to take her eyes from the woman. "Come," the Russian commanded.

Odd followed her down into the basement where the ceiling was so low Lena's grey head scraped it in spots. "This laundry room. Your chore is laundry. Every day. You no lazy like Mell-ney. You do laundry before?" Odd nodded, which seemed to upset the woman. "Say words: yes ma'am—no ma'am. Don't nod. Who can hear nod?"

"Yes," Odd said, as quick as she could. "I've done laundry before." She liked to be clean. In her nine days alone at the motel, Odd had twice washed her one set of clothes in the sink and had hung them over the shower curtain to dry.

"Good." Lena went to the washing machine and began pointing at the dials. "This—here. This—here. No use hot water. Is waste. No use second rinse. Is waste. Use this much powder. No more. And don't let machine bang. It disturb Vadim. Is bad. Is troubles. You understand?"

"Yes."

"Good. Come." Lena led her through the one door in the laundry room to a narrow hall. A single bulb hung from the low ceiling and it's light fell on a number of closed doors. She went to the first one on the left and opened it to show Odd a small square of a room. Inside was a single bed and dresser.

"This Mell-ney room. She oldest. She get own room. Keep out unless she say ok."

Odd began to nod, but stopped the move abruptly. "Yes, Ma'am."

Lena shut the door and went to the next door. "This Maria and Tanya room." Without knocking, the foster-mother opened the door. Two girls sat on the floor playing cards. Both had deep tans and black hair. As usual Odd categorized them as Mexican. The younger of them seemed about Odd's age, the older one was maybe fourteen or so.

"Girls, this Odd," Lena said as an introduction. Both girls applied insincere smiles to their faces. Their eyes, however, were judging and suspicious. The Russian went on, "They no good girls. Maria wants baby. Is very, very stupid. You no stupid, Odd. You no want baby, right?"

The question had never honestly come up. Odd couldn't take care of herself let alone another person.

Then there was the issue of her eyes. Who would want to be a family with her? Who would want her as a mother? No one.

"I don't want a baby."

"Good. No babies. You hear me, you two? No Babies!" Lena said with her hands on her hips. Her scowl cowed the two girls, both of whom stared down at the cards in silence.

Shutting Maria and Tanya's door, Lena pointed to two more doors on the left. "Is bathroom. Keep clean. No long showers. Is waste. Three minutes only." She held up three fingers, pushing them into Odd's face. "No more or I flush toilet. It get very hot. You no like. This is storage room. You stay out."

"Yes Ma'am," Odd replied as Lena paused to take a breath. The Russian then opened the last door. Inside was a bunk bed, two small dressers and barely room to walk. It was so cramped Lena didn't step in. A girl sat on the lower bunk. She had lank, dirty blonde hair and a face ravaged by acne.

"Kristen this Odd," Lena introduced. "She new girl. She sleep here." Lena pushed Odd into the room with a smile and a nod. She gestured to the top bunk. "Is your bed. Keep clean. Keep all made."

Odd glanced around the cramped space. None of the furniture matched and the carpet had turned threadbare. On the walls, covering over badly peeling paint, were a number of posters and pictures of horses. Odd liked them, but they seemed a little childish for a girl of Kristen's age, which she guessed at sixteen or seventeen.

Lena turned off her smile. It happened as if a switch had been snapped down within her face. "Get

Odd some clothes," she ordered Kristen. "Three of everything. Three shirt, three pant, three sock. You have underpants?" This last she asked of Odd.

Odd hadn't had underwear in a few months. "No, Ma'am," she mumbled. Embarrassed she sent her eyes down to the carpet.

"Three underpants, too," Lena sighed. Looking put out at having to supply underwear, she left, shaking her head.

From the bottom bunk, Kristen eyed Odd for a moment and then pushed by her, mumbling something under her breath. Odd was left alone in the tiny room. Besides Kristen's bunk there wasn't really any place for her to sit. Her own mattress practically reached to the low ceiling. The top of the taller of the two dressers was cluttered with make-up, hairbrushes, barrettes and the like. There was even a small jewelry chest on it that lay open displaying a confusion of earrings, necklaces, and pendants.

Odd gave it a curious glance only. All the make-up and jewelry in the world wouldn't help her appearance, though she did like to have her hair brushed out. Still she didn't touch anything. Instead she went to what she suspected was her dresser—a squat three drawer affair—and climbed up on it. Kristen came back a few minutes later with a handful of clothes.

"Thanks," Odd said, hopping down to take the bundle from the much taller girl. The clothes overflowed her short arms and most went on the floor. Odd began to fold them again. Nothing seemed to match.

"So, what are you in for?" Kristen asked, lying back on her bunk and watching Odd work.

"In for? What do you mean?"

"Whatcha doing here? This is the bottom of the barrel. The Fedorov's house is like foster-prison," Kristen explained. "You'll rot away here never seeing the sun...except to go that crappy school. You had to have done something pretty bad to be sent here."

Odd thought about her petty sins and knew they weren't the reason. "Nobody wanted me, I guess." Saying the truth aloud stung. She felt the pain of it deep in her chest.

"Nobody wanted you?" Kristen scoffed. "Hell, nobody wants any of us. Why do you think they have to pay people to take us in? You think people do this out of the goodness of their hearts?"

"I was in a home once in Toledo. The family was kinda nice, they were gonna adopt one of their foster kids," Odd said, picking out a pair of brown jeans and a *Hello Kitty* long sleeve shirt. She considered adding another shirt on top of it. The Fedorovs must have thought heating the basement was one of those wasteful things, like using hot water to clean clothes.

Kristen snorted. "Thinking about adopting? Man, you are one gullible girl. *No one* gets adopted, believe me. I've been in foster-care for years and I've never seen it. Except there was one time these three kids all get adopted into the same home, and you know what?" She paused long enough for Odd to shrug. "The family sent them back after a couple of months! Like they were some socks they bought at Walmart. They just got tired of them or something and returned them. Can you believe that?"

From what Odd knew of people, she could very well believe it. She leaned up against her dresser with her clothes in her arms as a gathering depression took hold of her. It wasn't just her, nobody wanted any of them; it was a terrible thought.

"So why are you here?" Odd asked. Kristen had an abrasive way about her and made Odd nervous.

"Why am I here? Because I don't give a crap anymore." Kristen reached up and started picking at an exposed board on the bed above her. "They have me going to a therapist and he doesn't call it 'not giving a crap', he calls it 'antisocial personality disorder'. But that's all bull. I'm very social. You can ask all the losers around here. I try to be everyone's friend...I can't help it if no one wants to be my friend."

"I believe you," Odd lied. The truth was she didn't know what to believe, other than the fact that Kristen made her 'twitchy'. The way she picked at the wood with her lips drawn tight together—the way she looked at Odd, almost from the word go, with a sneer on her face—the way her eyes were flat, unemotional, unreadable—all this set off warning bells in Odd's mind.

"You better believe me," Kristen replied. "You know why? Because we're going to be best friends. That's why. You don't want to be friends with the rest of the losers here. Tanya and Maria? They're a couple of skanks. Maria's been pregnant three times! Can you believe that? And I know Tanya's had like a dozen boyfriends since school started."

Odd didn't know the term 'skank' but guessed it wasn't good. "Are you talking about the two Mexicans?"

Kristen's brows came together. "They're not Mexicans. They're from Guatemala."

"Oh," Odd murmured. She had never heard of Guatemala. It sounded ghastly and her mind couldn't conjure up anything pleasant about a place with such an ugly name. Mexico was a whole other story. She had always pictured Mexico as a warm, sunny place with white beaches and bright blue water. She never understood why anyone would ever leave it.

While she had thought on this, Kristen had continued badmouthing her foster-family. "And Melanie, she's a klepto. She always stealing stuff from her foster families. Even from the other kids. She's so stupid. She takes the stuff, turns around and hawks it at a pawnshop, and then sends the cash to her mom." Kristen laughed at this. "In a way you're kinda lucky. You got nothing for her to steal except them glasses."

"Yeah." Odd pushed them further up on her nose. In her heart she knew what was coming. "I'm going to go get changed," she said, turning for the door.

"You don't have to change in the bathroom. We're both girls." Kristen stood and in one-step was next to Odd. "Hey, let me see your glasses." Her hand was out.

Odd tried to put on her best smile. "I can't. I have eye problems and..."

Kristen took the glasses from Odd's face. "It won't hurt you none. How do I look?" Odd had turned away the second her glasses had been snatched from her face. Now she peeked up at Kristen, afraid of what would happen if she didn't obey.

Kristen moved her head about to show the glasses off from different angles. The action made her face turn sharply angular in Odd's eyes so that the girl looked like a wolf. Odd blinked in response.

"I bet I look like a...movie...star...what the hell's with your eyes?" The older girl asked, using one finger to lower the glasses down her nose. She stared for a half a second and then screamed, "Gross!" Kristen flung the glasses away. "You got some sort of disease?"

Odd scrambled after them. One of the cheap lenses had popped out; her heart ceased to beat at the sight.

"I'm talking to you!" Kristen hissed. "You got some disease that's catchable?"

With her whole mind focused on the lens, Odd ignored the much bigger girl until it snapped back into place. At the sound, Odd let out a sigh of relief and put her glasses back on. Kristen kicked her in the back. It wasn't much of a blow since the girl seemed afraid that whatever Odd's problem was could come up through her shoe. Yet it still knocked the wind out of Odd.

"No...it...won't hurt...you," Odd said in between gasps.

"How do I know?" The bigger girl demanded. "I bet you're a liar." She started to back out of the room, watching Odd with narrowed eyes. When she turned into the hall, it was with a loud carrying whisper, "Hey! Everyone! The new girl's a freak!"

Chapter 14

Odd took a step back, hit the dresser and, in a fit of desperation she looked around for a place to hide. The room was too small; too cramped and there was nowhere even for someone her size to wriggle behind or beneath. A second later the door opened and the other foster girls stared in at her. Odd's chin dropped to her chest as the strength drained from her thin, little body.

"Hey freak," Kristen called to her. "Take off your glasses. Show them your eyes." Odd couldn't move. She couldn't will her hands up to her face. To do so meant the worst sort of ridicule...however to deny the bigger girl, likely meant pain. Odd preferred pain. Those scars would heal.

Pushing her way forward, Kristen asked, "You want me to take them off for you? If you make me, you can kiss those sorry glasses goodbye."

Her glasses were her only bridge to anything resembling a normal life. She was willing to lose a hand before she lost them. "Ok...please d-don't touch my glasses," she begged. When she took them off, the reaction of the other teens came as no surprise. They flinched back, all of them, Kristen included. And then they stared with revulsion.

"Diablo," Maria hissed to her sister, pointing.

Tanya nodded emphatically. "Sus ojos son muy loco."

"I'm not staying in here with her....none of us

can," exclaimed Kristen to the others. "You have to switch rooms with her Melanie."

The doughy, pale brunette sneered, "Dream on. I'm not moving anywhere. You two freaks belong with each other anyway."

"That's not fair!" Kristen whined.

While all this was being said, Odd put her over-sized sunglasses back on and waited in misery, hoping they wouldn't throw things at her. It had happened before.

"I don't care if it's fair or not. I'm not giving up my room." Melanie turned and walked down the hall, calling out as she did, "Enjoy your time together, freaks."

Tanya and Maria left as well, walking sideways to keep any eye on Odd, just in case. This left just Kristen who was looking a sickly green. "I'm not staying in here with you. I don't care what. I'll tell my caseworker. They can't make me."

Odd said nothing.

"This is totally unfair!" Kristen suddenly bawled. "I'm...I'm going to make Mrs. Fedorov move you. You can't stay in here. You're diseased." Now Kristin's green color changed to a high pink at the idea of confronting her foster-mom. Nevertheless, she walked away still lamenting her unjust situation.

Odd didn't move. She had no hope. No matter what, she would make enemies by her very existence. If she was forced to live with Kristen, the much larger girl would make her life unbearable. If Melanie was forced to move, there'd be no peace in the basement; the two girls would fight and Odd would be blamed. She was always blamed.

An argument began on the main floor. Odd sighed. What would the world be like if she wasn't in it? Everyone would certainly be happier, she was sure of that. Was her mom happier? Was that why she hadn't come back for Odd? Had Karen Wyatt stepped away from her responsibilities just long enough to see how much fun the world was without Odd in it, and now couldn't force herself to come back?

The argument grew louder. Odd was impressed with Kristen. There was no way that Odd would ever talk back to Lena. The woman had a dangerous mean streak running through her—odd had seen it in her beady little eyes.

The two voices grew hot in their anger. One of them stomped their feet. There would be no winners in this confrontation, but definitely there would be at least one loser. Odd waited for the inevitable

Now, a louder shout—like thunder—ended the argument. Then footsteps pounded down the stairs. Troubles were coming. Vadim was coming to fix the issue in his way. Odd feared his way even more so than his wife's. Beneath her thin ribs, her heart rippled in crazy waves. She pressed her back to the wall between the two dressers and watched the door in a horror-stricken silence.

She had not long to wait.

Vadim slammed into the door, sending it careening back. He stood there with a cigarette clenched between his teeth, searching the small room with bitter, resentful eyes as his breath blew out of his round cheeks in hot, smokey-grey plumes. His fat-cheeked face was red and in a full sweat of anger.

Finally, his eyes fell on Odd and her knees

buckled at the sight of his fury. She didn't collapse all the way to the floor, however. Vadim caught her. He caught her by her long, straight blonde hair and hauled her up, dragging her from the room.

Odd wanted to scream at the pain, but she knew that sometimes screams brought on even more punishment. To keep from crying out, she bit the inside of her cheek. And to save her hair she grabbed hold of Vadim's thick wrist and pulled herself up. He dragged her down the hall to the storage room. There he flung her in.

She banged up hard against a pile of boxes, knocking her, for the moment, senseless. The door shut taking the light with it. Lying on hard cement, Odd touched her head, feeling the pain in her scalp—she began to cry. Her tears were part fear and part pain. What was Vadim going to do with her? She could hear him in Kristen's room. It sounded like he was tearing the place a part.

Something heavy thumped into one of the walls, causing it to shudder. This got Odd moving.

Without a window, the room depended on the slim cracks around the door for its meager light. It was enough for Odd. Though she could hardly see in bright light, her night vision may have been without equal. It took a moment for her eyes to adjust, but when they did, she saw the stacks of boxes and moved through them to the rear of the room. There she slid behind a pile taller than herself.

Seconds later Vadim came in. Haphazardly he threw aside boxes making a little clearing. He then pulled a thin, stained mattress in from the hall and let it flop to the ground. He left again only to return a second later with an armful of clothing. These he dumped on the mattress.

"Stay!" he bellowed, before leaving. Odd did as he commanded; she didn't even move out from behind the boxes. Crying, she kept herself hidden, though eventually the tears stopped. In fact, perhaps due to the stress that she was under, she fell asleep in an odd half-kneeling position.

Sometime later, Lena woke her. "Odd-Ree?" She called standing just in the doorway. She had flicked on the overhead lights—effectively blinding Odd.

"Yes?" the girl answered from behind her boxes.

"Come," Lena said.

Wincing with stiffness, Odd extricated herself. She went to stand closer to her foster mother, yet didn't come within reach. Lena gave her a beaming smile.

"So, what you think of room?" Lena asked, waving a hand at the boxes. "Nice, huh? You like?"

"Do...do I like it?" Behind her dark glasses, Odd's eyes blinked rapidly as her mind reeled. Was this how they expected her to live? Shut up in a windowless room for the rest of her life? "I don't like it."

Lena sighed, and then shrugged, "Too bad. It is this, or B wing. You don't want that. They are terrible cruel there. You no believe me, ask girls. They tell you. Very bad stuff happen in B wing."

"I can't ask the other girls," Odd said. "They all hate me. They think that I'm contagious. It's not true. I was born this way."

"Here, we do this," Lena replied. "Tomorrow, we go doctors—eye doctors. He tell us you no contagious. Great. You stay wit Lena, ok?"

"Will I get to sleep in a normal room?"

Lena pretended to think it over. "Maybe. We see what the time it tells us. You nice. Girls, they start to like you, then yes."

"What about Vadim? Will he like me?"

Lena was far less convincing thinking this over. "Him? He funny man. For now just stay out of his way. Stay down here and you be fine, ok? Is good plan?"

Odd said yes, but knew, deep inside, that she wouldn't be fine. Kristen had been more right than she knew. Odd had been sentenced to foster-jail. She was looking at a six-year stretch and the time was either going to be served at Lena's or in the B wing. What a horrible choice! Living underground like a rat, or living in a cage—like a mouse among rats.

Her pathetic life seemed to be spiraling away from her. How low could she fall? Sadly the truth was she had a ways to go; there was still school to deal with—the worst torture of them all. Nothing was worse than eating alone, sitting alone, and being alone, all the while surrounded by hundreds of normal people. It made her want to cry just thinking about it.

The staring, the laughter, the over-the-top, feigned revulsion, and perhaps worst of all, the snide comments about her intelligence. In her twelve years of constant motion, Odd had been to school maybe two-hundred days total. Her mom could never be hassled with enrolling her and Odd purposely never brought it up.

She could read well when the lettering was large, but her writing could only be called childish and she knew next to nothing about grammar or spelling. She could do math, working out simple problems in her head, but in science she lacked even the fundamentals.

Quite literally Odd would have been shocked to hear that the earth wasn't flat. It sure seemed that way to her. Everything about science was a complete mystery to her. Yet worse was history, where she knew ten times more incorrect 'facts' than actual facts.

But for all this, Odd had a native intelligence that rarely led her astray. Thus it pained her to no end to hear the taunts about how stupid she was.

Odd looked up at Lena. "Can you home school me? You teach me stuff yourself, here?"

The very notion queered Lena's face as if she had eaten something unpleasant. "No. I don't do that sort of thing. You go to school with other children. Is right. What grade are you in?"

Odd didn't know. "Fifth or sixth, I think. I don't know where I'm supposed to be. I don't do well in school."

"Da. Is ok. We find out tomorrow." Lena turned thoughtful, staring at the boxes nodding her head. "You are special needs kid. That's good. You are special needs eye kid, too. This all add up. You stay wit Lena. We get you to level three and I get you pretty dress. What you think? You like pretty dress?"

Yes, Odd loved pretty dresses. It was her greatest desire to seen as a normal girl and normal girls wore dresses. However, she didn't want one if it meant being one of the special needs kids at school. The humiliation wouldn't be worth it.

Odd shook her head. "I'm not a special needs kid. I'm not a retard or nothing."

Lena glowered at this in silence for a minute. Then she stepped full into the room shutting the door behind her. "Odd-ree. I try to be nice wit you. Is difficult. You stay wit Lena, there is conditions, da? Or you go to B wing. Is very bad place. They hurt you there. You are too small and all children big. Too big. You understand?"

She had the picture. Odd nodded.

"You stay here. Is better. Is not great, but is better." Lena looked around again sizing up the cramped space. "We move some boxes. Is ok. You live in this room. These are conditions, or you go and I get new kid. Normal kid. Is up to you."

Odd had no choice. "I'll stay."

Lena smiled. "Good. Here are conditions: You sleep here. But is secret. If asked, you stay wit Kristen. No allowed to live in storage room. What do they know? I live in closet for five years. Is ok. Not great, but is ok. Now, two: you go to school. You say you no read and write. You stay wit special kids. They nicer. They no make fun of you. Is good, da?"

Odd stared down at a box marked: dishes-broken. Why would they keep them if they were broken? Maybe they were just chipped or cracked. Odd didn't know, but just then she felt like those dishes; useless, put away out of sight—tucked in with other damaged and unwanted goods.

"Ok," she said, despising herself. "I'll do it."

Chapter 15

Odd ate lunch in the storage room. Alone.

A knock came at the door. "Yes?" Odd replied to the sound. Nothing more was heard. She peeked out. There in the hallway sat a plate, upon which lay a sandwich, a handful of potato chips and a plastic cup of water.

Odd ate slowly. Then she stared at the boxes. Then she fell asleep. When she woke, she put her dishes in the hall and shut herself back in the room. She went back to staring at the boxes. Other than a few odds and ends, most of the boxes were labeled: clothes. Each was then sub-marked girls or boys and then broken down by size.

She quickly became bored with the view.

"Six more years," she whispered. She would have to look at the boxes for just six more years. Every day the same dull view until she couldn't wait to go to school. There she'd be gawked at and whispered about. Some kids would throw things. That's how it would go, and none of the rest would have the courage to stop them. Nor would any of the kids have the backbone to be her friend. She would hate it with such a passion that before long she'd yearn for the solitude of her room of boxes.

Back and forth it would go; hating, in turns, each aspect of the life she was currently living.

"Please God, I'm being good. Please send my mom back to me," she prayed. There was no response.

Did God hate her? Was it just her demon eyes or had Odd been much more of a sinner than she thought? She tried to recall all the lies that she'd told or the things that she might have taken. It wasn't a long list and eventually her mind wandered. She went from memories, to daydreams.

Hours went by this way, until a knock came at the door of her storage cell.

She was up in a flash. "Yes?" she called out, hurrying to the door. By the time she opened it, she just saw a wisp of dark hair retreating up the stairs. It had been either Tanya or Maria leaving her dinner. At Odd's feet sat a large bowl of soup, a piece of bread and another cup of water.

As she had at lunch, Odd ate very slowly. She savored every bite...except for the cabbage. That she couldn't savor, yet despite its nasty taste and slimy texture, she ate it. With so many lean years behind her, where her mom would drink away the last of their money instead of buying food, Odd never passed up a meal. And it was a rare day that she'd leave anything but crumbs behind.

When she had finished, Odd placed the bowl in the hall and went back to her room. An hour later, one of a thousand sighs escaped her lips. She didn't notice. Odd was too busy thinking about her mom. Wondering what had happened to her. Where she had gone; why she had left in the first place. Was there even a chance that Odd would ever see her again?

"Maybe she knows about the arrest warrant," Odd said aloud. "Maybe that's why she hasn't come back." It certainly made sense. If Karen Wyatt came back now, she'd just end up in a jail even worse than the one Odd found herself in. She'd be in a real jail with mean guards and vicious prisoners, with tall fences and locks on the doors...

"No," Odd said. "I don't want that for her. God, please keep her away. Don't let her go to jail." She paused listening, not knowing what, if anything to expect. When nothing happened, she breathed out a shaky sigh. "There...that's that."

Now she was truly alone.

The next morning, Odd pushed aside the boxes—since she liked to be on the right end of a lock she had barricaded her own door—and ran to the bathroom. She had no idea what the proper protocol was, who went first and all that, but she had to go and nature always held first priority. Afterward she saw that a towel, soap and other toiletries had been set aside for her. There was even a hairbrush for her, which made her smile.

Though she wanted to dally under the water, Odd thought it best not to tempt Mrs. Fedorov and her threat of flushing a toilet. She dried off, put on her new-ish clothes—stained, dark jeans and a blue t-shirt with writing so faded nobody could read it— and went back to her storage cell. There she waited on breakfast passing the time by fishing around in the boxes that were marked in her size.

The pickings for anything not already torn or stained were slim, yet she was able to add a soft blue hat that was shaped as an acorn and a pair of mis-matched black gloves to her wardrobe. Neither really went with her green coat that her mom had picked up somewhere for her, but Odd didn't care very much. She'd be warm at least.

Commotion, the type in which a gaggle of teenage girls competed for bathroom rights, ran through the house. Odd went to the door and listened to the muffled voices and waited. And waited. Gradually the house calmed. She went and sat on a box and did nothing, but wait.

"Have they forgotten about me?" she asked. Going to the door, she cracked it enough to listen. Someone was in a shower on the main floor, while the television yakked away in the living room. Odd went to slip out but as she opened the door further she saw that someone had put her breakfast outside the door already.

"Oh man," she grumbled. The food—a bowl of cheerios and two pieces of toast—had been there for quite a while. The toast was cold, the milk was warm, and the cheerios had the consistency of yesterday's cabbage. She ate it all.

A while later: "Odd?" Lena asked, tapping on the door and then opening it.

"Yes, Ma'am?" Odd had just finished her last spoonful of milk.

Lena smiled at her. "You like room, da? Is good like I say?"

Odd had been lonely and bored. Already she missed seeing people and the idea of living there, hidden away like a secret embarrassment, hurt her. She shrugged at the Russian. What good would it do to complain?

"Good," Lena said, reaching out to pat Odd's head. "You like it. Room grows on you. Very homey. And remember is secret, da? Just us know. What happened yesterday with Vadim? Is secret. Family have its squabbles. No one needs to know, da?"

So being dragged by her hair was another secret that Odd would have to keep to herself. How many more of these "secrets" would she have to endure? Probably a lot. Of course she had a choice: the B wing.

"Da is secret," Odd said to the Russian woman. This caused Lena to laugh.

"Good! I teach you Russian. Now come, we go make you level three." Odd strained to smile at this. Like her true mother, Lena looked to make money off of Odd's deformity.

The Fedororovs had an unexpected car. Odd had thought it would be a junker like Beth's truck, but it was a long black Cadillac. Every angle of it gleamed.

The inside was as nice as the outside. "You like?" Lena asked with a smile.

"Da. Is good," Odd replied, making Lena laugh again.

The woman backed out of the garage. "Is American dream," she said, turning the car up the street. Odd couldn't look out the side windows without her vision becoming distorted, but she could look ahead without a problem.

She kept her eyes out for any recognizable landmarks and as she did she asked, "You came to America for a Cadillac?"

Lena stuck out her lower lip and shrugged. "Yes and no. We come for chance at car. In Russia...I mother, and Vadim work in factory. We never have chance at nothing. No home, no car, no college for son Pyotr. Here, we get all this. If you get car someday. Make it Cadillac. Is good."

"I won't ever be able to drive," Odd said. "My eyes can't see well enough."

"Oh, then you get different American dream," Lena replied, seemingly indifferent to Odd's plight. "Every dream not same. America is land of opportunity. Don't forget this. You can do what you want. Freedom is good."

The girl gave the Russian woman a smile that she didn't feel. Odd couldn't do what she wanted to. What she wanted to do was go to California and find her mom, but that would never happen.

"Do you know where California is?" Odd asked.

"Is long way," Lena said with a sour face. "I know why you ask. You forget mom. She no come back for you. You stay wit Lena."

Odd deflated at this which caused Lena's eyes to narrow. Clearly her foster-mom didn't like the idea of her money-train heading off to California. To placate her Odd said, "Ok...I mean da."

Twenty minutes later Odd stepped out of an elevator and into the reception area of an ophthalmologist office. Odd had been to her share of these and no two had ever differed in any meaningful way. From the posters of eyeballs adorning the walls, to the receptionist with the perky smile and perfect skin, they all looked alike.

"We are having an appointment wit..." Lena squinted down at her own handwriting. "Dr Miller."

"The emergency appointment, right?" the receptionist asked. Lena showed her the name on the paper, while Odd stared at the woman's perfect skin. How did she do that? There wasn't a wrinkle or blemish visible. The young woman went on, "I'm sorry, but Dr. Miller is backed up and it's going to be a bit. Can you take a seat and fill out these forms?"

The forms consisted of hundreds of questions of which Odd could only answer two: her name and her mother's name. It took a long time to even answer these two since Lena's ability to read English was only slightly better than Odd's.

After a while the girl lost interest and turned to something that did interest her: a boy. He looked to be a year or two older than Odd, he had sandy brown hair and a quick smile. She had seen plenty of cute boys and rarely gave them a second look since she knew they'd never have anything to do with her. But this boy was different. He wore dark glasses too, and by the way his hands moved Odd could tell he had trouble seeing as well.

"Can I go talk to that boy?" Odd asked Lena.

Lena looked up from the form with a scowl and a sheen on her upper lip. Deciphering all the questions had caused her to break into a sweat. "Why?"

"I just wanted to see if he's got the same problem with his eyes as me."

The Russian squinted at the boy. "Ok...but no babies!"

This she said loud enough for the nearby receptionist to hear. The woman only barely raised her thin eyebrows in response.

"No babies," Odd whispered, feeling heat run to her cheeks. Getting permission from her foster-mom was the easy part. Actually going over to the boy was far more difficult.

Telling herself that he had the same problem as she did helped. She was sure he would love to know that he wasn't alone in his suffering. Taking a deep breath, she went over to him and sat down in the seat next to his.

"Hi, I'm Odd..." Her mouth went suddenly desert-dry and she had to swallow before she could spit out, "...dree."

Chapter 16

Immediately she wanted to kick herself for calling herself 'Odd'. If he had red eyes too, he probably wouldn't think it nice for someone like her to go around calling themselves that.

His quick smile came as she butchered her own name. "Nice to meet you," he answered with such coolness that Lena's warning: No babies! Sprang to the forefront of her mind. He then added, "I'm Rob...bert."

She grinned at this, but shyly so with her head down. "You're making fun of me and you don't even know me."

"Sure I know you. You're Odd...dree."

"You can't know someone with just a single name. Even if it is broken in half," Odd replied, watching his face. He had a light spray of freckles that ran up under his glasses when he smiled. They made her curious to see more.

"It's a start to getting to know someone," Robert said.

For some reason this caused a silence to come between them. It was as if they both suddenly realized that they were speaking to a member of the opposite sex. Odd found herself looking up at a picture of a giant eye. Her hands had become moist.

"I...uh..." Robert mumbled and then shut his mouth.

This caused Odd to turn back to the boy. She saw him lick his lips and run his hands over his jeans.

He was nervous as well! This plucked up her courage.

"Do you have red eyes?" she asked—the real reason she had come over to him.

"What? Red eyes? Is this part of a joke I'm not getting?" He gave a nervous little laugh as if she was trying to put one over on him. "My eyes are blue, or so they tell me. Why?"

Odd deflated slightly. "It's nothing. Just a hunch that went wrong is all." She looked down at her hands in her lap and then realized what the boy had just said. "You don't know if your eyes are blue or not? Are you color blind? I am a little. I can't see red. Whenever anyone says something is red, it looks kinda brown to me."

"What color do you see when you see brown?"

"Just brown...I think," Odd said, her brows furrowing behind her glasses. "You never actually know what a color really is. But what about you? You can't see blue?"

"I can't see at all."

Odd sat back in her chair with her mouth hanging open. "You're blind?"

"Yeah, that's what I meant by I can't see."

Sudden embarrassment struck Odd dumb. She had no clue what to say and felt silly over the way she had prattled on like an idiot about her color-blindness.

He sensed her discomfort. "It's ok. It's not catching. You can still talk to me."

"I'm sorry. It's just I feel so stupid thinking my problems are so big when you..."

Robert interrupted, "Look, don't start feeling sorry for me. And don't go patronizing me for my 'bravery'; it's what most people move to next."

"But you are brave to me!" Odd exclaimed "I know I'd just die if I was all alone out there, wandering around blind. Not knowing where I was or what sort of people were after me."

"Well that's just it," he countered. "I'm not all alone. I have my parents and my brothers and sisters. They look out for me."

"Oh." He had more than Odd did. Right then she knew she'd give up her eyes for a real family. Not just a drunk who was paid in beer and gin for peeks at her freak daughter or a romp in the back of a truck in the parking lot, but a real family. A normal family.

"And I'm not exactly helpless by myself," he continued. "I do tons of things on my own." He paused, swallowing loudly. "How old are you?"

"Twelve..." She added in a hurry, "...and a half. What about you?"

"Fourteen. I just turned it last week. My parents took us to Anthony's to celebrate. You ever been there?"

Odd thought for a moment but couldn't place the name. "Is that a bar?"

He laughed at this. "No. It's a pizza place. Its got the most killer New York style pizza I ever ate. You should go sometime."

"Sure...that sounds...I bet it would be wonderful." When she could get it Odd went nuts for pizza.

"What's wrong?" Robert asked. He put his hand out to her and touched her knee.

She lowered her voice to a conspiratorial volume. "My foster-mom won't take me there. She's..." Odd couldn't figure out how to tell this boy about how she was a virtual prisoner. "She's...she's..."

"It's ok," Robert said in a whisper. "I think I understand."

Odd laughed over this. The laugh didn't contain so much mirth as it did bitterness and pain. "Actually, you can't possibly understand. I'm not trying to put you down, but no one could. Not unless they've lived my life."

"You kinda make me—the blind kid—feel sorry for you," he said without joking.

This brought a rueful smile to her face. It was a smile that didn't belong on a twelve-year-old. Yes, she could see...not well, but she could still see. However it's what she had seen: anger, bitterness, hate and even the specter of evil, that made her realize that having eyes—if this was your only view—wasn't all that great.

"You should feel sorry for me," Odd said. "I met a lady who tried to keep me from wallowing in self-pity by telling me that there's always someone worse off than I am. I haven't met that person yet. But you have, Robert. You've met me."

"Then it's my lucky day. Do you want to talk about it? I'm all ears."

She shot a quick glance at Lena. The Russian was still sweating over the questionnaire, but it didn't mean that she couldn't hear. "I don't think so," she whispered. A second glance around the waiting area revealed something that she had missed earlier. "Where's your mom?"

"I'll tell you where my mom is if you tell me where yours is. Your real one that is."

Odd groaned and put a hand through her blonde hair. "You don't stop do you?"

"Nope," he said cheerfully. "I persevere. That's how I get through the tough spots in my life. My dad says talking helps and so far he's been right. So maybe you should give it a try."

"Persevere," she said thoughtfully. The word was new to her, but she deduced its meaning from their conversation. She liked it and she liked Robert. He was easy to talk to. With a big breath she said, "Ok. I'll tell you. My mom left me. Criminal abandonment they called it. Now she can't come back without going to jail and I can't go to her because..." There were many reasons. The biggest one being fear. She was afraid of starving to death, of freezing to death, of coming across another person like Mitch. She was afraid of getting lost and ending up in Guatemala. "I can't go find her because I'm afraid."

"Find her?" he asked in disbelief. "Why would you want to? She left you. You should go look for your dad. No one ever goes looking for their dads. I'd go looking for mine. Nothing against my mom, but my dad is a great man."

"My dad ran out on my mom while she was pregnant with me. I don't even know his name."

This toned the boy down. "Oh, sorry. Still I don't see why'd you want to go find your mom. Foster-care can't be as bad as being abandoned."

The windowless storage room flashed into her mind. The volcanic anger of Vadim. The nasty pinch Lena had given Melanie. The insults. The haggling over money. The meals left at her door. To the Fedorovs she wasn't a person, so much as a way to make money with the least amount of work. How long could she endure that?

Odd shrugged in response, then realized the boy couldn't see the move. "You'd be right if I was normal. There are nice families out there who are good to their foster-children, but I...I'm...I can't go to one of them." She leaned in close and whispered, "I'm stuck with her. It's not so good."

"I'm sorry," he said, patting her knee for emphasis. His hand there was nice. Odd was very aware of it. No one liked to touch her, but whenever they did, her body honed in on the sensation like a compass' needle finding true north. "Why don't you think you're normal," he asked.

This time her grin was a genuine one. "You're asking all these questions, why?"

"I left my book at home and, even if I hadn't, you're much more interesting."

She swallowed at that. His words had come with one of his nice smiles and now the hand on her knee felt hot. She liked it.

"Well?" he asked after a few seconds of silence.

Odd didn't want to answer his question. She liked him and didn't want him to know that she was ugly. Yet she didn't want to lie to him either.."How long have you been blind?" she asked in attempt to change the subject.

"Since birth," he answered straight away. "Why don't you think you're normal? You sound normal. Do you not look normal?"

"I'm ugly," Odd answered in a whisper that barely carried to his ear. Suddenly she wanted him to remove his hand. It had gone stiff on her knee at her words.

His look became sad and his hand grew soft

again. He said, "Sometimes it's good being blind. My world can be so simple. To a blind person being ugly or pretty is all about how we are treated, not about looks. So to me you are very beautiful. You've been nice to me when you didn't need to be."

"Thanks," she said. "But I'm glad I'm not blind. The world would be filled with ugly people if I were. Except for you, that is."

"Really? Then I'd prefer you were blind. We could then be pretty together." He said this with a strain to his voice.

The look and the words confused Odd for a moment and then she understood. "You don't think you're handsome? No one's told you?"

He blushed. In a snap his cheeks went a wild red. He stammered, "Well...my mom says stuff, but you know all moms have to say that sort of thing. So you never know the truth."

When Odd's mom was sober she insisted Odd keep her glasses on. When she was drunk she called her names like horrid and beastly. When your own mother couldn't call you pretty it could only mean one thing, you were dog ugly.

Odd tried not to think about that. Instead she looked at Robert's full lips and his soft hair. "Believe me, Robert, you are very cute."

His blush reached maximum temperature. He chuckled, embarrassed. "Thank you, I guess. Now we're perfect together. You're beautiful to me and I'm...I'm cute, I suppose." Suddenly his knee started jiggling up and down. "Um...tell me...um, are you allowed to go on dates?"

The question stunned her, sending air shooting

out of her lungs and none seemed to come back in. Her mouth came open as if it knew she should be saying something, however, her mind roared with an ecstatic scream—a *boy just asked her out!*—blotting out any words that might have formed there.

He swallowed again loudly. It made her realize she hadn't answered and she blinked a few times trying to think past the swell of feelings within her. They weren't good thoughts.

In her heart, she knew it would never happen. Lena would never allow her to leave her storage cell, not for a date. No Babies! Odd sat back in her chair, glum but so happy at the same time. "No. I'm sure I can't. I think I'm too young anyways, though it sounds nice. I've never been on a date before, have you?"

His handsome face sank at the word 'no', but he rallied, "No. You're actually the only girl I've ever asked. I'm O for one."

"You didn't really ask, you know," Odd said. "You just asked if I was allowed to. Maybe if you asked for real you wouldn't be O for one."

He considered this, still burning red in the cheeks. "Do you want to go out with me?"

"Yes, I really, really want to...when I can. But that might not be for a few years." How many years? she wondered. Six? Would Lena ever allow her out? Or would she rot away in the basement as Kristen had said?

"When you're ready, I'll take you to Anthony's or somewhere better if you don't like pizza."

"That sounds really nice," Odd said. There came a lull in the conversation as both thought about the date. Odd glanced up and found Lena staring at her. She turned back to Robert. "So where's your mom? Did she have to go back to work after she dropped you off?"

"No, I took the bus. She should be here any minute."

This floored Odd. A blind kid riding the bus. "How do you know when it's your stop? Aren't you afraid that you'll miss it and go riding around the city forever?"

"I was a little at first, but after a while it became easy. I've memorized the major cross streets of each of my bus routes, so if I ever go too far, I just backtrack. Mostly people are nice and tell me."

"Wow." Odd had never ridden the bus by herself. The moving traffic, the chaos, the people, all made it almost impossible for her to see straight.

"It's really nothing. You just have to trust people," he added.

Odd laughed at this. "You don't want to be called brave, but trusting people? That's the bravest thing I ever heard."

"Robert, who's your friend?"

Odd Jumped in her seat. A lady in a black leather coat stood smiling down at her. Though she seemed as a nice a person as Odd had ever seen, her gaze still sent a lance of guilt and fear though Odd's chest.

"I'm...I'm Odd," she answered. A second later, at the woman's puzzled look, Odd spat out "Dree...I'm Audrey." Robert snorted in laughter at this.

"Nice to meet you, Audrey. I'm Mrs. Hoover."

"Hi." Odd didn't know what else to say. Robert cleared his throat a little.

This made Mrs. Hoover's smile expand across

her face. "Robert, I'll just be over there filling out all these silly forms so you can talk to this pretty little miss."

Odd sat dazed as the lady went to talk to the receptionist. When she had moved out of earshot, Odd asked, "She called me pretty...is she blind too?"

Robert leaned in close and whispered, "No. She has twenty-twenty vision. You must not be as ugly as you think. If you were she'd have just called you my 'little friend' and then later would have hinted that you weren't so pretty. She's not very subtle."

"Well, I do have my glasses on. I'm not so bad when they're covering my...covering me."

Robert brought his hands up to her face. "Take off your glasses, let me feel. I'm a pretty good judge."

Odd started to panic at the idea of anyone seeing her eyes. "But...I don't think..." He took the glasses off for her and she slammed shut her eyes.

Both of his hands slipped over the contours of her face. They ran across her eyelids and brows. Gently touched her lips and nose. They even ran along the underside of her chin. She could barely breath and she trembled in fear that he would proclaim her ugly.

"Full lips...high cheek bones, small chin. I love your nose...and your full eye lashes. Soft smooth skin. Does that tickle?" She had squirmed under his hand.

"Yes a little. Can I have my glasses back, please?"

"Anything for a pretty girl like you."

She pushed her glasses onto her face, not believing her ears. "A what?" she asked.

"My mom was right. You're a pretty little miss."

Odd shook her head feeling her heart go light in

her chest. It felt to be beating so high it was practically in her throat. That was twice in the last few minutes someone had called her pretty. She wanted to cry. She wanted to laugh. She wanted to...

Harsh words interrupted her mad joy.

"Come away from that boy, Odd," Lena said from across the room. "Don't bother him no more."

"I wasn't bothering him," Odd replied in a little voice.

"Sorry for her," Lena said, apologizing to Mrs. Hoover. "She lie. She has lying tongue. She no good kid. Is bad. Very bad. Come, Odd."

What was going on? She had just been called a liar. Did Lena mean they were lying to her about her prettiness? Was that it? Odd hadn't lied at all. What was going? In her confusion, Odd had kept her foster-mom waiting a second too long.

Lena's face went hard. "Come, Odd!"

In horror, Odd saw herself rise from the chair. Her body was completely numb, yet it still moved as if controlled by another being. She went to sit by Lena.

"What did I say?" Lena demanded in a harsh, carrying whisper. "I say no babies!" Odds mouth came open to protest but no sound could come out. Her humiliation had struck her dumb. "Don't deny. I saw you let boy touch you. Is first step."

Odd didn't try to deny anything. She could only sit there with her mouth hanging open in astonished disbelief until her tongue felt dry and useless.

"Ma'am?" the reception asked Lena. She struggled to keep her smooth face from displaying disgust at Lena's rudeness. "I have an examination room ready for you. You can wait there for the doctor."

Chapter 17

In order to hide her burning shame at what had just happened, Odd kept her head down as the receptionist walked them back to an empty room. Once they were shut in together Lena unleashed her wrath on her foster-daughter.

"What you say to boy? Huh? You tell him about storage room? Is this what you say? Or you say about Vadim? What?" Each question was punctuated with a slap to the back of Odd's head. This made her eyes spin.

"Nothing. I didn't say nothing," she wailed, cringing away from her foster-mom. "We just talked..."

Lena stared hard. "About what?"

Odd almost mentioned how Robert had asked her on a date, but that would have meant more hitting and more lectures about No Babies! Instead she said, "He's blind. We talked about how he gets around the town on a bus even though he can't see."

"Then why he touch you? Why you let him."

"Because he was nice...his mom called me pretty and...and I didn't believe her...and..." she just sort of trailed off not knowing what she could say that wouldn't upset Lena.

"She call you pretty?" Lena snorted. "She no see eyes! You no pretty wit those eyes. But...but maybe she think you pretty enough for her blind son?" Lena went to a chair and settled her bulk down, thinking. "Possibly. This possible."

Odd more than hoped it was possible. Blind or

not, Robert was handsome. Never in her wildest dreams had she ever thought a boy as handsome as he was would ever consider her. And he had more than just considered her, he had asked her out!

The thought made her ecstatic, yet this was counter-balanced by the presence of Mrs. Fedorov. What she had done in the waiting room couldn't be undone and, even if Odd was to see Robert again, she didn't think that she'd be able to look him in the face.

In a fit of melancholy, Odd went to one of the chairs and slumped down on it. Lena straightened her with a pinch at the back of the neck.

"You sit straight," the Russian warned. "And make sure you tell doctor how much eye hurt. Da? Eye hurt! Need specialist or maybe surgery."

"But they don't really hurt unless there is too much..."

Lena came to stand over her. "You listen. Vadim, he no like you. Me? I don't know. Maybe yes maybe no. The other children, they hate you. They make troubles. They call caseworkers—is troubles. You go...if you no get third level pay, Vadim, he kick you out."

Odd's head drooped to her chest. Did it matter? Her life would be full of pain whether she was in the B wing or not. Defeat ran through her and it escaped in a long sigh.

"What, you no care?" Lena asked with eyebrows raised. "You should! You want boyfriend? In B wing you have lots. They put bag over you head and do things to you that you no like. You go in sweet girl, but when you come out...not so sweet. Have disease. You ruined for all time and no one want you. Not even blind boy."

The image of Mitch pressing down on top of her came to mind. It made her mouth go coppery with fear. "I...I don't want to go there." But she didn't want to stay with Lena either.

Just then the doctor came in. "Hi, I'm Dr. Miller." He pointed at *the* chair, the one hung with confusing eye gizmos. "Please have a seat over here." Odd had to take a second, her mind still clinging to the image of Mitch. When she did the doctor pulled up his own little stool and asked, "So Audrey what brought you in today?"

Behind her glasses Odd flicked her eyes to Lena; the woman was watching her very closely. "Um...I guess...I think I'm here to see if there's anything more wrong with me."

Lena nodded.

"Anything more wrong?" the doctor repeated. "There's something wrong with you? Have you been diagnosed with any..." he glanced down at the paperwork Lena had filled out. "Your history is pretty thin."

"My last eye doctor told me I had ocular albinism, nystagmus, and a congenital defect of the retina where the first two layers are fused into one. But I don't know what any of that means."

As she rattled off the memorized words, Dr Miller's eyebrows went up. "Interesting. Let's have a look. Can you remove your glasses...good. Fascinating." The doctor peered in at Odd's eyes, shining a bright, painful light, first into one and then the other. In seconds her red eyes were dripping with tears. When he finally sat back, Odd was nearly blind and could only make out the blur of his white coat.

"Is bad, da?" Lena asked, coming to stand next to the doctor and peer in at Odd. "All these stuff is bad?"

Dr Miller took a moment to answer, searching for a way to explain the diagnosis. "Well, it's not good. Though the appearance of it is probably worse than the acuity issue. Simply, ocular albinism is albinism that affects the eyes only." At Odd's blank look he tried to explain, "Albinism is a lack of pigmentation. Have you ever heard of an albino?"

Odd hadn't. Lena wrinkled her brows and said, "Is all white person, da?"

"Right. Here let me show Audrey." Dr Miller had a laptop computer on a counter in the room. He tapped away at it for a few seconds and then turned the screen towards Odd. It showed a man who was so white he could've been a corpse bled dry of blood.

"Is that going to happen to me?" Odd asked, her heart a trip hammer in her chest. It was one thing to cover up her eyes, but there was no way she'd be able to hide every inch of her. Even the man's hair was bone white.

Lena looked hopeful.

"No," the doctor replied. "This is a man with full albinism. Ocular albinism affects the eyes only. It won't spread. I guarantee it."

Odd melted back in the chair. "Oh, good. That's something."

Lena wasn't so happy. "You sure? This man, his eyes blue. Odd, she have red eyes. Maybe something different, something worse?"

The doctor gave Odd a reassuring look before

turning to Lena. "No. It is definitely albinism. Audrey just has the rarest form of it. Normally it presents in color as a very light blue or brown. She's also atypical because she's a female. Females are carriers of the gene; it's generally males who are afflicted."

"My last doctor said that I have the rarest eyes on the planet," Odd said.

Miller nodded. "Yeah, he was right about that, too. If there are five other people alive today with eyes like yours I'd be surprised."

"But...but what about other big words you say?" Lena asked, tugging at the doctor's white coat. "Is bad, da?"

He shrugged. "I'm not going to lie to you. It's all bad. We never want to see this in a patient. But it won't get worse, that's the good news. Except for the nystagmus. Nystagmus is that movement of her eyes. Mrs. Fedorov come here. See how her eyes act like an old time typewriter? They go to the right slowly and then zip back to center. That will get worse if we don't treat it."

Lena nodded. "She need surgery, da."

"No. She won't need surgery. She can control the movement by doing simple eye exercises."

"I already do them," Odd put in. "See watch." She went through her nightly routine: forcing her eyes hard to the left, then to the right, up, down and then crossing them.

Lena watched with her lip curled.

Dr Miller, however, watched approvingly. "Good. Just try to hold each position a little longer. Count to three before going to the next. That will help a lot. Now, I want another look at your retinas. Hold still."

He brought out the light again and seared Odd's eyes. "Ok. I'm seeing the retina pretty well. It's the wrong color obviously. Yeah...it's malformed. The dark red shouldn't be visible like that." He clicked off the light and waited as Odd blinked away the echoes. "I take it you can't see the color red?" Odd shook her head. The doctor continued, "And everything goes wonky every once in a while?" This time Odd nodded. "How is your depth perception?" he asked.

"Depth? You mean under water? It's not very good in pools with lots of people around, but I went to a lake once and swam there and I could see almost as good as I do on land."

He chuckled at this. "No. What I mean is do you see the world flat, like a picture, or do you see objects one in front of the other?" He held his hands a foot apart.

"I see it ok. Just as long as you don't move them too fast."

"Interesting, yours is a very special case." the doctor said, making a note in his paperwork. "I can tell you why you don't see fast moving objects very well; it's because of the fused retina. In a normal eye, light comes in through the pupil, and to put it simply, goes through three layers and is transformed into a chemical-electrical impulse that your brain interprets as sight."

Odd's mouth hung open. She thought she knew what chemicals were: ammonia and bleach, things like that. As well, she thought she knew what electricity was: the stuff that ran in the walls to make the light bulbs and the radio work. But what they had to do with her eyes, she couldn't fathom. Lena was right there with her, she blinked at the doctor in uncertainty.

He took a deep breath and tried again. "The light...the images of the world around us goes through the retina in three stages and this how we see. But with you Audrey, the light doesn't move front to back: one-two-three. It goes one and two at the same time. In essence the light doesn't go backwards so much as it goes sideways. This slows down your ability to focus on a swift moving object and may warp it as well. Do you understand?"

It did to a point. It meant that Odd saw things differently than other people. Of course she already knew this. She gave him a nod. "And this you fix?" Lena asked.

"No, it's not possible," he answered shaking his head. "Usually even glasses will only help so much since the issue isn't the shape of the eye. She is extremely lucky in one regard, there doesn't appear to be much foveal hypoplasia. It's another problem that is nearly universal with people suffering from ocular albinism, but for some reason hers is minimal."

Lena didn't look happy with this answer. "What if this get worse. Odd go blind maybe?"

"No. Don't worry about that. Her eye and retina are fully formed—not perfectly formed—but formed. She probably won't suffer any vision loss except for the usual degradation common with age."

"Oh," Lena said. Her disappointment had Dr Miller frowning at her in confusion. She ignored his look and pulled Odd out of the chair. "Well, this waste of time. Come, Odd. We take you to new school now."

"Wait! Hold on," he cried. "There are more tests we need to run...glaucoma at the least!"

Lena was already though the door. "No. Glaucoma for old people. Test are waste since you no fix eye!"

Chapter 18

"Is waste my time!" Lena grumbled. "Get in car."

Odd grasped the handle. She didn't pull up on it. Instead she pictured the B wing of the Social Services building. All the fences were quite tall; they curved inwards at the top, making it impossible to scale them. She pictured the older kids there—she saw in her mind their anger and building hate for the world. They would hurt her. They would belittle her. They would do things to her...bad things.

These were facts. She had to think about these facts in order to open the door to the Cadillac. Otherwise her hand would never do it on its own. She had to remind herself that there were worse places than Lena's. Or at least there was one worse place.

With great reluctance Odd climbed in and buckled up.

"This your fault!" Lena growled.

Odd guessed that this was a fact too. Her own mom had always blamed everything on her as well. Odd was sure that on her tombstone would be written the words: Odd Wyatt—Died—All Her Fault.

"You should make better try!" Lena went on. Odd just sat there, knowing from past experience the futility of trying to defend herself. "You no even say eye hurt. Why? This I tell you to do, but you no do it!"

Odd waited to be hit. Being yelled at and then hit was the norm. However, Lena turned her anger on

Dr Miller. "Is doctor so stupid! How he say you eye is good...no need surgery? You look like demon!" Lena seethed rocking back and forth in the car with hands white on the steering wheel.

"You do better at school. You make yourself into level three or there be troubles. You no worth level two. No at all! Make yourself most special of special kids. You understand?" Lena said this and to emphasize her point she screwed up her face into an over-the-top caricature of a disabled person.

Odd understood. Lena wanted her to pretend to be a drooling idiot, all for the privilege of living in a windowless storage room in a house where she was despised. A sigh drained out of the little girl. She was lost. It seemed incredible that living with Lena was the best she could hope for.

If only there was someone for her to turn to for help. There wasn't. Not even the nice people she'd met would be of any help. If she ran away to Father Marino, or Gary the bartender, or Mr. McCew, they'd only turn her over to Social Services, thinking they were doing the right thing. She'd then be right back where she was, or worse.

There was only one person who could help her—Karen Wyatt. Odd knew her mom wasn't a good person. She lied frequently, stole every time she thought she could get away with it, and used people, especially Odd. And she could be mean. She could be vile and nasty, again, especially to Odd, yet for all that she'd always protected her daughter. Perhaps not in a perfect way, but in a way that had worked.

Without her Odd didn't have a chance. Odd nodded. Lena had been asking something that seemed to require a nod in answer. Lena went back to berating her and Odd went back to dying inside.

A bus pulled up next to the Cadillac. They were both traveling at the same speed which allowed Odd to look at it without getting sick. Desperately she searched the dark windows in the hope of seeing Robert. He wasn't one of the three people on the bus.

How did he do it? A blind boy wandering around the city? *If only I had his courage*, she thought.

What if she did? Then what? Would courage get her to California? Not likely. Would courage allow her to stand up to Lena and Vadim *and* keep her out of the B wing? Definitely not. What good would it do?

I could get on a bus all by myself, Odd concluded. It was something. A tiny baby-step. She knew it would take a million baby-steps to get to California, yet she didn't think she had much of a choice but to try. She could never fake being a drooling idiot, at least not for long, and that meant she'd never get level three pay for Lena.

Purposely, she looked away from the bus. Buildings streaked by in a flash of undulating silver and melting glass. In just a second her stomach churned, unpleasantly.

"Mrs...Fedorov...I'm going to be...sick," Odd gasped.

"No, you wait till we get to school then..." Lena stopped in mid-sentence. Her eyes went wide. "Not in Cadillac! We pull over. We pull over hold on. No sick in Cadillac, no sick."

Lena pulled into a parking lot of a restaurant and Odd got out saying, "I'm...going to the bathroom." She went slow, clutching her stomach, taking small steps until her world righted itself in her vision. She was going to run away. That was her plan. She had no clue where she was and truly no clue where she was going to, but that didn't matter. What did matter was that she was trying.

Just the simple act of walking away from the car felt wonderful. No longer was she a leaf being kicked along by the wind. For the first time in her life Odd felt empowered, energized by the action of her little faltering steps. She would go into the restaurant, stop into the bathroom, and then slip out the back door. And who knows what lay beyond it?

Her mind pictured a gleaming bus with the word CALIFORNIA written in huge letters across the side. Waiting for her at the door stood Robert, with his easy smile and fine spray of freckles. They would board the bus holding hands and head for the back where...

Her dream and her plan were interrupted by the simplest thing. The restaurant door was locked. Squinching up her face, she strained to see into the window, nothing moved in the darkness beyond. Just like that, her energy and empowerment disappeared from within her.

Now what?

Lena would take her to school, of course, but could she run from there? Or did they keep close tabs on the 'special' kids? She believed they did. In her few times at the different schools that she had been to, she remembered seeing the special kids being escorted in little groups or working one-on-one with the special teachers.

But then how could she get away? Odd's main problem lay in the fact that she couldn't actually "run" away. Because of her eyes, running was simply beyond her. The most she could do was simply walk away and hope not to be noticed.

"Odd!" Lena yelled from the idling car. The little girl jumped, and a sudden guilty sweat broke out on her forehead. Feeling as though her intentions were readable at thirty feet, she turned to face her foster-mom, figuring to get yelled at for even contemplating escape. Lena did indeed seem upset. "Is closed! You no just stand there! Go to bank." She pointed at the building next door.

It was true, Odd could go to the bank. Why hadn't she thought of that? It was such a simple thing, yet taking the initiative and walking over to the bank had never crossed her mind. How was that possible?

"Because I don't think for myself. I let everyone think for me," Odd whispered. This was true. Whenever she was with someone, she let them do all the thinking, feeling she wasn't smart enough to contribute.

That would have to change and change in a hurry.

Giving Lena a little nod, Odd turned to the bank and began walking. As she did her eyes swept around her, hoping to see something recognizable, but this wasn't a part of the city that she had ever been too. They had left the tall, glass and steel buildings behind and for the most part, squat, red brick structures surrounded her.

"Can I use your bathroom?" Odd asked a tall security guard who stood just inside the front door of the bank. The very sight of his uniform and the large black gun at his hip almost had her turning back to the supposed safety that Lena offered.

"Are you a customer?" he asked. Odd's drooping face was enough of an answer for the guard. "Sorry, customers only. Have a nice day."

Now what? If she went from building to building Lena would get angry at the delay and force her back into the car. Odd began to feel a growing sense of urgency. Giving the guard a wan smile she said, "You have a nice day too." As she said it, her eyes fell upon a second entrance to the bank. "Can I go out that door?"

He shrugged. "I guess."

She went to it as fast as her eyes would allow and, in seconds, she found herself walking down a side street, her decaying Converse sneakers slapping rhythmically on the sidewalk as she went. Rude calculations drawn up in her mind gave her a minimum fifteen-minute head start. Lena would only sit so long in the car before her impatience, and a need to scold, would drive her into the bank.

And then what would Lena do? Call the police? Call Social Services? Drive around looking for Odd herself? There was no way to tell. Odd just had to go with the worst-case scenario and find a place to hide and quick. Looking to lose herself in the maze of streets, Odd took turn after turn; down a block and then to the right a block, down a block and then to the right.

She did this four times before she came upon an idling police cruiser. Her guilty feet stumbled at the sight. How long had it been since she had ran away? Had they been alerted yet? She didn't know. Odd held her breath and walked past the car. Inside, sat a man eating; he watched her as she went. She couldn't fake a casual air. Her body was stiff with fright and, if she had been touched, she probably would have screamed.

Only when she had left the car a block away did she wipe at the sweat that lay cooling on her forehead. Her stomach began to ache. She might have been a mile away from Lena, but she was only a hundred yards from a police officer and if he got a call about a missing girl, he could be on her in seconds.

Odd had to get off the streets. The only problem lay in the fact that nothing around her looked inviting to a girl who was so obviously destitute. The shops lining the streets: boutiques, salons, cafes, would all send her packing in seconds. She had to find a library or a...

"Yes!" Odd whispered.

Two blocks away a tall sign indicated a supermarket. It was the best that she could hope for under the circumstances. She could sit in the bathroom at the supermarket for a good hour before anyone would bother her. After that—she had no clue what would happen. Her mind dwelt on all the possibilities and the more it did the more she realized the idea of the supermarket didn't seem like such a good one after all. An hour was far too short a time period for hiding...in fact it seemed just long enough to get the surrounding area abuzz with the news of a missing girl. Not only that, if she was seen going in, she'd be essentially trapped.

Panic began to eat at her. The sensation was akin to having grit grinding in her soul and it stopped her halfway through the parking lot. What on earth should she do? The smartest thing to do wasn't to hide, but to get miles away as soon as possible. But how? She could hitch a ride, but that meant standing on the street for everyone to see. She could take a bus except that she had no money and even if she had, again it meant sitting on a main road—waiting; a perfect target.

Once when she was much younger Odd and her mother had stolen a ride in the back of a moving van. It had been an uncomfortable time, pitching to and fro, but they had crossed Indiana in four hours. For Odd, the same sort of truck would have been perfect, but there wasn't one in sight. The closest thing to it was a Suburban with its back hatch up. A lady in a heavy blue parka stood emptying her shopping cart into the rear of it.

As Odd stood there, the woman dropped a bag of oranges and the contents of it rolled around on the ground, going off in all directions.

"Here you go," Odd said, holding up two that had come her way.

"Thanks. You're a dear." The lady smiled, running wrinkles out of the corners of her eyes. She had a kindly face that was older than Odd's mother, but not by much. Odd glanced into the back of her big vehicle—the seats were high-backed—she could hide in the third row, easily. Odd walked away from the Suburban and the lady in the blue parka. She didn't go far, before she stooped to slowly untie and retie her shoelaces with hands that shook.

The audacity of what she planned scared the little girl. Stealing a ride seemed too close to actual stealing for her liking and her mind began to ask questions that were better left unasked. Was hopping a ride like this illegal? And what would happen if she was caught? Would it be the B wing or actual jail?

The fear within her began to act against her need. The shaking in her hands began to travel up her arms, but then, out of the corner of her eye she watched as the lady slammed shut the hatch and turned to return the cart. Without delay, Odd stood and went to the Suburban as quickly as she could, all the while keeping her eyes on the woman's back.

The woman was closer to the cart return than Odd was to the SUV, but the little girl in the dark glasses had both an urgent need and a numbing fear pushing her on, and she climbed into the Suburban, shutting the door, just as the lady sent the cart crashing amongst the others.

Odd was too afraid that she'd be seen climbing over the back seat to get to the third row so she turned herself into a tiny ball of human flesh and hunkered down in the foot-well behind the driver's seat. Seconds later, the lady in the blue parka got in and drove straight east, pulling over once to let a police cruiser zoom by with its sirens wailing. Odd shivered and shook in fright, while her breath panted out of her uncontrollably.

By a miracle the woman didn't hear her.

Chapter 19

Once the police cruiser went on its way, the lady switched on the radio. She began to sing along to the music, off-key. This little human idiosyncrasy helped Odd to relax. It was just a drive, nothing more. If the police were after her they were heading the wrong way.

With her eyes closed, Odd allowed herself to be lulled by the sound of soft rock and bad singing, and in this way she traveled for many miles. Or at least for many minutes. Sitting in the foot-well, unseeing as well as unseen, she had no idea of their speed or direction. Only when the lady stopped at stoplights did Odd dare to open her eyes and look out.

There was never much to see as her angle only allowed her to look upwards. She could on occasion see street signs and these she would squint at, slowly reading them with silently moving lips. None were familiar until they took a turn and a few minutes later, she saw that she was on 5st street.

She'd never heard of 5th street, but the street crossing it she had: Broadway!

That was where the *Lucky U* was, and the bar with the pretzels, and Mr. McCew. And most importantly, if her mom was back in town that's where she'd be.

Odd popped her head up. "Excuse me?" she asked in a little voice.

The lady in the blue parka screamed. The Suburban slalomed left and then right as if it had hit a slick patch of black ice. Odd's stomach turned a flip and she had to slam her eyelids down as the street in front of them appeared to take on the consistency of a stormed tossed sea.

"What are you doing in my car?" the lady shrieked.

"I...I only...I...I'm gonna get sick!" Odd wasn't lying. She began to pant to hold her terrible breakfast down. The lady wasn't helpful at all, though she wasn't being intentionally mean. Her sudden fright, coupled with the idea of someone vomiting in her car, had her driving in a stop and go reckless manner as she struggled to move her huge car through traffic, out of the left lane and into a parking spot on the far right.

The second the woman pulled up onto the curb Odd opened the door and dropped to her knees. By the barest of margins she kept from vomiting. The lady watched; disgust at Odd's gagging turning her once smiling face into a sick grimace.

"What were you doing in my car?" she demanded a second time, as soon as it became apparent Odd wasn't going to hurl.

From her knees, Odd replied, "I needed a ride—badly. I'm sorry that I scared you."

"Needed a ride?" the lady asked. "What? That's...that's...why aren't you in school?"

There wasn't any good answer to that other than a form of the truth. "I have eye problems...I don't go to school. I mean a normal school." This was true; technically her mother had taught her some things and others she just sort of picked up as she went along.

Her answer seemed to calm the lady. "Oh. Where's your mother then?"

"She's just down the street." To herself, Odd added—*I hope*. "She's at a bar, over by..."

"A bar!"

"I...I mean she's at a motel near a bar." Again, she thought—*I hope*.

"Oh," the lady said. For a second she appeared to be at a loss for words, but then she remembered her ire. "Well, you shouldn't break into people's cars. It's rude...and probably against the law."

"Yes, Ma'am."

"I have half a mind to tell your mother what you've been up to," the lady paused and looked around at the seedy neighborhood. "Or maybe I should call the police."

At this, she produced a cell phone from her coat pocket. Odd's insides began to shrivel at the sight. However, the lady didn't dial; instead she gave it a sour look.

"They probably have better things to do," she murmured and then turned her sour look to Odd and stared for a long while. "Hmmm... Do you need a ride? A proper ride to your motel?"

The question caught the twelve-year-old off-guard. "I...I uh..." she stammered trying to think. What would the lady do when they got to the *Lucky U* and Odd's mother wasn't there? Call the police, or worse, call Social Services? "No...thank you. The motel is just around the corner. I'll be fine." Odd could only hope that this was true. How far Broadway stretched, she didn't have a clue.

"Well ok," the lady said, looking slightly at a loss. "But no more getting into strange cars like that. It's dangerous."

"Yes, Ma'am. I won't," Odd replied, backing away. "And thanks by the way...bye." The little girl didn't give the lady a chance to say anything else. Odd turned to make her way back to Broadway, hoping the dirty motel would be in sight when she turned the corner.

It was not.

Not only that, nothing looked familiar. Guided either by instinct or luck, Odd turned south, which was in fact the direction in which the Lucky U lay. Yet it lay miles away. At first she walked with purpose and determination, but after three hours she plodded slowly along, staring in restaurant windows as she passed them. Her stomach demanded food. There was none to give it.

Eventually, she started to pass the same bars that she had stopped into the week before. This time she didn't bother going in any of them. If her mom had come back she'd have gone to Gary's or the *Lucky U*. Odd decided to save her energy and go there first. The only good aspect of her long trudge was that for the end of January the weather couldn't be any better. After a few miles she pulled off her gloves and hat. After another couple she unzipped her coat, while sweat dripped down her nose.

As she walked her mind strayed over people in her life: Did her mom miss her, or even think about her? Was Lena out with her two nasty dogs hunting for her? Was that horrid Mitch fantasizing about her and planning his revenge? Was Father Marino worried about her and praying for her?

She thought about the blind boy, Robert most of all. Her mind hung on a daydream of him; in it they were both miraculously cured of their eye problems and instead of finding her mom, Odd went to live with his family.

This kept her going. By the time her feet had blistered she saw the *Lucky U*. Gary's bar was closer by a couple of blocks, but Odd had most of her hopes pinned on the motel.

Despite the pain in her feet and the feverish desire to find her mom, Odd approached the hotel warily. Mitch was the last person she wanted to run into. Slipping around the back she entered through a door he wasn't likely to use. The place hadn't changed a whit in the five days she'd been gone. Phil hadn't changed either, literally. His clothes were the same stained ones she'd last seen him in and his stubble looked not to have progressed at all.

"Hi Phil," Odd said, trying her best to show a sunny disposition. Phil rolled his eyes and let out a tired breath when he turned to see who had disturbed his show. She kept the smile in her voice despite the quick depression that gripped her when she saw his reaction. "Have you seen my mom? Has she come by at all?"

He groaned. "No she hasn't and you know what? She's not gonna. Ok? She left you here and she ain't coming back. It's time you figured that out."

"But..."

"There ain't no buts!" Phil yelled. "For whatever reason she don't want you, alright? And don't start with the tears!"

It was too late for that. Like a sun shower that brings rain out of the blue, Odd's tears ran from beneath her glasses. Turning away to hide her eyes she lifted her glasses and wiped them away, but they kept coming as if her head was filled with water and had sprung two small leaking holes.

Nothing Phil had said was at all surprising, yet he had said it in such a way that Odd could no longer pretend it wasn't true. Her mom had left her. There could be no more hiding from that fact.

"Sorry for bothering you," she said, running her coat sleeve across her eyes.

"Well take your sorry rear-end out of here. This ain't no orphanage."

"Ok. I will," Odd said, walking with tired steps to the side door that she had entered from. She hesitated before going out. The day had been nice, but the night would be cold. The thought made her want to find a corner of the motel lobby to hide in and curl up.

"You gotta push that door, dummy," Phil said, still with his feet on the counter. "It ain't gonna open by itself like at a fancy hotel."

"Phil, where's California? How do you get there?"

"That's simple. Head west until you hit the Pacific." He chortled at this. Odd didn't see the humor in it, but then again she didn't really understand the word Pacific. She'd heard of it before, but couldn't connect it with a definition.

"Pacific?"

"Yeah, it's a freakin ocean," Phil replied in a softer tone. "You know, a great big bunch of water that you can't even see all the way across. You'll know it when you see it."

"Thanks, Phil," Odd said quietly. Just as she opened the door the grubby man behind the counter called out to her.

"Hey kid! Hey Odd? Don't try to go to California. You'll never find your mom there. It's too big. There's like fifty million people there. I bet you don't even know what city she's in. All that'll happen is you'll end up lost."

Odd hadn't turned in the open door. What did it matter if she was lost here or there? She stared out at the bleak city. "Thank you for the advice," she said in all honesty. Phil had given her about as much kindness as he was capable of and she truly appreciated it.

Chapter 20

The afternoon had worn away at some point and the low sun turned Odd's mind to the thought of shelter. Did she dare make another attempt to sleep in Father Marino's church? The idea made her nervous. If she had been a social worker, it was the first place she'd look. And that meant others would be looking there as well.

She couldn't chance it.

In fact it had been dicey even going to the Lucky U. With that thought in mind she went through the alley, heading north, parallel to Broadway. After a couple of blocks she crossed over. Between a chophouse and an oil-smelling mechanic's garage, up three irregular steps, she ducked into Gary's bar. Only a handful of customers made up the late afternoon crowd and an empty section of bar beckoned her.

A low groan escaped her as she got off her feet.

"Hey, what can I get..." Gary said coming over. He stopped in mid-sentence at the sight of Odd.

"I'm not here to beg, I promise," Odd said as quick as she could. The bartender's lips had come together to form a hard line.

"That's all good and all, but I remember telling you not to come in here without money. Do you have any?"

"Some." Odd had fourteen cents. She rushed on as Gary's eyes looked to get angry. "Do truckers come in here? My mom ran off with a trucker and I'm trying to find out if anyone knows a trucker named Jared who goes to California and back."

His shallow anger had dissipated at her question. He breathed out a long sigh. "Your mom still hasn't come back?"

She shook her head, feeling her eyes want to tear up. With a hardening of her young heart, Odd crushed her eyelids down, blinking hard.

"I'm sorry to hear that," he said, patting her hand. "Truckers? We get a few, but none that would go to California. You might try the Black Irish Pub."

The named seemed familiar. "Is that the one up Broadway?"

"Yep. Two blocks this side of the overpass. They've got a good-sized parking lot. I think that's what attracts the truckers."

Odd slumped on her stool. "I just walked down from up there."

Perhaps out of habit, Gary poured her a glass of ice water and asked, "So what have been doing to keep yourself from freezing to death? You aren't doing anything...bad are you?"

Odd chugged down the water, gasped and replied, "Social Services."

Gary smirked. "They let you hang out in bars? Or did you run?" She put her head down as answer. He filled her glass again. "Come on, Odd. You shouldn't give up on people so easily. Give it another shot."

"I would, but..." Odd paused to slide down her glasses showing off her eyes. "No normal family wants this hanging around them. If I go back, it will be to their juvie detention wing for the violent and unwanted. That's where they put you if you can't get a family to take you in after three days."

"Oh man," the bartender said as Odd polished off the next glass of water. She hadn't had anything to drink since breakfast.

Running her arm across the back of her mouth, she asked, "Do you know anything about California?"

"Yeah, I've been there. It's a lot warmer than here."

"Warmer?"

Gary grinned at her excitement. "Yeah and the sun is always shining. You'll fit right in with those glasses. Everyone wears them. I mean everyone. They may not wear underwear, but they sure as hell wear sunglasses."

Odd pulled them off and gave them a long look. "I hate my glasses...but I can't live without them. Funny, huh? They're sort of like a crutch that a cripple might use. I bet every crippled boy hates his crutch as much as I hate my glasses."

"You're probably right," Gary said, reaching for her water glass.

It was then that Odd realized that someone was staring at her. She fumbled her glasses back onto her face before turning to see a man she vaguely recognized.

"You're the red-eyed girl, isn't you?" The man was pretty red-eyed himself. It wasn't even five yet and already the man seemed halfway drunk. Odd felt a shiver of fear run through her. Drunk people could be unpredictable as well as dangerous and Odd didn't have anyone left to protect her.

"Yeah, I guess," she mumbled. Her quietness caused the man to lean closer in to hear.

At her words a grin lit his face. He spun her

chair around. "Freddy, you gotta see this. It's the coolest thing ever," he said to man at a nearby table. "This girl has—honest-to-God—demon eyes! You'll flip when you see em. Go ahead little girl, show em."

While she had been talking to Gary the bar had filled somewhat and now a good thirty people were staring at her. Odd tried to turn, but the man had arms that were bigger than her thighs and he held her in place with ease.

"That's right! Everyone has to pitch in a buck, or she won't show. Truss me it's the coolest. Come on let's see those dollars...come on."

Some of the bar patrons looked skeptical, while others grew excited and dug out money. Many of these excited people crowded in close and Odd recognized their leering faces from the time her mom had brought her in. Behind them, drawn forward by their perverse curiosity, the skeptics pressed forward as well.

"I'm not going to do it." Odd said in a terrified squeak of a voice. She turned her head to Gary for help, but the man wasn't looking at her. He had his eyes on the people in front of her. His bar had turned from a sleepy little dive into happy active place in seconds.

"What?" the drunk asked. Odd again tried to lean back away. The man seemed honestly confused by her actions.

"I saw this a couple of weeks ago. It's the freakiest thing," a woman with leathery looking skin and faded tattoos said. "Come on sweetie. You can use the money. I can tell. Come on don't be shy."

Her foul breath, a combination of beer, cigarettes, and rotting teeth had Odd turning away. The little girl almost gagged, but then felt someone touch her glasses. Odd slammed them back to her face, feeling the plastic bite into the bridge of her nose.

"No!" Odd yelled as more people pressed closer to stare. "I'm not a freak."

"Sweetie, no one thinks you are," the leather-skinned lady said, wafting more of her repulsive fumes Odd's way. "You're just...one of a kind."

"Let her be!" Gary roared out. "If she says no, then the answer's no." He came around the bar looking hard and cross. The patrons wilted before him.

"We was just having some fun," said the drunk. He still had his thick-knuckled hands on Odd's arms, but they had gone loose. "This place needs some fun, you know."

This dimmed Gary's ire. "Yeah, I know. But we can't have it at someone else's expense. Odd come away from there." Keeping one hand to her glasses and one arm across her skinny chest, Odd went to him. He put an arm around her shoulder and said, "Come with me."

He lead her through the greasy-floored kitchen to the back door and looked on the verge of kicking her out, but then he paused, thinking. He turned to a dented door and brought her into a room with a desk. It was obvious the room had never been cleaned and neither had the desk. Gary walked her across a floor carpeted in old bills and receipts and sat her behind the desk.

"Wait here for a few, ok?"

He didn't wait for an answer, but went away immediately. Was he going to call Social Services? Should she run...and, if so, to where? She didn't have the energy to run. Feeling overwhelmed and exhausted she laid her head down on the desk and, amazingly, she fell asleep. It was a short nap, however, and she came awake with a start when the door to the office opened.

"I'm sor..." she began, thinking it was Gary coming in but it was one of his wait-staff, an older woman with very fake red hair. Odd had seen her before. The woman gazed at her with squinting, mean looking eyes. She carried on a plate one of Gary's huge, delicious hamburgers.

"Here go. The boss was gonna bring it back his self but we're getting busy upfront. You need any ketchup, hun?" The woman's eyes may have been mean, but her tone was kindly. This didn't make sense to Odd.

"No, thank you."

The woman stared, forcing Odd to wait to eat. The little girl saw that the waitress was trying to peer through the dark glasses at her red eyes. Odd lowered her head.

The waitress tapped her on the arm. "Sorry. I shouldn't stare like that. It's just so...so different, you know?"

"Yeah, I know."

"I got bad eyes, too. I can't see worth a damn...I'm mean worth a darn. All my customers call me Cranky-Candy because I'm always like this:" here she scowled and then laughed. Odd could only guess that her real name was Candy. She had a nametag pinned to her heavy bosom, but the lettering was too small for Odd to make out.

"When you squint it does make you look a little angry," Odd said. "I thought you were mad at me when you came in."

"No. I just need glasses. I keep meaning to get them, but I never get around to it." The waitress patted her arm. "Eat. Gary will be by soon, K?"

Odd ate...and ate. She concentrated on the fries—they were never much good the following day and she planned to keep some food for later. And by the time Gary came in she was stuffed, and still three-quarters of her burger was left uneaten.

"You didn't like it?" he asked.

"No, it was really good. I'm just saving some for tomorrow." Just then her tomorrows looked as hungry as her yesterdays had been. "I'm sorry if I let you down. I know the bar woulda done better if I had let them..."

"Shush!" Gary interrupted. "You got nothing to be sorry for. I should of stepped in sooner, but I actually thought that you'd take the money."

"I'd rather starve than be a freak."

"I understand. I really do, but..." Gary paused, while his eyes shifted around. "But without a mom and no one to take care of you, you'll need money."

Her dinner rolled in her belly and an anxiety started to quiver her chest. "You—you want me to go out there and let them see?"

"No. I don't. I just want you to understand that there may come a time that you'll need to."

Odd looked at her hamburger instead of at Gary. She wouldn't be a freak. She'd walk to California before she'd ever let herself be one again.

Gary saw the stubbornness in her demeanor. "So what are you gonna do?" he asked. "Are you going down to the Black Irish and ask around for a trucker?" Odd nodded. Gary shook his head. "Not all bar owners are as nice as me. I can tell you who's ever running that joint isn't going to like a little girl wandering around his place asking where her mommy is."

"I don't have a choice," Odd said.

"How bout this? I'll see if Candy don't mind going up there with you after her shift at ten. She don't live to far away."

"Ten?" That was hours away. "The trucker could be gone by then."

Gary shrugged. "Or he could be just showing up. Or he could be halfway to California. You have no clue who this guy is. I mean there could be a hundred Jareds down there, but more likely there isn't any."

"I guess you're right."

"I am right. I'm right about a lot of things and one of them is you can't be walking the streets by yourself at night. It's way too dangerous. There are bad men around. Real bad men who would love to get a hold of a girl like you—you know why right?"

Odd nodded. She knew alright, Mitch had taught her a valuable lesson.

"Then take this warning to heart," Gary said. "I'm not throwing tales at you to try to scare you. These guys are for real. They are looking for little girls out all by themselves and there are more of them than you might realize." Gary started pacing. "The things they do—they should be locked away forever."

Whether he meant to or not, he had scared her. "I'll wait...and thanks for all your help."

Gary stopped his pacing. "I'll be even more help. Afterwards I'll have Candy drop you off where you're staying..." Odd opened her mouth to say that this wasn't necessary, but he held up a hand to forestall her. "She owes me about a thousand favors, so don't worry about it."

Odd was very worried. She wasn't staying with

anyone or anywhere for that matter. What would Candy say to that?

He continued: "Now I'm doing this for you. You gotta do something for me. Give foster-care another try, please. You can't be roaming the streets. Already you're like a stray cat...one that I've fed once too many times."

Sitting warm and full bellied, Odd thought that being a stray was a far better alternative to the Fedorov's basement jail or the prison of B wing. She said nothing to Gary.

"Promise me," he demanded.

"I...I can't, Odd said.

Chapter 21

"Odd, please! You're being unreasonable."

She hated the idea of making Gary in the least way mad; especially after all he had done for her. "I can't make that promise without lying to you. Do you want me to lie?"

"No! I want you to see that it's your only way to be safe." Gary slammed a fist down on his desk. The sudden movement warped her vision so that his arm looked huge, while his body had shrunk and seemed a distant thing. Odd cringed, more at the strange sight than any fear that he'd hurt her. Gary misjudged her response and moved away to lean up against the wall.

For a minute he stared up at the ceiling. "Look, I've got to get back to work; I've got a good crowd upfront. I'll help you like I said, but that's it. If you come in here again without your mom or at least a guardian, I gotta call social services. I'm not trying to be mean. I'm trying to help."

"You aren't being mean," Odd replied. "And I really do appreciate all that you've done for me."

"I'm just worried that my help may end up getting you hurt," he said. Looking glum he left her.

She would get hurt whether he helped or not. The thought wasn't cheerful, but the truth of it left her apathetic long enough for her to fall back asleep amongst the papers littering the desk. When Candy shook her awake, Odd felt slow and stupid until the night air perked her up.

"The Black Irish," Candy said as they walked towards a little rust and orange colored Honda Accord. "It's been an age since I set foot in that place."

"Are there truckers there, you think?" Odd asked. The interior of the Honda was better cared for than the exterior.

"Oh yeah. There's a whole bunch of warehouses on first and it's the nearest bar. Here, you forgot this." She held out a to-go bag. Inside sat the remainder of Odd's burger.

"Thanks...and thanks for wrapping it." Odd stuck it in her pocket. " Gary told me you live up this way."

"I rent a room from a friend. It's a bit cramped having all your stuff in one room, but it's cheap. Where are you staying?"

Odd sucked in her breath. "Well...it all depends on if we find my mom up here. I...I just can't believe she took off with a trucker. Are truckers nice?"

Candy didn't seem to notice the change of topic. "Truckers? Eh. Some are, some aren't. It depends. You know what truckers really are? They're stinky!" She laughed and Odd joined her though she wasn't sure why.

Probably because of her nap and her full belly, Odd felt good like she hadn't in a long time. If it was only summer, then she wouldn't have a care in the world. If it had been, she could go find a golf course, curl up on the soft grass, and sleep there.

"Why are they so stinky?" she asked Candy.

"Because they're always driving. For days and days they sit in their big trucks doing nothing but sweating."

Odd never knew this about truckers. "Then why would my mom take up with one?"

It was mostly a rhetorical question, but Candy answered, "Because they act like sailors half the time. They'll come into town; get their paychecks and blow it all before leaving again."

Big spending always attracted Karen Wyatt's attention. "There it is," Odd said pointing at the pub.

"Yep. Just keep your glasses on and don't do any talking." Candy pulled into a parking spot near the front. "What was this guy's name?"

"Jared."

Getting out of the car, Candy appeared confident. "There can't be that many Jared's. It's not the most popular name in the world."

The Black Irish Pub wasn't exactly in full swing. All told maybe forty people sat drinking beer and watching the TVs on the walls. For the most part the place was dimly lit and Odd had to peer over the top of her shades to get a good look around.

Her mom wasn't anywhere to be seen. This had been expected so Odd wasn't greatly disappointed.

Candy went to the bar. "Excuse me. I'm looking for a trucker named Jared."

The bartender was a hugely fat man sitting on a stool in front of the beer taps. From there he could pour and pass out drinks without moving. "Don't know no Jared," he said without taking his eyes from the nearest TV.

"I'll ask around," Candy replied with a strain to her smile. The man made a noise suggesting that he couldn't care less what she did. At the third table they went to, Candy got lucky.

"Jared? He went to the toilet. Had to take a dump."

Candy's smile became brittle at the remark. "Thanks." She turned to Odd and whispered, "What did I say about the smell?" Odd had to face away to stifle a giggle.

"Hey, Jared! Your wife and daughter are here," one of the truckers at the table called out. "They want their alimony check."

"What are you pulling?" laughed a portly middle-aged man, walking up. He wasn't bad looking, just past his prime. When he caught sight of the two females a slightly nervous expression overtook him. Candy nudged Odd.

"Sir? Is your name Jared?" she asked, just barely louder than the TVs surrounding the room.

"Yeah?" His nervousness became more pronounced much to the amusement of his friends, who elbowed each other as they whispered jokes back and forth.

"My name is Odd...Audrey Wyatt. I'm looking for my mom, Karen Wyatt. She went with you to California a couple weeks back."

This silenced the men around the table. Jared looked back and forth between Candy and Odd with his mouth working silently. Finally he gushed out, "Well yeah, but she wanted to go. I didn't make her."

"Do you know where she is?" Odd said in a rush, excited by the fact that she was at least one-step closer to finding her mom.

Jared shrugged. "She left me in L. A. for another dude. We..." He couldn't go on as his friends burst out in raucous laughter. He came in close and said, "Let's talk outside."

Once in the parking lot he lit a cigarette, which he didn't so much as smoke as used to add flair to his words. Odd took a step back and tried not to watch as he talked. The constant motion of the orange ember had her getting dizzy.

"Look, I didn't even know she had a kid," Jared said right off the bat. "She just said she was looking for a good time. Wanting to find a good guy to settle down with. I was game for a little company—I mean it's a long way to L.A. and back. Everything was good at first until she started spending too much of my money. She kept giving me promises about paying me back once we were in L.A."

"But that didn't happen, did it?" Odd asked. She'd heard this lie too many times before.

"No. She just hung around these bars flirting with every guy around. She said it didn't mean anything. She said she just liked being the center of attention." Jared paused to take a drag on his cigarette. "Anyway, after three days I'm thinking we were gonna be leaving, but she shows up with some old dude and says we're done. It was the last I saw her."

"And she didn't mention me once?" It hurt Odd to ask the question. Jared just looked down and kicked a pebble for an answer. After a deep breath she asked a less painful one, "Do you know the name of the guy she met up with?"

"No. Sorry. All I know was that he repaired shoes. I thought that was the dumbest thing ever, but she called him an entrepreneur. What a joke!"

Candy put her arm around Odd's shoulder and pulled her in close, but Odd wasn't done yet. "What about the name of the bar?"

Jared squinched up his face, looking up at the stars. "Something...Cantina. I don't remember. I do know that it was on Long Beach Boulevard near Fifty-fourth."

"L.A.—Cantina—near Long Beach Boulevard—near Fifty-fourth," Odd repeated. "Got it."

Candy looked at her aghast. "You aren't thinking about going to California, are you? Cuz that's just crazy."

"It's not crazy," Odd replied. "Without my mom there's nothing for me here except the cold, and Gary said it's warm in California. Is it?" she asked Jared.

He finished off the last of his cigarette, flicking the butt into the street before answering, "Oh yeah. It's hot out there."

"You can't go. Your mom abandoned you!" Candy practically yelled. "She left you here to...to die for all she cared."

Did Candy think that this was new information for Odd?

"I know!" the little girl replied, angrily. "You think I don't know this? I know it better than all of you, but what choice do I have? Are you going to be my mom? Are you going to take care of me and buy my clothes and send me to all those expensive doctors that she won't?"

Candy stepped back shaking her head. "I don't have the room or...or..." she trailed off lamely.

"If you're not going to do it, who is? Social Services can't do it. They can't find anyone who will take a demon-child. What about you Jared?" Odd yanked off her glasses. "Do you want this for a daughter? Will you kiss me goodnight and read me bedtime stories? Will you love me?"

The man was totally unprepared, both for the questions and the wild eyes of Odd Wyatt. He stumbled back, saying, "What? What is that? What the hell is wrong with your eyes?"

Odd ignored him and turned back to Candy, who flinched at the sight of her unadorned eyes in a tiny but obvious way. "I know I have the worst mom in the world," Odd said, calming a little. "No one needs to tell me that. Someone just needs to tell me what I'm supposed to do without her."

Chapter 22

Odd's emotions kept her warm for a little while. After that she pulled on her hat and gloves and zipped up tight. It was after eleven and she was doggedly walking in the direction she hoped was west. A slapping sound accompanied each step. Her right converse was coming apart.

"Just hold on for two-thousand more miles," she said to it. Two-thousand miles was simply a concept beyond her ability to comprehend. All she knew was that it was an impossible distance to walk. Regardless, she kept going—if for no other reason than to stay warm.

A half-hour later she came upon railroad tracks and an idea blinked into her head. She could hop a train. She knew it was possible having overheard a conversation between a couple of old rummy-drunks at a slimy bar one time.

In her mind she could picture the words written in large letters along the side of some of the trains: Union-Pacific. The pacific was where she wanted to go, but what was Union? Was that another ocean? And if so, which way was Union and which way was Pacific?

Odd went and stood on the tracks looking first one way, then the other. California lay in the west. The sun set in the west, but that had been hours ago and she was now far too turned around to know which way that was.

It hardly seemed to matter. There wasn't a train

in sight. Odd decided to keep heading the way she had been.

"The Union Ocean...the Pacific Ocean," she said, sampling the words. They sounded right. After another two miles Odd was really dragging, but she pushed herself on towards a large industrial building. Steam vented from at least three different places—and steam meant heat. Passing empty loading docks Odd hurried to the lowest of the billowing white clouds emitted from a stumpy-looking chimney.

She couldn't reach the steam until she rolled a barrel over to it and climbed up. "Oh my. That feels good," she whispered as the heat blasted her hands. The enjoyment of her hands only lasted so long before her frozen toes demanded their own heat. Letting a sigh escape her, Odd climbed down.

Within seconds she realized what a mistake it had been to put her hands in the steam. Her gloves were now wet and beginning to freeze. Quickly she tugged them off. "Now, what am I going to do?" In seconds her hands were even colder that they had been. She tucked them into her jacket and leaned back against the chimney.

She could feel the hot bricks through her jacket! In a flash she turned and put her numb fingers against its rough surface. This felt so good that she went so far as to hug the chimney. After a minute she rotated herself and put her back to it as well.

"Well, I won't freeze," she said, turning again. "But I won't get any sleep either." She needed some way to trap the heat—something to cover her over. "A box!" Odd giggled in excitement and began to run back to the loading docks she had passed. After three steps she pitched onto her side. It was hard to run when the ground seemed to undulate beneath your feet.

Odd got up and this time went slower. At the dock there had been a large green bin filled with broken down cardboard boxes. Grabbing up a large one, she tugged it back to her chimney and erected it where the chimney and the side of the building formed a little rectangle. It wasn't a perfect fit, but it was good enough for Odd to begin sweating a few minutes after she climbed in.

Unzipping her coat, and partially opening the front of her box helped to regulate the temperature and very soon the tired, stressed little girl was sound asleep. It wasn't a long sleep, however.

The sound of someone stumbling along, cursing at the dark had her red eyes opened wide straining to see through the opening in her box. At first she trembled in fear thinking it was a wino or a bum or some perv like Mitch, but then she heard a girl exclaim in anger: "Hell no! Hell no." A second later the anger turned into a pitiful crying. "And...and you deserve it."

Odd peeked her head out of the box to see who the girl was talking to, but saw she was all alone. The girl tilted her head back. Her hand gripped a clear bottle and she drank straight from it, before coughing and sputtering.

She then took a deep breath and drank again with the same results. "One more...one more." She tipped the bottle vertically, draining the last of it and then threw it away. The girl then laid down and began weeping. The sound of it went right to Odd's soul causing an ache to settle in her chest.

She's going to freeze to death, thought Odd. But

just then a long, moaning whistled sounded. Odd caught on in a hurry. The girl wasn't going to freeze to death; she was going to let the train run her over. Odd scrambled out of her warm cocoon and hurried to the tracks.

"Hey...hey," she said hurrying as best she could. The girl jumped in alarm and then reflexively grabbed the ice-cold rails as if she thought Odd had the strength to pull her off. Odd came down to her level. "You—you can't do this. A train's coming and—and it's going to hurt real bad. You don't want that do you?"

The girl, a teen of about fifteen according Odd's sensitive eyes blinked tears and confusion up at her. "Go away! This is none of your business."

Behind Odd, the train came into view a mile or so away. Odd very deliberately went around the girl so that the onrushing train's light was in her face. The idea of the steel beast coming at her from behind gave her the shivers that wouldn't stop.

She began tugging on the girl's hand; it was as cold and white as snow. Her face, however wasn't. Even in the dim light Odd could see that there was something wrong with it. She seemed almost green is spots.

"It is my business," Odd replied, though in what way she didn't really know. "I...I can't let you do this...because...well, because you're trying to kill yourself right in my front yard."

"What?" The girl looked around at the tracks and the fence beyond them and then back at the building. "What're you talking about?"

"I'm a runaway and that right over there is the house I built to keep me warm."

"But that's only a box. It's not a house," the girl responded accurately though a bit slowly, perhaps from the alcohol.

"Still, it's warm. There's this chimney right up next to it that keeps it good and toastie. Come on, you can spend the night there with me."

The girl looked at the box for seconds. They were anxious seconds for Odd as the train was speeding towards them and already she could feel the rails trembling beneath her hand. The girl didn't seem to notice. All she saw was the box and clearly it had brought up some long forgotten memory. Her tears came harder and then a spasm went down her back.

"No. I can't. I have to do this."

The train was only a few hundred yards away; it's front light sending a long shadow out behind Odd. The red-eyed girl bent lower and said, "You're not going to die tonight."

"Yes I am."

"No! You're only going to wish you had," Odd said with sudden anger making her voice rise. "You're going to flinch at the last moment and the train is only going to run over your feet. They'll get crushed down to mush, but you won't die."

The girl licked her lips and then with eyes that had gone wild she looked down at her feet for a second and then back up at Odd. "Ok...ok," she said with fearful desperation, using Odd to pull herself up.

"Come on," Odd said and gave a final look to the onrushing train. It was still a good hundred yards away, but from that distance its powerful front light burned into her malformed retinas. "We can't just..." Odd started to say.

When the light struck Odd, the girl stared into her face with frank horror. A second passed and then she screamed a full-throated, larynx-tearing shriek. She had seen Odd's eyes with the light beating right into them. In the dark it must have been a particularly hellacious sight.

She took off running—screaming and stumbling as she went. Odd did her best to hurry after as the train rushed past them letting out another long blast from its horn, while the thunder of its passing rattled the air in her lungs. The train seemed to frighten the girl even more than Odd's eyes had and she ran up the embankment where she attempted to scale the chain link fence that ran for miles along the tracks.

Whether from the cold or her insobriety, the girl couldn't get much of a purchase and her grip weakened while she was still halfway to the top. She collapsed just as Odd came up.

"Please God, no," the girl kicked out at Odd trying to keep her at bay. "What are you? A devil? Get away from me! Get away!"

The train drowned out her shrill cries.

Just out of reach of the thrashing legs, Odd stood waiting. When the air had calmed from the passing of the train and the girl finally stopped kicking, Odd said, "I'm not a devil or a demon or any of that stuff. I just have a birth defect in my eyes. You know what an albino is?"

"Yeah. But they're all white with pink eyes and you're like normal colored and your eyes are red...and not just a little red. They glowed!"

"You weren't supposed to see that," Odd said, with her head down. "Nobody handles that very well. I have more than one problem with my eyes, but I'm not a demon...or not a very scary one at least." Despite Father Marino Odd hadn't given up on the idea just yet.

Though in this case it was a joke. The girl lifted her head at it in understanding but didn't crack a smile. "A birth defect?"

The smaller of the two girls nodded emphatically. "Yep. Ocular Albinism and a congenital overlapping of my retina." Odd tried to make it sound like it was nothing. "It's not catchy or anything. You have to be born this way."

"Oh."

"My name is Odd Wyatt. I ran away from this evil foster-family where they were going to keep me prisoner. I'm twelve and my mom abandoned me about two weeks ago. I have most of a hamburger down at the box if you're hungry."

It was her life story in a nutshell. Odd wanted to get through it quick so the girl would know that she was normal. It didn't seem to work. The girl only swayed against the fence blinking largely.

"What's your name?" Odd tried again.

"Connie...Angeline," she said, breathing very heavily. "I...I think I'm going to be sick!"

Almost immediately, Connie went to her knees and began retching. Odd came down beside her as the first of the vomit splattered onto the gravel. The little girl then began humming a song, while her hands went into Connie's long brown hair and began braiding it to keep it out of the vomit. After the hair was braided, she continued to hum while rubbing Connie's back in a soothing way.

"Thanks," Connie said, sitting back, looking at

Odd with indistinct, bleary eyes. "How can you stand to do that?"

This made Odd laugh. "I have to do that for my mom two or three times a month so it doesn't bother me much." The truth was that it didn't bother her at all. In fact, she liked it. It was one of the few times that she felt needed. Odd liked to feel needed.

Connie's head rolled on her shoulders as if it was a weight to great for her neck to bear. "Man," she said. "Whenever I get near anyone puking it makes me want to hurl wicked bad."

In its strange way this was complimentary to Odd and she grinned at the words. "Are you getting cold? You can stay in my box...or I can walk you home or something. Whatever you want."

"I can't go home...I won't," Connie said, pointing an errant finger in Odd's general direction, as if warning the girl with it.

"Then come with me to the box. It's warm."

The girl nodded and then scrambled around on the loose gravel, her drunken legs working against themselves. "I don't think I can get up," she said with her mouth hanging open. A thin line of drool swayed from her lip; she didn't notice.

Ecstatic that Connie would come stay with her, Odd wiped away the drool and said, "Here, let me help you."

It became quite an effort for Odd. She tugged and heaved on the drunk teen until Connie stood swaying to an unfelt wind. Then cheerfully, and quite chattily, Odd walked the staggering girl across the tracks to her cardboard home.

It was another operation to get Connie into the

box. Odd likened it to putting a pile of cooked spaghetti into a straw.

Arms and legs went everywhere and Odd worked up quite a sweat in the process. She couldn't be happier. Odd had a friend. Whether it was just for the night or for longer, she didn't know nor did she really care. All that mattered was that she wasn't alone. Still grinning, she curled up to Connie in the now tight box and together they fell asleep like cats.

Chapter 23

The following morning, long before Connie stirred, Odd lay with her eyes open, thinking: what would drive a girl to commit suicide? Boy trouble? Had she been dumped for another girl? If so, that wasn't much of a reason in Odd's mind.

Or maybe it was a bad home life? Did her dad beat her? She had looked strangely green and splotchy in the low light the night before. The twelve-year-old wanted to roll over and get a better look at her new friend, but she restrained herself with patience beyond her years.

As long as Connie slept, Odd would lay there unmoving so as not to disturb her. It was a habit she had formed out of necessity by growing up with an inconsistently abusive drunk for a mother. There was never any way for Odd to know what her mom would be like when she woke up after a bad night. Her early morning attitude could run the gamut from groggy to spitting-mean.

Eventually she felt Connie stir—then stiffen as she came awake. The older girl's head came up as she looked around at the box and then at Odd. With her sunglasses outside the box Odd kept her eyes shut.

"Good morning," the little girl said.

"What?" Connie began to sit up. "Oh! Jeeze. My head...oh."

"We should get you some water. It helps with a hangover."

Connie pushed herself up, bumping her head on the top of the box. "Does it? I...I don't feel well."

Odd stayed where she was, still with her eyes closed. "Water and Tylenol and maybe some crackers is really the best."

There was a silence then. Odd could feel the girl looking at her. "Do you have red eyes?" Connie asked with a touch of disbelief to her voice. "Did I really see that?"

"Yeah, but it's not catchy or nothing," Odd said in a rush.

"Let me see?"

Letting out a long breath, Odd rolled over and looked up at Connie, expecting the worst—expecting to see revulsion straining the lines of her face as she stared in dread fascination at Odd's deformity. Instead it was she who gawked.

Connie was beautiful. Even hung over and just awake after sleeping in a box, Connie was a lovely creature. She had a tangled mane of rich, thick brown hair; her large eyes were of the same color as her hair and were set above a very pert nose and full lips. Only in her complexion did her looks stray from splendor. Though her skin was smooth and so soft looking that Odd wanted to reach out and touch her, it was also not the right color. Her face was a canvas of green and yellow bruises below the half-moon of a purple shiner beneath her right eye. There were even marks on her neck; little dark blue dots formed a ring around her throat.

The girl had been beaten. Embarrassed for her friend, Odd looked away. "I'm gonna get my glasses."

"Is it that bad?" Connie asked, touching her face

with gentle fingers. Still, she winced.

"I...I...It..." Odd stammered, not wanting to hurt the girl anymore than she had been. "It will all go away soon and when they do you'll be the prettiest thing to..."

"I don't want to be pretty anymore," Connie said, tearing up. Why it was so, Odd didn't know, but the tears made Connie even more stunning.

"You're crazy," Odd said touching the girl's shoulder. "Any girl would love to look like you."

"Then why do all the girls hate me? Everyone thinks that I'm after their boyfriends...or...their husbands."

"Husbands?" Odd asked. "How old are you?"

"Fifteen."

"Fifteen! Who would think a fifteen-year-old would..." Odd stopped at Connie's expression. Odd had seen sadness on people's faces before, but those looks had been counterfeits, weak forgeries of real pain compared to the look on Connie's face. "You...you tried to steal someone's..." Odd couldn't finish the sentence.

"Do you believe in heaven?" Connie asked after a minute went by in silence.

Odd believed in hell. Heaven, with all its senseless rules and unknowns confused her. She couldn't tell up from down about God, but to her, evil was very real. "I hope there is a heaven...for people." *And for me, I hope*, she added to herself.

"I think there's a heaven, too. I mean, I hope so or all of this is just such a waste. You know?" she asked Odd. "That's what I was thinking last night...that there had to be a heaven and it had to be better than here. That's why I wanted to...you know, lay down in front of that train."

Connie stared far away without seeing the brown of their cardboard box inches from her face. "I was scared, but I didn't think I had a choice. You can only do so many things wrong before...before they won't let you into heaven, right? And if they don't let me in, then I'll have nothing." Tears came again. Great round jewels. Pearls of the soul. And Connie only grew more dazzling. Odd, though smaller and far weaker, wanted to go to her and protect her.

"You could pray," she said, trying her best to be helpful. "Or...or...I know a priest. He can take away your sins and then you'd be a shoe-in for heaven. But, really, you don't need to die just yet."

"What else is there for me?"

"Have you tried talking to your parents?"

The words had the effect of a tremendous slap to Connie. She rocked her head back in misery. "Who do think did this to me?" she cried.

Now it was Odd's turn to feel as though she had been struck. "Oh, I'm sorry. I didn't know." Fearful of losing her new friend she cast about in the loose jumble of thoughts careening around in her mind. "You can still go to go to the priest...he's awful nice. You can trust him. Or we can call the police...your dad shouldn't beat you. It's against the..."

Connie interrupted, "Shut up! You don't know what you're talking about! It's my mom who beats me. She thinks I let...I let him do...the things he does to me." Connie couldn't go on. She went to her hands and knees and crawled out of the box.

"But...I didn't know," Odd said in confused desperation. The little girl plunged through the opening after Connie. She paused only long enough to grab her glasses and the hamburger from atop the box and her gloves from the ground. These were now stiff and frozen. She then hurried after the older girl who was trudging up the embankment to the railroad tracks.

"Hey! Wait up," she cried, fretting that she'd never be able to catch up with the older girl. Even on flat ground Odd could barely run, but the ladder-like railroad ties had her eyes distorting the truth of reality just at a fast walk.

"Please wait," Odd tried again before casting a frightened look behind her. She feared a train would come along in secret and crush her. There was another reason that made her look back: Connie was striding off in the wrong direction.

The rising sun blazed its light straight into their faces and threw their shadows out behind them—westward. Every step carried Odd that much further from her destination.

Finally, she yelled out, "Stop! You're going the wrong way."

Connie took a few more steps and then stopped, looking about her as if trying to comprehend her surroundings. She then let out a hysterical laugh that put an end to her tears. Wiping the last of them from her face she said, "How do you know I'm going the wrong way? I don't even know where I'm going."

"You're coming with me to California."

At first the older girl laughed again after a crazed fashion, but then she turned sober and thought for a few moments wearing a frown on her face. She then stepped lightly up onto one of the rails. From where Odd stood the girl seemed very childlike. Not childish, and not an adult either. Somewhere in the perfect in-between where balancing on a railroad track came without thought. "California? Why would I want to go there?"

"Why do you want to stay here?" Odd asked right back.

Connie didn't have an answer for this, so she said, "I don't have any money to get to California."

This made Odd grin. "Neither do I. But we can catch one of the Pacific trains. They go all the way to the ocean and supposedly California is somewhere near it. That's why I said you're going the wrong way. The ocean is that way." She cocked a thumb behind her.

For some reason Odd felt inordinately proud of this tiny bit of knowledge. Had she been asked where anywhere else was she would've been at a loss. But she knew two facts about California: it lay in the west and it was warm.

"I...I don't know," Connie replied. One of her feet slipped on the rail and for a few seconds she tottered off balance but then she threw out her graceful limbs to steady herself. "I guess I could. I can't ever go back home."

Odd was overjoyed. "Cool! Do you want to get some water first before we go? And...and I have a hamburger. It's fresh from last night...but now it's frozen. We could put it in our pockets till it's warm or..." Odd glanced at the chimney that she had slept next to. The steam still poured out of the grate. "Or we could heat it using that steam. It's very hot."

"I am hungry. It was probably all that puking I did."

Feeling gay over the prospect of having a friend, Odd laughed and tried to step up on the rail as well. She slipped off only after a second. "My mom is always hungry after puking. But she doesn't call it puking, she calls it up-chucking."

Connie opened her mouth to say more, but just as quick shut it again and pressed her lips tight. Odd knew she had something to say, but wasn't going to push. They had plenty of time together; California was a long ways away.

A plastic grocery bag lay hung up on one of the railroad ties near Connie. "Grab that bag, willya?" Odd asked her. "If we don't keep the burger covered it'll get all wet. It happened to my gloves and now they're frozen, see?" She held them out.

The steam heated the hamburger better than either of them could've imagined. It was delicious and Odd was ravenous, but she gave Connie the lion's share of it, content to see her friend eat. Afterwards they sat with their backs against the chimney with their legs sticking straight out enjoying the morning.

They were side by side; arms touching and Odd felt the greatest desire to hold Connie's hand. She resisted, but couldn't help smiling up at her every few minutes. A glow sat within the breast of the little girl. A glow she hadn't felt in ages. It was happiness. Connie had seen her eyes yet still she was right there next to Odd—they were even touching!

Odd almost couldn't contain herself. She wanted to laugh and pet Connie's hand or maybe kiss her cheek. But she did none of these things: Connie wasn't in the mood. Rather, sometimes she was and sometimes she wasn't. She'd smile out of the blue and then cry. Or she'd stare out at the railroad tracks and her head would go back and forth.

She barely spoke and so Odd rambled away enough for two. This surprised the little girl since she had never been much of a talker. Of course she never had a friend stay with her for so long before. When she was younger it was the parents of would-be friends that would warn their children away from her. As she got older the children her age seemed to grow in spitefulness so that Odd began to shy away from them. They were so invariably hurtful that she found it nearly an impossibility to open up. And then when she did...it had always ended poorly.

"Are you ready to go?" Odd asked after they had sat for a while. "We should try to get us some water before the next train comes."

"You're being very nice...but I don't know if you really want me to go with you. You don't know what kind of person I am. Bad stuff is always happening to me; I'm not a lucky person to be around."

Now Odd abandoned restraint and grabbed Connie's hand. "You're the luckiest thing that's happened to me in...in, like forever. I thought I was going to have to go to California all by myself but now I have you. Come on. It'll be fun and besides it'll get you away from your problems."

The girl shuddered and then rubbed her belly. "We'll never get that far away," she said.

Chapter 24

"When's the next train coming?" Connie asked from her perch on the rail. They had been standing, waiting in the cold air for ten minutes and in all that time the older girl had balanced there easily.

Odd marveled at her. She seemed possessed of a natural grace that looked out of place in this industrial setting. Her steps along the rail were light and unerring. It was as if, left unmolested, she'd never lose her poise. How tall she appeared to Odd. Tall and elegant; and slim. Not skinny like Odd but willowy and fine and perfect.

Again, Odd felt an overwhelming desire to touch Connie, to touch that elegance and take some of it for her own. However, she feared that touching Connie would have the opposite effect. That she'd blemish the girl in some way.

Odd peered eastward before answering her question, "I don't know. I think it depends on how far the Union ocean is."

"The what?"

"The Union ocean," Odd answered. "This is a Pacific-Union train track. The trains head all the way to the Union...I think, before they turn around and go back to the Pacific. I just don't know how far it is."

Connie had the beginnings of a smile on her face. Just a glimpse of one, like a blossom on the verge and Odd smiled herself, trying to coax it out. "What?" she asked.

The smile emerged, blooming splendidly despite the bruises around it, and with it came a high laugh. Odd knew she'd said something stupid about the oceans or the trains and she knew that she should be embarrassed by it, however, Connie's laughter was joyful. It was a wonderfully happy sound that Odd had caused.

"What?" she said again, laughing along. "The trains don't go all the way to the Union?"

"There is no Union ocean!" Connie said, still laughing.

"Is there a Pacific ocean?" Odd asked.

For some time Connie couldn't answer. She even came down off the rail and sat holding her belly as she laughed. "Oh...that hurts," she said, crying and laughing at the same time. Odd sat next to her and couldn't help giggling along.

Slowly, gently, Connie's laughter ran down like an old watch, becoming less and less. Finally she wiped away her tears and said, "Yes, there's a Pacific ocean. It's all the way west. And all the way east is the *Atlantic* Ocean—not the Union."

"Then why do they call the railroad the Union-Pacific? Why isn't it the Atlantic-Pacific?"

"I don't know why," Connie said with a shrug. She then peered in closer at Odd's face. "How old are you, again?"

Odd understood the question. It wasn't a question about age. "I'm twelve, but I'm not one of them special kids. I just haven't been to school much."

"In that case you're lucky," Connie replied. "You haven't missed a thing."

"Oh...that's good." Odd turned to squint back

towards the sun. She longed to go to school more than anything. As a little girl she would sneak off and watch the other kids—the normal kids—flying high on the swing sets, or playing kickball, or just running around, laughing. Sometimes they'd scream with laughter, or shriek with it. Sometimes they'd become overwhelmed by laughter and lie on the ground panting.

She'd see the girls in little packs, talking and touching each other's hair. They'd play house, while the boys hovered nearby acting like little fools. The boys would push each other or dare each other until one would go racing in and steal a baby doll or a teapot. Then the whole lot of them would begin a mad, swirling chase punctuated always by the happy laughter of children.

Odd wanted to be one of those happy schoolchildren so bad it hurt. "Hopefully a train will come by soon," Odd said quietly, staring up the tracks."

"Did I say something wrong?"

"No. No, of course not. Just wondering when a train's coming is all."

Connie laid her hand on Odd's, causing the little girl's cheeks to go red. "Odd...I don't want you to feel stupid because of that ocean business. There's lots of stuff I don't know. I don't know anything about...politics, and I don't really care either. And calculus? With all those symbols and equations, it's like a giant puzzle. I get nervous just thinking about it. Just because you don't know everything there is to know, doesn't make you dumb."

"I guess."

"I don't think you're dumb," Connie said. Odd kept her eyes down. The older girl then took Odd's little hand in both of hers. "You wanna hear something weird? Girls always think they're dumb...except the super brainy ones. But, your average girl will find some way to think she's dumb. It's true."

Odd's brows came down below the tops of her glasses. "You don't think you're dumb, right? Because, I think you're very smart."

This made Connie smile, but when she laughed it wasn't a happy one. "Sometimes I think I'm smart and then this happens..." she pointed at her face. "...And then I just don't understand the world. Nothing makes sense and I have to ask myself what did I do to deserve this? I think that if I was really smart I'd be able to figure it all out."

"Maybe it's like calculus—you know a puzzle." Odd had never heard of calculus before, but she understood puzzles. Her life was one great big puzzle that she couldn't hope to fathom. Her days came from an incalculable horizon and left her to run together down a deep well where their memories mingled and became confused.

"I guess so," Connie said with a long sigh. "Who knows? Maybe we aren't supposed to figure it all out." Connie fell silent and began tracing patterns on the back of Odd's hand. She laughed suddenly. This time with more cheer. "Here's what's really funny: girls always think they're dumber than they are, but boys always think they're smarter than they are. You ever notice that about them?"

Robert Hoover's freckled face came immediately to mind. He had seemed very smart to Odd. However, he wasn't the average boy, she was sure. For one thing, not every boy had such cute freckles, nor would they ever be brave enough to venture through the city alone the way Robert did. Odd could scarcely believe...

Just then a long blast of a train's horn shook the morning. Both girls jumped, reminded by the sound of what they had been sitting waiting for. They slid down the embankment and hurried to a spot where the little rise wasn't so steep. The train, a great, beastly steel snake slid into view from the east. It didn't seem to be moving as fast as the train from the night before, but still Odd was very nervous.

Her insides vibrated at the idea of jumping on board a moving train—no matter how slowly it was going. What would happen if her eyes went screwy right when she went to climb on board? Would she fall under the wheels? Would they chop her legs off? Despite the cold morning her hands became damp with sweat. She wiped them on her brown pants and saw Connie doing the same. They smiled at each other.

Connie's smile however was a thin crooked line on her now paper-white face. She had gone so white that her bruises stood out in sharp relief.

"It'll be ok," Odd said to reassure her. She didn't want her new friend to be frightened. Above all else Odd wanted her to be happy. "You'll see. It'll pull up right here and we'll jump right on."

Connie took a step back. "What about the conductors? Won't they be mad? They'll kick us off."

Looking at it head on, Odd couldn't tell what sort of train it was. Regardless she said, "It's not that type of train. It's one of them boxcar types. I betcha the conductor or engineer stays way up in the front and never walks all the way back. You'll see."

A minute later Odd was proven wrong. Then again so was Connie. The engine came rattling by, pulling behind it an immense number of open cars, each piled high with coal. The two girls could only stare. The only place they could've sat was atop the coal, twenty feet in the air.

"Now what?" Connie asked. She now appeared smaller—hunched over. Her shoulders, her face, even her thick brown hair drooped, heavy with depression.

"Uh...uh...maybe we could wait for the next one," Odd said, turning on a smile she didn't really feel. She had a sudden desperate fear that her new friend would leave her if things didn't go right. "Or we could go get something to drink. Do you know if there's anything around here?"

"Yeah, but nowhere I want to show up looking like this." She touched her blackened eye and then grimaced.

An idea formed in Odd's mind—one that she could barely put into words. "You...you could borrow m-my glasses. They're very big. They'll cover half your face." With her head down, Odd slowly took them off and held them out. Handing over one of her lungs would've been less of a sacrifice.

"Thanks. That's real nice of you." Connie slipped them on. "How do I look?"

Odd didn't want to take her eyes from the ground but not to look would be rude. She gave Connie a quick glance, trying to hide her unseemly eyes behind a gunfighter's squint.

"You're very beautiful. Like a movie star," Odd told her. This made the older girl flash a white smile, which Odd reluctantly looked away from. She felt weird screwing her face up the way she was.

"Like what movie star? Who?"

"Um...I don't really know any," Odd stammered out. "I just think you're beautiful."

The girl's smile dimmed. "Well, I'm tired of being beautiful. It's got me nothing but trouble."

Odd couldn't understand that at all. She would've traded places with Connie in a second. She didn't want to dwell on the negative, however. "Let's go get you that drink? What do you say?"

Chapter 25

Connie didn't live too far away, and knowing the area, she directed them to the nearest supermarket where they could get some water. Odd found this news worrisome and walked as if her head was mounted on a swivel.

"Aren't you worried that your mom will drive by or something?" she asked. Connie's mom had to be a fiendish brute of a woman. Her dad she pictured to be a tiny wimp. After all, what sort of man would allow his wife to beat one his children?

"No. I bet they don't even know I'm gone," Connie replied, staring down at her feet as she walked. Every once in a while she kicked a can or a rock. "I was gonna leave a note...you know, a suicide note, but I got too drunk and it came out sounding stupid, so I threw it away. I figured that it didn't really matter, they know what they did to me."

"They? I thought you said it was your mom that beat you up. What did your..."

Connie cut her off, turning with a glare, "I don't want to talk about it!"

Odd went meek as a mouse. "Sorry. I didn't mean it. Ok? I won't bring it up anymore. I promise."

Connie stewed in silence as they walked, but this gradually gave way to a slack-faced depression that Odd couldn't snap her out of, though she made several attempts.

The water helped to revive her somewhat. It

helped Odd as well. She felt a thousand times better. The two of them went back and forth, taking turns guzzling from the fountain at the back of the store, drinking enough between them to shame a camel.

"Are you ok?" Connie asked, wiping her lips with the back of her hand. "You keep rubbing your forehead."

Without her glasses Odd felt terribly exposed. From the second she'd handed them over she had either squinted around or kept her head down and her hand up across her brow in the hopes of keeping her eyes from being seen. However, she couldn't say this to Connie. The girl would then feel awkward about having borrowed the glasses.

"It's nothing. It's uh..."

"Brain-freeze?" Connie asked, filling in an excuse nicely. "I've got it too. No more water for me. Come on I've got to use the bathroom."

Odd didn't really have to go, but she went anyways with a giddy charge inside her over the invitation. Girls went to the bathroom in groups. She had seen it happen time and again, yet having been friendless all her life, she'd always gone by herself. That morning she walked into the three-stall bathroom as if experiencing it for the first time. She went in beaming a foolish smile.

Connie didn't notice. Hurrying to the first stall she went in and seconds later drew in a sharp breath. Then she groaned.

This took the shine off Odd's penny and it was her turn to ask, "Are you ok?"

"It's...nothing," Connie replied somewhat evasively. "I just have a tummy ache."

"Do you want me to leave you alone? I can wait outside."

Odd started to head for the door, but Connie's quick and anxious reply stopped her. "No. Don't leave me. Just...just stay here with me."

"Sure." Odd opened the door to the next stall and sat down. The glow from being invited to "Go to the bathroom" was fading rapidly. In its place concern for her new friend filled her. Connie's groaning became more pronounced.

She stifled it a minute later when the bathroom door opened and a whistler came in. Odd could only catch the barest sight of her; however she could track the lady around the bathroom by her constant whistling. She sounded like a lovely bird singing to its mate. It was as out of place in the bathroom as Odd's smile had been.

"Odd, I'm going to need...I'm going to need some help," Connie whispered, trying to pitch her voice lower than the whistle. "See if you can get some—you know."

"Some what? Toilet paper?" Odd began to take apart the spring holding her roll in place.

"No. I mean tampons," Connie said.

"Oh. I don't have any. I'm not ready for that sort of thing." Odd had only a hazy notion of a woman's cycle owing to her mother's frequent and crude remarks concerning it. However, what she did know didn't jibe with the way Connie was acting. It wasn't at all like how her mom did.

The whistler flushed and then washed her hands to a jaunty tune, pausing only long enough say, "Here you go, Hun." Through the crack Odd could catch only part of a blue vest and a braid of black hair and then she was gone.

Almost too late Connie called out, "Thanks!" right before the door shut. Her voice shook and that made Odd nervous for her.

"Are you ok? Really?"

"Yeah." In contradiction to the word she groaned again.

"Does it sting...like a cut?" Odd had never got a good answer from her mom on this one. Where did all the blood come from?

"A little," Connie replied. Her voice carried a grimace with it. "The pain's deeper."

"Sometimes my mom gets cramps when she has her period," Odd said. Seeing a chance to be helpful to her friend she added, "I used to rub her back to make her feel better. Do you want me to rub yours?"

Odd went to get up but Connie heard and said with a little panic in her voice, "No. Please just stay there."

The little girl sat back down and for a long time there was silence in the bathroom. Connie broke it by sniffling quietly. Her friend cried in the stall right next to her and Odd didn't know what to do.

"Odd?" Connie asked.

"Yeah?"

Except for her crying Connie went quiet again for nearly a minute before she said, "I think I did something really wrong. I...I..."

More tears could be heard, but now they were tears of sadness, not of pain. Suddenly, Odd had the feeling that she was back in Father Marino's confessional. What would he do in a situation like this?

"Why don't you start at the beginning?" Odd asked in a solemn voice.

It took Connie a few tries before she finally spat out, "I've been having s-sex with m-my step-father."

Odd's red eyes grew huge at this. Her dainty hand went to her mouth to keep herself from audibly gasping. She didn't have a clue how to respond so she said nothing.

Connie's crying grew louder. Between the sniffling and the hitching of her breathing, she said, "I...I...It...It's been going on for years. Not like every night, but every few months he'd sneak into my room."

Goose bumps flared on Odd's arm. She rubbed them away without noticing. "Did you tell your mom?"

"No. He said he'd hurt me, and her, if I did. He said he'd kill us. You see?" Connie asked. Odd nodded to the grey wall of the stall. It almost seemed as though Connie saw this. She continued, "You have to understand, I didn't have a choice...I didn't have a choice. He would've killed us. Anyways, it started to get worse in the last year and..."

Connie seemed to be choking on words and Odd couldn't blame her. The question—How could it get worse?—ran around her head unanswered.

Finally, Connie found her tongue, "...and my mom started to suspect what was going on...she blamed me."

Odd wasn't appalled by the statement. It was within the norms of her life to be blamed for anything—even something as outrageous as that. "It wasn't your fault," she told her friend. "You know that, right?"

The grey wall next to Odd's head thumped from

a blow. The little girl jumped back, startled.

"I know it wasn't my fault!" Connie cried. "My step-father knows it's not my fault...even my mother, deep down, knows it. But what good does that do me? I still get blamed."

She paused, taking deep breaths. When she went on she seemed more controlled, more cold, "My mom saw how George would look at me and she would get furious at me and call me a slut even though I never wore anything that was nice at all. I never-ever would with him around. He's so gross! I mean I haven't worn a dress since the eighth grade. And I never wear pajamas. I sleep in jeans and a sweatshirt—but still he would come. I don't get it. I just don't get it."

"I don't get it either," Odd agreed, thinking about Mitch. "My mom says men have needs...but it doesn't seem normal."

"I don't know what's normal anymore," Connie said, "I know George isn't normal. He's a perv. I shoulda killed him instead of killing my..." Connie stopped in mid-sentence. An intensely awkward silence filled the space between them before Connie finished her sentence, "...my baby."

Aghast, Odd leaned back away from the wall. "You—you killed a baby? That's awful," she said, unable to hide the disgust in her voice. She had never heard of anything so horrid before.

Connie's anger blew out like a candle to be replaced with tears. As she tried to explain, Odd could hear her hands pawing at the steel wall. "It wasn't a real baby...I mean it hadn't come out yet. They said it didn't even look like a baby yet. Like it was a blob or something."

"What? A blob? I don't understand."

"It was still inside me, growing, and they...they made me get rid of it. My mom made me get an abortion. She took me down to this clinic and lied and said I had this scumbag boyfriend. And...and..." Connie broke down again, her words becoming unintelligible.

Odd's head went in circles as if she couldn't decide to nod or shake. The last minute of conversation had quite overwhelmed her. Blobs? Babies? Abortions? The words jumbled in her head. She knew what all three words meant, but taken together they became senseless.

How do you equate a baby with a blob? And the word abortion? The definition: terminating an unwanted pregnancy suddenly became something else with the words: 'killing a baby'.

Yet there was one word Connie had used over and over again that struck home more than any others. "It," Odd repeated the word in a soft whisper. The baby hadn't been a baby, but an "It".

Odd was an "It". She'd always been one...just a thing. Something not quite right. Something different from the rest. Something to be loathed and hated and ridiculed. Something unwanted. Something abandoned. Something forgotten. Something that could be killed with impunity or left to die on its own in an unknown city.

In silence, Odd struggled against sudden tears. Some were for Connie, who wept alone in the grey cell next to her own and some were for her baby—the it—the voiceless thing; who knows where it was. And some of the tears were for herself; a girl who couldn't be any more lost.

Unzipping her coat, Odd used her silly Hello Kitty shirt to wipe her face. "Did you want to keep the *baby*?" she asked, purposely emphasizing the word.

"I think so," Connie said. "I didn't want to kill it at least. I mean the part that was him I wanted to kill. Whenever I thought about it I wanted to take a kitchen knife and cut it out myself. But then I would think about how it was part me, too. What happens if it was a girl? What would it look like? Would it have..."

Odd heard the word 'it' once too many times. In a rare display of temper she slapped her hand against the grey wall, the flat of it shaking the stall and cutting off Connie's words. "Stop calling her, 'it'!" Odd practically screamed. Before she knew it, she was out of the stall and heading for the door.

"Wait! Don't leave me...please," Connie pleaded in misery. "I won't use that word anymore. Please."

In the mirror, red demon-eyes caught Odd's attention and stopped her in her place. She looked hellish even to herself. Who was she to judge anyone? Who was she to make demands on Connie? Odd was nothing. Little more than the 'it' that had just been killed.

She fled back to her bathroom stall and shut away the image of the nasty girl with the red eyes.

"I'm sorry I yelled at you," Odd said to the grey wall. "It wasn't my place to say anything. It just sounded so..." she wanted to use the word uncaring, but thought it wouldn't be a good choice. She tried a different track and quickly wished she hadn't. "What would you have named her if she was a girl? We could call her that, instead of it."

Abruptly, Connie's misery intensified to the

point that Odd's tears came back in a rush. The older girl's mourning swept away any thoughts of self within Odd and she felt the pain of Connie's tears as if they were her own.

"No...no...no. No names! I just want to forget," Connie said through her weeping.

"It wasn't your fault, Connie. They made you do it."

"No. You're wrong." Connie's voice dropped low and quiet. "That isn't a good enough excuse. I was the baby's mother. I should of protected her. I should have done...something."

"Like what? If they wanted to get rid of the baby they would've found a way."

"I could've run away," Connie replied. "I thought about it...but I never had the courage. Oh, Odd, why didn't you find me sooner?"

"I wish I had." In her mind Odd pictured Connie with a baby, both wrapped in soft, white linen. They cuddled together warm and content; at peace. Both were angelic.

Chapter 26

An hour later the two girls trudged back to where they had met the night before to wait upon another train. Connie moved listlessly while Odd did everything she could to please her companion.

The older girl's mood yo-yoed from deep despair to teary, giddy laughter depending on the slight variances in the world around them. A shiny penny had her smiling in triumph as if their luck had changed, while the sight of a dead squirrel had her blank-eyed and staring at the corpse.

Odd hurried her to their box before anything worse could befall them. In particular she worried that Connie's mom was out searching for her, or worse, that the police had been called.

Though the industrial complex next to which they were squatting, hummed and teamed with busy men, their box lay in a tight corner and as yet hadn't been noticed.

"Why don't you take a nap?" Odd suggested once they had crawled in and arranged themselves comfortably. Connie looked pale from the trip to the grocery store. "I'll keep watch for a train."

Connie nodded once and closed her eyes. Odd remained vigilante for the next twenty-minutes and then she too closed her eyes. The warmth and snuggled soft form of Connie were simply too much for her.

A watch turned out not to be needed. The sound of a train's roaring engine had her sitting up and blinking in a daze. "Connie. A train's come by. Connie? Wake up, so we don't miss it."

Connie pushed her thick brown hair out of her bleary eyes. "A train? Is it the right kind?"

Odd peeked out as the engine slipped by. Behind it came a menagerie of cars: cattle-cars, boxcars, empty flat cars—even cars carrying other cars.

"Yeah. There are some boxcars we might get onto. But we have to hurry." She climbed out and waited for her friend who groaned as she stood up. Odd took her hand and lead the way as fear began to mount as a pain centered behind her breastbone. The train wasn't moving fast, yet up close it looked terribly frightening to the little girl.

She began to get woozy. "Are you sure you want to do this?" she asked Connie.

"Yeah, I'm sure." Connie yelled over the sound of the train. They were very close now. Her brown eyes held a fierceness that sucked in Odd's breath. "I'm never going back there, Odd. Never! It's either this or..." Odd knew and she didn't much blame the girl, but she feared for her nonetheless.

"How do we do this?" Odd yelled back. "How do we get on?"

Connie watched the train cars go by, zipping her head back and forth, looking for the right moment. "Grab the bar at the end of the train! Then pull yourself up."

It sounded easier than it turned out to be. Connie went first. She grabbed at a bar, flailed, found a grasp, but couldn't pull herself up. Odd watched in horror as the train dragged the older girl along. She thought for sure that Connie would fall beneath the wheels, but somehow she rolled away clutching her stomach.

"Are you alright? Connie? Connie?" Odd screamed as she hurried forward. Curled in a ball, Connie lay crying holding her mid-section.

"I'll never get out of here," she said through her tears.

"You will! I promise...are you hurt?" Odd asked squatting down close to inspect her friend. Connie shook her head and Odd knelt back in relief. "Thank God! You had me so scared. When you fell...I... thought..."

The sight of the train stopped her words. Odd watched in amazement as the train gradually slowed. Car after car passed them gently by, until even the last one slid away, but still the train slowed.

"Do you think someone saw us?" Connie asked her voice pitched higher than normal. Her brown eyes had never seemed bigger as she stared far away towards the front of the train.

Odd looked over the top of her dark glasses, squinting at the distant engine. It seemed indistinct to her. "I—I can't tell. But I doubt it. They would've had to be looking back at us and who would drive a train like that?"

Connie got to her feet, swatting the dirt from her clothes. "When's it gonna stop?" Already the last car had run a hundred yards further up the tracks. They started after it. Unconsciously Odd picked up Connie's hand and held it. Both of their palms were damp.

Ahead of them the train slowed even more and then came to a clanking, shuddery halt. The girls came closer, moving in towards each other as they went. It was the sight of the last car that had them so nervous. It was an engine car just like the one in front. Both of them knew there was a chance that someone was in it looking out at them. With the dark windows they couldn't be sure.

"Hello!" Odd called out at ten feet, but got no response. She tried again coming up abreast of the iron horse. "Hello? I don't think there's anyone home. Do you want to go up there and check? Maybe the door's open."

"Me?" Connie asked in surprise.

"Yeah...I'm no good at climbing." Odd was no good at many things. "Go on. I'd rather ride in there than any of the cars."

"But my stomach. I felt something pull inside me when I tried to get on the train."

Odd looked up at the train. It seemed very high up to the little girl. Along with her many other issues, she suffered from vertigo and even a little height could make her dizzy. But since Connie clearly wasn't going to make the attempt she would have to.

Knowing her wool gloves would slide on the metal, Odd tugged them off and put them in her pocket. She then took a deep breath and started up. If it weren't for her eyes it would've been an easy ten-foot ladder climb. Instead she sweated and gasped as the cold metal appeared to twist and reshape itself beneath her fingers.

"You ok?" Connie asked.

"Yeah...fine," Odd said with what little breath her panic would allow.

"Odd, the knobs right there. What are you doing?"

Just then Odd was hard pressed to release even a single finger of the death grip she had on the rungs.

Eventually her fear that she would tire allowed her to release the rung long enough to twist the knob. It wouldn't budge. Immediately she started down.

"Hey, try knocking."

She paused just long enough to thump the door with a single fist and then hurried to get to the spinning earth. No one answered. Gaining the ground Odd stood with shaking legs and had to unzip her heavy coat to let her nervous sweat dry.

"I hate heights," Odd explained when Connie offered her a bewildered look. "Even that little bit made me dizzy."

"That's crazy! You were only, like right there. I could touch your foot if I wanted to." Connie shook her head in disbelief. "I guess for you that was pretty heroic then."

Odd could feel her cheeks going hot. "Stop making fun."

Connie reached out and took Odd's little, shaking hand in hers. They started walking up the tracks to the next car. "You are brave. If I had been as brave as you I would have ran away a long time ago. I wish I had."

Odd couldn't stop smiling at the praise. She smiled so hard her cheeks began to ache. Gradually, her smile faded as they progressed up the tracks. Every one of the boxcars was padlocked, leaving them with the cattle-cars as the next best option. It was a terrible option. The cars were long rectangle boxes with open grating for sides.

Each of the girls looked upon this option with trepidation. "It's gonna be too cold," Odd said. "When we get up to speed."

Grimacing, Connie showed her desperation to get away at any cost. "We'll go in that one, behind the red box-car. If we stay in the middle at the front...and keep low, it won't be so bad."

Connie spoke only to convince herself. She didn't wait for a reply from Odd, but only tugged the girl along. Odd knew that it would be more than just cold. The wind would rip over them—stripping the heat from their bodies.

Despite knowing this, Odd didn't fight the tug at her hand. She went along willingly, knowing she would gladly suffer the cold for this girl she'd only met the night before.

Connie was her friend after all.

Chapter 27

Their cattle-car, as Odd thought of it, smelled of cows and in not in any way that one would think of as good. Still it was clean. The floor looked to have been newly hosed down and gleamed a dull aluminum up at them. Odd would have preferred more dung if it came with straw to bed down into.

By unspoken agreement the two girls cuddled together at the head of the car. In order to stay warm they clutched each other in a broody silence brought on by another gloomy fit of Connie's. Odd sensed the darkness, the sadness, the despair coming from her older friend and seemed powerless to change it. After awhile, the silence felt like a net around her that she had to shed no matter what.

Odd began jabbering away. She told Connie about Lena and the foster-prison. She told her about the B wing, and Mitch, and the priest. Mostly, however, she talked about her mom until the sun stood almost straight up above them. Without any warning the train started with a jerk. The move surprised the two girls and, as if they were tired of being depressed, they shrieked and then giggled.

Much to Odd's disappointment, the train moved at a pokey little pace as it wound through the city. She wanted to get to California as soon as possible; it was her hope to be most of the way there by dinner. The sights that the train offered held even more disappointment for the two.

The train slipped in and out of the seedier neighborhoods that adjoined industrial sections of the city. The haggard buildings were uniformly ugly—grey concrete draped in curtains of multi-hued graffiti. The streets and alleys they passed were littered with refuse and what little vegetation she saw looked to have died long before winter had come. The sight disheartened Odd.

"Does California have cities that look like this?" she asked.

Connie didn't hesitate. "Probably. Every city has their poor neighborhoods and their rich neighborhoods. But it is warm and they have beaches. That's what I'm looking forward to most. What about you? Why do you want to go?"

"To find my mom."

Connie's bruised face contorted. "Your mom? Didn't you mention being abandoned by her? Why, on earth would you want to find her? So you can punch her in the nose?"

"Because she may not have abandoned me on purpose," Odd said, sitting up. Here the buildings sat further back from the tracks which allowed her to see without her eyes going batty on her. "She may have been trying to get back to me this whole time. And besides...no one else will take care of me."

Connie sat thinking, looking out at the passing scenery. They were in a suburban neighborhood now and the train began to pick up its pace. "Maybe if you don't find your mom, you and I can take care of each other."

Odd's heart skipped right over two or three beats before she broke into a wide grin. "I'd like that a lot."

"You'll have to change your name to Rodriguez, though." When Odd's nose crinkled in puzzlement Connie explained with a laugh. "It's my diabolical plan.

You see we're gonna need new identities."

"And you want us to be Mexican?"

"Yeah, but only at first," Connie replied becoming more animated than Odd had yet seen her. "The first thing we do is try to look like Mexicans. A few days on the beach will work for me. But you...we might need a wig to cover all that blonde hair."

"But..."

"Don't interrupt," Connie chided. "Here's the beauty of pretending to be Mexicans: No one does it! I mean, who would? So if someone says they're Mexican you're gonna believe them, right?"

"I guess," Odd replied feeling slightly lost.

"So once we have Mexican identification we then get fake American identification."

Odd had to scratch her head at her friend's logic. "This doesn't make sense. Why don't we start off with fake American identifications?"

"Because that would be illegal, dummy."

"What? It's illegal for Mexicans too," Odd contradicted.

"Not really," Connie wore a smug look as she said this. "It's a felony if you or I try to have forged documents, but Mexicans get caught all the time with them and they never go to jail."

"Really? Doesn't the government send them back at least?"

Connie shook her head. "No. They set up trial dates and tell them to come back at such and such time. And of course most don't. Who would come back just to get deported or sent to prison? No, they just go steal another person's identity and start over."

Odd thought the idea was completely

outrageous without a chance in the world of working and she said so. "It'll never work. I'll never pass for a Mexican, no matter how much time I spend at the beach. I don't tan; not at all. I just burn and then peel and then burn some more."

Connie frowned at this, but the brightened in a flash. "You won't have to tan! Tell me, what would an albino Mexican look like?" She had a finger pointed at Odd as she asked. "Right? You see? If anyone doesn't believe you, just take off your glasses."

The train began to accelerate and the first touch of wind played with Odd's long blonde hair. She tucked it further under her acorn hat. "You just came up with this idea? Just now?"

"Naw. I've wanted to run away for years. I just....I wish... I had," Connie's face went dark as another gloom doused her mind. "All this time I thought I was protecting my mom from harm, but I wasn't. I think she's known for ages what he was doing to me, but, she refused to see. How do you do that? How do you pretend that your daughter isn't being...raped?"

Odd could only shrug and reach out for the older girl. However, Connie didn't want to be touched. She pulled away and stood up on the rocking train, moving to the steel bars of their rolling jail cell.

Connie put her hands on the horizontal bars and looked out at the wintering suburbs. "I couldn't do it. I couldn't make my daughter live in the same house with a rapist...or a child molester! That's what he really was. When he first started messing with me I was your age, maybe even younger." Suddenly Connie gripped the bars and shook them with all her strength.

Not remembering that the car was meant to hold cows, Odd foolishly became alarmed, worried that the girl would either break one of the bars and fall off the train or tip the whole car over. She crawled over to her new friend and tugged at her coat.

"Hey...it's ok. It's not your fault. None of this is your fault," Odd soothed, touching Connie's leg and rubbing it gently.

"I did something to deserve it. I just don't know what."

Though she felt infinitely safer huddled on the metal flooring, Odd decided to stand to be closer to her friend. The view, the last of the suburbs, was a lot more pleasant than the industrial area of town. The houses grew larger. Their yards—wide, tended lawns with the remains of flower borders—sprawled across the landscape. With the view Odd felt once again the secret wish of being normal, of being a part of a normal family. The feeling tried to creep out of her heart and take over her mind.

She had to push it aside. Her friend needed her and besides, she reasoned, fairy tales were for children. What slipped by in front of her eyes could never be her life.

"You didn't do anything, Connie. You said yourself that you never did anything to provoke him. You can't blame yourself if you're just naturally beautiful."

"I must have done something," she replied hollow voiced.

"Stop it!" Odd said, showing a touch of anger. "This is your mother's fault. Not yours. It's her job to protect you. She's the one who's supposed to keep you safe. You're the innocent one here."

"I'm the innocent one?" Connie asked, shaking her head as if amazed at the words. Just then a strong cold gust of wind whipped around them. Odd had to turn her face away from the wind it was so cold, but Connie looked straight into the bitter air. Her hair blew back in rolling waves and her brown eyes sprung tears from nowhere. Again, her beauty took Odd's breath away.

"Go sit down," Connie said in an easy tone. A smile of fate turned the corners of her lips upwards.

The request had Odd blinking in confusion. "Why?"

"Because we're coming to a river."

"Oh don't worry about that. I like rivers...and water in general." Odd turned to look at the view. An instant later she screamed and clutched at Connie, holding her in maniacal wrestler's grip.

The land had dropped away in a cliff and the river wasn't just a few feet below them, it seemed hundreds of feet away—straight down. The train bucked and swayed along a single track with only a foot or two to spare on either side, and a slim lattice of metal to keep the unknown tonnage of the serpent-like machine from plunging off the precarious edge.

The world swam in Odd's eyes and she climbed down her friend as though she were climbing down a short tree. Connie smiled at her. "I warned you."

"Yeah...I'll listen next time," Odd said in a shaking voice. Connie breathed out a long sigh and stepped up on the second bar. Her hair blew around, flaring out from her head, flickering and snapping in all directions like soft brown flames. Her coat had been open and now the edges of it flashed back away from her body like the wings of a terrific bird. "What are you doing?" Odd asked, as a sudden spike of fear shot through her.

"I used to be afraid of heights," Connie reached higher and pulled herself up another bar. "Yesterday. I used to be afraid...yesterday. Now I'm not. We're so high up, but we could go higher and I wouldn't be afraid."

"Get down! I'm afraid for you."

"You're not my mother, Odd." Connie said. Odd could barely hear her. Connie went to the next rail. Above that was an opening that a slim girl could slip through quite easily. Connie stared at the opening for a moment and then began nodding at it, while her breath grew heavier in her chest.

"Connie, what are you doing?" Odd felt terror rip through her heart. The look Connie wore: a placid far-away stare didn't jibe with her present position hundreds of feet in the air coasting along a thin set of rails. "Connie! Get down, please."

"I don't want to. I want to fly away." She turned from her high perch and looked down at the little girl. "Don't be mad, Odd. It's not you. You've been good to me." She took a good hold and swung a leg up.

"No!" Odd screeched. She jumped to her feet, but at the sight of the river so far below her knees buckled and her eyes spun. The car seemed to go over on its side and she flailed trying to find the ground. It came up slow but jarringly, knocking the air out of her.

It took a moment to right her mind again and when she did Odd saw Connie had one leg through the opening already. The little girl tried again to stand but to no avail. Her eyes and her fear wouldn't let her. She got to her feet, only to feel the blood draining from her head, turning her already pale face a shade lighter than alabaster.

Shaking from head to toe, she sank to her knees, panting and moaning in fear. "Connie, please," she wailed. "What about becoming Mexican? What about California?"

"I can't go with you," Connie said. "I—I don't deserve it. This way is better."

Odd held out a trembling hand to the girl. With her fear almost paralyzing her it was the most she could do. "Connie, stop. You are the victim here. You didn't do anything wrong."

"I killed my baby!" Connie screamed, her eyes blazing in misery and anger. "I swore that I'd never be like my mother! I swore that I'd be different, that if I ever had any that I'd protect *my* babies." Her tears came unstoppable, gushing out of the well of her soul in torrents. "But I'm worse than even she was. I killed *my* baby! You hear me! I killed her."

"But you were forced to."

"I could've run away...but I was too afraid." Connie turned from Odd and looked out at the river. "I'm not afraid now." She pulled herself up, working her other leg through the opening.

Odd's vision blurred with her tears and she shut the demon-eyes that had so plagued her. She climbed to her feet with her blind hands outstretched and walked forward. With the wind and the sound and the rocking of the cattle car, Odd felt as if she were walking to her death, that the walls of the car had evaporated and any second she'd step out into the cold air and hurtle to her death.

A whimper escaped her throat, but she kept going and the next second she found the wall and the next after that she found a piece of fabric that she could only assume was Connie's coat. Still with her eyes closed Odd hauled on it struggling against the weight above her.

"No!" Connie shouted. "Let go!"

Odd didn't listen. She found a grip on Connie's waist and pulled the struggling girl down on top of her. They landed on the floor of the cattle-car in a heap. Connie spun in Odd's grip trying to get away, but Odd held on in the only way she could. She grabbed a fist full of brown hair.

"Let go or I'll punch you in the face. I swear I'll do it!" Connie yelled. Odd felt a splash of wet on her cheek and she opened her eyes in time to see a huge tear fall and blear her left lens. Above her Connie sobbed. Her right hand she had balled into a fist.

"Then punch me," Odd said. "But I won't let go, ever." She meant it, too. This girl—this broken girl was all she had in the world.

"You h-have to let me go," Connie said through her tears.

Odd didn't. Instead she gently pulled on the lock of hair in her fist until Connie's cheek was close enough to kiss. And then she planted a soft, little girl's kiss on Connie's bruised face. This little thing drained the older girl of energy and she slumped over onto her back breathing heavily and running tears into her hair.

Chapter 28

"I wish I could be like you, Odd," Connie said after a while.

At first Odd giggled at this, then she rolled on the floor of the car, laughing until her sides hurt. Connie didn't share her amusement. She stared out at the dull forest they were buzzing through—the river with its suicidal drop lay miles to the east

"Don't waste wishes," Odd advised in a serious tone, when she could breathe again. "My mother used to say that. She'd say: 'Don't wish for a peanut butter and jelly sandwich. If you're going to wish for something, wish for a steak.' So if you're going to wish, Connie, don't wish to be like me."

"But I do," she insisted. "You're very brave..."

Odd interrupted with a snort and then more laughter. "You don't know what you're talking about! Until last week I was even afraid to step into a church because I thought God would zap me with lightning. And earlier, I could barely climb that little ladder. The rungs looked like they were twisting under my..."

"That's what I'm talking about," Connie cut in. "You're afraid but you do things anyways. If I was as brave as you I would've stood up to my step-dad. Or I would've told my mom a long time ago. Or I would've run away before they made me...before they made me...do it."

"I don't feel too brave," Odd said. She heaved a sigh. "What I feel is cold. Why don't we go to the front of the car?"

Connie groped her way forward and laid down where they had been earlier. "I think I'm too afraid to live. I'm afraid of everything. I'm afraid that they'll catch us and make me go back home. I'm afraid of freezing in this car. I'm afraid of starving to death. I'm afraid of where we'll be tonight, where we'll sleep, and how we'll live tomorrow. I'm even afraid that they'll stop and put cows on board. What do we do then?"

"Then my wish for steak will come true." Connie didn't smile at Odd's little joke. "Try not to worry so much. I can help you with one of those things," Odd said, coming to a kneel beside her friend. She pulled off her warm hat and snugged it down onto Connie's head. Next she tugged off her gloves. "These may be tight, but they're better than nothing."

"No. What about you?" Connie tried to push the gloves back at Odd.

"My coat's too big for me. I'll snug up inside it." Turtle-like Odd pulled her arms in and did her best to tuck her head in as far as she could. It didn't go as far as she hoped. She then draped herself half over Connie, blocking out the worst of the wind for the girl.

They moved together trying to get comfortable and Connie seemed to find a good position. Odd thought she had fallen asleep when a mile or two passed in silence and then Connie whispered, "I'm afraid my baby won't forgive me."

Odd moved not a muscle at this. She could think of nothing to say that would in any way help her friend. Who knew what a baby would think? Did they only have one shot at life? Or did you get to go around again—like a ride—if you wished? Did a soul go right to heaven or did it puff out of existence? Who knew?

As she pondered this, the train rocked after a soothing fashion and they slipped through a great belt of forest where the air was closer and the wind less. Odd fell asleep.

When she awoke the cold had progressed and the sun had turned in the sky. It had been on the left side of the train when they first started moving but now it lay high up and just to the right of the front of the train.

Are we still moving west? Odd wondered. Whatever direction it was, the temperature wasn't improving as she had hoped it would. They were zipping along at a tremendous speed. On their left a highway ran parallel to them and on their right lay empty fields. Nothing could block the wind ripping over the two girls.

The cold had a burning sensation as it found every weak spot in Odd's slight armor against it. Cold stole down her neck at the back where her thrift store coat lifted slightly and it crept up her ankles where her short socks did nothing for her. The worst parts of her were her feet. Her gaping Converse sneakers held the heat no better than a tissue would. Yet still she cuddled closer to Connie, trying her best to cover the girl as well as possible.

"I'm freezing," Connie said with a voice that shook. Her head had come up from Odd's chest. The little girl shoved it back down.

"Try not to move. It let's all my heat out." There was a little barrier between her chest and Connie's head that trapped a tiny bit of heat.

"But my legs! They're turning to ice."

With the greatest reluctance, Odd sat up and looked at her taller partner. There would be no way she could cover her completely. "Face away and tuck into a ball...bring your knees up," she ordered over the wind. Connie did as she was told and Odd curled around her acting like a blanket. Now the little girl was in a far worse and far colder position. Connie's back seemed not to give off any heat whatsoever and Odd's body temperature clicked down by degrees.

Not for a second did she complain.

If she had known the day before, just after running from Lena, that her future entailed the possibility of freezing to death with an actual friend, she would've ran faster.

Odd snugged closer. The train ride became a slow, raw torture. Eventually her muscles began to tire from the constant trembling and the need to hold herself up against her friend. More and more, as the trip progressed into the late afternoons, her body would give out, and she would slump over. Always it was a fight to push herself closer to her friend.

Her feet were long numb and her knees felt to be freezing into place like rusted machinery, when the train finally began to slow. It seemed a dreadfully tedious process to Connie who couldn't wait to get off. She had hopped up at the first sign and had the door pulled back. There she stood in the opening trying to work her frozen limbs into warmth.

If she had seen her, Odd would've been alarmed at how close to the edge her friend stood, but the little girl still lay in a ball, nearly senseless. All she knew was that the train had begun to slow and the wind had diminished to nothing. The rest of her mind thought of little more than the terrific pain that seared her skin and the fearful numbness that seemed to be deeply rooted in her feet.

"Hey, Odd, do you think that this will ever stop? Odd? Odd!" She could hear her friend's feet thumping on the metal flooring and then hands gripped her shoulders and turned her. "Odd? You ok?"

"Cold," Odd mumbled. "Can't—feel—my—feet."

Connie's eyes went wide. "What? Why didn't you say anything?" Quickly she yanked off the borrowed hat and gloves and pulled them onto Odd. The older girl then began rubbing Odd's limbs working them through their range of motion, trying to get the blood flowing.

A minute later Odd shrieked in pain. First one foot, then the other erupted in sudden agony. The feeling was similar to the pins and needles sensation that frequently happened when her foot fell asleep, except this was far, far worse. She writhed on her back, but then the pain grew too great and she took to massaging her feet through her shoes while weeping uncontrollably.

Seeing her misery and unable to help in any meaningful way, Connie cried as well. Eventually she took off Odd's shoes and placed Odd's near-frozen feet against her own skin under her coat.

"Oh my gosh!" Connie cried out as the soles came in contact with her stomach. "You should have said something. You should have switched positions. Wow! I thought I was cold. You know if we had gone much further, you could've died."

"It was my idea to take the train, remember."

Odd said, feeling stupid at how horrible it had been. She had known it was going to be cold but she had no idea how bad.

"That's going to be the last time..."

A heavy vibration shook the train and it came to a jolting halt. Connie stopped rubbing. The silence that followed unnerved Odd enough to get her to sit up and look around.

"Where are we?" she asked

Connie could only shrug. As far as Odd could tell they were nowhere. In the west the sun had disappeared below the horizon and surrounding them were trees and fields. Of lights or cars or houses, none were visible at all.

Chapter 29

"Do we get off the train?" Connie asked. "Or what?"

For Odd the only answer was yes! "I can't take anymore cold." Fearing that the train would suddenly start moving again she hurriedly put on her shoes, grimacing as she did.

"But where do we go? There's nothing here." Connie had a wild look about her. "I mean, I thought that there'd be a station, or something, or people."

"Maybe the station is up ahead," Odd suggested. "This train's like a mile long after all."

This idea got Connie excited and moving. She helped Odd down. Hand in hand they started toward the front of the train—Odd limping badly—however it didn't take long for them to discover a nice, warm train station wasn't awaiting them.

"I think we need to go talk to the conductor," Connie said, decidedly. "I'm freezing which means you must be simply ice. I don't think we have any choice."

"I guess. I don't know what else..." Odd stopped as the train abruptly started again. Connie hurried towards it, but Odd held back. "Wait! Don't get on. It could be hours before it stops again."

"Odd face it. We're lost," Connie countered. "This is the middle of nowhere."

Odd grabbed her friend, feeling certain that she'd freeze to death if she got back on the train. "Please, no."

Though Connie couldn't see the look in Odd's eyes, she could hear the pleading in her voice. "Fine. We'll freeze out here instead of on the train." A minute later, Connie waved as the last car passed them. "Good-bye train. So, do you know how to make a fire?"

Odd felt such a surge of relief over not getting back on the train that she joked, "Yeah, with matches and gasoline."

Connie smirked at this. "I bet you don't have a pocket full of gasoline do you?"

Playfully Odd dug in her pockets. "Nope. I have a hairbrush and fourteen cents. That's everything I own."

"So what do you wanna do?" Connie asked, stooping to pick up a heavy stick. "Our choices have slimmed down a bit. We got...death by freezing or death by wild animal attack. Take your pick."

Odd clutched at Connie's arm searching the darkness. "Wild animals? Really? You mean like a bear or a tiger?"

Connie laughed. "You are so precious! There are no tigers in Illinois." The older girl paused looking around at the coming night. "At least I think we're in Illinois. We were this morning at least."

Odd rarely knew or cared to what state her mom dragged her to next. However she did care about being eaten by a wild animal. "Then what kind of wild animals does Illinois have?"

"I'm not sure. Maybe bears or wolves."

In no way did Odd like the sound of that. In growing fear she stared around at the strip of forest and the fields lying fallow. Then she saw that they weren't exactly in the middle of nowhere. "Hey, wait a minute.

Those are fields, like for corn or something. That means there's got to be a farm around here."

They wasted no time hurrying to the fields. Once there, they came upon a dirt road and far down it a light shone. In excitement and hope the two girls rushed toward it. Odd hobbled, miserably, in silence. Her feet, somewhere between frozen and thawed, sent shocks of pain up her legs. Had she been alone she would've cried at the pain, instead she walked with her toes curled in and her lips pressed hard together.

"What are we going to say when we get there?" Connie asked.

"Maybe we can ask to do some work in exchange for a place to stay? I bet they have chickens. We can feed them or change their litter boxes. This one time I got a free burger just by asking to do work."

Connie curled her lip at this. "It sounds too much like begging. I don't think I can do it."

"Then we should start becoming Mexican like you said," Odd replied. "It's a good time. It's dark and we're all covered head to toe...do you know any Spanish?"

"A little. I'm taking Spanish as my foreign language. But this isn't going to..."

Odd grew excited and cut her off. "Can you say: do you have work?"

"Please, Odd. You're not listening to me." Connie said. "This isn't going to work. I never really thought that I'd actually try to become Mexican. It was just sort of a game."

"We won't know if we don't try. How do you say it?"

Connie squinched up her face, thinking. "I don't

really know. Uh...tu trabajo...or something like that. Maybe it's tu tienes trabajo. I think."

"Tu tienes trabajo," Odd repeated, committing the words to memory. "Pretty simple. I betcha their Spanish is worse than yours either way."

"Then we shouldn't be speaking it," Connie argued. "What good is it if they can't understand us?"

Odd shrugged off the question by shushing her friend. They were getting close to the source of the light. It flickered gold against a dark background. Strangely, the farmhouse and its attendant out-buildings were completely encircled by a belt of trees and low shrubs. They seemed purposely placed to act as some sort of barricade. But what the vegetation meant to keep out Odd couldn't figure. Not a person for certain, she could slip in between them with ease if she wanted.

The house itself, two stories high, gave off a pleasant feeling. Compared to the crumbling barn, that couldn't look anymore spooky, it showed that a loving hand still resided within. Not a shingle sat askew, not a crack could be seen in the white paint.

When they drew up close a dark beast of a dog cut loose with a terrifying racket, warning them to stay away. The white of its teeth shone clearly in its snarling mouth, making Connie pull back.

"Come on," Odd urged. The dreadful pain in her feet outweighed her fear. She needed to get inside desperately and so she rationalized, "It probably won't hurt us...it's old, I think. And look, it's on a chain. We can go around it." Connie hesitated and Odd added in a whisper, "We don't have a choice."

Of that she knew she was right. The next house could be miles away and she was beginning to think something really bad was happening to her feet.

They started to the left only to find there was a lot more length to the chain than either of them imagined. The dog kept back at first, growling, and barking with raised hackles, but then, as that didn't keep the two girls away, it darted forward with its jaws gaping wide, its huge teeth glinting in the low light.

In a rush, the beast went for Connie, who screamed and stumbled back, falling. The sudden movement in front of Odd twirled her world. The dog and her friend seemed to mold into a hideous creature that was beyond imagination. One thing was fact in the little girl's mind: Connie would be torn apart in seconds if she didn't react. Since her eyes were useless she snapped them shut and threw herself forward in the blind hope of getting between Connie and the dog.

She didn't make it. The dog, old or not, was too fast and Odd's outstretched hands came in contact with its heavily muscled back quarter. Yet this action did save Connie from being mauled. The dog, sensing an attack from the rear, pivoted like lightning and sunk its inch-long fangs into Odd.

Chapter 30

Odd felt almost no pain. A quick, sharp sting and then nothing. She even felt an otherworldly calm as her muscles simply went limp, as if in surrender to fate. Perhaps it was an instinctual response triggered when in the jaws of a deadly beast—a way to show that she was no longer a threat.

At seventy-two pounds compared to the dog's one-hundred and thirty, she wasn't close to a threat. The dog had her by the upper arm, with its top teeth through her bicep, while its lower teeth were caught up in Odd's coat.

In a foaming fury, it shook its triangular head hard left then right. Odd went to her knees, held up only by the great strength of the dog. The beast then pivoted, torqueing its upper body, and sent Odd flying like a boneless ragdoll.

Still there wasn't pain. Even landing on the frozen ground didn't bother her. She'd felt the moment of weightlessness when she was in the air, heard a long, *crump*-like sound and when she opened her eyes, she saw stars by the millions in the dark sky above. They were pins of light and by the way she could see them with such edged detail she knew she'd lost her glasses.

Normally she would've considered this a calamity but now she knew only a vague uneasiness. A second later the glasses were totally forgotten as the dog hurtled at her face with its jaws gaping. Odd saw it coming, yet still felt not the slightest touch of fear.

Everything was moving far too fast for her to take in.

"Ike, no!" A rough voice called out in sharp angry tones. Just like that the dog stopped with its jaws agape above her face. In irritation it blew out a heavily scented blast of dog breath that Odd found strangely interesting, and then it trotted away, not giving her a second glance.

Though she was dazed, Odd said with a single-mindedness born of desperation, "Tu tienes trabajar?" The dog attack had put her even more in need of work—and shelter.

"What?" the man asked, anger showing even in the one word.

Had Odd said the phrase wrong? Slower, she repeated the phrase, "Tu...tienes...trabajar?"

A figure rushed to her side.

"Odd! Are you alright?" Connie knelt over her with eyes grown huge in fear for her friend. At the question, Odd's numbness began to fade and stinging pain shot through her arm. She barely noticed. Compared to the agony in her feet the dog bite was simply uncomfortable. Connie unzipped her coat and gasped.

"Oh jeeze! You're bleeding."

Odd could hear footsteps approaching in the dirt yard. "Connie...my glasses," she whispered. Having a dog see her eyes was one thing; having a person see her eyes terrified her. If the man saw the demon in her they'd never get work.

Connie couldn't understand this, however. "Forget your glasses! You're bleeding."

"That's not my fault." The owner of the rough voice came up to them. From Odd's vantage, lying stretched out on the dirt, the man seemed like a giant. "You two was trespassing. And when you trespass, you get what you get."

Odd didn't second-guess this for a second. She couldn't afford to. Ignoring her wound and her pain, Odd squinted up at the man, "Sorry about bothering your dog, Mister. Do you have any work?" Her single mindedness stemmed from the thought of the coming night and the promise of bitter cold that carried on the wind. She feared the pain the cold would bring.

"Work?" The man seemed perplexed at the question. "What? How old are you?"

"I'm...I'm..." Being twelve hadn't helped the last time the question had been put to her. Still she didn't want to lie, so she went with a modified version of the truth. "She's fifteen," Odd said, pointing at her friend with her good arm. Connie's mouth came open at being brought so unexpectedly into the conversation, though nothing came out.

"Fifteen?" the man spat out the word as if it offended him. "Where are your parents? Why are you running around my yard disturbing my supper?"

Odd's mind had begun to form answers until the man had mentioned supper. When he did, she suddenly noticed a heavenly aroma coming from the open door of the farmhouse. Her breakfast—four small bites of a leftover cheeseburger—seemed ages in the past.

"I...I..." was all she could manage. The man turned to Connie with a questioning look.

"We're lost," she managed to say. He moved closer and looked at her face. Even in the dim light her bruises were obvious. Embarrassed she dropped her head.

"Lost, huh?" Clearly he wasn't convinced.

"Who's out there with you?" A woman called from the house. The man was tall and broad shouldered, but was very old. He had a ruddy face that only an iron could've got the wrinkles out of and his fine white hair blew in the chill wind like wisps of rising steam. The woman's voice suggested great age as well, yet also a sweetness that stood in contradiction to the man's scowl. Odd pictured a plump Mrs. Claus.

"Just a couple of runaways," he hollered back. Odd cast a swift look at Connie. The older girl seemed to be in shock. What was he going to do with them?

"Well, have them in for a bite," the woman answered.

"For the love of Pete!" The man turned, kicked a rock, and then stood for a moment with his hands on his skinny hips. "You heard the boss." He pointed at the doorway.

They were going to get food! Connie tried to stand her friend up, but Odd's feet were like frozen cord wood. The pain ached past any numbness and she stifled a scream before collapsing. The man let out an exasperated breath.

"The dog got your coat for crying out loud. If you think you're going to sue me for a bad back or a whiplash..."

Connie interrupted him, "Her feet are frozen. She doesn't have snow boots or anything."

The man came down to Odd's level. Quickly she turned her face away, hiding her eyes. She could feel him touching her ankles and feet, probing here and there. He sighed again, this time in worry.

"Up you go," he said and then hoisted Odd aloft

in his long arms and brought her to his chest. Gently, he held her as a mother would a baby. The feeling of being carried this way was so foreign to her that she clutched at him tightly, afraid. He laughed at this, his anger gone in a flash. "I won't drop you, Sprite."

The man carried Odd into the house, which smelled wonderfully. How it appeared she didn't know. Her eyelids were crunched down hard. She wasn't going to ruin this by opening them.

"Move them periodicals, Mother!" he groused. "I have to put her down." Odd could hear some movement and then the man made a cranky noise in his throat and said, "Here, I have to put you down, Sprite. You're gonna have to stand for a bit—Mother's got a bad back, you know."

He placed her down next to a fine old couch. She clutched at the back of it for support with one hand while the other went to cover her face. Peeking through the cracks of her fingers she stared in fascination at the room around her. It was perfect. Large and heavy, matching furniture of some sort of dark wood sat upon deep, soft, white shag carpeting. There was a log burning in the fireplace and every few seconds it would crack loudly to remind them of its presence. Pictures adorned every wall and in them Odd saw the old couple. For the most part they smiled out at her surrounded by an amazing number of children.

This was a place for family.

Connie stared around as well. Her faced looked both sad and cheated at the same time. Odd could almost read her thoughts: Why couldn't I have grown up here?

With the man grunting under stacks of

newspapers and magazines that had been sitting on the couch the woman turned to the two girls. "Well, let's have a look at these two runaways." At this both Odd and Connie cast their eyes to the floor. The woman, who bore no resemblance to Mrs. Claus, as she was tiny and frail, glanced over Odd quickly and then went, "Ahh," at the sight of Connie's face.

"Oh dear. Oh dear. Abe, did you see this? Someone has hurt this girl."

"Yup, I saw."

For long seconds, the old woman peered with straining eyes as Connie turned red from embarrassment. The woman clucked and shook her head in anger at what she saw. "And what about you?" she asked turning to Odd. The little girl quickly snapped her fingers closed, but still held them in front of her face. "Let's have a look at you."

Odd caught a glimpse of a small, strangely bruised, and splotchy hand before she closed her eyes. The old woman made a note of approval at not seeing bruising, but then she gasped at the sight of the blood seeping from beneath Odd's torn coat.

"Abe, she's bleeding."

"What? No she ain't."

"She is!" the woman rejoined crossly. "I'm not blind. Come let's lie you down. Why didn't you say something, Abe?"

"It's not like I had my specs on," Abe said a little hurt. "I thought Ike just got her by the coat. I figured if he had bitten her that she would've screamed."

"She's really brave," Connie explained in a little voice.

All this Odd heard, but didn't see. She felt Abe's strong hands gently put her down on the couch and then she felt the skinny spidery hands of his wife as she pulled back the coat. The old woman mumbled disapprovingly.

"Look at what your dog did!"

Behind her eyelids, Odd could sense Abe leaning over her. "It's not so bad. We can clean those wounds out easy. And don't go blaming Ike. He was just doing his job. You see, Sprite we get lots of transients and them long-haired hippy types come off the railroad..."

His wife interrupted, "We should take her down to the county."

"What?" Abe exclaimed angrily. "The county? They ain't nothing but democrats. We don't need them, Peach. She'll be fine, won't you Sprite."

"Yes sir," Odd replied, taking an immediate dislike to democrats. If Abe didn't like them it was good enough for her. Not to mention, by 'county', Odd understood that to mean Social Services.

"See that?" Abe said with a smile in his voice. "Sprite here knows what's what. And besides you know that idiot Sheriff Vernon will want to put down Ike as a repeat offender. Damned democrats."

"Stop it with that democrat business," Peach snapped. "These bites could get infected."

Chastened, Abe said in less rancorous voice, "Maybe, and if they do then we'll go down to town for sure, I promise you. It's her feet that have me nervous. Let's get them cheap, china-men shoes off you, Sprite. Gently now."

"Oh! That...that...hurts," Odd gasped. There was

no holding back the pain now. Tears came down her face; a second later something soft brushed them away.

"Ok, I've seen worse. I've seen worse," Abe said in a soft tone. "You ain't gonna lose any of these little piggies. See if you was to have any blistering or there was any white or grey patches that would tell a man that you got yourself a case of frostbite, but...Sprite? You can look. It ain't scary."

"Go ahead, dear," Peach said. "Your feet look ok. If that's what you're nervous over."

"She can't," Connie said as there came an awkward moment when Odd refused to open her eyes. "She's got an eye problem. She needs her glasses, but they're out in the yard...I'd get them, but...the dog is out there."

"Oh, he won't bother you now that you've come in..."

"Abe, she afraid. Get the glasses for her please," Peach sighed. "What's your name, dear?"

"Odd," came Odd's timid reply.

"It's Audrey and I'm Connie. Thanks for letting us come in like this."

"It's nothing...and here you go Audrey."

Odd felt her glasses being slipped onto her face. What a relief it was not to have to keep her eyes shut. Sitting up a bit she looked down at her feet and gave them a little wiggle. It was like trying to wiggle her ears—they barely moved.

Abe came in with a bucket of water. "Sit up, Sprite. Now, I don't want to scare you, but this is gonna hurt. A lot. When I was in the Ardennes, this sort of thing would..."

Odd's harsh gasp cut him off in mid-sentence.

She had just put her feet in the water. "It hurts! The water's too hot!"

This pain made her previous agony seem like nothing. It felt as though her feet were burning. She tried to pull them out of the bucket, but Abe easily held them down.

"No. Keep them in the water," Abe soothed in a soft voice. "There you go. The water's not hot at all. It's just your feet are so cold. Now where was I? Oh yes, the Ardennes. It was back in forty-four. Back before even your mother wasn't born. I was with the 99th at Lanzerath and we held up the Germans for ten hours! Oh, you wouldn't believe how cold it was, but with all the fighting and the gunfire and the constant threat of their panzer-tanks roaring all over the place, I didn't realize my feet had near froze right off."

"The—99th—what?" Odd asked between gasps, desperate to keep her mind off the pain.

Abe frowned at her. "The 99th infantry division of course. You know World War two? General Eisenhower?" He paused as the two girls only stared at him. "You had to have heard of Ike?"

"The dog?" Odd asked, her nails digging into the sofa cushion.

"No! President Eisenhower. What do they teach you in school these days?"

Odd had no idea who Eisenhower was. She didn't even know who the current president was, nor did she know exactly what he did as president. And what she did know about the US government, like much of her limited store of knowledge, was also factually incorrect.

Connie had heard of Eisenhower. "He was

president in the fifties, right? Just after Truman?"

Abe beamed at her. "Right as rain. Ike was a great man. I met him once." The old man held out his big right hand. "He shook my hand and clapped me on the back. Told me what a great job I was doing. This was back in February of '45, right after the battle of the Bulge. "

Peach came back into the living room carrying a white box adorned with a red cross. "And Abe has been in love with him ever since."

"I ain't," Abe growled. He wore a scowl for his wife, but it didn't reach into his eyes.

"Enough with your politics, Abe." Peach knelt, groaning her way slowly to the floor next to the bucket. "You'll bore these two clear to death."

"No he won't, Peach...Ma'am...Mrs. Peach, I mean," Odd said. "It helps takes my mind off the pain. And it's very interesting." This last wasn't exactly true. It was interesting enough, but what she really liked was the kind way in which Abe spoke. His gravely, old voice rumbled out, reminding Odd of a cat's purr, and was strangely comforting.

"And it ain't politics, either," Abe added. "It's fundamental history. Stuff that should be taught in the first grade. They teach you about World War two, Audrey?"

She'd heard the term before, but not in school. Drunken bar talk could ramble incoherently over many subjects. What she knew about World War two consisted mainly of the fact that the French would be speaking German if it wasn't for the U.S. She didn't know who the French were, or why it was such a big deal what language they spoke.

When Odd hesitated Connie spoke up for her, "Odd hasn't gone to school much." The little girl turned red with embarrassment.

Abe saw this and tried to peer through Odd's glasses with sympathetic eyes. "Well, school only get's you so far, Sprite. The rest of it you do for yourself. Hard work. Perseverance. Honesty. These are worth more than a college education to me."

His rough hands were gentle. He pulled back Odd's coat as he spoke, exposing her blood stained shirt. This he carefully tore so he could see the bite marks on her upper arm. "Though it never hurts to go to school and learn all there is to learn, just remember there's more to life. Ok?"

"Yes sir."

"Sir...I like that. It's proper. Your parents taught you manners at least."

This wasn't true. A gentleman in a bar in Dayton, disgusted by the way Odd had chewed her food with her mouth open, had taught Odd manners. He had also taught her how to hold a knife and fork correctly and to sit up straight—like a lady.

Abe smiled, peering in at the wounds, "Yep, Ike got you good. It ain't nothing though. Three deep gouges—a couple of scrapes. I've seen worse. The peroxide, Peach, if you'd be so kind."

"Will it sting?" Odd asked. Her feet no longer burned with the same intensity as they had. They now ached deep into the bones. All the same she'd had about enough pain as she could stand.

"Nope." Abe spread the first jagged hole as wide as it would go and poured clear liquid into it. In a flash a gush of pinkish-white foam frothed out, running down her arm. Odd gasped at the sight and just like that, her eyes rolled up in her head.

Chapter 31

Voices strayed into the jumble of dreams and images that ran through Odd's mind. She had fainted, yet as some point her exhaustion, hunger, and overwhelming stress, had caused her blackout to rollover into an actual form of sleep. Though at best it could only be called an unkempt fidgety doze.

The voices intruding into her slumber were at once known and friendly as well as strange. They belonged to people she hardly knew—people she would trust her life with, if necessary. She hadn't a single reservation about any of them; her mind had categorized them as *good*.

Hearing her own name brought her, reluctantly, around. Immediately she came aware of the pain that had been an undercurrent to her dreams. Her feet ached and her upper right arm shot out lances of pain at the slightest move. She cracked a fearful eye to look at her wound, afraid it had gotten larger somehow.

The first thing she noticed was that someone had removed her glasses. The white bandage around her arm was the second. She'd also been practically swaddled in a thick downy comforter. Odd couldn't remember ever being snuggled in something so soft and warm.

Now she turned her head the slightest and looked out through squinted eyes to see the old couple talking to Connie. They sat in the kitchen, just off the living room. Her friend talked through huge mouthfuls of mashed potatoes and steak; she seemed only to pause when she drank from a tall glass of milk. She talked about Odd. What she said turned the little girl's cheek as red as her eyes.

Connie didn't hold back. She told them everything that Odd had ever mentioned—including what Mitch had tried to do to her. At the recounting of this, Odd trembled and cried in shame. On a certain level she knew that what had happened wasn't her fault. She knew that Mitch was some sort of nasty perv. But—but what did he see in her? Why had he chosen her to try to do that thing to? Did he see something in her that was like him in some way? Was she nasty as well?

Ashamed, Odd slid beneath the comforter.

"That poor girl," Peach said. Odd could tell by the change in volume that Peach had turned toward her. Under the cover, Odd froze, not daring to breath. She wanted them all to look away and ignore her. She wanted them to talk about something else altogether.

Abe came to her rescue. "Yep, sounds like she's had it tough...but what about you?"

At first Connie tried to sugarcoat her story—the bruising wasn't as bad as it looked—she had fallen and hit her head by accident—her mom had only lost her temper the one time. Abe saw right through it. Peach warned him not to press for answers, but he did regardless and soon Connie broke down and told the truth—even about the baby. Hearing the tale a second time hurt Odd's soul even more than it had at first. It made her want to hide in the comforter forever.

A part of her knew that her own mom, the woman that she was so desperate to find, might have done the same thing as Connie's mom. Thinking on this and hearing her friend weep forced Odd out of the comforter. She didn't want to be alone. Finding her glasses on the coffee table—thankfully Connie hadn't said a thing about her eyes—she slipped them in place and hobbled to the kitchen.

"Maybe you shouldn't be up," Peach said, struggling her ancient body out of her chair.

"She's up already, Peach." Abe stared at Odd angrily; his faded blue eyes set hard. He then thumped the table with a large fist.

"I—I'm sorry." Odd stopped in her tracks. "I—I'll go back to the couch." She began to turn back when Abe stopped her.

"What? Your dinner's right here. Come sit down."

Odd hesitated and by then Peach had her by the shoulders guiding her to a seat at the table. "He's not mad at you, dear. He's angry over what's been happening to you two."

"Damn right!"

"Abe! Watch your tongue," Peach admonished.

The old man turned and dropped his gaze to the table. "Darned right—then. I am mad. How some people treat their children. It's unbelievable...unbelievable!"

"That's enough, Abe." Peach hurried to the stove and brought back a cut of steak bigger than both of Odd's hands. Next to it sat a heaping pile of mashed potatoes topped with butter. Odd's mouth came open at the sight and she nearly forgot her manners. As she hurriedly grabbed her knife and fork, Abe cleared his throat.

"Oh yes...thanks a lot. This looks so good," she said.

Peach smiled at this and said, "Let's let them eat in peace...we should go talk."

Connie shared a worried look with her friend. When they left she said, "What do you think they'll do with us?"

Odd had to wait to answer. She had shoved three heaping mouthfuls of food into her mouth and hadn't yet chewed. "This—this is so good! I don't know what they're gonna do." Famished as a winter wolf, she went back to eating. Just then, getting the next bite crammed between her teeth was all she cared about.

After a few minutes of utensils clinking and scraping, of sighs and the occasional small, girlish burp, Connie asked, "You think they'll call the police?"

This question alarmed Odd enough for her to hesitate before putting the next hunk of steak into her mouth. "Did we do something wrong? Did I hurt Ike?"

Having finished most of her huge portion of food, Connie was only nibbling, but she still managed to spray Odd with a few specks of potato as she laughed loudly. "You? You hurt Ike? Ha-ha, that's too funny. That thing is a monster." She paused and the laughter died and her smile drooped. "Why did you do it, Odd? Why'd you go after the dog like that? It could've killed you."

Behind her glasses, Odd blinked at the question. *Why had she?* "I don't know. It just happened so fast that I didn't have time to think."

The older girl's eyes seemed to stare past the dark glasses and burn into Odd's red eyes. "Instinct? You saved me by instinct?"

Though *instinct* was a rarely used part of Odd's vocabulary she understood the word. In this case it was the perfect word. When Ike attacked with his thick muscled body and wicked sharp teeth, Odd had felt that natural impulse to help someone in need.

"Yeah, by instinct." Sitting at the table, thinking and kicking her feet, which swung well off the kitchen floor, Odd discovered there was more to it than just instinct. Purely by accident, Odd had found that one person who might have been worse off than she was. But she couldn't say that. Never could she say that. To tell someone that they were worse off than an abandoned demon-child was plain mean. "Just instinct," she repeated, yet even as she did, a feeling as ethereal as smoke tried to make itself known within her.

"And what about on the train?" Connie asked. "You could have frozen to death. Was that instinct too?"

On the train Connie had been weak, mentally, still overcome with the desire to kill herself. She hadn't tried hard to keep warm; in her malaise even the basics such as balling up to trap heat had escaped her. If anyone had been in danger of freezing to death it had been Connie.

"I think so," Odd replied, sensing there was a lie to her words. There had been more to it than instinct, but Odd couldn't force her mind to admit the ethereal truth of what had motivated her.

Connie gave a long sigh and then went back to finishing off her food. Odd caught up quick and scraped hers clean almost at the same time. She leaned back in her chair and just like that an intense weariness had her yawning like bear.

They could hear the couple having a discussion that ranged over the spectrum of emotions and volume. Sometimes the girls could hear one or the other grow angry or frustrated and their voice would rise. At least twice Abe could be heard to grouse: "Damned democrats", further cementing Odd's dislike for these vile creatures.

The talk took so long that Odd put her head down on the table and began to nod off, but just at that moment, the couple came back in.

"What are you going to do with us?" Connie asked. Her full lips were drawn in, invisible, and her face paper white apart from the bruising. Odd could see that she feared desperately that they were going to send her back home.

Abe came to sit in front of his half-eaten dinner. "Well we haven't really decided. A lot depends on the Sprite, here. If her wounds heal up nicely, then we'll see. But if they don't and they get infected, then the matter's out of our hands. We'll have to take you into Springfield and that means questions we can't answer."

Connie looked to Odd as if the little girl could force herself to heal properly. "They only hurt a little," Odd said to reassure everyone. "They're not bad at all." In truth, any sudden movement sent a grimace across her face.

"You are one tough cookie, Sprite!" Abe laughed.

"Does that mean we can stay?" Odd asked. "You won't send us up to Springfield?" To her Springfield sounded like a state penitentiary.

Abe gave her a smile that so crinkled his face that it looked as though it had folded in on itself. "We have to give those bite marks a couple of days to see what happens. And yes, in the meantime you can stay with us."

"Thank you," Connie said, relief obvious on her face.

"Since you two have had such a long day, we should probably get you to bed," Peach announced. "We'll put Connie in Anna's old room and Audrey can go in Jacob's. Can you carry, Audrey upstairs?" she asked her husband.

Abe looked at Odd closely. "I don't know, Peach. The Sprite ate half a sack of taters and most of a cow all by herself. She might have gained twenty pounds."

"I didn't," Odd insisted. "I swear. I ate only what Mrs. Peach gave me." She was actually quite nervous over this. Both because she didn't want to be seen as a burden—an over-eater, and second because she *really* wanted to be carried up to bed.

If Odd had ever been carried to bed, she couldn't remember. What she could remember was waking up alone in the back seat of strange cars, with the sun coming up. Or in back-corner booths at bars, shaken awake by the surprised morning crew, and once she came to under a pool table in a dive pool hall in a city she'd never seen before. Odd had never given this much thought. It was simply the way her life went.

But now she had the chance to be carried to bed—something she knew happened all the time to normal kids—and she didn't want to miss out. "I'm very light. Everyone says so. They say I'm small for my age."

"Oh, don't worry, Sprite." Abe picked her up

easily, cradling her as he'd done when he had brought her into the house. "I may be old, but I still swing my own axe. You ain't nothing more than a feather to me."

His cheek wasn't exactly smooth next to hers, but she didn't mind a bit. He smelled of earth and soap. She breathed in the scent and closed her eyes. As they went up the stairs in his slow measured step, Odd's heart began to beat heavier with the secret hope that there would be children's books in Jacob's old room and that Abe would read her one.

It was not to be. The room had been the home of a much older boy. Upon shelving along the wall were a dozen trophies of different sports. Neat stacks of books and magazines, as well as footballs and frisbees and trading cards and knickknacks of all sorts were arranged in order on the dresser and desk. Odd would've preferred a girl's room, but loved it nonetheless.

"Here you go." Despite his talk of strength, he breathed heavily with a slight rasp. "Tuck on in." When a grimace of pain passed over her features, Abe caught the look. "I'm sorry what Ike done to you. He's a good dog, but he can also be hell on strangers."

"It's ok," Odd replied. "We were trespassing...and it doesn't hurt much anyways."

He put a fluffy blanket over her. "We'll see in the morning. G'night, Sprite."

With her left hand Odd reached out quick and caught hold of his sleeve. "Mr. Abe? What's a damned democrat?"

This got Abe laughing so hard he began to cough wetly. "First off, no cursing...leave that to me. Second, I raised six children and fourteen grandchildren and I know a ploy to stay up late when I hear one."

"I'm just curious is all."

"Well if you're still curious in the morning you can ask Peach."

Abe was right, Odd didn't really care. She knew it had something to do with politics but that was about it. What she wanted was to hear him speak in his rumbly voice. She wanted to be able to touch those giant hands and watch the wrinkles of his face become valleys when he smiled.

She tried again to engage him, "Does she know more about democrats than you?"

"Oh yes," he said, flicking off the light. "She is one. G'night." He left a very stunned Odd staring at the crack in the door. Peach is a democrat? How could they possibly be 'Damned' if she were one? In her mind she had pictured a race of evil rat-faced people and now her little vision was all topsy-turvy. No one was nicer than Peach.

Odd couldn't fathom it and, after yawning a few times, she decided to let the matter rest until morning. With care, she took off her glasses and set them on a small table that sat next to the bed. She was just trying to get comfortable—her right arm throbbed if she laid it in its usual position—when someone appeared in the doorway.

At first Odd thought it was Peach, but then saw the wild mane of curly hair. "Odd? Are you still awake?"

"Yeah."

"Can I sleep in here...with you?" Connie asked, moving into the room before the question had fully slipped from her mouth. "I'm feeling lonely."

"Sure!" Odd exclaimed in excitement. Though she was confused as well. Odd had never in her life felt less lonely than she had in the last three hours. Gingerly, she moved over to allow her friend under the covers.

"Thanks..." Connie wanted to say more but she hesitated. Odd could wait for whatever the girl wanted to talk about. She couldn't be happier curled up next Connie. Eventually her friend said, "Did you see all those pictures of their kids and grand kids? How do they do that?" At this Odd giggled, thinking Connie was talking about making babies. The older girl chided, "No, I'm serious. They all seem so...happy."

"I guess, maybe because Abe and Peach are so nice."

Connie laid there quietly for a time. Odd could tell that something still bothered her. She guessed that the pictures had her friend hurting. There had been many, many photos of babies and toddlers. A painful reminder of what had happened to her. Odd snaked her left arm under Connie's head and pulled her in close.

"Odd," Connie said, almost begging. "If...I mean, when we get to California, can I stay with you and your mom?"

Odd could not be more content. Lying in the softest bed she'd ever touched, warm and cozy, with a full belly, protected by two loving adults and a mean ole dog, cuddling with a girl who was part best friend and part sister, she sighed out the word, "Yes," and then fell asleep.

Chapter 32

At dawn Odd woke with her right arm aching, Connie snoring, Ike barking and some creature making a long 'waah' noise. She was in heaven. Despite knowing her pain would slacken if she moved her arm she remained perfectly still—moving would wake her friend.

On the floor below, Abe stomped around trying his best to be quiet. He even tried to curse quietly. "Ike shut up! There's people sleeping. Damned dog." Odd heard this plain as day. When a teapot began a high whistling—a whistling Abe clearly couldn't hear—Connie rolled over, freeing Odd who slid out of bed.

As always she planted her glasses on her pert nose before heading down to the kitchen. Abe sat reading the newspaper, oblivious to the teapot.

"Good morning, Sprite," he said brightly. The fact that he was obviously glad to see her, made her flush pink with joy. "Did that damned dog wake you?"

"No, just the sun. I get up when the sun gets up. Your water's boiling."

"Oh my!" Abe showed his age as he moved with gimpy motions from his seat to the stove. "Thank goodness you saved me from burning water once again. I can't cook a lick. My whole job in the kitchen is to make Peach her tea and stay out of the way. I'm not all that good at either."

"What's that—*waah*—noise?" Odd asked.

"Just our goats," Abe said. "They're hungry for

breakfast. You wanna go see? You can help me feed them." Odd grew too excited and moved too fast. Reaching for the back door, sent a lance of pain through her arm. Abe saw, but said nothing.

"It was only a twinge...really. It's feeling a hundred percent better. Practically good as new," Odd said, moving her arm with her teeth gritted together behind a phony smile.

Abe opened the door. Striding into the dirt back yard he said, "I'm gonna have to look at that later. Here, grab up that bucket."

Odd picked up a rusting little bucket and followed after Abe who was heading to the decaying barn. Part of the barn was in good enough shape to house half-a-dozen goats. As soon as they entered the creatures started a fearful bleating.

"Why are their eyes like that?" Odd saw that the goat's eyes weren't normal. Their pupils weren't round but rather rectangular and worse they were horizontal, unlike any animal Odd had ever seen. Ironically, they looked freakish to the demon-eyed girl.

Abe grew alarmed. "What do you mean?" he asked, taking a hard look at his animals. "They're normal...that's what goats look like."

Odd pulled her glasses down for a better look. "They sure are weird."

"They sure are," Abe agreed. "But as long as they keep giving me milk, I'll keep them around."

This was another weird aspect of the goats that Odd was having trouble with. All six were females and had enormous udders for their size. Odd felt her cheeks turning a little red at the sight.

Abe took no notice. "See that bin? Open her up,

scoop out a bucketful and we'll get these animals fed."

Doing everything left handed didn't escape Abe's notice, but Odd couldn't help it. The lid to the bin was heavy and hurt her right arm too much to lift, as did digging out the grey pellets. She forced herself not to make a peep or screw up her face in any way.

"Now just dump that over the fence...just not in a pile. Spread it out." Abe watched with his hands in his pockets against the cold. Odd barely felt the cold; the animals entranced her. "Now, let's get 'em a treat. This here is alfalfa. They love it. You can feed it to them through the wire. Just keep your fingers on this side; you don't want to lose one of them."

The herd crowded over to where Odd squatted and she took turns feeding each. "That's enough you pigs!" she scolded, after her supply of alfalfa had run out. "Go eat your pellets."

"Good job. You don't want to over-feed them. Goats can get ridiculously fat. Now all we have left to do is run that spigot for a few minutes and we're done." Odd needed two hands to turn the knob. Again she went to great lengths not to let her pain show. Abe watched her closely. "That's enough, Sprite. Good job. You have the makings of a good farmer."

Odd couldn't help grinning at the compliment and Abe grinned right back. They walked in silence back to the house. A heavy aroma of buttery eggs greeted them. Peach, looking twenty years older than she had the night before stood at the stove in an old housecoat, squinting at the eggs.

"Good morning, Mrs. Peach. I fed the goats." Odd felt the greatest need to tell everyone about her accomplishment. "Can I help you make breakfast? I can only make toast, though."

Peach blinked sleepily before responding, "Wash your hands first. The bread is in the second drawer down." Odd did as directed and soon found that Peach was less of a morning person than Abe. Only after her second cup of tea did she start to look refreshed.

About the time Odd had the toast done Connie came down. Obvious anxiety had her looking pale. "I got nervous when I didn't see you in bed."

"I was out with Mr. Abe. He let me feed the goats!" she said triumphantly. "They eat like pigs and they have weirder eyes than me..." Too late she stopped. A silence enveloped the kitchen.

Connie quickly filled it, covering for her friend. "Breakfast smells wonderful, Peach. Can I help with anything?"

The old woman shot her husband a glance before saying, "Just grab those plates, dear."

Peach had made more than enough food. The two girls stuffed themselves silly in an hour-long binge. Not until Abe took the plate away did Odd stop nibbling at the bacon. She sighed happily when he did and leaned back in her chair.

"Thank you Mrs. Peach. Everything was so good."

Peach gave a little head tilt and said, "You're welcome. How's your arm feeling today?"

Odd's smile froze on her face. "It's practically good as new."

"Then you won't mind us taking a look at it," Abe said He moved in close, groused at his wife for blocking the light and the gently pulled back the bandage. Odd was afraid to look, so she looked at Connie instead. Not a good move. Connie went white at the sight and then began to chew on the inside of her mouth.

"Is it bad?" the little girl asked, still unable to look.

"Oh, I don't know," Abe replied, touching around the deepest and most jagged wound. "What do you think, Peach?"

After a long squint, she answered, "I was expecting worse." At this, Odd looked. The good news was that the wounds looked to have closed, the bad news was that they looked red and swollen. As her husband had done, Peach touched the wounds, even seeming to take their temperature with the back of her hand. "Yeah, they don't look so bad. But only time will tell."

In Odd's opinion it took far too little time. By dinner, two of the three wounds were hot and red. By the time Abe tucked the two girls into bed they were oozing pus. All day long Odd pretended not to feel a thing. It was an easy thing to do. She hadn't lived a better day in her life.

Connie broke out of her depression the second she heard Peach proclaim the wound didn't look so bad. After breakfast Peach took the two girls shopping at a nearby town. She bought Odd a warm pair of brown boots and a pink sweater to make up for her ruined *Hello Kitty* one. Connie received a hairbrush to tame her wild hair and a matching set of hat and gloves.

In the afternoon, while Peach took a needle and thread to Odd's coat, Abe took them on a tour of his farm on the back of a big green tractor. The metallic beast chugged slowly, leisurely along in the cool air, while the old man told story after story. Some of these were exciting—his times in the war—but most were funny and they laughed until they were close to falling off the tractor. Connie had such a good time that she appeared to glow with happiness. She held such an attraction that Odd couldn't help kissing her hand whenever the wind swept her dark hair back. When they pulled up in the yard, Abe killed the engine and helped Odd down first. They both turned to look at the fifteen-year-old girl still on the tractor.

"She's prettier than the sunset," Abe said. This was saying something since the western horizon was aglow in gorgeous colors. Odd could only agree.

After another huge dinner meal, Abe entrusted Odd with the evening feeding of the goats. Feeling important, she took Connie by the hand and led her out to the barn. There they fed and watered the goats, chatting like happy birds.

"Can you wake me up in the morning?" Connie asked, an hour later as they brushed their teeth with new toothbrushes. "I want to feed the goats again with you and Abe."

Despite a greedy little feeling inside her that wanted the morning to be her and Abe's time alone, Odd didn't hesitate to say yes. What was good with two could be great with three.

Chapter 33

Ike barked. The sun flashed its light. Connie snored. Abe cursed...and Odd smiled. For a long time the little girl lay snuggled warmly next to Connie. No feeling had ever been so grand as waking up this way and the sensation that had been ethereal the day before could hardly be ignored now. It made her chest ache. It made her breath swell in her lungs and it made her mouth want to smile.

Giving in, she smiled huge. She did this despite her fear that the dog bites were worse. They began throbbing as soon as she woke and she was afraid to move. Yet eventually she had too. No way did she want Abe to start feeding the goats without her. Slowly, carefully Odd extended her right arm.

It hurt. She couldn't move it without having to stifle a groan. Looking under the bandage sent the air out of her lungs. The redness had advanced; a streak of it had begun to run up to her shoulder. Quickly she pressed the bandage back in place.

"Connie?" Odd whispered. "Connie? Time to get up," Odd became louder giving the girl a shake. "Connie! Come on now. The goats are hungry. Come on, come on, get up."

"I changed my mind. Let me sleep."

Had her arm been feeling good, Odd would have allowed her friend to sleep in, but she didn't want to chance Abe seeing how badly she was hurt. "No. I can't do that. This is a farm. If you want to live here, you have start acting like a farmer. Let's go."

With help from her red eyes, Odd finally roused a sleepy Connie out of bed. The little girl had forgotten to put her glasses on and when Connie roused herself enough to protest, she caught sight of Odd's malformation. It shocked her into higher level of consciousness.

Odd didn't even notice, her aching arm preoccupied her too much. Not until Connie handed the sunglasses to her did she even think about her eyes. "Sorry about that."

"There's nothing to be sorry for. I'm ok with your eyes," Connie replied. "Tell me, have Abe or Peach seen them yet?"

"No. And I don't want them too. Not until we know what's going on with us. They..." Odd paused listening. The goats had begun their clamoring. "We'd better hurry."

Abe gave each girl a smile and wished them good morning. Odd wanted more and hugged him in his chair before tugging the big man up with her one good arm. "I want you to see Connie feeding the goats. She's an expert already." The greedy part of her wanted to do all the work herself and show off to Abe, but she feared that he would see her arm wasn't healing the way it was supposed to. So she stood with Abe, complimenting Connie at every opportunity.

"The teapot!" Odd cried, after a few minutes. A tiny whistling had got past the noise of the goats. Abe scurried off. The two girls went to hand feeding the goats and were silent for a time. Connie lost in thought. Odd lost in worry.

"I could live here forever," Connie said, as she

gave into the goat's incessant pleading for more Alfalfa from the goat in front of her. "Would you stay with me, here, if you could?"

Odd didn't hesitate to answer, "Yes." Her quest to find her mom wasn't about finding Karen Wyatt exactly. Odd had set out looking for love—even a tiny scrap of it, which was all Karen had ever offered. But here on the farm she had found bushels of it.

Connie came in close and Odd thought the girl would hug her. Instead she moved in to whisper: "Could you ask Abe if we can stay here? I think he just adores you."

"Me?" Odd giggled at the thought. "No, he thinks you are beautiful. He said you were prettier than the sunset. And I think so too." Connie actually blushed at this. "And besides, I don't think I can." Actually Odd could ask and desperately wanted to, but the truth about her arm held her back.

"Please?" Connie begged. "For me? Ask for me? I get the feeling they'd never say no to you."

Odd, who couldn't say no to Connie, swallowed any more objections. "Ok...ok. Just give me some time. I have to find the right moment."

"No, now is perfect."

"He'll ask about my arm," Odd said, dropping her head. "I don't think it's healing right."

Connie pulled her deeper into the barn. "Let me see." Odd lifted the bandage. "Oh jeeze! I think it might be infected."

Odd pushed the bandage back. "What does that mean exactly? Infected? Can it get better on its own?"

"An infection means there are germs in there. But if they go away on their own I don't know," Connie said with a half-shrug. "Does it hurt?"

"Just a little bit. Mostly when I move it."

Connie zipped up Odd's jacket. "Then don't move it. I'll make sure to do everything for you. And I'll get that peroxide from the first aid kit. We'll put some more of that on you. Until it heals more we have to find some way to keep anyone from looking under that bandage."

At first this was easy.

During a breakfast of seemingly endless waffles Odd was quick to bring up a subject that she knew would last an entire meal: democrats! Abe immediately went on a long tirade. Peach sipped her tea, rolled her eyes and eventually pulled her hearing aids out and set them in the middle of the table.

Finally she'd had heard more than she could stand and slapped his hand. "That's enough you ole grouch!" She turned to Odd. "Don't get him started so early or he'll be at it all day."

Odd grinned and Abe chuckled at it. He then crossed his arms. "Being honest and being grouchy aren't the same thing."

"With you they are," Peach said and then purposely turned her back on him. "I'm going into town again. I have to go to the library. Do you two want to come with me? We can have lunch at the Greek place."

Connie greeted this with excitement. Odd had to fake her enthusiasm. Libraries were fine places to warm up, to take a nap, look at pictures in magazines, but only if Odd was alone. With others around it was a place to show off her inability to read beyond a fourth grade level.

There would then have to be explanation as to

why, which would eventually lead to questions about her crazy eyes and then would come the demand to see them. And then what?

Abe must have sensed something in Odd's behavior. "You'll love the Greek place, Sprite. The owner, Spiros, makes the best lamb kabobs. They're spectacular."

"But Spiros is a democrat," Peach chided. "Aren't you afraid you might catch something?"

With her mind still on the thought of germs, Odd asked, "Like what would he catch?"

Abe touched his temple, "A softening of the head."

Peach poked him in the chest, "No, you'll get a softening of your hard heart!"

Looking slightly wounded, Abe pulled Odd's chair right up next to his. "I bet the Sprite here thinks my heart is plenty soft. Don't you?"

He gave her a warm squeeze around the shoulders. Odd paled from the pain in her right arm. Connie saw it and hopped up quick, coming to Abe with her arms wide. "I think your heart is already soft." They hugged, but it was less spontaneous and less heartfelt than the one he had given Odd and Connie came away with a strained smile.

"You win, Abe," Peach said, getting to her feet. "You've turned these two against me. Now I have three republicans in the same house. What will the neighbors think?"

"What neighbors? The goats?" Abe cackled at his own joke and stomped off.

"He's an old goat!" Peach said with a warm smile. "Ok you two. Time for your baths. Connie why don't you go first on account of all that pretty hair. It must take forever to dry."

"Sure thing, Mrs. Peach. And if you want I'll be a democrat with you."

The old lady laughed that sounded somewhere between a gag and a cough. "That would be great, but only when you're older. Now get. A storm is supposed to be moving in this afternoon and I don't want to get caught up in it."

Connie left wearing a look that spoke of more gloom. Odd started after her but Peach plucked at her sleeve. The woman's wet blue eyes were looking questioningly at Odd's right arm. She opened her mouth to speak, but Odd, worried what the woman was going to say, spoke first.

"Why didn't Abe hug Connie like he hugged me? Doesn't he like her as much?"

Peach blinked in surprise at the question. "Oh, that? No, he likes her just fine. That's just him being a man. You see men—after all this time on earth—have yet to learn thing one about women. I can see his mind working. He thinks that since Connie's step-dad molested her, then she'll be wary of any father figure. Even a harmless old goat like him."

Odd could understand his reluctance. "I think she needs him. She needs all of us." The one thing Connie hadn't mentioned the first night was how she and Odd had met. Nor had she brought up the terrifying time on the train when she had hooked her legs over the rails as it sped high over the river.

"Yes, she's been through a world of troubles for one so young," Peach agreed. "But what about you? How are you feeling?"

"Me? I'm doing great. Here let me do the dishes," Odd jumped up too quickly and felt her head go suddenly light. Regardless she went back and forth from the table to the sink in such a hurry that Peach could only stand there blinking after an owl-like fashion.

"I guess you are doing better," the old lady said.

Odd stopped at the sink and held onto it. Two minutes of work had cleared the table and left a sheen of sweat on her forehead. "Yep. I'm gonna be as good as new in no time." She fought to keep her food down.

Chapter 34

At the library, Odd watched as her friend went through the books. Connie barely looked at a single one. Mostly, she just let her hand run along the bindings, while her eyes stared off at nothing.

Eventually Odd pulled Connie aside. "You ok?"

The girl hadn't been seen to smile since breakfast. She had shut herself up in the borrowed room after her shower and wouldn't open the door for anyone but Peach.

"Yeah, I'm fine," Connie lied.

Connie had become so listless in her depression that tiny Odd, with only one good arm could push her into one of the library's leather bound chairs without a problem. "Did Peach tell you why Abe didn't give you a hug like he hugged me?" Odd asked.

"Yeah, he thinks I'm broken, mentally. He thinks I hate all men now."

"No, that's not it," Odd insisted, frantic to make Connie see that Abe did indeed like her. "He's just taking it slow. He doesn't want to scare you off by being too loving. I think if some guy had tried to hug me after what Mitch did I probably would have screamed." To lighten the mood, Odd let out a half-hearted "Eeek!" The little scream seemed to sap what little energy Odd had left. She slumped onto the arm of Connie's chair.

The scream had Connie smiling for real. It didn't last but a second. "Am I screwing this up for us? Am I ruining it? I love it with Abe and Peach. They're wonderful. The house is so warm all the time and the goats are so neat to have around."

"I could do without Ike." Odd hadn't set one foot in the front yard without Abe right near her side.

"Yeah, he always gives me the shivers when I see him staring at me." Another smile came and went. "Tell me it's going to be ok."

"It will, somehow," Odd replied, rubbing her temple. A fever had begun cooking her on the ride into town. As it progressed she'd found the old truck becoming more and more unbearable with each mile. And now, in the library her head had begun to ache.

"How?"

Odd had to shrug. "Somehow it will. I really believe that you'll be fine. I think Abe is so furious over what happened to you that he'll keep you even after...even after they take me away." The little girl hadn't known her tears were so close until, just like that they were running down her face. Finally admitting the truth to herself—that her dream was coming to an end—cracked that dam and the tears gushed.

"Take you away? Is it your arm? Is it really bothering you?" When Odd nodded, Connie got up quick and put her in the chair. The older girl knelt beside her friend. "I'm not going to leave you. We're a team."

"We were a team," Odd said, lifting her glasses enough to wipe her eyes. "Once I go to the hospital they'll figure out who I am. After all, how many girls with red eyes do you see running around? And when they figure it out, they'll ship me back. But you can stay. I want you to stay; they'll be good to you."

Connie's misery grew, becoming loud in the small library. "But—but they don't love me. You do. You saved me and kept me warm and fed me and did everything for me. You love me. I can't lose you."

Despite her growing exhaustion Odd laughed. Her tears, which she had just checked, sprung anew. Inside her the ethereal feeling that had shown rare glimpses of itself had been named: love. "I do...I really do love you. It's so strange. It's like I found a long-lost sister on a rail road track."

"You found a drunk sister!" Connie smiled through her tears as well.

"Shhh!" the librarian hissed. The girls giggled.

"Abe and Peach will love you too," Odd said. Connie began to protest but Odd put her hand to the girl's lips. "They will. You're sweet and beautiful and kind—the perfect big sister. They will love you. And just think how it will be...can you imagine Christmas at the farm?"

Connie's mouth came open and her eyes were far away. Odd's were, as well, as she pictured the farmhouse decorated for Christmas. There'd be a huge tree covered in tinsel and bulbs dominating the living room. Stocking would line the mantle, hanging over a roaring fire. The house would fill with the aroma of pine needles and pies, of turkey and stuffing and gravy. And carols would warble out of Abe's antique Zenith Cobra-matic until the record would begin to skip.

Where Odd was going the place would smell like bleach, the walls would hold nothing but the scrawling, indecipherable mess of graffiti. Music would be either angry rap or death metal. Unless, by some curse, Odd were to be sent back to Lena's. Then

Christmas would be spent in the storage room in solitary confinement.

Connie sighed in hope; she wanted the picture perfect Christmas so bad it hurt. Odd sighed in quiet desperation; she wanted it too, just as badly. She wasn't going to get it, all because she had saved her friend from a vicious dog.

The greedy part of her screamed in rage.

Odd, however, smiled. She loved Connie. It was out there; the words had been said and acknowledged. They couldn't be taken back. Odd loved Connie, but she didn't love her as she would a big sister. She loved Connie as she would a little one. One that couldn't do for herself, one that had to be guided and protected.

"You'll be fine, Connie. As long as you let them love you. Will you promise me to try?"

"I will."

"No. You have to say it better than that," Odd demanded. "Say: 'I promise to let them love me and take care of me and I promise to...to be good and be happy'. Go on, say it."

Connie took a deep breath. "I promise to let them love me and take care of me and I promise to be good and be happy...but it's not so easy as that, Odd. Everything keeps coming back to me. I keep having these dreams...where I'm holding my baby. We're on the train over that river and the wind is blowing so bad and it's so cold. I try to wrap her up, but she isn't moving. She's quiet. I'm so afraid that it's too late. That I already let her freeze to death. And then my parents are there..."

She stopped in mid-sentence and took a long shuddery breath before finishing, "They are yelling at me to throw the baby into the water...to get rid of the evidence. Only I can't do it. She's like glued to me. They keep yelling—pushing me to the edge of the train—demanding that I get rid of the useless blob. But I can't do it. I can't throw her away like that, not all alone. So I jump off with her."

Odd took her friends hand, something that only a few days before had made her heart thump crazily in fear and excitement. She took it and kissed it and felt warmed by it. "I'm sorry. It sounds so scary."

"It is, right up to the end."

Odd nuzzled the hand, loving the feeling of it so much that she almost missed what Connie had just said. "Up to the end? That's the worst part." The older girl said nothing. "Connie, that's the worst part of the dream. They practically hound you into jumping from the train!"

Connie shrugged, "Yeah. But when I'm in the air, falling, I know I'm free. I know they can't hurt me anymore."

"But they can't hurt you now." Odd gripped the hand, squeezing it nearly to the point of pain. "As long as you're on the farm you'll be fine. They won't have a clue where you are. You'll be safe."

Now Connie smiled and gripped Odd's hand back. Again the smile slid away as if the gears holding it in place were slippery with oil. "What about you? Will you be safe? Everything you've said about that nasty foster-home and the prison they were going to send you to..." Connie got the shivers. She then straightened her shoulders. "I've made my promise..."

Odd interrupted, "And what was that promise?"

"Um...to be good and happy and let them love

me...as long as I'm on the farm," Connie said, looking up at the ceiling as she did. "Now stop interrupting. You have to make your own promise. Promise me that you'll escape and come back to the farm."

Though that seemed the easiest promise in the world to make, it really wasn't. What would happen if she did? Wouldn't the farm be one of the first places they would look? Wouldn't Abe and Peach get in trouble? Maybe even go to jail? And what would happen to Connie? They'd ask questions about her and it wouldn't take much to figure out that she was a runaway too.

Going back would ruin their lives. Yet Odd felt sure that Connie wouldn't understand. Not with the way her mind sat so precariously balanced. "I'll try." In her mind Odd finished the sentence—I'll try to keep you safe.

Chapter 35

Before they went to the library, the threat of a winter storm had been lost on Odd. The morning had been practically warm, while the cloud cover had been generously interspersed with dazzling blue. However, by lunch the world had become a dull heavy grey.

Abe gave up hating democrats long enough to enjoy a meal of lamb, rice and warm pita bread. He laughed with an old bear of a Greek, named Spiros, who kept up a ruddy complexion by nipping at a bottle of clear liquor that smelled like licorice.

"Opa!" he would shout with each shot.

"Stop it! This is too early for Ouzo!" a matronly woman shouted from the kitchen.

"No dear. We'll be closing early. You'll see. Abe says we'll get a foot of snow by sundown. And he's never wrong about the weather."

"I'm never wrong about nothing," Abe added.

The Greek turned his large head back to Abe. "Then explain your vote for Nixon!"

"Ok, maybe one time I might have been wrong, but..."

The two took to arguing good naturedly, while Peach chatted with some ladies at a nearby table. Connie, in a food stupor, sat languidly brushing her hair, turning it wavier with every pass. And Odd pushed her food around. She liked the bread. Everything else she had trouble putting in her mouth; her appetite left her as the fever began to turn her cheeks red.

"Careful or you will turn yourself into a lion," Peach advised Connie. Indeed her hair seemed to be growing into a rich brown mane. "Why don't you do Audrey's hair? She looks a little down."

The suggestion surprised Odd and without thinking her hand went to touch her blonde hair. It seemed all right. Why would they want to touch her hair? Connie seemed eager to.

"Is my hair ok?" Odd asked.

"It could use some brushing," the older girl replied coming behind Odd's chair. "And it could use a trim and layers...it's too straight."

Odd wanted to be defensive about this, but she lacked the energy and the knowledge. She didn't know what Connie meant by layers. Was she suggesting Odd wear a wig perhaps? Or maybe extensions, which didn't make any sense since Odd's hair already hung halfway down her back.

"Do you use conditioner?" Connie asked, staring at the hair intently.

Conditioner and proper clothes were, for Odd, luxuries her mom had never been able to afford. Gin and tonic: yes. Shoes or a haircut for her daughter: no. Once they had stayed at a nicer motel, bought and paid for by one her moms "friends". Odd had used conditioner that one time.

"No, not really" she replied, embarrassed.

"Your hair is so soft, I was just wondering."

Odd felt a hitch in her chest at the simple compliment. Compliments were rarer than conditioner in her world. Connie began running the brush through the top of her hair and said, "Take off your glasses...it'll be ok. Just keep your eyes shut."

Odd did, placing them neatly on the table. After that she was in heaven. Connie ran the brush through her hair back and forth. She then teased it into a million different shapes. It felt so good Odd wanted to purr, knowing then what a cat must feel when subject to a prolonged caressing.

Other than her mom, no one had ever touched her hair and with her mom it was a rarity. Her mom did nothing but shear off three or four inches off the back every few months.

"Peach, who are these pretty young ladies," a woman asked, interrupting Odd's perfect moment.

"This is Connie and Audrey. They're staying with us for a while...friends of the family. Girls, this is Mrs. Reed."

Connie was quick to put out her hand. "It's nice to meet you."

Odd, on the other hand was effectively blind. Reaching for her glasses she accidently knocked them off the table, forcing her to then scramble on the ground for them while trying to peek between her fingers.

"I'm sorry. I'm sorry. The light hurts my retinas." Finally she got them in place and popped back up. "Mrs. Reed, it's nice to meet you."

The woman was a good decade or two younger than Peach, which still put her in the category of really old in Odd's book. She flashed a welcoming grin at the little girl, shook hands with her right, and with her left she touched Odd's hair.

"I love all this pretty hair. I'm so jealous! When I was just a girl..." her voice faltered. "Are you feeling ok?" she asked Odd. "Your head seems quite warm and you're flushed. Peach, look how red she is. And feel her forehead."

"Oh my. Is it the dog bite?" Peach came over looking worried. "It's time we took you in to the doctors," she said after putting the back of her hand to Odd's forehead and neck. She shook her head sadly. "Sorry ladies to cut our visit so short but we have to get a moving. Abe, we need to go to the hospital."

"Please, can we go by the farm first and drop Connie off?" Odd begged, having just told her friend how safe she'd be there.

Abe cast a look outside at the already swirling snow. "No, I'm afraid not. The truck's tires are getting worn we shouldn't trust them in really deep snow. But it'll be ok. We will just tell them that you two are friends of the family...which you are, so there's no lie there."

Connie tried to smile as if everything would be ok. "Come on, Odd. You don't look good and I don't want you dying on my account. I'm the big sister, remember? I should be looking after you, not the other way around."

Odd allowed Connie to lead her out into the blistering cold of the storm where she shivered and shook all the way to the hospital. During the ride they held hands and stared out the window. Odd was afraid of what was coming, but her fear was muted by her fever which made her sluggish. Connie, however, showed hers fully in the lines of her face, in the jangle of her knee as it bounced up and down, in the way she chewed at the inside of her mouth.

Once at the hospital, they were routed away from the emergency room and sent to the Urgent Care ward a floor above it. There the tension in the little group mounted. Abe and Peach huddled close, filling out forms, and whispering to each other conspiratorially, while Odd leaned on Connie, using the bigger girl to hold her up.

Eventually they were led to a little room where Abe explained to the nurse about the dog bite and the infection. The woman asked a few easy questions and then took Odd's blood pressure, her temperature, and her pulse. After this came a question of payment.

"You don't have an insurance listed for Audrey..." the nurse left off with an expectant look.

"We'll be paying by credit card," Abe replied. "You do take credit cards, right?" Odd opened her mouth to object, wondering how much a visit to the hospital would cost, but Peach shook her head. A quick authoritative move that had the little girl snapping her jaw shut.

"Oh yes, credit cards are fine," the nurse answered. She then brought them to a single bed enclosed in a curtain. "Here you go, honey. Put on the gown and we'll get a doc back here as soon as one's free."

When she left the little group sighed in unison. So far no one had asked a single question concerning Odd's relation to the couple. This didn't last long however.

A relatively young doctor entered a half-hour later just as Odd was beginning to nod off to sleep. He introduced himself as Dr. Philips and shook hands all around.

"So dog bite. I bet that was scary," the doctor said, congenially.

Odd glanced to Abe before answering. He

nodded to let her know it was ok. "A little."

"And was this your dog?"

"No. It's Mr. Abe's. His name is Ike and he's not mean really. We were just..." Odd left off wondering if they would they get in trouble for trespassing too.

"Messing where you shouldn't have been messing?" the doctor asked, filling in the blank. It was close enough to the truth for Odd to nod. The doctor smiled and then turned to Abe. "Mr. Hewitt, just to let you know we will have to report the incident to the health department."

Reporting an incident to the health department sounded a lot like trouble to Odd. She wanted in some way to defend the beast that had practically torn her arm off. Abe saw this and patted her leg.

"Ike is a good dog, Audrey. Don't worry about him."

"And one last question. I'm guessing you two aren't Audrey's parents, can you tell me your relationship to her?"

"Odd is a friend of the family. She will be staying with us for a while." Abe said this while looking at Odd. Despite her pain and fever and fear, Odd took in a sharp breath. He had invited her to stay! She sent a look to Connie and the two girls shared a smile.

"And are you her guardian...legally?" Abe shook his head at the question. The doctor seemed like a very nice man, but he had very shrewd eyes. "In order to treat her I'll need her parent's consent...but I'm guessing you won't be able to get that so easily. Am I wrong?"

"No. You're not wrong," Abe answered in a

slow voice. "Can we talk somewhere private? This is a special case."

When they had gone the two girls pummeled Peach with questions: What were they talking about? What would happen to Odd? What would happen to Ike? Could Peach drive Connie back to the farm before anyone thought to ask about her?

Peach waved all this away. "We'll wait and see. I'm sorry Connie but I can't drive like I use to. In the snow I'm practically useless. In fact I'm a danger to everyone."

They could do nothing but wait. When Abe came back in he looked not just old, but haggard as well. "I had to tell him the truth about you, Odd. He says he has to contact Social Services no matter what. I'm sorry."

This hurt, but Odd wasn't much surprised. A lifetime of being kicked to the curb had prepared her for exactly this sort of thing. The farm had always been just a fantasy to her—a dream. A part of her knew that any happiness was fleeting and would be stripped from her sooner rather than later. That was the way it had been. That was the way it would be.

What life hadn't prepared her for was the love that felt like a bomb inside her chest. It wanted to explode out of her in every direction even then, even after fate had ground her down under its unyielding heel. "What about Connie? Is she safe?" Odd asked.

"We didn't talk about her. I kept everything focused on you. He doesn't have any reason to be concerned about her."

"Good," Odd sighed out the word, relieved for her friend.

Connie wasn't relieved, however. She hopped up and snuck a peek out through the curtains. "It's not good. We can't let them have Odd. I told you where they'll put her. In with the criminals. She's too small! And with her eyes..."

"Connie!" Odd hissed to shut her up.

"They have to know," Connie insisted.

Just then the doctor cleared his throat before pulling back the curtain. "Hi there," he started a touch sheepishly. "I just got off the phone with someone at Springfield Social Services. They have an Audrey Wyatt listed as missing. They're sending someone up to collect you."

A stony silence greeted this. No one said a word, but only the doctor found it awkward. He tried to explain, "I'm sorry. I wish there was another way, but I could lose my license to practice medicine."

"There is another way," Connie interjected. "Just give Odd her medicine and we'll go. No one will know, and no one will care. We'll take better care of her than any Social Services people!"

The doctor opened his mouth to reply, but Odd, afraid that her friend would slip up and let it out that she was a runaway too, interrupted, "Stop it Connie, please. We knew this was going to happen to me. And where would I to run to, anyway? They have *your* address at the farm. I can't go back there."

Connie heard the word *your* distinctly and it made her head drop. It signaled two things: Connie had a home now and Odd didn't.

Chapter 36

Abe stood his tall frame up and said, "Peach, maybe you should take Connie down to the cafeteria and get some hot cocoa in her." When they left, Abe gave the doctor a hard stare. "You gonna do anything that might actually help her? Treat her wounds? The girl is sick. Isn't making things better what you're *supposed* to be doing around here?"

Odd felt a flush strike her skin. Abe was in fury!

The doctor, doing his best to ignore the abrasive words, went to Odd. "Let's take a look at what that dog did to you—this may hurt," he warned. She turned away and silently glared at the wall. She hadn't been angry with the doctor before, figuring he had just been doing his job, but now that Abe had shown his anger, she felt her steam rise.

The doctor removed her bandages, probed and prodded, soaked the wounds, and dug into them to clean out the pus. He fretted about what sort of pain she was in, commented about the size of the wounds, and asked about the dog. Stoic as a veteran Odd ignored both the pain and the doctor.

In all her young life she had never allowed herself to stew in anger as she did that afternoon. She let it fester to the exact second that Abe did. When the doctor left—wordlessly—Abe smiled as if a joke had passed between them, and just like that Odd felt her spirits bloom.

"Connie is right. You are a tough one, Odd."

At first she smiled at the compliment, then her mouth drooped a touch. "Could you call me Sprite? I like that better."

"Of course, Sprite. I didn't mean to be so familiar. But what about Audrey? It's very pretty, do you like that?"

Odd thought on it. As she did, a part of her mind wondered why she was bothering to care what he called her. They would be coming to take her away soon. She tried to bury the depressing thought.

"No, Sprite is better. When you say it you make me feel special."

"That's because..."

Just then a nurse came in saying something about broad-spectrum anti-biotics and dehydration. The little girl tried to go back to being stoic, only Abe's eyes wouldn't stop smiling even if his mouth wasn't. Still she barely twitched at the sting of the IV.

"That hurt?" Abe asked.

She had always been afraid of needles but with his fading blue eyes on her and his compliment of her toughness still warming her ears she forced herself not to react.

"It was nothing."

Abe sat back wearing a proud look. "That's my girl."

At this all stoicism left her and she silently blinked away tears until the nurse left—in a huff. She had been as ignored just as the doctor had. Then Odd cried great, fat tears.

"I'm going to miss you," she said, hitching out the words.

"Oh, Sprite, I'm going to miss you, too."

It took only seconds for Odd to calm down enough to tell Abe not to miss her. "You can't. Connie will know. She needs to be somebody's girl right now. She needs it more than me."

Suddenly the curtain was thrown back and Connie stood there looking amazed. It took a second for Odd's eyes to catch up and right themselves from the quick motion. It also took a second for Connie to find her tongue. "How...how can you say that? How can you be thinking of me...watching out for me all the time? How?"

"Because I love you," Odd said, still stunned by the girls unexpected appearance.

"But you were doing it right from the first moment you saw me. You pulled me off that train track and you didn't even know me!" Connie came and sat on the bed, oblivious to Abe, who had been as startled as Odd at her sudden appearance.

Odd gave a shrug. "I don't know. Lovers sometimes have love at first sight, why can't best friends?"

"I don't know why they can't...maybe they do," Connie reasoned, looking at Odd still with amazement in her eyes.

Abe stood and stretched, looking taller than usual. "Connie? Where's Peach?" When she told him that his wife was still in the cafeteria he drew back the draping about to go join her, but stopped at the sight of a police officer pulling up a chair against the wall opposite Odd's curtained chamber.

"What's this?" Abe asked.

"Just protocol," the officer replied. "The girl's a runaway. That makes her a flight risk and we wouldn't want that—not on a day like this."

"What a waste of taxpayers' dollars! She ain't going nowhere," Abe griped walking past the man. Odd had to agree. Fleeing was going to be her top priority, but she'd had enough of the cold to last a lifetime and wouldn't try just yet.

Odd didn't like the idea of the police officer being able to look in on them and so she nudged her friend to close the drapes. Connie was only too glad to do so. She shut them, keeping her face averted as if she were one of the Ten Most Wanted fugitives. Even with the curtain drawn the presence of the man curtailed conversation and the next couple of hours dragged by.

Eventually, just as the sun set behind the clouds, turning a dark day into a dark night, the social worker showed up. Odd had expected a woman, but it was a man in his thirties. A soft man with a bulging mid-section and a receding hairline.

"All right," he said, bustling through the curtain. "Which one of you is Audrey Wyatt?"

Odd wanted to tell the man that he had taken too long and that Audrey Wyatt had already left, but she lacked the cheek to try. Instead she raised her hand. "Oh great." the man said, in a tone that seemed filled with forced cheeriness. "Let's get you unhooked from all that stuff and get you back where you belong."

This set the room to simmering. No one believed she belonged anywhere but the farm. Hard looks went back-and-forth between the two adults and the two friends. Just then the policeman got up with a weary sigh as if his guard duty had been an arduous backbreaking chore.

"You got things under control." It was a

statement not a question. "I'm heading up to the roof to take a smoke break if you need me."

Abe rolled his eyes, which almost set Odd to laughing. She could imagine the word 'break' had galled him since the officer had done nothing but flip through magazines all afternoon. The old man ambled to his feet and came up to the social worker. He came in very close and towered over him, holding out his hand.

"I'm Abe Hewitt."

"Hi, I'm Dave Willings. Thanks for..." The old man took Dave's soft hand in his big, callused paw and gave it an easy crushing squeeze, causing Dave to swallow once before continuing. It didn't look like Abe had meant to hurt the man, rather it looked as though Abe was trying to form some sort of bond through the handshake that lingered a second or two longer than a normal one. "Thanks for taking care of our Audrey," Dave finished.

Our Audrey made Abe's eyes go flinty but he smiled, nonetheless. "Where will you be taking her?"

"Um...tonight we'll go back down to Springfield and tomorrow," Dave paused and looked through his paperwork. "She'll go back to the induction center that she was processed through."

"The B wing?" Connie asked suspiciously. Dave gave her a sharp look, his eyes lingering on her fading bruises.

"It just says the induction center, Miss...?"

Connie ignored the suggestion that she say her name. "I bet that means the B wing. Look, she's too small for that place...and with her problem..."

Odd began to worry that her friend was bringing too much unwanted attention on herself. "Connie, please. Don't worry about me."

"Someone has to worry about you," Connie said, and then turned to the social worker. "Mr. Willings she's too..."

Abe put a hand on her shoulder. "That's enough Connie," he said with the gentle force of a father. It shut her up immediately. "Look Mr. Willings, my wife and I want to know about this foster-business and I figure you're the man who's in the know. Can we take her on? Would that be allowed?"

Dave didn't allow Odd to feel the rapturous joy the question brought for more than a second. "No. I'm sorry. She's under Kendall County's jurisdiction. You can talk to them, but I'll tell you now, you'd be wasting your breath. The counties all have specific rules and they never bend them."

"That's crap!" Abe growled, glaring about the room.

Dave surprised Odd with his response. "Yeah, it is crap. There's a lot that's crap in the system. At the same time there's a lot that's good. Mr. Hewitt, Audrey seems like the type of girl that will find an easy placement in a good home."

Connie jumped up in anger. "No, she won't! She's...special...Odd show 'em your eyes."

Odd dropped her chin to her chest. "No." What good would it do?

The older girl came to Odd's bedside and grabbed her hands. "Please show 'em. They'll put you in the B wing for sure if you don't."

Abe gave Odd a long look. His stare seemed to penetrate the dark glasses. Odd turned away. Peach, who had been sitting quietly, running her hands over themselves in her anxiety, asked, "What exactly is this B wing all about? The two girls seem scared to death over it."

"My guess. It's an alternative placement program. Usually kids who can't adapt to the foster system are place there."

"Violent kids? Druggies?" Abe asked.

Dave gave him a sympathetic look. "Yeah, I'm afraid so. However like I said, Audrey is the type of girl who's an easy placement. No eye problem is going to stop people from wanting her."

Connie wasn't going to be stopped so easily. "What if there was? Look at her Mr. Willings. Look how small she is. What would happen to her if she had to go to that alternative place?"

"It's not going to happen."

Abe didn't like the answer. "You've been pretty straight with us so far. Why don't you answer the question?"

"Because I don't want to scare Audrey unnecessarily. Yes, those places aren't good. Things happen there. Kids can't be monitored every minute of every day, you know."

"See, Mr. Abe," Connie said grabbing Abe's sleeve in desperation. "He said it...*things happen there*. We can't let Odd go."

A great sigh escaped Abe. "I don't know what you expect me to do. The B wing does sound terrible, but I'm with Mr. Willings. Sprite is a great kid, she's sweet and loving and tough. She's going to find a good home. Maybe even a better one than ours."

"That's not possible," Odd said. "I've never been in a home better than yours. It's the best."

"No!" Connie stamped her foot. "Odd you show 'em right now, or...or else." Her eyes flicked towards Dave. She was threatening to turn herself in.

"Connie please, no. It won't do any good. Don't make me," Odd begged. The older girl set her face in stone with only a second twitch of her eyes as a response. Odd was stuck. She felt like a criminal being forced to remove her mask. It would mean Abe would know what she really was—a demon child. But saving Connie was worth it.

"Alright, but Mrs. Peach has to leave first. I...I don't want you to have to see me like this. Please," she added when Peach didn't move. Abe, who looked to have guessed Connie's meaning gave his wife a little nudge.

After she left, Odd took off her glasses and opened her eyes. Her eyes were not only red but huge as well. Had they been blue eyes, or brown, or green, people would have gushed compliments over how large they were. But since they were the eyes of a demon, their size only made them more freakish.

Dave, Abe, and even Connie, who had seen them before all stared in silence. Odd gave them a good look before putting her glasses back on. She then asked the question that had her chest quaking in fear.

"Mr. Abe? Am I still your Sprite?"

Chapter 37

Abe had trouble finding his voice. "Of...of course. Of course you are. Nothing will change that, Sprite. But...but what was that?"

Connie cut in quickly before Odd could answer. "That's the reason she can't go back into foster care. When people choose a kid—it's like they're picking out a puppy. There's even a little window where you can see the kid sitting there just like at a pet store."

"You've been in the system before?" Dave asked.

The question brought on a longer silence than the exposing of Odd's eyes. Finally Connie nodded, her head bobbing slightly. "Twice in Will County..."

"Connie!" Odd practically screamed. She had to keep her friend from saying anymore. "Stop...this isn't about you. This is about me. I'm the problem here..."

"It's ok, Audrey," Dave said sadly. "You don't need to cover for her. I knew Connie was in trouble the second I walked in the room. Lost children always have a look in their eyes."

"I'm not lost," Connie whispered. "I'm exactly where I want to be and I won't leave. I won't go back." Suddenly she shouted, "Look at me! I. Won't. Go. Back!"

"You'll be safe, Connie. We have counselors who..."

"Who don't do anything!" Connie interrupted, a vicious note in her voice. "They never believed me before, or if they did they didn't do a thing to help. I'd be in foster care for a couple of months and then they'd ship me right back home. And nothing ever changed—ever—except all the kids at school thought I was some sort of loony."

Peach came in, cast a quick, nervous look at Odd, and then went to Connie. "There, there child. Abe what do we do?"

Dave answered for him, "There's nothing you can do." He then pitched his voice low, "You've already broken a number of laws. It's illegal to harbor or aide minors the way you have. But don't worry, nothing will happen to you unless you try to interfere again. For better or worse these girls will have to go back north."

Abe was a stone, a rock, an iron statue. His anger seemed to have welded his joints in place—all but his jaw. "Better or worse? How can you say that? This girl was raped and then beaten, repeatedly! And Sprite here was made into a prisoner in the basement of some woman's home."

"I don't know what you want me to do. The law is the law."

Abe's great hands turned into fists, each the size of Odd's head. "What I want is for you to do the right thing—not the legal thing—the right thing. Go back to Springfield and tell them these weren't the right girls. Tell them they were our granddaughters. Do that and I promise I'll treat them like my own."

"I'm sorry. That's not the way it works."

Abe's face screwed up, his wrinkles turning on themselves and a single tear escaped from the soul that Odd knew to be so soft. He then turned and cast a single glance at the police officer. Who knows what a younger version of Abe would have done, violence possibly, but this old one suddenly went limp.

"It's ok," Connie said, touching his arm. "Odd has promised to escape and I...I promised to be good, but I'm going to escape too."

Dave breathed out heavily and rang for the nurse to disconnect Odd from the tubing of her IV. This she did bringing out a bottle of pills that looked alarmingly big. She handed them to Odd, but said to the social worker, "One pill twice a day; morning and night. Make sure she finishes the bottle."

"Are we free to go?" Dave asked her.

"Paperwork, paperwork. I gotta get my work done now. Ten minutes."

Ten minutes to say goodbye? Ten minutes before her life would be over and hell would begin? It seemed like such a short time. Odd didn't want to miss a moment of it. "Can you leave so I can get in my clothes?" She demanded of the social worker. When Abe started to go Odd grabbed his shirt. "I don't want you to go, just turn your head."

When she was all buttoned up she got to her feet on the bed so that she stood a head taller than Abe and hugged him. He smiled up at her. It was sad smile, however. "You're big for a Sprite."

"What is a Sprite anyway?" Odd asked, refusing to let go of his hug. Hoping he would hold her forever.

"Oh, it's like a fairy or a pixie. A tiny thing just like you." He picked her up easily and set her down in front of Peach. The two hugged. It didn't last the forever that Odd wished.

The little girl then stood there not knowing what to do or say that could fix what was happening. She had been prepared to go to the B wing but that was only when she thought that Connie would be safe. Now it felt like someone was rubbing salt in her wounds. She wanted to be mad at the older girl, but Connie had exposed herself for Odd's sake. Connie had stood up for her. A first in Odd's life.

Connie gathered up the strength to make proper goodbyes. She thanked Abe and Peach for everything they had done for her and Odd, giving them each a long kiss on the cheek and then hugging them. After that she sat next to Odd on the bed and stared at the floor, as Abe and Peach murmured to each other.

Odd counted seconds. It took her a bit to work out how many seconds ten minutes was, but when she did she started counting. At six-hundred she breathed deeply, fully expecting the nurse to be punctual to the second. She didn't come back. Odd whispered, "It's been ten minutes."

This set a fire under Connie. She jumped down from the bed, paced the room frantically for three turns, and then came back to Odd with her sole possession in her hand: the hairbrush.

Connie began running it through Odd's hair. "You're going to escape. You hear me?" The words came out just below a whisper.

"I don't think I will. The B-wing is like a prison. They have everything: locked doors, barred windows, barbed wire fences." Once inside she knew that there would be no escape.

"I know," Connie said breathing into her hair. "You're going to escape today. Here, in just a minute."

"But..." Odd tilted her head at the police officer.

"Don't worry about him. I'll make a diversion so

big he won't notice that you've gone for ages."

Odd turned to stare at Connie. How could this even be a topic of conversation? They hugged to cover their low whispering. "I'm not going without you." Odd said.

"You are," Connie insisted. "Didn't you tell me that it made no sense for both of us to be hurting? One of us has to create a diversion and it should be me. The fact is...I'd run, but without you I think I'd curl up and die. In fact...I'd want to die. You're the one with all the bravery. We both know I will never make it on my own."

This was true. Without her, Connie would have killed herself twice over. She seemed to lack the will to live, even at the farm. Yet, somehow, she was being strong enough to give Odd this chance. And how badly she wanted to take it! How badly she wanted to run back to the farm and be greeted with hugs by Abe and Peach. Right then it was all she wanted.

However, she knew that she could never go back. The social worker had warned: laws had been broken. Odd wasn't going to be the reason Abe went to jail.

Connie saw her hesitation and added, "Remember the promise you made me?"

"I do, but I can't go back to the farm. They'll get in trouble."

"Then go to California," Connie hissed.

The thought of California with its sun and beaches reminded Odd of another reason she couldn't escape. "But all the snow. I'll freeze to death."

Connie paused, seeming to consider that. "Maybe that would be better."

Dying in the snow was better than going to the B wing? At first Odd thought Connie was crazy, but then a sullen depression swept her as she remembered the sorts of kids there. They were societies least wanted. And what's more, they knew it. It showed in the nasty anger in which they did everything. They couldn't cross a street without their rage showing through.

Her life there would be six years of hell. Compared to that the snow didn't seem so bad. "I'm going to miss you," Odd said and began to cry.

Connie didn't cry. Her eyes stared at the crumpled bedding. "You would miss me either way." She then blinked and gave Odd a strained smile. "Here take this. It's all I got and I won't be needing it." She pressed the hairbrush into Odd' hands and asked, "Are you ready?"

"Yeah."

"Here's the plan," Connie said, after taking a look back at the police officer, who still thumbed a magazine. Abe and Peach sat in stony silence. Dave the social worker leaned up against the nurse's station, looking tired.

"You're going to show the cop your eyes. While he's distracted, I'll be halfway down the ward before he even notices. Everyone will think I'm the one running. All you gotta do is walk down to that exit and you'll be outside in ten seconds. Do you remember which way west is?"

Odd knew. She pointed west, feeling suddenly small. "I'm scared."

"You know what's funny?" Connie asked with a little laugh. "I'm not. I think this was how it was to supposed to end. Give me a kiss." Odd kissed her friend's smooth cheek, while Connie gave her such a fierce hug that Odd gasped, and then laughed.

Connie was serious, however. "Go on."

After a big breath, Odd walked past Abe and Peach trailing her fingers so they touched the old couple. She went up to the police officer and removed her glasses.

He didn't look up.

"Yeah? You gotta go to the bathroom or something?" he asked.

"Look at me," Odd commanded. For the first time in her life she purposely let her eyes blaze into someone else's. She held them wide and unblinking.

"God! What the hell!" the man practically shouted, flipping the magazine up as if Odd was attacking him.

Peach called out from behind her, "Audrey, what are you doing."

Despite the strong desire not to, Odd ignored her and continued to stare directly into the policeman's shocked face. When Mitch had seen her eyes it had been an accident a quick flash. When drunks at a bar had paid three dollars a pop to look blearily into her face, her eyes were always heavy lidded and half-closed from embarrassment. When the eye doctors gazed at her, the lights they used practically blinded her, so that she squinted. But the cop got the full force. It rooted him in place for thirty seconds as his mouth worked and his head shook as if he were seeing something unnatural. In a way he was. She was a defect.

"Doctor Phillips! Get over here," he cried eventually. "There's something wrong with this girl's eyes." The terror in his voice had the doctor hurrying over, Dave came right behind him. Odd slipped on her glasses and faced them.

"What is it? What's going on?" the doctor asked, in a rush.

"Her eyes! They're all red. They're..." He left off what every drunk in every bar had ever said: *they're demon eyes!*

"I have pink eye," Odd said simply.

"Pink eye?" the doctor said in disgust at the commotion such a common ailment had evoked.

Just then Dave caught on that there was someone missing. "Where's the other girl?"

So far Odd's distraction had proved so great that no one knew where Connie had gone. Was Odd supposed to give them a hint? If she didn't they could spread out and search the building, making it tougher for her to escape.

Odd waited, as the men stared about them and began swinging the curtains aside. After about half a minute, she pointed at the door Connie had breezed through as everyone had come running at Odd. "She went through there." It was a stairway door marked with a little symbol of a helicopter. Knowing that Odd would be fleeing downwards, Connie would be moving up. Odd guessed that she would be a few floors up by then.

All heads turned in that direction.

"That's the roof access," the cop said. His words were quiet and full of meaning. Odd smiled as all three, the police officer, the doctor, and the social worker ran for the door.

"I'm going to miss you Mr. Abe. I'm going to

miss you Mrs. Peach," Odd said, walking away from the bewildered couple. "Thanks for everything." She then gave a little wave, turned and headed for the other exit. She didn't hurry, mainly because she couldn't. Stairs were difficult on her eyes and she depended heavily on the railing. But she was only one floor up and Connie had been right at how quickly she made it outside.

The snow hit her immediately, freezing the tears on her face. Odd zipped up tight, shoving her blue acorn hat hard down onto her head and wiggling her fingers into her gloves. She had to force herself to stop crying. The snow helped with that; it simply hurt too much to keep it up.

Immediately she began heading west. Unfortunately, that took her directly across the front of the hospital, so she detoured into the parking lot to use the cars as cover in case someone came out looking for her. No one did.

They were still chasing around after Connie, Odd figured. The girl had promised a very good distraction and so far she had kept her word. She was probably racing around the hospital going from floor to floor at top speed. The thought cheered Odd, who was in a great need of cheering.

The idea of searching for her poor excuse of a mom did not fill her with a great deal of enthusiasm. What if Odd did find her? Had Karen Wyatt changed in the last couple of weeks into an actual, loving mom? Odd highly doubted it.

Up ahead the parking lot cleared and a forest grew at its curb. Odd figured she would walk under the cover of the trees for awhile and then, if she hadn't frozen to death first, go back to the road and try to hitch a ride. After all who wouldn't stop for a little girl in the middle of a snowstorm?

She was still in the lot, however, when she heard, "Oddd!"

Hearing her name, Odd jerked around making the snow turn spirals in her eyes. She put out an arm to steady herself and looked around for Connie. It had been a female voice and there was only one person within a hundred miles called her Odd.

"Odddd!" the cry came again, high up on the wind. Odd looked up at the roof of the 4-story hospital, about fifty yards away, there stood her friend on the edge of the roof. With arms out stretched Connie stared upward. "I'm not afraid!" the girl yelled.

She didn't look toward Odd, but Connie had to know where she was. The girl had made sure Odd knew which way west lay. Which meant Connie was speaking to her. Odd wanted to scream back, but hesitated, she could see men advancing on her friend. Odd ducked behind a car, watching.

"I love you! I'm not afraid!" Connie hollered again.

Why wasn't she afraid of being so close to the edge? Odd wished she could yell for her to get back. The girl stood just too close to a very long drop. It started to make Odd's insides hurt. The men came closer and Odd could see that one was definitely the police officer. Thankfully his gun remained in its holster; his empty hands he held out.

With one last: I love you. Connie turned her back to the edge. Odd slumped in relief. She had almost played the part of decoy too well. The men all stopped, their arms dropping, but Connie didn't move toward them as she should have. Instead she just stood there with her arms out, her coat once again billowing like wings. Then she fell backward, dropping four stories to the concrete below.

Chapter 38

Odd did not see her best friend die. The girl flew down to the ground and just before she struck, a hand, heavy and gnarled, came down over her glasses. Nor did she hear the dreadful sound of a skull cracking open on concrete. Just before it did, Odd screamed out in pain. She screamed in mortal agony. So powerful was her scream that it felt as though her soul peeled away from her insides and shrieked out of her.

After that, she grayed out. Odd was semi-consciousness, not really aware of her body or mind. Things happened to her and things happened around her, but it felt to be happening to someone else.

Gnarled hands lifted her limp form and brought her to a truck and laid her inside. The truck was driven away and Odd laid there, uncaring where it went. The driver cried and thumped the wheel with a callused hand. He swore and punched the windshield and then swore some more. He cried harder, sometimes sounding like a child and sometimes like an old man—weak and decrepit. In all this she could hear Connie's name being said repeatedly and sometimes her own.

Yet it wasn't her name that she heard. The driver didn't say 'Odd' or even 'Audrey'; the little girl heard someone calling out her real name:

"Sprite? Sprite?" Only one person called her Sprite.

Abe called her name gently in that deep rumbly voice, but Odd pretended not to hear. She began to think and feel again. The name had brought her around, but just then she didn't want to think or feel. Her insides were precariously balanced between breathing and not breathing and she was trying hard to tip the balance away from breathing.

She didn't want to breathe. To breathe in meant to breathe out and with every breath out she wanted to scream, and bawl, and yell, and demand that the world take it back!

"Sprite, you're scaring me," Abe said.

That was a lie. Odd couldn't scare anyone. Her arms had the thickness of twigs. Who could she scare? No one. It was the opposite that was true; Odd was afraid of everyone. Even Abe. If he raised his fist to her...but he never would.

"Sprite, please."

Sprites were fairies. Weren't they just small demons? "This is my fault. Let me out here. You're not safe."

"No. we're going to Springfield. I'm going to..."

"Let me out here!" Odd cried, pulling herself up. "Abe, you're not safe with me. I'm cursed. I'm a demon."

"You're not."

"You saw my eyes! What else would you call it? The doctor's have a science word for it, but all it means is that I'm cursed! My whole life has been one big curse."

Abe pulled the truck over to the side of the road and turned to Odd. "Sprite, you can't blame yourself. Everything that happened before Connie met you drove her to do this. It had nothing to do with you. In fact, judging by everything I heard and saw the last few days, you might have been the best thing that ever happened to her."

"She was the best thing that happened to me. I never had a best friend before and now...and now..." Odd stopped and looked out the window, letting her tears come. "And now she's gone and all I have to remember her by is this." Odd looked at the hairbrush—a cheap piece of plastic that she would cherish forever. "I wish I'd had something to give her. I wish I had a necklace or a diamond...I would've given her anything."

"You did," Abe said. His crooked index finger touched her cheek, and caught a huge tear. "You gave her happiness. When you two were together she was always smiling and laughing. Do you think she smiled much before she met you? Because I don't. And even...even on that roof," Abe paused to wipe his own tears away. "Even on that roof she sounded...she almost sounded thankful. Like you had taken away her fear. She said, 'I am not afraid.'"

The snow grew deeper around them with every passing minute. Odd stared at the swirling chaos above and the serene perfect white blanket below. The two didn't make sense. "Abe, you can't trust the tires on this old truck, remember? Please turn around and go back. I don't want to be the reason you get into an accident. It'll be ok in the B wing."

"No," Abe said fierce and hard. He put the truck in gear and got it going. "Things might have been different if I took Connie home when you asked. The one thing I'm sure of is you don't belong in foster-care. People are mean. They're mean to anyone different."

Different? Did Abe see her as different now that

he had seen her eyes? Odd's mouth came open to ask. She shut it just as fast. Of course he did. How could anyone look at her and pretend otherwise. A second wave of sadness struck her and she cried again—this time out of self-pity.

Odd felt her selfishness grow to bounds she had never allowed before. In silence she cried over the terrible life she had been given. She moaned over her red eyes, her lack of money, her constant hunger, her crappy trashcan clothes, her pathetic mom. If her mom had only killed her just as Connie had killed her own baby... she went on until she noticed Abe sniffling.

"Abe, don't..." Odd stopped. She had been about to try to soothe his sorrow but she stopped. Why did she have to soothe anyone? Shouldn't someone be soothing her? Didn't she deserve that sort of thing too, like everyone else? Sudden rage filled her throat with bile. She wanted to spew it all over Abe in a great torrent of profanity. But she wasn't good at swearing; instead she slammed her elbow into the window next to her. Pain from the dog bite flared—she didn't care and she hit it again.

Abe ignored her, which only set her teeth gritting together. She went to hit the window a third time when he said, "She was so sweet. So beautiful." Didn't he care that Odd was going to wreck his truck?

"I hate this stupid truck!" Odd said. She looked around for something that her puny strength could destroy. Only the rear view mirror looked weak enough. Gripping it with both hands, she yanked it off and tried to break in two. Even in her rage she was too weak.

Still Abe seemed not to notice. Or if he did he was confused. "I'm so sorry," he said. The words didn't coincide with her action. They made no sense—she was the one who had just broken the mirror. What did he have to be sorry for? Everything was Odd's fault, not his.

In the space of a second, her confusion doused her anger. She then forgot how she had decided not to soothe him.

"It's not your fault...I'm just not thinking straight," Odd said. "And...and Connie was sweet and beautiful. But she didn't want to be beautiful..." Odd suddenly laughed, tears running as she did. "She said she hated her beauty. How strange is that? Something that I'd kill for, she hated."

Odd slipped off her glasses and looked at herself in the mirror. How wonderful would it be to look like Connie? How fantastic.

But wait! What about being molested like Connie? And how great would it to be raped like Connie? Or to be beaten.

"I hate people," Odd said listlessly.

Abe shook his head as if to say *no*, but what came out instead was: "Me too."

They drove on, each by turn either crying or trying to calm the other. By the time they reached Springfield Odd thought she was all cried out. She felt dead inside—in her core, behind her breastbone was an empty pit, hollow and black.

"Where are we going?" she asked, looking at the drab city. Even with a coating of snow the squat, rectangular buildings were a depressing sight.

"The bus depot. I'm going to put you on a bus to Los Angeles. I don't know what else to do with you."

"I wish I could stay with you," Odd said.

"More than anything, I wish you could, too. Them damned democrats—they wouldn't never allow it!" He was angry, but him saying this made her laugh.

"You hate democrats, but you love one. You know that doesn't make any sense."

"Yeah," he whispered. "Right now nothing makes sense. When you find your mom, make her love you. Make her see what a good girl you are, Sprite."

"How?"

"I don't know."

Odd didn't see how that could possibly happen. She could only go back to her mother and hope that she wouldn't be abandoned again. Anything more was simply a fairy tale. Odd gave the old man a pat on the leg. "I'll figure it out, don't worry. Oh...I'm sorry about your mirror. And I'm sorry that I got you in trouble with the Social Services guy. Will you get in too much trouble for bringing me here?"

"I don't care what they do to me. They're just as much to blame for Connie's death as her parents...making her go back there!" Abe struck the wheel again. "They can do what they want to me. I know I was right."

He paused in his anger, squinting out into the snow. "There it is. I haven't been here in years. I came to this same bus station back in '42 when I went to enlist, and my boy, Scott...I dropped him off thirty years later when he was heading off to fight the commies in 'Nam."

Odd didn't know thing one about the commies in 'Nam. "Did he live?"

"Oh yeah. He came back a little nicked up but was fine. He died a few years ago—some sort of cancer. Now don't give me that look. Scott lived a good life and was happy. It's all we can ask of God."

The old man pulled the truck into the lot and went inside the station, but not before telling Odd to keep low. He came back with a ticket in one hand, his wallet in the other and a worried look on his face. "That was more expensive than I thought it would be. Here..." He dug in his wallet taking out all the cash tucked into the crease. "Forty-two dollars. I wish I had more. I thought the bus ride would be close to thirty dollars. It was the last time I rode the bus."

"I'm sorry," Odd said. "I'll pay you back, I promise; though it might be a little bit." Her mind flitted back to Connie's crazy idea of pretending to be Mexican.

"Don't be a silly girl," Abe groused. "You don't owe me nothing. In fact take this too." Odd looked on in amazement as Abe battled his wedding ring over his thick knuckle and pushed it into her hand. "It's the only thing I have worth pawning."

"I can't...I can't take this. I've been nothing but trouble to you. I don't deserve it."

"First off, shut up. Second, find someone you can trust...a priest or a teacher to help you pawn that. I can give you my phone number if anyone needs to talk to me and get my permission. And third..." Abe swallowed loudly. "Third, Sprite, you deserve far more than this. You deserve to be loved and you deserve a family. And you ain't trouble, neither."

Abe grabbed Odd suddenly and pulled her in close. Unbelievably, he kissed her on the cheek. For that one second Odd forgot all about Connie. She breathed in the giant of a man and smelled his aroma of earth and soap. Odd fell into him and gripped him tight.

"Before you came, the high point of my day was watching *Wheel of Fortune* in the evenings. I've been in a rut for years, like I was just killing time, waiting to die. But you...you and Connie...you two came in and turned me around—just like that. And Peach, too. I've never seen her happier, not in years."

"But the ring. Won't Peach get mad?"

"Only if I take the opportunity to go astray like an old tom cat," Abe replied with a smile. "She'll understand don't you worry. Now it'll be time to board the bus soon. Look you're gonna have to make a switch to another bus in Denver. I'll ask the driver to show you which one it is so don't fret."

"Ok." She would fret no matter what.

On a piece of paper, Abe scrawled out his name, address, and phone number and tucked it into her front pocket. Then the two sat watching the clock on the dashboard tick away. A bus pulled up. Some people got off, some got on. Suddenly Odd was terrified of leaving the old man. California seemed like a million miles away—too far away from him—too far from the farm—too far from home.

With a nod to her he pushed the heavy door of the truck open and stepped out. They went to the bus where Abe talked briefly to the driver and then came back to Odd.

"Give me a hug," he said, his voice shaking. She didn't want to let go.

Chapter 39

The bus started out less than half-full and Odd had a seat to herself. There, she curled up and cried, not only over the loss of Connie, but also at the loss of Abe and Peach. She'd never be able to go back to the farm.

She didn't have a seat companion until they reached St Louis a few hours later. There, so many passengers boarded that not a seat remained empty. The bus quickly began to stink; mainly of body odor, but also of old cigarettes. This dulled her mind and she sat in a stupor.

The first person to occupy the seat next to Odd on her long journey smelled strangely of mint. It turned out to be the only pleasant thing about him. The mint smell came from the type of chewing tobacco he used. Every thirty seconds or so he'd spit into a large plastic cup and soon this held a small ocean of vile black liquid that had Odd's stomach turning over.

He also presumed that, since Odd wasn't large, he could fill part of her space. One of his elbows hung way over into her chair and she was forced to retreat up against the window like a cornered rabbit.

Unfortunately he didn't remain on the bus for long. Odd sighed in relief when he got up and hoped the next person would be a more agreeable companion. A swarthy man in clean blue jeans, wearing a very white cowboy hat took his place. He seemed not to like Odd from the second he sat down and he too spread out, and not just his elbows. The seats weren't very wide. Odd pushed herself into the corner as far as she could go, but still the back of the man's hand kept touching her thigh.

He appeared to sleep a lot, but his hand seemed awake and restless. And searching. Odd didn't know what to do other than to sit there as meekly as possible with her legs drawn in tight and hope that he got off soon. It made the night a terrifically long one for the poor girl. When she wasn't worrying over the man, she was fighting off depression over the past and anxiety over the future.

Odd was still awake when the sun came up—stiff from sitting in the same position for nine hours. When they hit the Colorado border, the swarthy man got off. While the bus re-fueled most of the passengers took to wandering around. Odd went to the bus driver, mostly because she was bored and wanted to stretch her legs, but also because she was anxious about being alone.

"Are we almost to Denver yet?" she asked as way of small talk. He had looked at her a few times as she stood next to the pump doing little besides kicking pebbles.

He yawned and stretched. "Oh, a few more hours. We gotta stop in Limon first."

Odd pulled out her ticket and then pursed her lips together. The lettering was too small for her to make sense of it. "Will this get me on the bus to California?"

He didn't bother to look at it. "I told your grandpa it would and he told you. You shouldn't doubt him. I mean, why would he lie, right?"

Grandpa? Odd like the sound of that. "You're right, he wouldn't. I guess I'm just nervous."

The driver worked the handle of the gas pump back in its cradle, saying, "Don't be. I'll point you in the right direction when we get to the Mile-High City."

Odd, who had been all set not to be nervous, started with a jump. "What did you say? Is...is Denver really a mile up?"

The man laughed at her expression. "Yeah, it's a mile above sea level, but don't look so worried. Just don't go running around. The air is so thin you'll have trouble breathing."

"Ok," she replied, knowing that there wasn't a chance on earth that she'd be running around in a city so high up. Odd got back on the bus wearing a sheen of sweat at her neck despite the chill morning. A mile high city? Who would build a city that high? She pictured Denver with great skyscrapers towering on the edge of a cliff. In her mind its streets were narrow with deep rocky chasms dropping away forever on either side.

A shudder went through her. How long would it take someone to fall a mile? It had taken Connie only a couple of seconds to die. She had simply leaned back as if dropping onto a soft bed, as though she were going to sleep. She probably didn't even have time to be afraid. Odd hoped that was true. The words *I'm not afraid* sang through her mind. Oh, please let that be true!

The bus idled there for a while, just as it did at most of its stops, giving her time to become more depressed than she had been. To add to the black cloud that seemed to hang above her, was the ugly desolation of eastern Colorado. It wasn't at all what she had imagined the state to be. As far as her warped eyes could see the land looked dead and dry with sparse, tired-looking weeds and scrub the only living things.

This view didn't change for the next few hours, not until they were practically in Denver itself. She didn't know it was Denver until the driver called to her.

"Hey...little girl. This is you." He pointed out the door.

Odd looked out the window, wondering if a joke had been played on her. They weren't a mile in the air. There weren't cliffs or chasms; it wasn't even hilly. "This is Denver?" she asked coming off the bus and staring around. "Aren't there supposed to be mountains here? And didn't you say we'd be a mile up?"

The man gave a weary chuckle and said, "We are. It's just the slope up is so gradual you can't really tell. Now about those mountains, follow me." They went around the side of the bus depot. "What do you call those?" The entire western skyline ran high with white topped peaks. They were like a wall, a barrier to the other side of the world.

"Isn't California that way? Is there a road that actually goes up there?"

"Oh yeah. It's beautiful."

The driver showed Odd where to go for her transfer and told her not to worry. This she ignored. She sweated out the minutes, twisting the ticket in her hand, as her toes went numb with cold. Other people waited inside the station, but she was too afraid to miss her bus so she stood outside.

She worried for nothing. The bus came, people got off, she got on, and it left. The mountains were indeed beautiful. Sitting alone, she stared in wonder at the views. Majestic peaks, rushing rivers, gorgeous forests, but mostly what she saw was the back of her eyelids. Her infection and grief, as well as her sleepless night kept her asleep until they were well into Utah.

She woke to find herself with her head in the expansive lap of a toad-faced old woman. Bleary-eyed, Odd made to sit up, but soft hands that ended in what felt to be talons held her down.

"There, there. Go back to sleep," the toad-faced woman crooned. "It's ok with Grammy."

It wasn't ok with Odd. "No...no thank you. Please let go." The woman tried to hold Odd's head in her lap, while the little girl squirmed.

"Go back to sleep—go back to sleep."

"Stop it!" Odd didn't yell, but the words were harsh. The woman released her grip, giving Odd a hurt face.

"That's no way to treat your Grammy!"

Odd sat up straighter to look over the seats. The bus was mostly empty and no one was within three seats of them in any direction. Why was this woman there?

"Go sit somewhere else...please." Odd wasn't one for confrontation, especially not with adults, and very especially not with strange, scary looking adults.

"When we get home you are in for one hell of a spanking. How dare you talk to your Gammy that way! Oh, the sass! You'll get a spanking and I'm gonna wash your mouth with soap. That'll teach you some manners." Too quick for Odd's eyes to follow, the woman reached out and pinched her arm savagely.

Odd stared, aghast. Who was this lady? What was going on? Should she call out for the bus driver to help her? She hadn't really paid attention to this driver. What if he believed the woman over Odd? Would she be forced to go with this evil hag?

The word evil rang up an idea in Odd's mind. With a shaking hand she pulled down her glasses and looked at the woman. "Go sit somewhere else," Odd commanded in her quiet, little girl's voice.

One second of silence went by before the toad-faced woman screamed and threw herself into the aisle. "Demon! Help! She's a..."

A screaming woman on his bus caused the driver to react. He stomped on the brake with more pressure than he realized and sent the woman tumbling up the aisle, still screaming. By the time the bus pulled to the side of the road everyone was awake and eyeing the disheveled woman like she had a disease.

"There's a demon! That girl's a demon. Someone do something!" the woman wailed. Odd only shrugged her shoulders, doing her best to look meek. It wasn't difficult. The woman's reaction was far more extreme than Odd had expected and she was in a state of panic that people would now demand she show her eyes as proof of her humanity.

The driver came back and barely cast an eye in Odd's direction before turning to the woman. "There's nothing here. Either calm down or get off the bus..."

"But that girl's a demon!"

"Alright. Off the bus. Let's go."

The woman immediately sat, looking contrite. "No...I'm not at my stop. I don't get out here. I get out at Cedar City. Not here. My son is gonna pick me up at the station. He promised."

With a tired sigh and a final warning to the woman to remain seated, the driver got the bus going again.

Not a minute later a girl—a strange girl with

black, spiked hair and facial piercings—came from the back row and sat across from Odd. "What did you do? That old biddy, like, freaked out. I never saw nothing so funny when she went rolling up the aisle."

Now that it was clear that no one was going to confront her, Odd was able to smile. The woman had been funny, after all. "She wasn't right in the head. She thought I was her granddaughter...and then she just went crazy."

"People are so, like, weird. So, where you going?"

"California. Los Angeles—have you heard of that?"

The girl snorted. "Uh...L.A? Who hasn't? I'm going there myself. I'm going to be a star. Ultimately, I want to be a movie-star, but I'll take TV if that's what I can get."

"Wow." The girl's conviction impressed Odd. She slipped into the aisle seat so she could get a better look at her piercings. "How do you become a star? Is it hard?"

"Here's the deal, Lil' Sis. It's all up to fate. I'm destined to become a star—so I'll become one. People with my same fate get discovered all the time. Walking down the street, sitting in a park, whatever. They're just minding their own business and just like that some director comes up to them and asks: *Hey, you wanna star in my movie? You'd be perfect for such and such role.* You see?"

"Yeah, I think so." Knowing that she was ignorant on so many subjects, Odd rarely doubted people. If this girl said people in the movies were discovered this way she didn't question it. She only questioned what sort of movie the girl would star in.

Odd couldn't watch movies, but she did like to look at pictures of stars in magazines. This girl looked like none of them. She had tiny silver dumbbells going through both her eyebrows and her ears, dots of silver pierced her cheeks next to her mouth, and tattoos ran up her neck. In Odd's opinion she would've been prettier without them.

The girl went on, "I've known since I was, like, a little girl that I'll be a star. I even changed my name to Desty—you know short for Destiny? Pretty cool, huh?"

Odd nodded and the girl went on...and on. Desty talked for hours with surprising stamina. Odd didn't mind. She had been bored and lonely, and when she wasn't sleeping, her mind kept stealing back to the image of Connie dropping gently backwards, replaying it over and over again.

Finally, after about three hours had passed, Desty ran out of things concerning herself to talk about. "You're the quietest girl I ever met. You should tell me something about you. I don't even know your name."

"My name is Odd. It's short for Audrey."

"Odd? Naw, stick with Audrey. You know, like Audrey Hepburn. Odd doesn't sound good. So are you going to L.A. to be a star too? You got the big movie star glasses...hey, can I try them on?"

Odd sent a hand up to her glasses and she leaned back. "No. I'm sorry but the light hurts my eyes. I need them. And I'm not going to be a star. I'm going to California to fi...to be with my mom."

"That's cool. Mom's are cool, right?"

Odd agreed, but with only a nod. Sometimes moms weren't cool. Sometimes they were horrible, but sometimes horrible was better than being alone. And, with Connie gone, Odd had never felt more alone.

Desty then spent the remainder of the trip sleeping or talking. Odd slept when Desty slept and listened when Desty spoke; there wasn't anything else for her to do. The landscape varied little throughout Utah, Nevada, and southern California. Desert and more desert. A dry, barren wasteland that did nothing to help her depression.

Eventually, long after the sun had set on her second day of travel, the lights of Los Angeles greeted the weary girl. At first they lifted her spirits, but then, slowly, as the size of the city began to unveil itself to her, Odd sagged in her seat.

"Do you know where Long Beach Boulevard near Fifty-Fourth is?" she asked. By now the bus had filled again and Desty had moved over next to the little girl.

"No. I've never been here. Which stop are you getting off at?" Odd wanted to say the Los Angeles stop, but got the feeing there might be a few of them. She shrugged which made Desty stare in amazement. "Isn't your mom meeting you?"

"No. All I know is she's at a bar on Long Beach Boulevard near Fifty-Fourth."

"A bar? That's messed up. How are you supposed to get there? Do you have any money for a taxi?"

Frugal by necessity, Odd had spent only four dollars in the last two days. She had purchased a bottle of soda and had been refilling it with water at every other stop. She had also bought three very small bags of chips, which she had spread out over the two days. She was famished and had begun daydreaming of the mountains of food Peach had made at every meal.

"I've got some money...thirty-eight dollars. But I should..."

Desty shook her head. "Thirty-eight dollars? You better hope this bar is close. My boy friend says the taxis are outrageous out here. They even charge you for sitting in traffic. He says you can go like six blocks and they'll charge you ten bucks because the traffics so bad."

"Oh." Odd was wondering what sort of walk she would have in the immense city, when Desty snapped her fingers.

"I got an idea. My boy friend will give you a ride. You'll have to pony up your money, but we'll get you there."

"How much?"

Odd feared to part with even a penny. What would happen if her mom wasn't at the bar? She'd need money for a place to stay for at least a night, maybe even two and she had to think of food as well.

"I don't know, twenty. Probably not more than twenty. It depends on how far it is." Desty said, and then went on a long one-woman lecture over the wonders of her boyfriend, which, as it turned out, in no way jibed with reality.

An hour later a sharp, angular faced young man took one look at the twenty dollar bill and another look at Odd, torqued his face into a look of disgust and said, "Hell no."

Chapter 40

"That's way down past Compton," the boy said. Odd classified him as a boy mostly because of Desty, who was eighteen, and the fact that he dressed like your average teenager with sagging pants and a baseball cap cocked at an angle off the side of his head. On the man side, he had length to him, towering over Odd, and his hair had already begun to recede.

"So?" Desty replied in a whiny voice. "Brute, she's got money. Thirty-eight bucks."

Brutus—as he called himself—thought this over, looking at Odd with a calculating eye. "I guess I could."

"But I can't spend all my money. I still have to..."

"Then you'll never get there, will you?" Brutus said with a nasty tone in his voice. "A cab will run you fifty bucks, easy. Or you could walk, but you'd never make it through Compton. Hell, you'd never make it *to* Compton. You know how many gangs there are between here and there? You know how many pervs there are roaming the streets?"

"Odd, it's only thirty-eight bucks," Desty said reassuringly. "It'll be cool once you get to your mom's. Here, let's have the money."

The pair had so thoroughly intimidated Odd that she handed over all of her cash. In her heart she knew it was a bad idea. Yet what could she do? Los Angeles wasn't like Toledo, or Juliet, or even Cleveland. Los

Angeles went on forever. At this time in the evening, a bus could zip through all of Cleveland in twenty minutes, but they had been on the bus for an hour after Desty told her they were in the Los Angeles, and there was so much more to it still.

"Brute, do you have any grass?" Desty asked, giving a twenty to her boy friend. "That bus ride really has me wired."

The boy snatched the remainder of the cash from her hand with a smile. "Nope, but now we can score some."

At this point Odd became an afterthought. Brutus loaded Desty's bags into the bed of his Ford Ranger—neither of them commenting on Odd's lack of luggage—and then stowed the girl in the cramped back seat. They drove off, going God only knows where, and Odd could do nothing but hope that they would get her to her destination.

They didn't. Instead they drove into a seedy looking neighborhood, and pulled up in front of a house, the front yard of which was strewn with all sorts of trash and rusting car parts. Brutus tasked Odd with guarding over the bags and the truck, and went inside. Odd wondered at the wisdom of this. What could she do if someone took them? Scream? No, she wouldn't scream. She wouldn't do anything to call attention to herself.

Odd locked the doors and slunk low into the back seat, jumping at every sound. Soon her lips started quivering and her hands took to shaking; she pulled on her gloves and acorn hat. Wasn't California supposed to be hot? The temperature hovered around fifty degrees, which wasn't bad, but sitting in the cold truck, Odd was uncomfortably chilly. She had expected it to be warmer.

Laughter—wild, braying laughter—erupted from the house. Then came giggling and snorting. This went on for over an hour. By the time Brutus and Desty came out—still giggling over something—Odd had retreated turtle-like into her coat again. Her mouth drooped at the corners as she remembered showing Connie her turtle imitation when they had been freezing on the train.

"Can you drop me off now?" she asked, trying not to wrinkle her nose as they came in. The two stank of pot and cigarettes.

"We'll get you there, don't worry, Lil' Sis," Desty said. "Hey, let me see those glasses." Before Odd knew it her glasses were snatched from her face. Quickly her hand came up to block her eyes from being seen. "How do I look? Brute, what do you think?"

"Like a bug," he said and then began to giggle, his facing turning red. "You look like a bug."

"I don't! Do I?" she cried, turning on the overhead dome and cranking the rear view mirror around to herself. "I look like a star. They wear these big glasses to keep from being recognized. Duh."

With her hand poised above her forehead, Odd said, "I need my glasses back. My eyes hurt without..."

Still admiring herself, Desty interrupted, "That's all in your head. These aren't prescription, you know. They're just normal sunglasses."

Odd didn't know what she meant by prescription, a word that always meant pills in her mind. "I know but the light hurts my..."

"It's dark out!"

"Just give the girl those stupid things." Brutus

tore the glasses off his girlfriend and flung them in the back seat without caring where they went. "You look better without them, babe. So stop your pouting. And you," he turned to Odd, who was just righting herself after finding her glasses. "You should be a little more grateful. Destiny takes you under her wing all the way from Provo and this how you repay her? You should be damn happy that she's letting you tag along with us."

"I—I am grateful, but I want to find my mother. You said you'd drive me. I just..."

"And I will!" He turned to Desty. "Give that brat a hit of your sess-pipe before I lose my temper. She needs to calm the hell down."

The pierced girl cast a dark look back at Odd. "No way. I'm not wasting primo sess on her. You'll be good, won't you, Odd? You don't want to ruin Brute's high. He gets a little cranky when that happens."

"Too late for that," Brute said, cramming a cigarette into his mouth. He worked the Ford hard, sending Odd thumping back. "You know what? I don't think the bud was all that good. The flash was good, but now? Nothing!"

"It'll be ok, Brute. When we get to Pam's, she'll hook us up real good." Desty rubbed her boyfriend's shoulders and then looked back at Odd. "You'll like Pam. She came out last June; right after graduation, to get her start singing. Did I tell you she sings?"

"Yes. On the bus." She'd heard all about Pam as well as a great many other people that, supposedly, she'd 'just love'. After meeting Brutus, however, Odd doubted it.

Desty sat back, looking dreamy. "Right. On the bus. That was a helluva trip. *The wheels on the bus go round and round. Round and round...*" she sang until Brutus flicked on the radio, cranking it to decibels that had Odd's eardrums quaking.

"I hate that damned song," Brutus snarled.

Desty only giggled, turning beet-red. "This is why you should never-ever drink tequila. It makes you so cranky even good sess can't make you happy. You know what you should drink...how old are you, Odd? Twelve? Screwdrivers, that's what I drank when I was twelve. And it's good for you. All that vitamin C and pulp and Smirnoff. So don't worry about that. Pam will set you up, too."

Brutus drove them into another, seedier neighborhood, which even had Desty looking around, no longer giggling stupidly. "We ain't got nothing like this in Provo," she said.

"You ain't ever been more right," Brutus agreed. "But you'll be fine. Just act like you belong."

They allowed Odd to come in this time. It was a toss-up whether it would've been better to shiver in the car than to go into the foul smelling den, but the neighborhood was just too scary for Odd to stay alone outside.

The house reeked of smoke and drugs, of unwashed bodies, sour milk, and garbage. If she had food in her stomach it likely would've come up. As it was, the little girl turned green and glanced around wondering if anyone would notice if she vomited on the threadbare carpet.

She didn't think it likely. Everywhere she looked people sat stoned, or baked, or tripping, or drunk, or all of the above. For the first hour, Odd stuck close to Desty and her horror of a friend, Pam. Never in her life had Odd ever seen anyone so riddled with holes. Steel pierced her nose, her eyelids, and eyebrows, her cheeks, her lips, her mouth and her forehead. The worst of all was her tongue which sported three steel balls, front to back, right down the middle.

It made her almost impossible to understand and, coupled with the many drugs in her system, she sounded very much like a retarded kid. Even Desty eyed her with an uncomfortable look until she became too drunk to care. All the while, Odd kept to herself, though a few people inquired about her after an uncaring fashion.

"Searching for your mother? That's cool." This was about the extent of the interest shown in Odd. And this was just fine with her. She wanted, above all else, to be left alone by these vile people. Even the nice ones made her skin crawl. It wasn't just the piercings and the thousands of tattoos the crowd sported, many of them looked diseased. Blistering sores decorated so many mouths that Odd couldn't help but flinch back when spoken to.

Eventually, Desty went into a back room with Brutus where Odd could not follow. So the little girl waited for them on a cracked leather couch in a hallway. Next to her came and sat an Asian girl that Odd figured was about sixteen. She wore a short mini-skirt and a white button up top that hung too far open.

For the moment she was disease free, but it wouldn't last. "I'm so wasted," she said to Odd as soon as she flounced down. "I never been to a party with so much weed!"

Odd didn't know what to say. "Your panties are

showing."

The girl looked down at herself for just a split second before exploding in laughter. "They are! You're so right, dude." She began to work her skirt down but not before a grubby looking man came over and ran his hand up her thigh. She didn't seem to care. Nor did she seem to know who the man was. Odd wanted to choke from his smell.

"Hey, there's a free room downstairs," the man said, his hand going as high as nature would allow. "Let's go talk."

"Talk?"

The man pulled her up. Immediately she sagged and he was forced to almost lift her. "She has a boyfriend," Odd said, feeling protective. She didn't like the hungry look on the man's face, or the empty look in the Asian's eyes. The words had the man second-guessing himself. Leaning back he stared down the hall, trying to see into the living room. Odd added, "He's pretty big."

Unceremoniously he dumped the girl back onto the couch and left, perhaps in search of easier prey. "I have a boyfriend?" she asked and went back to laughing. "Dude, I don't think so. It's sooo weird. Boys don't really date anymore. It's like they're only after one thing and when you give it to them, bam! They're gone. You know what I mean, Cindy. Wait! Ha-ha, I'm Cindy. That's so funny."

Odd smiled to be polite. "My name is Odd." This got Cindy laughing again. She couldn't seem to stop, not for many minutes, until at once she did. And when she did, she promptly fell asleep. Odd did her best to cover Cindy, whose clothes were hiked and open in the most revealing ways. She then set herself as guard over the unconscious girl until around eleven when she noted that the party seemed to be moving to a different location.

"Cindy!" Odd said giving the girl a violent shake. "Get up. Everyone's leaving." The girl blinked up at her stupidly, something Odd didn't have time for. She felt desperate to get out front so that she wouldn't be left behind by Desty and Brutus. "Get up, let's go!"

When the girl could stand on her own, Odd pointed her to the front door and pulled her along. "Hey! Desty?" The girl from the bus was just climbing into Brutus' very full Ford Ranger. "Desty, what about my ride?"

"Oh...it's you," Desty said, slurring her words. "We thought you left already."

"Left?" Odd asked, looking into the cramped back seat and seeing every possible spot filled with bodies. "You were my ride. How could I have..."

Brutus interrupted her, "Desty stop talking to that little pain in the butt. We gotta go. The weed's gone—it's time to move on."

"But, my ride."

"Sorry, Odd. Maybe next time," Desty said. She shut the door with a heavy thud.

Odd's heart began a mad thumping at the idea of being left behind. The little girl stepped up on the runner to look into the truck. "But you promised...and you took my money. If you're not going to give me a ride, then I...I want it back."

"I would if I could, Lil' Sis, but Brute spent it on the weed. Now get off the truck before you get hurt." A chorus of voices from the back seat yelled and cursed in agreement. Odd didn't budge; she gripped the door with both hands.

"No! You owe me a ride," Odd insisted. Making any sort of demand and standing up for herself were very rare occurrences in her life, but she felt she had no option. She had no idea where she was or where Long Beach Boulevard was. If she had known she would've turned away from the truck and begun walking, meekly—a tiny mouse in a world full of cats—hoping not to be noticed. However, with walking away not a choice, she became bold in her desperation and held onto the truck with tight little fingers.

Desty began prying at Odd's fingers. "We don't owe you anything, Lil' Sis. You're lucky you got this far. In fact you owe me for taking you to this party. That was easily worth...fifty bucks. Here, I'll just take these and we'll call it even."

Desty stopped prying at Odd's fingers and took Odd's glasses.

Chapter 41

Odd ducked her head—at first.

"Give 'em back! They're mine," Odd said, surprising herself with the anger in her voice. In her life she had been angry many times—there had been much for her to be angry over—but expressing it was an extraordinary phenomenon. "You know I have an eye problem, Desty."

"And I had one too. I didn't have sunglasses before, and now I do," Desty said with a nasty smile. "Thanks, Lil' Sis." The bigger girl began to polish them on her shirt.

Odd's anger spilled into a rage filled with impotence and screaming desperation. It was one thing to be lost in a sprawling city of four-million people—that she could handle. She'd find someone to help her with food, directions, maybe even a ride. In her heart she knew it could be done; she'd made it this far after all. However, she knew that there'd be no ride, no food, not even directions with her openly displaying her vulgarity. There'd be pointing, staring, whispering. There'd be an eagerness to get far away from her.

"Give them back, or..."

"Or what? You'll call the cops? You'll tell your mommy—the one in a bar somewhere here in L.A? You're not going to do jack but get off this truck before Brute scrapes you off on that fence."

Odd still didn't budge. "Give them back, or you'll be sorry."

The three people in the back all said, "Ooooh," as a chorus, before cracking up with laughter. Desty didn't share in the mirth. She had just noticed Odd's red eyes and was staring at Odd with her mouth hung open in horror. The little girl had lifted her head into the light given off by an overhead streetlamp.

"It's contagious, Desty. You'll look just like me," Odd lied in a calm voice. The quiet serious tone had Brutus' and the other passenger's attention and they too stared.

The staring, a silent, horribly embarrassing few moments, ended with everyone screaming in the truck in unison. Desty threw the glasses out the window, while Brutus first gunned the truck, and then jerked it to a halt, sending Odd flying.

Luckily Cindy had been standing right there the entire time and caught the girl. They fell together in a mash, which set the Asian giggling again.

"Cindy don't touch that girl," someone from the truck yelled. "She's got red eyes!"

Cindy took this as a joke. "You should see your eyes, Joan. You look totally baked." She then became insensible with laughter. The more the people in the truck tried to get her to see the supposed danger she was in being so close to Odd, the harder Cindy laughed. Eventually Brutus, with Desty urging him on, simply threw his hands up and drove away.

After finding her glasses Odd laid back next to Cindy and looked up at the few stars there were to see. Strangely, though the night was a clear, bright one, there weren't half as many stars out as she was used to seeing. Where were they all? Did stars experience day and night also? Was it nighttime for some of the stars?

Were they dark and sleepy? Odd certainly was.

Two straight days on a bus had left her a jangle of nerves with heavy eyes. Had it been even a little warmer out she could've fallen asleep right there on the front lawn of the drug-house, amongst the broken bottles and cigarette butts. Next to her Cindy appeared to have fallen asleep again. Looking at her, Odd wondered how she wasn't freezing to death. Her short skirt had hiked itself into a broad belt at her waist and her top was held closed by a scant two buttons.

Odd touched her arm and found that her skin felt freezing. "Cindy. Wake up! You're going to freeze to death. Where's your coat?"

The girl sat up blinking stupidly. "I don't have a coat, dude. Where's my shoe?"

Odd spotted it next to the front door. She also spotted someone staring out at them from the house. "Here, put it on. I think that creepy guy is watching us. You remember...never mind. Let's get out of here."

The little girl started walking Cindy to the street when Cindy pulled back. "Little dude! My car. I'm not walking back to Huntington."

"Is Huntington close to Long Beach Boulevard near Fifty-Fourth?"

The girl screwed up her eyes. "You need a ride? To Long Beach?"

How badly she wanted to say *yes*, but she could see that Cindy could hardly keep her bloodshot eyes open. "Are you ok to drive?"

"Dude, I drive better stoned than when I'm sober. It's like I'm hyper-aware that I shouldn't be driving and so I get all, like, super-para."

"Super-para? What does that mean?" Odd

thought that she meant driving fast and her hand stopped just as she swung the door out.

From inside the car, the girl spoke over the sound of her engine, "Super paranoid. You know when you're all freaked out and think every car behind you is an undercover cop. You'll see."

At first Cindy drove as well—meaning slowly—as she had said she would. Then she started weaving, her eyes drooping lower and lower. Odd did her best to keep her awake, asking the girl about herself and her family, where she lived, anything to keep her awake. Unfortunately this didn't help her driving at all—in fact, it made it worse, because Cindy tended to turn and face Odd when she spoke. It was as though she thought the car would drive itself, while she carried on a conversation.

Soon Odd's eyes whirled as they danced back and forth between Cindy, the road, and the rushing headlights that seemed always to miss them by inches. The only time Cindy would glance back to the road was when Odd would talk. Unfortunately, Odd wasn't in the most talkative mood. She was dog-tired and had the shakes from lack of food.

Yet worse than that Odd could only think of depressing topics: Connie's suicide, being forced to leave Abe and Peach and the farm, being abandoned by her mother. None of this she could force out of her mouth; it still hurt far too much. She dug Abe's ring from her pocket and stared at it, wishing it was a magic ring that would grant her wishes.

This gave her an idea and she started talking about a girl named Sprite. That girl had a beautiful best friend, who called her brave. She had grandparents who loved her and who gave her a magical golden ring that would bring her food when she grew hungry and a bed when she became tired. Sprite was on a mission to find her mother who had been swept away by an evil wind. With the help of the ring, she overcame many obstacles: ferocious beasts, evil men, and tragic sorrow. She went on a great journey and, in the end, she found her mother and the two lived happily together forever.

This spun out of her mouth with ease. Her imagination, honed through constant use, made it simple. What also helped was that she didn't really think Cindy was listening. The older girl barely blinked and never said a word until Odd finished her fairy tale.

"Cool story, Odd," Cindy said. "And you're Sprite, aren't you?"

"No, I—I'm not." Her cheeks felt red.

Cindy took her eyes off the road. "It's ok. I know you are. For one, you're not from around here. You're clearly parentless...I mean it's midnight and you're out partying. Heck, you even have the ring in your hand..."

Though it looked brown to her, Odd screamed, "Red light!"

How long it took Cindy to mentally process the scream, Odd didn't know, but it sure felt like ages before she pitched forward and the tires screamed. A moment later, with horns blaring, the nose of the car stopped, jutting well into the intersection. The sudden stop had the two girls bucking back and forth, and of course Cindy began to laugh.

"Dude...Dude...that was so totally close. We almost got hit. Did you see how close that was?"

Odd hadn't. Her eyes had been closed, hard, and

her teeth gritted against a collision she had been sure was coming. "Can you please look at the road when you talk? It's...it scares me when you don't."

"Sure, sure, no problemo," Cindy assured her. "I do that sometime, you know. I just like to see how the person I'm talking to..."

Odd interrupted, "The light's green. You can go."

This had the girl snorting with barely suppressed laughter. "I'll look for now on. Hey...where are we?"

"I don't know." Odd said. "I thought you knew where we were going."

Cindy blew out in exasperation. "I know where we're going...Long Beach. But where are we now? Hmm...Alameda and Del Amo. It's the one thing I don't like about pot. You get in your car and drive and when you look up you're like in the middle of nowhere. It's like: How did I get so far out in the boonies, right? You know what I mean? I think I want to go east. Hold on." Cat-like, with her sharp nails digging into the leather, Odd held on as the car darted left in front of oncoming traffic. "Yeah, yeah, yeah," Cindy said to the many horns blaring.

"There s-sure are a lot of c-cars for this late at night," Odd warbled in an attempt to make small talk. The lights of the cars they had cut across had blinded her and riding sightless with the pot-infused girl had her panicky.

"Midnight isn't late for Saturday night, Odd. It's the witching hour you know. You should put that in your story. I could be the witch. Dude! I'd make a good witch. You know what you...hold on."

The girls cell phone began to ring somewhere under her seat. Odd watched in amazement as she ducked completely under the wheel and retrieved it.

"Joan! You bit...I mean you...B...I...T...C...H. Where are you?" Cindy listened for a few minutes with barely an interruption before she exclaimed, "Dump the brat? No, that's mean. Hold on, Odd." The girl took a sharp right, hitting the curb with such force that Abe's wedding ring bounced out of Odd's hand and dropped to the floor.

Odd ducked down searching in a panic. It was nowhere to be seen. Running her hands all along the carpeting didn't help either. Quickly she undid her seat belt and turned her tiny body around to squat down in the footwell.

"Just a sec, Joan," Cindy said. "Odd, what're you doing?"

"I dropped my ring," she said, looking up to see Cindy staring down at her. Headlights from the opposite lane began to change their angle lighting up her face. "Cindy! Look at the road."

The car swerved hard to the right and Cindy burst out laughing. "I'm still flying, Joan. That was primo..."

Odd tuned her out. She had to concentrate. Her fingers ran along the metal of the underside of the chair, searching—searching. The ring had to be there somewhere. It couldn't just disappear. Just as Cindy broke out in another case of the giggles, Odd found it. Up until that moment she was so panicked at the loss of the ring that her sudden relief made her want to giggle as well.

"Hey, Cindy. I found my ring. It was sitting..."

Odd stopped talking as her eyes went wide. Cindy had turned at the sound of her name and as the words were leaving her lips again she saw the angle of the light on her face track from her left ear all the way to dead center. They were heading straight into oncoming traffic.

Chapter 42

Odd could do nothing but roll herself into a ball and hope that the collision wouldn't crush her completely. The car felt to sway like a rudderless ship and then noises of all sorts erupted around her: screams, horns, breaking glass and a long, ripping-grinding noise of metal tearing at metal. It sounded as though Cindy's car was actually eating another car.

She felt and heard, but did not see. She had been sitting in the footwell facing backwards and at the look of alarm on Cindy's face, Odd had closed her eyes as meager protection from what she knew was coming.

Now she sat there, blinking in the dark, the car still vibrating from the crash. She couldn't figure out if she had been hurt. Her upper right arm ached, but that was still the pain from Ike's bite. That was it. But what about Cindy?

Odd tried to turn her head in that direction, but something above her—something that hadn't been there before—prevented her. When she put her hand up she felt jagged metal. All around her was jagged metal, as if she were in the mouth of a steel beast.

Feeling a far greater panic over this than she had at the loss of the ring, Odd called out in a tremulous voice, "Cindy? Are you there? Are you ok?"

"Odd! Oh my God, are you alright?" The voice seemed strangely muffled.

"Yeah, I think so. I'm just trapped."

"Hold on!" Cindy called. Odd then heard a door

open and then many voices rising and falling. The voices were a blessing, but more of a blessing was the light that streamed in when the door opened. It filled her with immediate relief. However that feeling was short-lived. More lights came into view. Red and blue seemed to reach out and slap at the dark. The police were coming! They'd know who she was and they'd take her back.

That couldn't happen, not now, not when she was so close. Odd squirmed lower down so she could get a sense where the light was coming in and saw a gaping hole that ran at least ten inches wide toward the driver's side door. She didn't hesitate. Pushing as far back as she could, Odd shrunk as low as possible and slithered into the hole. On one side sat the plastic casing of the automatic transmission, on the other, part of the crushed-in console.

Odd opted to slide as far toward the gearbox as possible where the plastic was smooth, yet she still got stuck. The panic which had been controlled to a point by her action, now came screaming back. She was caught up around the chest and no amount of wiggling would free her.

"Help!" she screamed.

"Hold on," a man's voice called to her. "The fire department will be here in a moment."

"No, Mister. You have to help me. I'm caught on something and I can't get around it."

"Just wait..."

"Please no. It hurts." It did, too. Every breath sent the object cutting into her chest. Suddenly, she saw a hand that looked as black as midnight snake toward her. It felt around and then began yanking hard at something unseen. Each yank made her want to scream, but she didn't dare because she knew the man would stop. Finally the object snapped away and Odd felt blood run hot, down into her coat. She didn't care. She began squirming harder and then the hands were there again, pulling her and sliding her free.

"There, there child you're ok," crooned a black man with a shaved head and rimless glasses. He was tall and had to go down on one knee to hold the little girl up. For the moment Odd cuddled up to him, leaning against his chest, exhausted and shaking.

Cindy came up to them, walking like a zombie, taking slow uncertain steps. "I can't believe you're alive. I thought for sure that you'd be dead. No one could survive that." She pointed with a shaking hand at the remains of her car.

Odd turned and saw that the car had careened away from the oncoming traffic right into a row of parked cars before sliding partially under a pick-up truck. Where Odd had been sitting only a few minutes previous was completely crushed in. The little girl wanted to faint. Her head spun at the sight and her knees buckled, but the man was still holding her gently.

"That's a miracle if I ever saw one," he said. "You should thank God that you're still alive."

"Thank you, God," she said obediently. "And thank you too, mister. Thanks for pulling me out of there. You are very nice...but I have to go." Odd tried to pull away. The fire trucks were just pulling up, and behind them a police car elbowed its way through the late night traffic jam.

"No. No. Sorry, but you have to get looked at and they..."

Odd pulled harder. "I can't, please. Mister, I'm a runaway. I can't go back there. They'll send me back." The man opened his mouth but didn't say anything, seeming unable to come to a decision. Odd's hand went to her glasses. She would show him her eyes, perhaps frighten enough to make him let go of her.

However he did it on his own. "Ok. I won't stop you," he said , standing up. "Who knows, maybe God wants you to go, right? I mean if he wanted you dead, you'd be dead. And if he wanted you to stay, you'd still be trapped. I mean, really, that's a miracle. I still can't believe it."

"Neither can I." Odd had trouble understanding or believing anything. All she could think of was getting out of there. "Thanks for helping me," she said and turned to Cindy, but the older girl was lost in her own world and only stared dazedly at the wreck of her car as if nothing else mattered. Odd went around it and then slunk away, hoping that no one had spotter her. Someone did.

"Odd, where are you going?" It was Cindy. She had come around the wreck but didn't move any further toward the little girl.

"To find my mom. What direction is Long Beach Boulevard near Fifty-Fourth?"

The girl pointed with a limp arm. "I don't know. I just know that Long Beach is right down that street," she pointed with a limp arm. "Probably only a mile." Odd started walking again. "Good luck," Cindy called after her.

Odd kept walking. To turn meant to risk falling; she felt light-headed and weak. "Thanks...you too. Good bye, Cindy."

"See ya."

Odd walked the mile, looking for any bar with the word cantina in its name. There weren't any, which saved her from wasting her time. Long Beach was simply too nice for her mother's tastes. Not only that, the street numbers were counting down. By the time she got to Second Street, she could hear the waves and see a thick darkness ahead.

Her first time seeing the ocean wasn't in any way awe inspiring or majestic. Her head thumped with a dull ache. Her chest trickled blood from a still unseen wound and Odd was close to exhaustion. Still, she forced herself out onto the sand and struggled through it until she came to the water's edge. There she knelt, touched the water—felt its cold—and then tasted it.

"What the heck?" she said spitting to clear her mouth. The water couldn't have been worse tasting. Thinking that California wasn't anywhere near as nice as she had hoped it would be, Odd walked back the way she had come. It was slow going. Without the will or the energy to hurry she tottered on, sometimes using buildings to hold herself up. She didn't even need to detour around the scene of the accident; by the time she reached it, all the cars involved had been towed away.

Odd headed north, following the streets as they clicked slowly up. After twenty-five blocks she knew she wouldn't be able to make it much further. Her plan was to get to Fifty-Fourth and then ask where Long Beach Boulevard was. By Twenty-Fifth Street she began looking for a place to rest. Anywhere that was the slightest bit warm would suit her, but she didn't get lucky with a steam vent as she had before.

Instead she got lucky with a prostitute.

"Whoa, this ain't no place for a kiddie stroll, baby." The words had Odd looking around in slow surprise. She had been so wrapped up putting one foot in front of the other that she didn't see the small gaggle of women standing against on the corner. One of the three, wearing a short fur coat and an even shorter skirt stepped forward.

"The kiddies play in West Hollywood, not in Long Beach. So just move it on."

Odd lacked the strength to question this. "Ok," she said, before stepping to the side to detour around the women. She stepped too far back and stumbled into the street. Odd lay where she had fallen. The gutter was just too comfortable compared to standing or walking and her body demanded rest. She laid her head down in the cold street and listened.

"Get on up, you, before a street sweeper comes by and sucks you up!"

"Man, she's awful small to be all strung out. What a damn shame."

"I can't believe you. You so manipulated! You only think that 'cos she white. Look how many teenie crack-whores you find in Watts and when do I ever hear you crying over them? You whities all stick together."

"First of all, I ain't white. You ever heard of Mexico? You ever look at a map? The only white people we got down there are tourists. Second, Watts is a damn shame. That whole part of the city is one big shame...hold on...Hey, baby. You lookin' for a date. No? We could have some fun...If you ever get lonely you come on back. See ya. Bye...pendejo. Where was I?"

"You were running your mouth, that's where.

We gotta move that girl. A little kid laying in the gutter is bad for business. Inez, you do it since you care so much."

Odd heard the light clicking of stilettos on pavement and then felt a hand give her a shake. "Hey you? You can't lay here. Come on get up."

Her limbs had begun to go stiff with the cold anyway, so Odd pushed herself up and stood swaying, looking at a rail-thin Mexican prostitute dressed in a shimmering, tight, pink dress. The material appeared so soft that without thinking Odd reached out and touched the woman's side.

"That's soft. What is it?"

Inez looked down at her skimpy outfit. "I don't know. I think it's like some sort of cashmere knock-off." She then gave Odd a closer look. "Are you on crack? What are you doing, meth?"

Odd had heard of these drugs before. It was kind of hard not to have growing up in the places she had. "No. I don't do drugs."

"She on somethin'," one of the prostitutes said. "Look at her. She dancin' wit the wind."

"I was in a car accident," Odd explained. "I—I just don't feel good."

"Well that's your too bad. Go up the street and don't feel good up there. We got work to do still."

Inez gave the woman a sharp look. "You know what's wrong with you, Tiesha? You got nothing left inside you, and that's why you never pick up a repeat. They'd rather go jack-it than be with a ho who ain't got no feelings. Come on, girlfriend. Let's get inside and see what's going on."

Tiesha didn't look like one to stew over an

insult. "Go on whitey. See what Trey does to you when he finds out you ain't on the street."

The women had been lingering just down the block from one of those cheap motels that Odd had called home for most of her life. At Tiesha's warning Inez had stiffened, but kept walking.

"It's ok, Ma'am," Odd said to Inez. "I don't want you to get in trouble. I'll be fine." She didn't feel fine, however, and the woman in the pink dress knew it.

Inez guided her into one of the lower floor rooms of the motel. "Are you hurt? Take off your coat—without falling over! Here, sit on the chair."

Odd sat simply because Inez moved her to the chair and it struck her behind the knees. "I think all I got is a cut on my ribs. And it hurts where the dog bit me and my head is swimming," she said, seeing the prostitute in the light for the first time. Inez wasn't much to look at. She had wide gaps in her teeth, her nose looked squashed in, and her skin had been ravaged by acne at one time.

Yet for all that, Odd could understand why she would get repeat customers; she had a kind, personable air about her which was comforting and immediately friendly. "You were bit by a dog? Where?" Inez asked.

"Illinois."

"No. I mean where on your body?" This she asked with a smile on her face. Odd was too done-in to care about modesty and she stripped off her shirt. The gash on her lower chest wasn't bad, though the shirt was wet with her blood. She also sported bruising on her back and down her left arm where some part of Cindy's car had punched into her during the collision.

"Wait right here," Inez ordered. "I'm going to

get something to clean you up. I forgot to ask, what's your name?"

"Odd," she replied listlessly.

Inez wrinkled her face in amusement at that. "Odd? Ok Odd, is there someone we should call, while I'm at the office? Mom...dad, sister? Anyone?"

"No."

"You a runaway? Because, I gotta tell you that most of the girls working the streets are runaways. I think you should..."

Odd interrupted, "I'm not really a runaway like you're talking about. My mom got stuck out here and I came from Illinois to find her. I got picked up by Social Services and it's them I ran away from."

"Oh, that's different," Inez said looking relieved. "I was about to call the cops on you. Ok wait here."

Odd sat in the chair, half-naked. With the room agreeably warm she fell asleep in less than a minute. She woke sometime later, at Inez's touch.

"You were out of it, weren't you?" the prostitute said with a gentle smile as she cleaned Odd's wound. "This may become infected if you're not careful."

"I have anti-biotics for the dog bite. Will it help this cut too?" Odd had been taking her pills morning and night.

"I think so...I'm pretty sure," Inez answered as she started laying a string of Mickey Mouse band-aids across the gash. She glanced at the clock. "Look, I gotta get back to work." For a few seconds the two just looked at each other before Odd realized that she was being asked to leave.

"Oh, right. Sorry about this. I hope I'm not getting you in trouble." Odd winced as she tried to put on her stained shirt. There hadn't been much initial pain after the accident, but now she began to ache all over.

"Odd, what are you going to do? Do you have a place to stay?"

The little girl shook her head, zipping up her heavy coat. "No, but I'll find somewhere warm. Thanks for helping me."

It was Inez who now looked to be in pain. "I'd let you stay here, but Trey would kill me."

"Please, don't worry." Odd wasn't much worried. Worrying took energy and she didn't have any left. She would walk north until she fell over and after that she didn't much care what would happen to her. Odd made it to the door before Inez pulled her back.

"I can't do this. I can't let you walk out there. I got an idea! You can stay in the closet. I know it's not much, but it'll be warm." The prostitute ran to a dresser and pulled out some white sheets. "These are all clean, I promise. You can use this one as a pillow, and these three as bedding. What do you think?"

On the verge of collapse the twelve-year-old could only nod. Inez's smile then faltered a little. "Listen, two things: you gotta be out of here by ten tomorrow morning. That's when they clean the room. And...and...and if you hear anything, any moans or screams or anything, just keep quiet and stay in the closet. I mean it when I say we'll both catch a beating if you disturb any of the...guests."

Chapter 43

Odd didn't hear anything that night. Not even the door closing as Inez left her. She slept in a little ball with her sunglasses near at hand and Abe's ring pushed down over one of her thumbs.

In the morning she took stock of herself: right arm—healing; chest—sore to the touch; back and neck—aching. She then laid out her meager possessions: one gold ring—possibly magical, a hairbrush—filled with long strands of Connie's beautiful brown hair, a pair of sun glasses—gathering scratches, a half-filled water bottle and a container of fat pills, one of which she popped into her mouth immediately. And last, her warm gloves.

Her acorn hat was nowhere in the room and she had to wonder if it was still in Cindy's smushed car. She didn't care past the fact that now she would have to brush her hair more frequently. As she left the motel she took to running the brush through her blonde hair, thinking about how it was only a few days ago that Connie had done this for her. She remembered how good it had felt.

She walked north. Though it was still early she began to sweat and so she took off her coat, wrapping it around her waist, using the sleeves to tie a knot. The street she walked along had the name Cherry, which she mistook for cheery. It made her smile thinking someone would name a street that, but the smile didn't last.

It dropped the moment she came to a cemetery.

"All Souls Cemetery," she read from the sign. A place for the dead. It made her wonder if Connie had been put in the ground yet. She didn't like thinking on the subject, only the tombstones went on forever, or so it seemed to the miserable girl.

Would Connie get just get a little squat of a stone? One that would be covered over in grass and ignored for all eternity, or would her parents' guilt force them to get a great slab of marble topped with an angel?

"It doesn't matter," Odd said, using her gloves to wipe under her glasses. "She's in heaven now."

Eventually she left the dead behind.

Lack of food dragged at her. It had been four days since she picked at her lunch at the Greek place and in that time she'd had a few handfuls of chips and water. Still she plodded on until the street numbers began to rise into the fifties and she was all set to cheer when she got to Fifty-Third Street, but the next intersection was Plymouth Street and then Market and then Washington.

"Where's Fifty-Fourth?" she asked aloud in frustration.

"There ain't one. Not 'round here." A tiny black lady, old and so withered that she and Odd could look each other in the eye, stood right next to the girl. Odd had been so preoccupied looking up the street signs that she hadn't even seen her.

"Is there a Long Beach boulevard around here?"

The woman raised her scrawny arm and pointed west. "Bout a mile."

Odd thanked her, and strode off, hoping that there'd be a Fifty-Fourth street by the time she trudged that far. There wasn't, yet it didn't really matter. When she got to the boulevard she saw a shoe repair shop almost immediately.

"Shoe repair?" Odd said aloud as she closed on the shop. She had never heard of such a job before. It was an assumption on her part that most people were like her and simply wore their tennis shoes until they had practically disintegrated into nothing. It made her wonder how much work there could be in the field of shoe repair. Inside the shop, the mayhem of shoes, and boxes, and papers, and receipts certainly seemed to suggest that there was a great deal more work than she could have imagined.

"Hello?" she called out. Like a jack-in-the-box a man popped up from behind the counter. Before her eyes could adjust, Odd saw a man whose baldhead looked to be inflated to the size of a balloon and who had blue eyes the size of fists. Odd put an arm up in front of her face as if to ward the balloon off.

"Oh, sorry to scare you."

"It's alright," Odd replied, blinking behind her glasses. "It's just my...never mind. Is Karen Wyatt here? Do you know her?"

The man had been giving Odd a friendly smile and this now became brittle as if it had been coated in glass. "No. She's not."

Odd felt as though the wind had been drawn out of her own balloon; she didn't have the energy for a second quest. Still she was compelled to ask: "Do you know where she is?"

"Who are you?"

"I'm Odd," she said and then added, "Her daughter?" Mentioning that little fact seemed to constantly slip Karen's mind. "She did say she had a daughter, right?"

"Yeah, but she said you lived with your dad." Was this wishful thinking on her mom's part? Very likely. Odd gave the man a shrug that could've meant anything. He took it to mean he should go on, "Either way, she's not here. She's probably two doors down."

"A bar?" The word 'cantina' came too slowly to her mind. It hardly mattered, Odd was sure there would be a bar in the cantina. There always was a bar when her mom was concerned.

"No. It's bail bondsman company."

A sad fact about Odd's world: she had no clue who Abraham Lincoln was, but the twelve-year-old knew what a bail bondsman was. "Has she been arrested?" Odd had to wonder if she had come all this way only to find her mom in jail?

The man breathed out a sigh, as if the subject pained him. "No. Her new boyfriend, Bully, owns it."

New boyfriend. Odd wasn't at all surprised. Karen could churn through 'boyfriends' at a prodigious pace. Picking their pockets, literally as well as figuratively, as they kissed. Feeling low, Odd, turned to leave, but paused in the doorway. She wanted to apologize to the man for her mom's behavior only she was too tired to make it sound convincing.

Instead she said, "Thanks," and walked out into the bright California sunshine. Pushing her glasses firmly into place on her small nose, she went to the second business along the strip: Bulldog Bail Bondsman.

"Right—'Bully'—I get it now." She had wondered if she had misheard the shoe-repairman when he had said the name, Bully.

Strangely the interior of the business looked more like a pawnshop than anything else. There were guns in glass cases, lawn mowers hanging from the ceiling, guitars and drums and musical instruments of all types as well as an assortment of TVs and stereos.

A man sitting at a desk eyed her close as she walked in. He had a red face as if the California sun burned instead of bronzed; his hair—a uniform grey—had a military air to it and his eyes were grey as well and flinty.

He didn't address Odd in any way, he only stared.

"Excuse me, are you Bully?" she asked, her voice only a whisper under his intense stare.

"You are Audrey," he returned, not at all answering the question.

"Yes, I am. Is my mom here?" she asked in a rush. He waited three seconds to answer, though with Odd holding her breath it felt like three minutes.

"I'm not Bully. I'm Evan," he said. Odd nodded, vaguely. What did this have to do with her mom? He went on, "Up close you look like your mom...same nose, same little cockle ears, same brow line...but you're prettier."

Now Odd's head wagged from side to side. Was I just called pretty? she asked herself. And what did that have to do with anything? The man radiated calm—a dangerous calm and so Odd kept her aggravation in check. "My mom?"

"She's in the office with Bully."

Odd had to reach out and grab the edge of one of the glass cases. Her knees wanted to give out. She felt sick with relief, and hunger...and anger. Right then all three vied for supremacy within her. She pushed her anger back; it would wait. A cheeseburger could not—or pizza—or tacos—or anything.

"Where is the office?"

"You're not expected."

Despite the fact that the man had arms that were corded with muscle and a neck as thick as a tree trunk, Odd's anger crept up. "I don't care! Where's my mother?"

He seemed completely unfazed by the little girl's display of fury. "They think you're still in Illinois. I'm just warning you, Audrey. Remember: Forewarned is forearmed. Think about their reaction when you go barging in. Will they be happy? Will they rejoice to see you? or..."

Odd gazed back at the man. What was he trying to say? "Will they be disappointed?"

"I don't know exactly. Just be ready for anything."

Odd's relief turned to a jelly-like fear in her stomach. "Ok thanks, I will. Where are they?"

Evan stood up and beckoned Odd to follow him as he went through a series of doors to a far back room. He listened at the last door for a moment, knocked once, and then let himself in.

Inside, Odd saw her mom, looking better than she had looked in years. Her tan practically glowed. She sat perched on an old scarred desk and next to her was a thick-bellied man of about fifty. He gleamed with gold—on his fingers, his wrists, his neck, even his glasses shone bright.

"Evan? Is this a cli..."

It took a moment for Karen to grasp who it was

that stood just five feet away. "Odd!" she screamed in shock, cutting off Bully's words like an axe. "What—what are you doing here? You're supposed to be in Illinois."

Now Odd was thankful for Evan's warning. Her anger, that small part of her that had always been buried behind her fear—at least until very recently—leapt up inside of her. She struggled to back it down, thinking Evan knew something that she didn't.

"I came to find you."

"Me?" Karen began looking back and forth between Bully and Odd, bewildered. "All the way from Illinois?"

"Yes." The word was little more than a hiss. Odd's anger kept boiling up. Why hadn't her mom come back for her? Why hadn't she at least called, or sent money? And clearly she had money. Karen's outfit was new, her hair was recently cut, her nails were even manicured.

Bully shifted in his chair and casually commented: "She's like one of those dogs you read about in the freakin paper. You know the ones that get left behind in a move and then they show up months later all freakin bedraggled looking."

Evan spoke up quickly as Odd's lips formed a hard line on her face at being compared to a dog. "Your perseverance is admirable."

"Yeah, that's what I'm talking about." Bully said. After this came a long awkward pause. Odd couldn't find a thing to say that would come across as nice. Part of her problem stemmed from seeing the guilty look her mom couldn't hide. It only made her anger a greater force within her. Yes, her mom should feel guilty for abandoning her daughter. And, oh yes, Odd had every right to feel angry.

Before that moment, she hadn't known what she would feel when she found her mother. She had thought it would be a mixture of relief, of comfort, of warm security, knowing they were together at last and that they'd never be parted again. However, that wasn't at all what she felt. It would've required Odd to be self-delusional. Her mom had left her on purpose—that was a cold, hard fact. Another cold, hard fact was that Karen was quite obviously enjoying her freedom from motherhood.

And the last cold, hard fact that killed any sense of security in Odd was the knowledge that Karen Wyatt rarely let anything interfere with what she found enjoyable. In her heart Odd knew that Karen would leave her again or...send her away.

The seconds ticked by until Bully couldn't handle the silence. "Hey, this is a freakin' reunion. There should be hugs." Odd's last hug from her mother occurred during a New Year's Eve celebration two years before. The sudden clamor in the bar had woken Odd, who went to find out where her mother could be, only to have Karen practically fall on her in her drunkenness. She had received her hug and a second later, Karen had vomited down her back.

"Yeah, you're right Bully," Karen said, coming forward with arms outstretched. "Here, give me a hug."

When Abe had hugged her, she had felt safe and warm. When Peach had hugged her, Odd knew everything would be all right. When Connie had hugged her she knew love for the first time.

When her mom hugged her—there was nothing.

Even the bite from Ike had more feeling behind it.

"There you go," Bully said, smiling benignly. "This is a good thing. You saved us a two-thousand mile trip, Odd. Not to mention, now your mom don't have to worry about that freakin' pesky warrant."

"It'll go away?" Karen asked, showing true happiness.

Bully made a face. "What did I just say? Yeah, it'll go away. We show up in court with Odd. You say she's been with you the entire time and that they must've got the wrong girl and just like that it's gone." He snapped his gold encrusted fingers for emphasis.

Karen wasn't mollified. "I don't know, Bully. Her eyes. No one's going to mistake her eyes for somebody else's."

"Oh yeah!" Bully exclaimed as if just remembering that Odd had red eyes. "Let's have a look at them."

"Why? Why should I? They're red, ok?"

"Go on, Odd. It'll be alright," Karen said.

Odd glanced to Evan. The man gave the tiniest nod possible. His grey eyes flicked to Bully and then back to her. Evan wanted her to show her eyes to Bully. Why? And why would Karen want that as well? Normally her mom was mortified at the idea of Odd showing her eyes to anyone—for free.

Maybe it wasn't free.

Odd took off the cheap, convenience store sunglasses. Bully stared, and then whistled.

"Wow! Those are simply amazing. What do you think, Evan?"

Evan hadn't looked, something Odd was grateful for. Now, at his boss' command he came up and stared good and long in that calm way of his. "Does it hurt?" he asked.

"No," Odd lied. It actually burned. When people stared, it burned down into her soul.

"Of course it doesn't freakin' hurt!" Bully said laughing. "It's a birth defect and birth defects don't hurt. Karen, you were right! You were freakin' right. Her eyes are perfect."

This was news to Odd. "What do you mean perfect? They're not perfect at all."

"Odd, let me explain," Karen said. "When I came out here, it was on a whim. I thought I'd have a little vacation and then go on back. But then I met Bully. He's helping us get on a better financial footing..." Bully cleared his throat significantly and Karen paused. "What I mean is that he's going to help you."

"How?" Odd asked. Her tone dripped with suspicion.

"I have connections that's how," Bully answered. "There's this tour group that runs all year doing county fairs, summer festivals, things like that. They're basically only a sideshow only, but they bring in top-freakin'-dollar."

"Doing what?" Odd had never been to a festival or a fair.

Bully waved one of his gold plated hands. "It's a freak show."

Chapter 44

Odd heard the words. They struck her eardrums, the nerves jangled right into her brain, but from there the message became jumbled.

"What?" she asked in frank confusion. Bully went to repeat himself when Odd asked again, "What? A side show? A freak show? In a county fair? Don't they have rides there? I can't do rides. Ask my mom."

"She can't do rides," Karen agreed, looking fearfully from Bully to Odd.

"You know I'm not talking about freakin' rides, Karen. I'm talking about what we discussed already—putting Odd in a show. Now don't go getting soft on me! You knew it wouldn't be easy. But there isn't going to be no backing out. I put a lot of time and money into this already."

Karen gave Odd a pained expression. "Bully and I, we're trying to help you. I know it doesn't seem that way, but this is a good opportunity for you."

"You think joining a freak show is a good opportunity for your daughter?" Odd couldn't quite grasp how.

"I do. What else are you going to do with your life?" Karen asked. "You have no skills, no education. And even if you did we both know that no one outside a freak show can stand to look at you for long."

"I can't," Odd said quietly. *How could her mother propose such a thing?* "I can't do it."

Bully sat back in his chair, running his hands

over his girth. "You can and you will. It's already a done deal. And it won't be like you're going to be alone. I'm going to be your manager. Your mom and I will see you all the time."

"And when you're on the road you won't be alone either," her mom said. "There will be the other...performers."

"You mean the other freaks?" Odd asked with acid running from her tongue. How strange it felt to speak to her mom like this. Her whole life she had been cowed by her but now Karen seemed more a stranger than her mom. Or perhaps Odd had become the stranger, she didn't know.

Bully sat up straighter, looking mean, but Karen put a hand out and said, "Yeah, the other freaks. They know what you're going through. I bet they'll be there for you."

Odd would bet that the other performers were all on their way to the loony bin. How could anyone stay sane under those conditions: being laughed at, being jeered at, being a living horror? "I can't. I'm sorry."

"You can!" Bully said slapping the flat of his palm down on his desk. He blew hot air out of his nostrils for a few seconds slowly calming himself. "I'm sorry I yelled, Odd. From what I've been told this may be your only chance at a job, and a life, and a future outside of sitting in your motel room, afraid to open the door. You're only twelve so you probably don't know this, but life only gets harder."

"It's true, Odd," Karen said joining in. "This is your chance. I say take it."

"You're wrong about me. I'm no longer afraid,"

Odd said. In her mind she heard the echo of Connie's last words: *I'm not afraid.* They stirred something inside her and she turned and headed for the door.

"Where are you going," Bully asked suspiciously.

After traveling for over a thousand miles, Odd surprised herself by saying, "I'm going for a walk."

She left the building and immediately turned south. Within her lay one simple desire: to see the beach in the daytime. She wanted to run warm sand between her toes and splash in the shallows. After that, it didn't matter where she went. Her quest had ended in the harshest failure imaginable.

Wherever she ended up, it wouldn't be a freak show. That was out of the question.

The question shouldn't have ever been raised. The very fact that her own mother had brought it up, caused Odd more pain than she had ever felt. It dug at her, burning her insides, building a fire out of her once slight temper.

Her anger and disappointment kept her moving, at least for a little while. After a few miles, the last fumes of her energies were spent, and her feet began to drag. She took to lingering where the hot sun couldn't get at her, in the shade thrown out by the tall buildings. She felt like little more than a shadow herself.

Eventually she found herself at a complete standstill outside a burger joint.

For blocks the aroma had teased her and drawn her in and now she stood as close as she dared to the people sitting outside eating at umbrella-covered benches. Little birds flitted unseen among them, gathering up crumbs and sometime whole french fries.

Odd looked on in jealousy, her stomach eating itself in her starvation. Who would feed her now? Who would take care of her?

Nobody.

How long can a person go without eating? she wondered. It had been two days since she ate the last crumbs of her chips and four since she had a meal. Her head swam every time the sun beat down upon it and her body had taken to quivering and shaking. She figured that it wouldn't be long before she fell over and wouldn't be able to get back up again.

There is an alternative, a part of her mind said in a silky voice. *They will feed you at the freak show*. Odd pictured herself in a cage, squatting in a corner as tourists leered at her and threw scraps to get her to move.

"No," she whispered and forced the thought away. It was better to starve.

What about begging? You could do that to live," the hateful voice suggested.

And turn into one of those bums living out the remainder of their squalid lives beneath an overpass? That couldn't be her life either. But what could?

She had no idea.

Odd stumbled back to Long Beach Boulevard, her quivering legs barely able to hold her up. There she saw a man with flinty, grey eyes watching her. "Come here, Audrey. Your mom sent me to find you. We can get something to eat before we go back if you want," Evan said.

If she went to him she'd be fed. She'd get a job and she'd make money. She'd have a place to stay and she would be safe—and she would be in hell. Her alternative: a slow, hungry death. Odd headed for the beach, thinking it was at least a nice place to starve.

"You would rather try to make it on your own?" Evan asked, striding along easily next to her. "Impressive."

"I don't want to live like a freak. I don't want to be an animal in a cage. That's what I'd be you know: a freak animal in a freak zoo. People would point and rattle my bars and try to get me to do tricks. Little kids would scream when they saw my eyes, and the girls would all squeal and look grossed-out, and the boys..." In her mind she pictured the boys throwing stones.

"Yes," Evan replied to it all.

The word took the last of the steam out of her and she stopped. "You know?"

"Yes. Bully wants to make you into an 'attraction'. He wants to go with the whole hell-spawn, demon-child angle until you start to fill in. Then he wants to remake you into a sexy demon—a succubus."

With an effort Odd started walking again. "And you're ok with this?" she asked him.

"No. That's why we're walking instead of me dragging you back."

"Oh...thanks." Odd gave him a rusty little smile. He only stared.

"You amaze me," Evan said after a minute.

"How do I do that?" Odd asked, but then another question came to mind. "How did you know I was coming? You knew."

"I tracked you from Illinois. I wasn't actually there. I did it by phone and computer," Evan said. "But it amounts to the same thing."

"Why would you do that?" Odd's head began to

spin and she lurched into Evan.

"Because..." he paused and opened a door to a pizzeria that she hadn't even noticed. Odd was nearly overcome by the smell that struck her and she offered no resistance when he tugged her inside. "Because Bully asked me to check out your mom...Hey Veronica, table for two, inside please." A stout waitress with black hair escorted them to a table.

"This your daughter?" Veronica asked.

"I wish. A large pie, half pepperoni, half cheese and two cokes," he said to the waitress as they sat. Then he resumed his story, "So Bully asked me to check out Karen—he does that sort of thing all the time. Anyway, it takes five minutes to find out you were in foster care and that you'd been living alone at that junk motel. I even find out how you slept in the church."

The dark and the cool revived Odd slightly, but Evan's words were still making her head go round and round. "How did you find out about that?"

"It's nothing. Everything's on computers these days. All the reports, everything." He paused as the waitress dropped off their drinks and started up again after watching, with a smile, as Odd sucked down her entire drink in three long pulls. "So, a couple of days later, I'm curious about how you're doing. That first caseworker was really worried about you on account of your eyes. Lo and behold I find that you've skipped out on your foster-home."

"They made me sleep in a storage room," Odd said, sticking one ice cube in her mouth and putting another round one on her finger like a ring. "Was that in the report?"

"No, but I read about thirty complaints on those

parents. It's a wonder they're still allowed to take in kids."

"Yeah, it wasn't a good place. Do you know where I stayed the night I ran away?" She would have thought it scary if he knew. When he shook his head she chuckled feeling the caffeine hit her system, "In a box by the railroad!"

He nodded as if that made perfect sense. "But the next two nights you stayed with the Hewitts and then Abe put you on a bus Thursday night. He paid in cash, which I couldn't track, but he did get gas a block away and used a credit card. It didn't take a genius to know you were on the bus that had just left. And besides I knew you were coming to find your mother."

"Did you tell my mom where I was?" The real question that went unasked was: did Karen care where Odd was?

"No. I didn't have any real reason to and I was supposed to be looking into another matter. But since the two cases were related I decided to keep tabs on you. I was there when your bus pulled in and I followed after you to those two parties...I almost did tell your mom when I saw that car crash. I didn't think anyone could live through it."

"I dropped my ring and when I went to pick it up we smashed into the truck." Odd's mouth abruptly filled with water as a huge, piping hot pizza was set before them.

Evan didn't eat at first. He watched Odd chewing at the ring of crust until the center of the pie had cooled somewhat. Odd began to feel strange with him just sitting there watching her.

"Why didn't you tell my mom if you thought

that I died?"

"Because I don't like her. She doesn't deserve a daughter like you," he answered. As if this was his cue he then pulled a slice onto his plate.

"Like me? I ruined her life. I've been a weight dragging her..."

Evan flashed his eyes and growled, "Shut up that nonsense! That's only what she wants you to believe. The truth is she's foul and you're sweet and I think she's jealous of you."

"You don't know me," Odd said. "Maybe I'm just like her."

"You're not," he insisted. "This may be the first time we're talking, but it doesn't mean I don't know you. I've read the reports. I spoke to Peach and Father Marino on the phone. I know you're not like your mom."

Odd forgot to eat. She was still caught up with idea of him having spoken to Peach. A thousand questions came to mind, mostly about Abe and Peach, but what came out was: "Why would you do this if you didn't have to?"

"Because you fascinate me. You should be nasty like your mom...maybe even nastier after everything you've gone through, but you're not. You seem to bounce from person-to-person, relying totally on the kindness of strangers, which to me is intriguing since there's so little kindness in the world."

She took another bite, chewing slowly, wondering about Evan. "Why do you work for Bully? You seem nicer than him."

He took one large bite of pizza and then another so that Odd began to wonder if he would answer.

Finally, he said, "Because I stepped in it a few years back and he was the only one to give me another chance. People deserve a second chance and that's what I'm going to give you."

What did that mean? Suddenly his off-the-cuff comment to the waitress sprung to mind. She had asked if Odd was his daughter and he had said 'I wish.'

"Do you want me to be your daughter?" The idea was alarming to her as well as a little frightening. He had been practically stalking her halfway across the country. What kind of man would do that?

A smile struck his grey eyes. "No. You have a father already. Here in Los Angeles. I found him for Bully. I'm going to take you to him as soon as you're done eating."

Chapter 45

An hour later, still in a state of shock, Odd climbed out of Evan's car.

"Good luck," he murmured quietly.

"Thanks, Evan, for everything." She had repeated this phrase half a dozen times already. Evan had given her quest back to her—had given her a reason to live. He smiled just as he had done the previous six times. "I promise I won't tell," she added, again a repetition. Evan was risking his job by bringing her there. He stared at her before giving her one of his tiny nods.

"Go on."

She liked his quiet style and adopted it for the moment. "You go on."

Laughing, he did just that. Driving away with a single honk of his horn. Odd stared after him. Just then, her stomach—bulging with pizza—began to knot itself in fear over meeting her dad. Karen had always described him as such a monster, but Odd had never believed it, certain that it had been Karen's nastiness that had driven him away.

She had always pictured him as handsome, and smart, and nice. And now, standing in front of a giant glass and steel building she pictured him as rich, as well. Odd tilted her head far back to look at the towering building. A second later she found herself on her bottom.

The skyscraper had seemed to spin and she had

lost her balance. She giggled a little from a combination of embarrassment and nerves before climbing back to her feet.

With a deep breath she marched into the building. A security guard sat behind a desk. Normally he would be a person Odd would have skirted around, but she had a sense of belonging. She had a right to be there.

"Doctor Alstrom, please...he's my father." She loved the words coming from her mouth. Her father was a doctor! It gave her the tingles just thinking those words and she couldn't seem to stop.

She was Audrey Wyatt and she had a real father—and one who wasn't a bum, or a monster, or a jerk—he was a doctor. A type of doctor called a psychiatrist, Evan had told her. Being a doctor meant that he was smart, and Odd began to think that she could be smart, too someday.

Evan had also told her why he hadn't stuck around when Karen was pregnant. He had been her therapist and had an "indiscretion" with her that could have cost him his job. That had been over thirteen years ago and both Odd and Evan thought that enough time had passed for him to finally meet his daughter.

The guard, a sweaty freckled man in his late forties, looked at a computer screen. "Suite 2269. Take one of those elevators," he said, pointing to the far right.

2269? She wondered if that meant the twenty-second floor. Sure enough, when she stepped into the elevator she saw the rows of buttons. She pressed the twenty-two and had to swallow her fear as the car shot upwards.

"Just don't go near the windows," she whispered to herself. It would do no good to start screaming the first time she met her father. After the ride up she paused in the hall trying rid herself of the shaking in her limbs. They wouldn't stop.

"Just don't go near the windows," she repeated. Of course, that wasn't the only thing making her anxious. She was about to meet her father. What would happen when he saw her eyes? Would he cringe at the sight of her? Would he want to send her to the freak show as well? "Stop it. He's a doctor."

In her experience, doctors rarely cringed at the sight of her eyes. They were intrigued instead of being disgusted.

With that thought, Odd screwed up her courage. It wasn't courage to face her father, not really. It was courage to hope. Something that, before her lunch with Evan, Odd didn't think she was even capable of anymore. So far every hope had been taken from her—crushed out of her—and this was her last one.

"Doctor Alstrom, please," she said to a pretty receptionist.

"And you are?"

"Odd...Audrey Wyatt. I'm his daughter."

The receptionist narrowed her eyes at this. "He's with a patient, but he'll be done shortly. I'll let him know you're here."

It didn't seem very shortly to Odd. She couldn't hold a magazine due to the shaking in her hands and the other people in the waiting room seemed bothered by her pacing. She took to sitting on her hands and swinging her short legs above the elegant, pale green carpet.

The receptionist came out of a room at the end of the hall, "Miss Wyatt? I'm sorry but the doctor can't see you today. He asked me to give you this." She held out a note.

At the sight of it, Odd felt something turn sideways in her chest and begin to burn. She realized then that hope was a physical thing. It wasn't just an emotion. There was a part of her that was linked to hope by nerves, and muscles, and tendons, and when hope died, it hurt—badly.

"What does it say?" Odd could see the squiggles of indecipherable cursive.

"I didn't read it. Here."

Odd took the piece of paper and held it up to her glasses—first one way, then the other. Neither way made any sense. She looked around at the faces of the other people in the waiting room. Was there someone who looked trustworthy enough to tell Odd what she already knew was on the note—that her father didn't want to see her?

Really, there was nobody she wanted to hear something so dreadful from—not Abe or Mr. McCew not even Robert Hoover.

"Definitely not Robert," she whispered. She hadn't thought about the blind boy in days, which made her feel a little guilty. He would be the last person that she would want to know. She didn't want pity from him; she wanted something else.

But did she want pity from any of them? No. Odd crumpled up the note and looked for a waste paper basket. One sat near the receptionist's desk. She went to it dropped it in and then continued walking down the hall to her father's office. Since she couldn't read his handwriting, he would just have to *tell* her that he didn't want to see her to her face.

Odd didn't hurry, though she expected to hear a shrill cry from the receptionist with every step. She slipped through the cracks of the woman's attention and, in seconds, Odd stood in front of the polished mahogany door.

With only the slightest hesitation Odd walked in.

She'd been correct. Her father was handsome. He was tall and blonde, with strong Nordic features. These sagged as he looked up and saw Odd.

"So your mom sent you to try to pull more money out of me?" he asked. Before Odd could say a word he went on, "A thousand a month isn't good enough?"

"I—I don't know what you're talking about," Odd replied. Thinking he had her mixed up with another girl, she introduced herself, "I'm Audrey Wyatt. Your daughter."

He threw down the pen in his hand. "I know who you are and I know why you're here. It's ridiculous! Karen and I had a deal, and the deal strictly emphasized no contact."

Odd's mind wanted to spin away and pretend it didn't know what was going on. She forced it back on track. "So, you're paying my mom a thousand dollars a month to keep me away from you?"

"Yes...no. Look, uh..."

He didn't even know her name. "Odd."

"Odd—Audrey, you got it wrong. The money is for child support. For you to have clothes and food. That sort of thing. It's just...I have a family and a practice and I can't jeopardize them. If anyone found out about you I could lose everything."

He had to be lying—Odd couldn't believe she had that much power; she didn't think it was possible. On a shelf she saw a picture of her father sitting in a group portrait with a pretty wife and two little blonde girls. She went to it and studied the children, seeing little parts of herself in them...except the demon eyes, of course. "How could I do that? Make you lose everything?"

"Because I made a mistake a long time ago. A terrible mistake that should never have happened."

Odd was that terrible mistake. "Were these mistakes, too?" she asked tossing the picture onto his desk.

He caught the picture with deft hands. "No....and Audrey, you weren't the mistake. What I did—sleeping with your mother—was the mistake. I was new in my practice and...and your mother...well, it just happened. And now if people were to find out, it would be very bad."

Another shelf, another picture of his happy family. What would she give for her face to be in that picture? "I'm not looking for people to find out. I'm looking to have a father. I'm trying to be normal like everyone else and be a part of a family."

"That can't happen," he said.

"It can!" Odd shouted. "I can be right here." She pointed at the picture, just to the side of his oldest daughter...his second oldest daughter.

"Do you want to destroy me?" he asked in a tired voice. "Because that's what will happen if you insist on going down this road."

"What happened was so long ago that no one cares!" Odd's anger flared brighter at his flimsy excuse. "What about me? Do you want to destroy me? Do you even care what happens to me?" Odd yanked off her glasses. "Look me in the eye and tell me you care."

Her father leaned far back and the two stared into each other's eyes for all of five seconds before he turned away. "You want the truth?" he asked, speaking to the picture in his hands. "I don't. I don't care. I don't even know you."

"I'm your daughter."

"Really, you're not. These are my daughters. You're nothing but a stranger, demanding money."

Odd gripped the picture so hard she thought it might break in her small hands. "I never asked for money! I'm asking to be a part of a family. I'm asking for...love." She couldn't believe that word had come out like that. Instinctively she knew a girl begging for love would never get it, but there was no taking it back.

"I'm sorry," he said.

"I don't want your sorry or your money."

"I can't give you my love. It's just not that simple. You just don't love a stranger," he said still talking to the picture. He hadn't raised his eyes, and Odd knew he wouldn't as long as her glasses were off. With a sigh she put them back on.

"But you love them?" She tapped the picture.

"Yes."

"But not me?" He nodded at her question. She wanted to scream, *Why not?* But she knew the truth. "You don't love me because I'm really 'the terrible mistake'. If I hadn't been born, then sleeping with my mom would have been a little slip up...a what do you call it? An indiscretion. But with me here—standing in your office, I've become a thousand-dollar a month mistake."

It took him a moment to respond, "It's not healthy for you to think of yourself that way."

"Is it healthy to lie to myself?" she asked in a small voice. With his every word, her insides felt more and more empty. More desolate. More barren.

His answer surprised her. "Yes. Sometime it is."

So she was right. She was just one big terrible mistake. "Would you like me to leave and never come back?" Odd asked, putting everything on the table.

He didn't have to say anything. His eyes spoke for him: *Yes, please leave and never come back*, they said.

Her heart, now brittle as glass after the constant wear and strain of the inhumanity that had surrounded her for so long, broke, sending shards of pain ripping through her. She wanted to cry out, but she held it in. What good would it do? What good would anything do? What good would living do?

It wouldn't do any good. She had nothing left to live for. She had no more reason to hope; the idea of having a father had been it, the last shred of hope left to her. With it gone, something inside her—something that had been bending for years, snapped. Like her heart, a part of her broke. The part that cared about life.

Odd took another, longer, look at her half-sisters. They were cute, adorable, beautiful even. They looked sweet and innocent and were probably easy to love. Puppies, kittens, and babies—everything that was small and cute was always easy to love. Ugly, harsh things like Odd were the difficult things in life to love.

"I'll make it easy on you," she said, not to her father, but to the world. Like her father, the world had never wanted Odd Wyatt in it. She could see that now. All her life, everywhere, there had been signs that she had stubbornly refused to see. Now it was impossible not to.

Dropping the picture to the carpet, Odd left. Her father made no attempt to prevent her. If he had, she would've stopped at his slightest word and clung to him. But he said nothing. She went to the elevator, punched the top button and waited, but not for long. Not long enough for anyone to ask her why she was going up instead of down.

When she arrived at the thirtieth floor Odd felt a sort of listless surprise that she wasn't on the roof. But that didn't stop her on the final leg of her journey. A door marked with the universal symbol for stairs stood near at hand. She went to it thinking how easily Connie had found her way to the roof of the hospital. Odd would get to the roof as well. She was sure that it would be easy for her, too. The world wanted her dead and the world couldn't be denied for long.

She followed up the concrete stairs as though she were following in Connie's footsteps.

The door to the roof had a bar across it, and warning signs stating that an alarm would sound if opened. There was even a lock. Uselessly, it hung on its chain from a rail next to the door, which was propped open with a rock.

Easy.

It was all so easy.

A warm wind plucked at her as she stepped onto the roof. She allowed it to push her near the edge of the building. Again, easy. All she would have to do is go right to the brink and let her vertigo and the wind push her off. She looked out at the city as her blonde hair whipped around her pale cheeks. It wasn't a beautiful view; it was smoggy and tired looking. Strangely, it wasn't frightening.

Now she understood what Connie had meant when she had cried out, "I am not afraid." There was nothing left for Odd to fear. There was nothing left to cry over. Nothing left to rage against. All her life she had lived in fear and anger and sadness and it had done her no good. She had nothing left, and no one, left.

Her father paid to keep her away. Her mother wanted to place her in a zoo for deformed humans. Abe and Peach could be jailed for seeing her again. Evan would lose his job. Connie was dead. The truth about Odd was that she was poison. She was truly a demon and everyone who stayed with her for any length of time suffered. The little girl would end that suffering now in the easiest way she knew how.

Odd took out Abe's ring—the one regret she had was that she couldn't return it to him. She had never for a second thought about pawning it. Slipping it on her thumb she went to the edge of the roof so that her toes hung over. The wind rocked her and she waited, but the wind grew confused and pushed her back and forth, but not off.

Odd smiled, knowing what the wind was waiting on.

The wind wouldn't do this for her; if she wanted to die she'd have to do it herself. Odd let her arms fly out from her sides.

"I am not afraid!" she cried aloud and then

looked down. The street seemed an endless distance away. It spun round and round.

She swayed, and fell.

Epilogue

How long she fell, she had no idea. Her mind had switched off from the moment she felt the pull of the world sucking her down. It could have been a second, or it could have been an hour.

When she landed she became conscious of a single sweet note—the song of a gold ring vibrating in the air. The little girl opened her red eyes and saw the ring falling lazily, sending out rays of pure sunshine from its gleaming surface. Then it bounced upon the unseen ground and trilled aloud once again, leaping into the air. It fell again and then its melody rung out a third time and then went quiet.

Where had it gone?

Far above her, a tiny wisp of a white cloud, like a swan's feather against a bright blue sea, lay across the sky, pointing. Even before she turned her head, she knew it would point to the gold ring.

There it was. She scooped it up and stuck it back on her thumb where it spun in an easy, loose circle. The girl smiled at it, giving it a spin.

She then raised her head and looked out. Her view of the world didn't appear to have changed. She still seemed high up above the grit of the city. In fact, she realized with a jolt, she was still atop the building.

"What?" she asked in wonder. "What happened?" The girl sat up, her feet dangling over the edge, her heels thumping placidly against the glass. "How am I still here?" Nothing made sense and yet nothing needed to. The broken feeling inside her and the desperate need to end her life, were gone and in their place was a silent calm.

She filled her lungs with air as if breathing for the first time. It felt wonderful.

"Excuse me," a soft voice called to her. "Little girl? Are you ok?"

She turned to see a man, a thickset man with a deep, healthy tan and black hair, approaching her, crunching the gravel of the roof under his feet.

"I'm ok," she replied. She touched her shoulder where a dog had bitten her. It held a memory of pain. The same was true of her chest. The Mickey Mouse band aides were still there, yet the pain was distant. "I'm the same really. Where am I?"

"You're on the roof of the Davis Building."

She had never heard of it. "I mean is this heaven? Is that really heaven?" she asked pointing to the city.

His hands had been up, palms out and now they slipped down a little and he smiled. "Some people think so. It is the city of angels."

The City of Angels? Was this really heaven? She gave the city a better look, leaning back on her palms and kicking her legs against the side of the building. It sure looked the same as Los Angeles.

"I'm confused," she said.

"Well, you fell pretty hard," he replied coming a little closer. "And I think it messed up your eyes. They're all red."

Her hand went to her face and realized her glasses had disappeared. Had they fallen? Did it matter anymore?

"They're still red? Huh? I would've thought that they would have changed to blue or green. If I had my way they'd be green."

"I think you hit your head for sure." The man eased within a couple of feet of her and glanced over the edge. "Aren't you afraid?"

"It's not scary at all, now." In her mind, she heard an echo of voices crying out, *I am not afraid!* She knew the voices—one used to be hers. "Back, before, I was afraid of heights."

"Before what?"

"Before I jumped, silly." She decided she liked the man. With his brown skin, black hair, and thick forearms, he sort of looked like a cute bear. He seemed quite huggable.

"But you didn't jump," he said. "I thought you were about to. You sort of wobbled and you leaned way out. I was right over there behind that air conditioning unit and when you fell, you dropped out of my line of sight. When I ran around it, you were right where you are now."

She wrinkled her nose at him. "Really? Then I'm not dead?" She sure felt dead—or at least different. It was as if everything that had been broken inside of her had been mended. As if she had given away her life only to have it returned to her in mint condition.

"No. That is, unless I'm dead, too. And I don't feel dead," he remarked, stretching his arms out wide.

She inspected the man. "You don't look dead. And I'm guessing I don't, either. I just feel so strange. There are things that bothered me so much before and now, suddenly they don't." Finding her mom, for instance. That had consumed her for days and now she had to wonder why. Karen Wyatt had always been a nasty person. Had her quest really been about finding her? If so, it sure seemed like a waste of time now.

"That sort of thing happens when you have a scare like you did," the man said, easing down next to her.

There was a time when the little girl had been scared a lot and she'd never experienced this freedom of fear before. She figured the man was wrong, but didn't want to hurt his feelings. "So what brings you up here? The view?" she asked as way to change the subject.

"No, I was doing an inspection. I'm the building manager. That's sort of like a superintendant. The owner has too many properties to attend to so he assigned this one to me."

"Is being a building manager hard? I only ask because I'm looking for work...or I might be, if I decide to go back." Did she want to go back? Was there anything for her down there? She looked out over the city, impressed by its size, but not by its squalor. There was so much misery.

Her eyes then saw past the buildings and picked out the blue gem in the distance. The ocean. She remembered how she had wanted to see it in the daytime and how she wanted to feel the sand, hot, between her toes. The color reminded her of a boy's eyes.

Robert Hoover. The blind boy. The brave boy. The boy with eyes the color of the ocean. Was he enough to get her to go back? Him and the ocean? What about Abe and Peach? What about the gold ring that she felt she needed to return? What about the farm at Christmas? What about Evan and Gary and Mr.

McCew? Just picturing them she knew the answer: Yes. There was misery down there but there was also love and friendship.

The man watched the girl closely. "Any life worth having is hard if you do it right. My name is Gabe by the way."

"Abe?" she asked, in shock. Her mind hearing what she wanted it to hear.

"No, Gabe...with a 'G'. What's your name?"

"Me?" The question was tougher than it seemed. The girl she had been, the one who had waited fearfully in a musty motel room, was gone. This new girl had crossed the country. She had loved and been loved. She had hugged and been hugged. She had laughed and cried. She had lived and died. She had fed goats. That old girl had been a freak. This new one was simply a girl—a girl with red eyes.

"You can call me Sprite."

*

Author's Note:

Writing a novel is not easy, just getting it on paper takes hundreds of hours worth of work and then there is the fact that a writer must carry the story around in his head all day every day. When a writer is at lunch, he is thinking about his story, when he's chatting up a girl, he thinking about his story. And then there is the endless editing involved and the cover work and the formatting...writing is not easy, except when it came to writing *Sprite*. This was the one book that I thought truly wrote itself and every day I looked forward to find out what was going to happen to Odd. She had such a combination of innocence and hope that I felt more like a reader than a writer.

If you liked the character of Odd Wyatt, then you would probably also appreciate The Horror of the Shade's Katie Jern and The Apocalypse's Jillybean, both of whom have something of that innocent quality.

Finally, on a self-serving note, the review is the most practical and inexpensive form of advertisement an independent author has available in order to get his work known. If you could put a kind review on Amazon and your Facebook page, I would greatly appreciate it.

Peter Meredith

Fictional works by Peter Meredith:

A Perfect America
The Sacrificial Daughter
The Horror of the Shade Trilogy of the Void 1
An Illusion of Hell Trilogy of the Void 2
Hell Blade Trilogy of the Void 3
The Punished
Sprite
The Feylands: A Hidden Lands Novel
The Sun King: A Hidden Lands Novel
The Sun Queen: A Hidden Lands Novel
The Apocalypse: The Undead World Novel 1
The Apocalypse Survivors: The Undead World Novel 2
The Apocalypse Outcasts: The Undead World Novel 3
The Apocalypse Fugitives: The Undead World Novel 4
Pen(Novella)
A Sliver of Perfection (Novella)
The Haunting At Red Feathers(Short Story)
The Haunting On Colonel's Row(Short Story)
The Drawer(Short Story)
The Eyes in the Storm(Short Story)

www.ingramcontent.com/pod-product-compliance
Lightning Source LLC
La Vergne TN
LVHW020654110826
845149LV00012B/1998

* 9 7 8 0 9 8 8 8 9 8 0 4 2 *